FROM ALL FALSE DOCTRINE

Alice Degan

First published by Sexton's Cottage Books in 2014

Paperback ISBN 978-0-9938051-5-8

Cover image: St. James Cathedral doorway, 1923
(City of Toronto Archives Fonds 1266, Item 87)
Cover design: Alice Degan

For Mike

CONTENTS

From all sedition, privy conspiracy, and rebellion; from all false doctrine, heresy, and schism; from hardness of heart, and contempt of thy Word and Commandment,
> *Good Lord, deliver us.*

—the Litany of the 1918 Canadian *Book of Common Prayer*

PART I

Preaching to the Choir

Chapter One

THEY TOIL NOT, NEITHER DO THEY SPIN

"It isn't a question of actually believing the teaching," said Elsa, drilling two neat holes in the sand with the heels of her shoes. "It's whether or not they believe in the authenticity of the manuscript, that's all."

"Gosh, you had better hope that's all," said Harriet cheerfully. "It would be so tedious for you, wouldn't it, to have your research interrupted every so often by cultists wanting to worship the thing you were studying? In my department, now, we don't have such problems."

"Good heavens, Harriet—you study money! All *sorts* of people worship that."

"Oh, true. Have a grape while I consider a suitable riposte." Harriet proffered the tin of green grapes that had been nestled on the blanket beside her.

They were seated in the shade of a large blue sun-umbrella—Harriet's property, like the blanket and the grapes and the vacuum flask of iced tea and the basket that it had all been packed in. They had been there since noon; they had moved the umbrella several times to adjust their pool of shade, and the tea was nearly finished. The day had become blazingly hot, the sky arcing blue-white out over the lake, the water flashing in the sun. Because it was a weekday, the beach was not crowded. A few young people in bathing costumes ran or strolled, according to their preference; a few mothers lay in beach chairs while their children squatted over sandcastles by the shoreline. Elsa and Harriet sat under their umbrella with their books.

Harriet was the golden-haired, rosy, curvaceous one, radiant in a red bathing costume, her long curls tied back with a flowered scarf.

Elsa was willowy and long-legged—or, depending on her mood, tall and thin. She wore her much paler hair tightly plaited and pinned up. The black bathing suit she had on was the first one she had ever owned, this trip to the beach only her second since coming to Toronto four years ago. It was late August; the academic year of 1925–26 would not start for another two weeks. It was a period of waiting, of planning and anticipation. The hot, heavy summer air seemed to Elsa to be telling her to go slowly, not to be so eager to rush onward to the new school year. It was an irresistible suggestion, but she chafed at it.

"Cultists aside," said Harriet, "I am proud of you. It's not everyone who gets to write her Master's thesis on a newly discovered manuscript."

"Oh, I don't know that I will," Elsa corrected her hastily. "I'm only hoping Professor Gallagher will give me something on it. It is up to him, of course."

"Of course. But anyone can see he's keen on you. Becky Taylor's young man told me Gallagher never normally takes female graduate students. He'll give you this Orpheus thing, I'm sure of it."

"I do hope so." Elsa had now drilled her heels as deep into the sand as they would go. She took them out, stretched out her legs, and crossed her ankles.

The thought of returning to school, whether or not she got the *Bibliotheka Orphika* as a thesis topic, was immensely satisfying. All summer, with her brother's health in doubt and her parents worried about the crops, Elsa's MA, which she had been talking of as a forgone conclusion at Convocation, had seemed actually a fairly remote and unimportant possibility. Then her father had proved an unexpected ally, and even if she privately judged the reason for his about-face on the subject to be embarrassingly absurd, she was grateful for it. She had packed her bags with a feeling of unreality, not sure until she boarded the train whether the whole thing wouldn't fall apart at the last moment. But it hadn't, and here she was.

"I don't really know that I care for this book," said Harriet, turning it over to gaze critically at the cover. "My mother recommended it to me, and I suppose it is meant to be romantic—but I just can't help thinking that the characters aren't being sensible."

Elsa leaned over to look at the cover. "It has a picture of a nun swooning in the arms of a—I don't know, I suppose he's meant to be a knight? Were you really expecting it to be about sensible people?"

"He's a Templar."

"Not dressed like that, surely. He looks more like a court jester."

"No, you're right. He ought to have a big cross on him somewhere, oughtn't he? No, I suppose I didn't expect them to be sensible. I just wish they would at least *discuss* the possibility of her leaving the convent—perhaps it's not feasible, I don't know, but it seems like the sort of thing they should at least ask about. You know, you can't be sure until you ask."

"I think in that sort of book you can."

"Well, it's the sort of book one ought to read at the beach, anyway," Harriet said with a shrug. She eyed Elsa's little black library volume disapprovingly.

"I don't think you're in any position to be critical," said Elsa dryly. "I'm *enjoying* my book." She picked it up again. "Besides, it's not as if I brought Liddell and Scott with me to look up the hard words."

"You mean that gigantic dictionary that I saw you eyeing as we were packing our basket?"

"Go back to your wayward nun." Elsa flapped a hand at her dismissively. "Perhaps she will surprise you on the next page with a little dissertation on the manorial system."

She rearranged herself on the blanket to lie propped on her elbows, setting her text and her pocket dictionary in the sand in front of her. As she was doing this, two men in bathing costumes strode past quite close to their encampment. One of them—it was all she noticed from this vantage point—had very nice legs, sturdy and well proportioned. His companion's legs were too thin and hairy for beauty. Elsa looked back at her books, divided between being embarrassed and being annoyed with herself for being embarrassed.

"While it is yet midsummer," she translated aloud, "tell your slaves: 'It will not always be summer; build barns.'"

"What?"

"'Build barns.' Tell your slaves."

"'Is there then no other way?' groaned Sir Roderick, gazing out from the battlements toward the misty moors. 'Nay, my liege lord, the ordeal must be undergone. The cardinal will brook of no refusal,' intoned—"

"Oh, stop!" Elsa put her hands over her ears. "Why did your mother recommend this thing?" she asked when she had taken them away again.

"I expect because it's terrifically anti-Catholic. That's what Mother likes, mainly."

"Oh, I see."

Elsa looked down the beach toward the lake. The two men whose legs she had been comparing stood near the waterline, looking about vaguely, as if in half-hearted search of something. They were not very far away, but over the noise of a group of children nearby it was impossible to hear their conversation.

She studied them idly. They were young, but not very young: older than the undergraduate men who formed most of her male acquaintance. To judge by their hair and bathing suits, neither of them had been in the water. The one with the less satisfactory legs was the taller of the two, and thinner, and wore a flashy suit in green and yellow stripes. He was dark-haired and long-faced, and affected a pencil moustache, which suited him. His friend, who was just slightly shorter and wore a more conservative black suit, was better-looking all over: broad-shouldered and trim-waisted, with crisply wavy hair the colour of toffee, and a handsome face full of frank, boyish good humour. He was laughing at the thin-legged, moustached man, who had begun gesturing to different parts of the beach with great sweeps of his long arms.

"Oh!" said Elsa, pushing herself up from her elbows.

"Oh?"

"Harriet, I think those men are looking for their boat."

"Are they?" Harriet was eating grapes again, and did not look up. "How silly of them to have mislaid it."

"No, I don't think it's their fault. That's what I meant by 'Oh!' I think they're looking for the boat that I let those people take."

Harriet looked up at that. "That was half an hour ago, and the boat had been sitting there longer than that. They oughtn't to have left it alone so long."

"All the same, I think I had better go explain. Hadn't I?"

"It would be the decent thing to do," Harriet agreed. "I'll come with you."

She got to her feet, adjusted the knot in her scarf, and stepped into her shoes. Together they picked their way past the noisy children to approach the two men.

The handsome one saw them first—or saw Elsa, anyway. He was looking at her with a kind of intrigued half-smile, as if unsure whether she meant to be looking at him or not, when his friend, who had his back to the women, burst suddenly and loudly into song.

Harriet was so startled that she literally jumped. Elsa almost did too. He had one of those surprisingly high, powerful voices that you don't expect to hear coming out of a man.

"*Oh for the wings, for the wings of a DOVE!*" he sang.

"Do shut up!" his friend cried. "You're frightening people!"

"*Far away, far away wo-ould I—augh!*" He left off with an undignified squawk when his friend dove at him and wrestled him expertly to the sand.

"Be civil, Peachy," said the wrestler with mock sternness, getting to his feet.

"Psalm 55," said Harriet. "Mendelssohn, naturally."

The singer rolled over onto his stomach and goggled up at her and (to a lesser extent) Elsa. "Good heavens, Kit, females! Where did they come from?"

"They walked up, the way that people do on a beach."

"You have a terrific voice. Are you an opera singer?" Harriet demanded.

He picked himself up and brushed sand off the front of his bathing suit. "No," he said, thoughtfully, as if he had only just noticed this about himself. "No, I'm not. But you're right about Mendelssohn, of course."

"Can we help you at all?" asked the wrestler. "We're not completely mad—or we're not *both* completely mad."

His accent was lightly, refinedly English, and his eyes were very blue. He was still looking mostly at Elsa.

"We thought," she began awkwardly, "that … we ought to tell you—at least—you are looking for your boat, aren't you?"

It was her embarrassment at her errand, not his comeliness, that made her inarticulate. But she thought he was probably more or less used to having girls gibbering at him. He took it in stride, pleasantly.

"Yes, we are," he said. "That is, we were. It seems to have vanished."

"It was right about here, pulled up onto the shore?"

"Yes, just here. It was a hired boat, not actually ours."

"I'm afraid a family took it. A man and woman with three young children. They asked if it were ours, and when I told them it wasn't, they must have thought it was abandoned, and they took it and rowed away. I'm most terribly sorry. I ought to have stopped them. I didn't think that it must have been *somebody's* boat."

"I hope," Harriet put in, "that you hadn't left anything in it?"

There was a moment's glum silence.

"We shouldn't have, should we?" said the wrestler.

"Oh dear," said Elsa.

"It couldn't be helped—we were doing a good deed," said the

singer. He turned to scan the lake. "Is that them?" He pointed to a boat not far out, moving slowly and apparently full of children.

Harriet and Elsa said that they thought it was.

"They can't possibly be out long with all that progeny," the singer declared. "I suppose they didn't ask directions to Hamilton before they rowed off?"

Harriet and Elsa said that they hadn't.

"In that case," he said, "I feel sanguine about our chances of recovering our property, if we merely exercise patience and don't let that boat out of our sight."

"Terrific," said Harriet. "And in the meantime, you must allow us to buy you ice cream as an apology."

"Oh, we couldn't possibly," said the wrestler.

"Speak for yourself, my man," said the singer loftily. "I left an unfinished symphony on that boat. I would accept any amount of ice cream from any number of women."

"Oh dear," said Elsa again. She wished she would stop saying it.

"He'd written about three bars," said the wrestler. "The loss to humanity is trifling."

"Philistine!"

"I am frankly much more worried about our clothes."

"You ought not to be! Consider the whatsits."

The wrestler laughed. "Yes, well, I was rather asking for that. But I think it's verging on the beastly, all the same. You were the one who suggested we could leave our things in the boat and not pay for a locker."

"By 'whatsits,'" said Harriet critically, "do you mean 'the lilies of the field'?"

"That's right," said the singer. "Like the fellow said."

"You mean Our Lord Jesus Christ?"

"He does," said the wrestler. "You see what I have to put up with."

"Terrible," Harriet agreed. "You must absolutely let us buy you ice cream, under the circs. Come. You're not in a position to treat us, if you've left your wallets in your trousers' pockets in that boat, as I suppose you have. Well?"

"It's unanswerable, Kit. Unanswerable. We are not in such a position. Damsels, we must accept your charity." The singer swept a low, absurd bow. "Allow me to introduce myself. Peacham is my name. Peverell, to be specific, but my friends, as you will have observed, call me Peachy."

This, thought Elsa, was unhelpful. She had no intention of calling him "Peachy," and the way he had introduced himself had left her unsure whether his name was Peverell Peacham or Peacham Peverell.

"Peacham is his surname," the wrestler supplied helpfully. "Mine's Underhill. Christopher Underhill."

"But 'Kit' for the most part," Mr. Peacham insisted.

"Yes, but it isn't obligatory."

"Pleased to meet you both," said Elsa.

"Delighted! And I am Harriet Spencer, and this is my dear friend Elsa—"

"Nordqvist," Elsa added quickly.

"She thinks I don't know how to say it, but I do, and I was going to pronounce it *beau*tifully."

"I know you were. I'm sorry."

In Elsa's experience, people had two main ways of dealing with her surname. Either they adopted a cavalier attitude, apparently feeling that so long as it began with "Nor" and ended with "st" they were doing pretty well, or they enunciated with elaborate care—Norrrrd-ke-*vist*—which was worse. Harriet, especially when making introductions, had a tendency to fall into the latter category.

"Miss Spencer, Miss Nordqvist. How d'you do?" Mr. Underhill bowed in a much more restrained style than his friend. His pronunciation of Elsa's name was equally restrained. She was pleased.

There was an ice-cream cart on the street at the top of the beach, still within sight of the wayward boat, as Harriet pointed out. They walked up the beach towards it, four abreast, with Mr. Peacham and

Harriet in the middle. Elsa had fallen silent. She did not think of herself as shy, but she rarely had much to say in a group, especially among strangers. The heavy heat, with its encouragement to passivity and sloth, did not help. Harriet had no such difficulty; she shone in company.

"What was the good deed that you were doing when you left your things in the boat?" she asked the men.

"Believe it or not," said Mr. Underhill, "we were helping some children find a missing dog."

Mr. Peacham elaborated: "It had gone all the way up the street and was digging in someone's front garden when we found it. We managed to corner it and reattach the rope they were using as a lead. Quite a herculean labour, all told."

"The children must have been grateful," said Harriet. "I'm surprised *they* didn't buy you ice cream."

"I thought the same, personally," said Mr. Peacham. "I expect the financial side of the thing presented a problem—from the look of them, only a couple had any pocket money. They did, however, give us a frog in a jar by way of reward."

"We waited until they were out of sight before we released it under a hedge," Mr. Underhill added. "We didn't want to seem ungrateful."

"We were boys once too. Long ages ago." Mr. Peacham looked affectedly wistful.

Harriet laughed. "And pretty recently, too, from what I've seen. But what do you do when you're not rescuing puppy-dogs for waifs? *You* must be a professional musician, I guess."

"Ah! From the depths of my soul to the tips of my fingers, Miss Spencer, I am indeed a musician."

"Professionally?" Harriet repeated, prosaically.

"Oh, professionally—I profess it, yes, as the earth professes daffodils in spring."

"Or whatsits," his friend added irrelevantly.

"But then what exactly," Harriet persisted, "do you *do*?"

They had reached the ice-cream cart by this time, but a nanny and a couple of little girls were there before them. Mr. Peacham stopped and looked up at the sky.

"What does any of us do?" he asked, looking back down at Harriet. He draped an arm around his friend's shoulders. "We breathe, we love, we sing praises to our Maker, we eat bread in the sweat of our brows, we inch toward death day by day, but we *live* in every moment! That is what *we* do—isn't it, more or less, Kit? Sometimes we come to the beach."

There was silence. Mr. Underhill looked at his friend with undisguised affection. Elsa could see why. His enthusiasm was endearing. She half-expected Harriet to try again: "But how do you *earn a living?*" But she did not.

"I see," she said instead, smiling too. "And what are you doing at the beach on a Monday afternoon?"

"By a happy coincidence we both have the day off. You, I suppose, are women of leisure?"

"No, of great industry. We're university students. I'm a Political Economy major, and Elsa has her BA in Classics already, but she has come back to get her MA. We live at Victoria College—or we will, in two weeks. Elsa's come to town early and is staying at my house, to help me enjoy my last carefree days."

"Ah, scholars!" said Mr. Peacham rapturously. "You evoke happy memories, dear girl—happy memories. We were at U of T together—Trinity—aeons ago."

"Surely not aeons."

"You might be surprised," said Mr. Underhill. "We are alarmingly old."

"Indeed," said Mr. Peacham. "As a matter of fact, it's Kit's birthday—and how old do you suppose he is today?"

"Oh, I couldn't possibly—" Harriet began.

"Thirty," said Elsa decidedly.

"Elsa!"

"No, she's absolutely right," said Mr. Underhill.

"Oh, you don't look it!"

"Yes, he does," said Elsa. "Or sounds it, anyway. I think when men talk of being 'alarmingly old' without having a single grey hair, you can be pretty sure they have just turned thirty."

Mr. Underhill laughed. "If I could be sure I didn't have a single grey hair … "

"But you're younger, Mr. Peachy, aren't you?" said Harriet hopefully.

"Older," he confessed, hanging his head.

"By three whole weeks," said his friend.

"Well, all I can say is that you don't seem like thirty-year-olds to me," Harriet declared. "You seem quite young and unspoiled. I suppose you must not have fought in the War."

"We enlisted in '17," said Mr. Peacham, "but that was a little behind-hand of us, and we never shipped out. We missed the whole show. Nothing to boast about, I suppose, but that's how it was."

The nanny and the little girls had got their ice cream by this time, and their party had to attend to the serious business of choosing flavours. Mr. Peacham dithered for some time, finally settling on pineapple. Mr. Underhill chose vanilla. Elsa and Harriet both ordered chocolate, and Harriet paid for everyone.

"I guess," Harriet said to the two men as they strolled back down the beach, "that you have been friends since university?"

"We've been friends since we were twelve," said Mr. Peacham. "As a matter of fact, we're step-cousins."

"Is there such a thing?"

"Naturally. My aunt is Kit's father's second wife, hence his stepmother. Therefore I, her sister's son, am his step-cousin."

"I see," said Harriet. "And I guess you are both confirmed bachelors?"

"Oh, I am. Decidedly. I don't know about Kit."

This was evidently a joke, because his friend laughed at it, but neither elaborated. There was something rueful in the laughter, which made Elsa think that perhaps Mr. Underhill had recently been crossed in love.

"Now we have got our ice cream," said Harriet, "you must come back and sit with us, and we'll await the return of that boat-stealing family."

The men agreed readily, and they all made their way towards where Harriet's umbrella was planted in the sand. Mr. Peacham, not forgetting that Harriet had been able to correctly identify the song he had been singing earlier, began to interrogate her about her taste in music. Mr. Underhill dropped back to walk beside Elsa.

He smiled at her but said nothing, and went back to licking the drips off his ice cream. There was something undemanding about the way he smiled, as if it were not necessarily an invitation to conversation, just a gesture of goodwill. All the same, she found herself after a few moments talking to him.

"I hope you were not insulted by my saying you look your age."

"No, not at all."

"You don't, of course." He looked rather like a boy, particularly when he smiled, and particularly now, because when he had said he hoped he didn't have any grey hairs, he had riffled his fingers through his hair, making a couple of locks fall onto his forehead in a boyish way.

"No," he agreed. "I don't, really."

"Only I somehow thought that's how old you were. Harriet, of course, can't relate to anyone older than twenty-one, or thinks she can't—she makes an exception for me. I'm twenty-five." It was gauche of her to mention her age, she thought, especially since it was advanced for a university student. Clearly this was a subject she should just abandon. "I got started late—at U of T, I mean. My brother was offered a scholarship, but he's not well enough to take it up, so it was extended to his family, and that's how I was able to afford to come, and why I'm so much older than Harriet."

"Have you and Miss Spencer been friends long?" he asked, coolly sidestepping the awkward topic.

"Three years. Not long, not compared to you and Mr. Peacham. But it seems ages."

"It often does with friends."

"She started at U of T in my sophomore year, and we lived in the same residence. I noticed her straight off—well, she's the sort of girl you can't help noticing." Harriet and Mr. Peacham were far ahead of them by this time, and deep in their own conversation. "But for a long time we never had occasion to talk. I had my own friends from first year, and she was always surrounded by a crowd of girls from her own class—I mean her class at school *and* her social class. Then I overheard her one day giving a piece of her mind to some upper-year oaf who had made a friend of hers cry, and I thought: I have got to get to know that girl. So I invited her to my room to share some cake that I'd bought, and we discovered that we had the same opinion about several novels, and communed over our common disinterest in men."

That was how it had happened, but she realized too late that she should have ended that sentence sooner. She looked ahead to Harriet laughing up at Mr. Peacham and felt like a fool.

"We've not … maintained that disinterest," she said uncomfortably.

He said nothing, just offered her that same undemanding smile. She was impressed. She didn't think she had ever met a man who could have resisted saying *something* to that.

"It was different, actually," she said after a moment. "From the beginning it was different for both of us." She realized that wasn't very clear. "We weren't interested in pursuing husbands the way some of our friends were. We were purely interested in studying. But our reasons weren't the same.

"Anyway, we have been friends since then. You might think we would not have much in common, but I admire her greatly. She has such singleness of purpose, and such generosity. She's an heiress, but she has the ambition of forming a charitable foundation and opening a school for underprivileged girls—that is why she's studying Political Economy. And she never makes one feel inferior for not having expensive frocks or box seats at the opera."

"That is admirable, indeed. I daresay it took courage to invite someone like that over. I mean, if you didn't see yourself as part of her set."

"Courage? No, I don't think so. At least … I hadn't thought about it that way."

He shrugged. "Proof that you are generally courageous, I should say. But I may be wrong. I just met you."

"You did. I expect you're just impressed by the fact that I can talk to you without giggling. I daresay you don't get that a lot. Especially at the beach."

"Oh, why?" He gave her an innocent look.

Elsa frowned at him severely, and he cracked into a little, abashed (and very attractive) smile, and turned his attention back to his ice cream. She laughed.

Ahead of them, Mr. Peacham had broken into song again, this time in German.

"He is very talented, your friend," said Elsa. "What—if you don't mind my asking—what does he actually do for a living? Or does he not work?"

"He does," said Mr. Underhill. "He works as a shop clerk."

"Oh," said Elsa. She could see that there was something about this that displeased or saddened him, but she felt reluctant to ask what. They had, after all, just met. Perhaps, she thought, there was a class difference between him and his friend, as there was between herself and Harriet; only, judging by his accent, he was not the one in her position. Perhaps he saw it as a problem. "I suppose one can write symphonies in one's spare time while working at a shop," she said. "And one does have to earn a living somehow."

"One does," he agreed. "And one can."

They arrived back at the umbrella, where Harriet and Mr. Peacham had already seated themselves, Harriet in the shade, Peachy in the sun. Mr. Underhill sat down in the sun as well. Elsa joined Harriet beneath the umbrella.

Mr. Peacham, between mouthfuls of ice cream, was talking about an oratorio which he was composing—or had composed or was on the point of composing, it wasn't quite clear—for some entity or event called "Figgy's Sally."

"Are we back to the oratorio, then?" said Mr. Underhill. "What happened to the Symphony in … whatever it was?"

"C."

"As in 'lost at'?" Harriet suggested.

"Oh, very good!" cried Peachy. "That's what's happened to it. Anyway, I owe it to Sally to get to work on the oratorio. She's a great girl, and she's got her heart set on this. And it's not in any way her fault Figgy's stuff is so … unmusical."

Figgy, it transpired, was—or had been—a person, and Sally was his widow, or as near as made no difference, and wanted some of his unmusical poetry set to music. And Peachy Peacham, even when he wasn't rescuing puppy-dogs for waifs, was clearly something of a sweetheart. Anyway Harriet looked like she was thinking so.

"I think it sounds splendid," she said. "It's so good of you, and I'm sure she'll appreciate it. But speaking of splendid things—Elsa dear, tell them about your manuscript."

"Manuscript?" said Mr. Peacham. "What sort of manuscript?"

"A terribly ancient thing full of magical spells—tell them, Elsa."

"It isn't *my* manuscript."

"Whose is it?" Mr. Peacham seemed interested.

"It belongs to a Russian countess, who sponsored the excavation that found it in Egypt. This was only about a year ago—it was a major find. She has loaned it to a professor in the Classics Department at U of T, one of today's foremost Greek philologists, to establish its authenticity and prepare an edition, and … as I was one of his senior students last year, he let me spend quite a lot of time with it."

"Terrific!"

"It is, isn't it?" said Harriet happily. "She's a star student, actually, though she's too modest to say so. But tell them what the manuscript is."

Elsa warmed to her subject. "It's quite exciting," she admitted. "The only thing of its kind. The manuscript itself is from the fifth century, but its contents are probably much older. Professor Gallagher thinks, on the basis of the vocabulary, that it belongs to the Hellenistic era—that's BC, post-Alexander-the-Great, so not Classical, but ancient. It's called the *Bibliotheka Orphika*—the Library of Orpheus. You know Orpheus, of course."

"A musician," Peachy supplied, "though not, perhaps, a professional."

"Don't be absurd," said Harriet.

"Weren't there Orphic mystery cults in the ancient world?" said Mr. Underhill.

"Yes, exactly. It's that sort of thing. It's not magic spells, precisely—it's a whole system for using the power of your mind to transform yourself into … oh, all sorts of things. Anything you have ever wanted to be."

Peachy stared at her, wide-eyed. "It gives you instructions on how to do that?"

"Of a sort. They're very vague and mystical. There's something called the Pure Plain that the devotee is supposed to be able to descend to and receive spiritual instruction. Not, as in the Classical myths, the realm of the dead, but a sort of pure reality accessible to the individual will. Physical matter is conceived of as base and, well, basically evil, and 'spirit' as pure and capable of changing matter. And there are implications for human conduct—though to be honest, I can't imagine anyone ever took it very seriously. But it is tremendously interesting historically. The religion is otherwise undocumented, totally different from other Orphic cults of the time, and the Greek is unusual."

"Elsa is going to write her Master's thesis on it," Harriet explained proudly. "Or—probably, at any rate. Right, Elsa?"

"Hopefully." She really did think that "probably" was the right word; Professor Gallagher had seemed so pointed in showing the manuscript to her last year.

"But has anyone tried it out?" Mr. Peacham pursued. "I mean since they found it in Egypt, has anyone tried out the system?"

"I hope not," said Mr. Underhill mildly. "It sounds just the *faintest* bit heterodox."

"No," said Elsa, "I'm not aware that anyone has tried it. Although the countess who owns it is apparently eccentric, so she might have."

"How could she resist? What would you turn yourself into, Miss Spencer?" Mr. Peacham asked. "If you had this fascinating system at your disposal."

"Me? Nothing! I'd be scared to touch it."

"Oh, pssh! You then, Miss Nordquist! You're not afraid to touch it, obviously—but what would you *do* with it?"

"She'll study the morphology of the verbs or something, Peachy, you fool," said Mr. Underhill. "She's not doing her Master's thesis in experimental pagan mysticism. One hopes."

"No, indeed," said Elsa, laughing. "But I do know what I'd do if I thought it really worked. I *don't*—but it is the sort of thing one daydreams about. I would make myself into two people. That way, I could lead two different lives, without having to choose between them."

"What? You can make yourself into *multiple people*?" Mr. Peacham, who by this time was sprawled on his stomach in the sand, his ice cream finished, reared up on his elbows excitedly at this. "Why didn't you say so at first?"

"Oh, I don't know that it actually suggests you can do that. As I said, it's vague. That's just the first thing I thought of."

"Well! I know what I would do, though. Why stop at *two* versions of yourself? No, I'd take things a step further than that. I'd make the Peverell Peacham Symphony Orchestra, where I'd play every instrument; Peachy's Jazz Band, with Peverell Peacham on saxophone, piano, vocals, and drums; the Peacham Singers ... "

"And the Peacham Review, no doubt," said Mr. Underhill sarcastically, "to publish glowing notices of all your concerts. You'd do nothing of the sort, Peachy. Even you would not want to live in a world populated entirely by yourself."

"There'd be other people! That isn't what I meant, and you know it."

"But what would you do, Mr. Underhill?" Elsa asked.

"Oh, don't ask!" Mr. Peacham cried peevishly. "Would he sully himself with such a thing? Blasphemy and dark arts? My God! Frivolity, even!"

"Shut up," said Mr. Underhill. "I'll admit that if there were really supposed to be any power in the thing, like Miss Spencer I should of course be inclined not to touch it. But, to speak hypothetically, if I could turn myself into anything I wanted, I think I would enjoy spending at least an afternoon as a cat."

The others laughed, and Harriet agreed that it would be delightful, and told a story about her own cat, illustrating its keen enjoyment of life. For a while the conversation turned, as it always does under these circumstances, to anecdotes about cats that each of them had known. Elsa suspected Mr. Underhill of having changed the subject deliberately, but she was not certain of his motive. Something had been revealed in that discussion of the Orphic manuscript, she thought. She and Mr. Peacham had something in common, something that Harriet and Mr. Underhill, who would not have touched the thing that could transform them into a new person, clearly did not understand.

The topic of cats having been temporarily exhausted, Harriet reminded the men that they needed to keep an eye on their boat.

They spent a minute searching the lake until they had satisfied themselves that it was still out there, and still full of children.

"*Sister Agatha*, 'A Heart-Breaking Tale of Forbidden Love in the Dark Ages,'" Mr. Peacham read aloud. He had spotted Harriet's sensational novel, in spite of her attempt to slide it discreetly behind the tin of grapes. "I don't think I've read that one."

"I don't think you'd like it," said Harriet, artfully rearranging her legs so as to thwart his attempt to pick up the book. "It's full of evil cardinals and things. And Sister Agatha isn't your type of girl at all."

"No? What order do you suppose she belongs to, Kit?" He leaned boldly across Harriet to pluck the book from behind the tin.

"Some sort of heretical offshoot of the Poor Clares," said Mr. Underhill, deftly taking the book away from Peachy and handing it back to Harriet, who smiled gratefully at him.

"Spoilsport," Mr. Peacham muttered, sinking down to recline in the sand again. He hooked his thumb through a chain around his neck from which hung a medal bearing a small figure. "So that's the sort of thing Methodist girls read these days, is it? Hm. You *are* Methodists, I imagine, if you're at Vic?"

"They're in the United Church now," said Mr. Underhill.

"Oh, so you are."

"I'm not," said Elsa.

"No," said Mr. Underhill, "because Swedes are mostly Lutherans, aren't they?"

"I'm an atheist."

"Or because of that," he conceded, unfazed.

"Elsa, my dear!" said Harriet, a little irritably, "no one wants to hear that sort of thing when they're making polite conversation. Honestly, I don't know what to do with her sometimes."

"I'm sorry," said Elsa, because this was easier than getting angry with Harriet for trying to water down the conversation. It was Mr. Peacham, after all, who had introduced the subject of religion. But she thought Harriet was still put out by the incident with Sister

Agatha. To Mr. Underhill she added: "You are quite right about Swedes being Lutherans."

"I'm the one who should apologize," he said. "I was just trying to show off my knowledge of the world. *Is* your surname Swedish?"

"It is."

Mr. Underhill ate the last fragment of his ice cream cone and stretched out on his back in the sun.

"Shall we bury him in the sand?" Harriet suggested to Mr. Peacham.

"No!" said Mr. Underhill with surprising vehemence, half sitting up. "I mean, please don't. I'd rather you didn't." He looked ashamed of his outburst.

"He has a horror of sand," Mr. Peacham explained confidingly. "His ancestor was a pirate, you know, who was once marooned on a desert island. He survived—he was rescued by a merchant vessel—but he passed down the hatred of sand acquired in his ordeal."

"That's ... surely that's not true," said Harriet doubtfully.

"Not remotely," said Mr. Underhill. "It would be Lamarckian inheritance, for one thing."

"Goodness! And what's that when it's at home?"

"It's the theory that organisms can inherit traits acquired by their parents. It sounds good, but I'm told that's not how it works. One of my immediate ancestors is a zoologist."

"Well, the desert island part may have been a *slight* fabrication," Peachy admitted, "but I'm sure I remember you saying that your great-great-grandfather was a pirate."

"Really?" said Harriet, taken in again.

"No. Absolutely all of my great-great-grandfathers were gentlemen."

"English gentlemen," said Harriet. "Of course. But I'm not adept enough with accents to say what *part* of England."

"That's not your fault. I've a generic Oxbridge accent—but because I grew up at Oxford, not because I went to school there. Or only prep school."

"I get it. Because you left when you were a boy. But your 'immediate ancestor' the zoologist, I suppose he was a professor?"

"Indeed. He's retired now, but he taught at U of T for some years after we came to Canada."

"And what made him leave Oxford for Toronto?"

"Harriet," said Elsa, "don't interrogate the poor man."

Mr. Underhill laughed. "Peachy's aunt, mostly."

"Really?" Harriet was frankly astonished. "*Eminent Zoologist Immigrates for Love?* I don't believe it."

"These things happen," said Peachy. "Besides, you haven't met my aunt."

"I suppose. Look!" cried Harriet suddenly, starting up onto her knees. "They're turning towards shore—aren't they?"

The others followed the line of her pointing finger, and agreed that the boat seemed to have turned. But it was hard to tell, from this vantage, whether it was coming back towards the shore or travelling farther out.

"Perhaps we had better go down there to intercept it," Mr. Underhill suggested.

"I'll go," said Mr. Peacham, levering himself up from the sand. "Miss Spencer, you come with me."

"Oh, but that's not—" Mr. Underhill tried to protest.

"No, you two stay here," said Mr. Peacham firmly. "Someone ought to guard the umbrella."

Harriet looked at him doubtfully for a moment, then glanced at Elsa. "I—"

"Do come along!" Peachy cried.

"I'd better go," said Harriet, getting to her feet. "It doesn't seem as if he will take no for an answer." She did not look displeased.

"Quite right," said Mr. Peacham.

Elsa and Mr. Underhill watched the two of them hasten away

down the beach, Harriet tossing back her gold curls, Mr. Peacham leaning over to hear what she was saying. Mr. Underhill buried his face in his hands. Elsa laughed.

"Well, that was subtle!" she said.

"Wasn't it?"

"I'm sorry you got stuck here with me."

He frowned. "You know, I think of myself as a gentleman, but all the same, I don't think I'm going to let you get away with that. You were quite hard on me when I went fishing for a compliment earlier."

That made her laugh again. He stretched out in the sand once more, leaning back on his elbows. There was a pale scar on his upper arm that she would have said was from a bullet wound if she hadn't already heard that he had not fought in the War. Of course there were other ways that one could get shot. There was an attractive hint of delicacy in his colouring, a nice contrast to his sturdily masculine frame. She thought of asking if he wouldn't prefer to lie in the shade.

"There is something about this weather," he said, gazing out at the lake. "It makes one feel … "

"Indolent," Elsa supplied.

"Yes."

"Do you know, I am pretty sure your boat is headed *away* from shore now."

"I think you're right. Perhaps they'll come back directly," he suggested facetiously.

"Perhaps they will. I was a little surprised that Harriet agreed to go."

"Were you?"

"She's looking for something very particular in a man, and I'm not sure that your friend, delightful as he is … Well. She has a definite idea about how to talk to men, too—that is why she got annoyed with me just now, when she thought I was going to start discussing religion."

"You weren't?"

"Perhaps I was. She and I don't agree on the subject, but we're able to discuss it intelligently when it's just the two of us. But she thinks men don't want to hear that kind of thing from girls. I'm surprised she even told you we're at university. She thinks you don't like women to have serious thoughts."

"She's not wrong. A lot of us don't."

"I know. But Harriet doesn't want to marry a man like that. It's absurd."

"I see what you mean. For what it's worth, Peachy's not really a man like that."

"I didn't think so."

"And you?" he said nebulously.

"Me? I refuse to pretend to believe in things that I don't believe in just to be polite."

He nodded. "It's something I always discourage."

"Anyway, she needn't have worried—she knows I'm not the sort of atheist who goes around loudly trying to convince people not to believe in God."

"I'm glad to hear it. Although, if it were your idea of fun, I would listen politely."

"Would you?"

"Oh yes. Such is my gallantry."

"It won't be required, thank you."

He sighed affectedly. "It so seldom is, in this day and age."

"You wouldn't be afraid that I might convince you, if I tried?" she pursued. "Or is *that* the extent of your gallantry—that you would be willing to risk it?"

"You see through me, to some extent. I would't be afraid of it. I was raised an atheist."

"Really?" She had not, as far as she knew, ever met anyone who could say that.

"Really. Not a freethinker or a sceptic, or just someone who didn't go to church very much, but absolutely an atheist."

"So I have no need to convince you."

He smiled. "That is between you and your conscience. I meant that I've heard it all before."

"Ah."

He squinted up at the cloudless sky and said nothing. She wanted, or half-wanted, to ask whether he meant that he had really travelled precisely the opposite route to hers, from disbelief to faith, and if so, how on earth had he done it? And why? And with what, exactly, had he replaced the rationalism of his youth? But perhaps he had not meant that. He seemed, she thought, to enjoy being enigmatic; it seemed to suit him. By and by he looked down at her again.

"What were you reading?" he asked. "Not a heart-breaking tale of forbidden nuns, I don't think."

"Hesiod, the *Works and Days*." She produced the book, and offered it to him. "Do you read Greek?"

He grimaced. "Not so you'd notice."

"I'll read you some, then." She surprised herself—though not, apparently, him—with the suggestion. "I mean I'll translate it for you. It's quite good. It's all about farming and the value of hard work. The perfect thing when you're feeling indolent on a summer's day. Only … do come under the umbrella," she added, moving over on the blanket to make room for him. "You're very fair. I'm afraid you'll get sunburnt."

He looked up at her quizzically, and she realized too late how much that had sounded like something one would say to a small boy.

"I think I'll be all right here," he said. "But I should love to hear what Hesiod has to say about hard work."

So he lay in the sun, and she read to him about the changing seasons in ancient Boeotia, the best time to plant crops, the importance of praying to Zeus and Demeter, and when not to go to sea. The naïve instrumentalism of the pagan religion struck Elsa more forcefully than usual. Petition Zeus and Demeter for a good harvest, Hesiod advised his feckless brother; and wash your hands before you make an offering, or they won't hear you. And of course they might not anyway, because ultimately the gods' wills are unknowable. Dress them up as you would, she thought, this was what all mankind's faiths and creeds amounted to when you stripped them naked: rules for trying to get by in earthly life, and a mystical loophole whereby the divine power could do whatever it wanted without disproving its own existence. But she had been telling the truth when she had said she was not a proselytizer for unbelief; reality struck her as more a source of sadness than of satisfaction.

She paused to explain her translation of a difficult passage, and it became clear that Mr. Underhill hadn't been modestly deprecating his knowledge of Greek. He had studied it once, he admitted, but he hadn't paid very much attention at the time, and her grammatical explanation was lost on him. Somehow she found this perversely charming. His Latin wasn't a great deal better, he said, and though at one time he had been absolutely wild about Anglo-Saxon, that was mostly because he liked the way it sounded, and his professor had despaired at his laissez-faire approach to the philology. Elsa said sternly that she would have sided with the professor, and he said, "Of course you would."

But he seemed to enjoy listening to her. Fleetingly she wondered whether Harriet hadn't followed Mr. Peacham down the beach partly in order to allow something like this to take place. If she had—even if she hadn't—Elsa was grateful.

By and by she laid down the book, and said that she thought he might be growing bored. He protested that he was not.

"At any rate, that's as far as I'd read," she said, "and I don't fancy sight-translating for you. Not that I don't like you … "

In fact, she had been translating at sight for some time already. But she had reached a passage in which the poet advised that the right age to take a wife was when a man was thirty—"not much more nor less"—and she remembered the rueful way her companion had laughed when Mr. Peacham had suggested he was not a confirmed bachelor, and she had the sense to stop.

The sun had moved so that the edge of the shadow of the umbrella just touched his side. He lay with one arm crooked behind his head, the other hand lying on his stomach, on the black wool of his bathing suit. A gold signet ring on the ring finger of that hand caught the sunlight and sparkled. It was engraved with something that she couldn't make out. She imagined reaching out to run her hand up the back of his thigh, brushing away a streak of sand that clung to the soft curls of hair. She felt she could have sat there for a long time just looking at him. His eyes met hers, and she thought he knew what had been in her mind. And, somehow, he was not entirely happy about it.

"These two separate lives that you want to lead," he said, "what are they?"

She considered for a moment before answering. "One of them is a scholar who stays in Toronto, wins another scholarship after her MA, goes on to complete her PhD. She never marries. She devotes herself to a life of study. The other is a woman like my mother and my sister. A wife, a mother, with a beautiful house on a farm in Saskatchewan, and a husband, and four or five blond children. They are both happy, but they inhabit different worlds. They have hardly anything in common."

"And … which of them is the real you?"

It was a funny question: not "Which of them do you think you most want to be?" but "Which of them is the real you?" Yet it was a question she could answer.

"The one who stays in Toronto. The one who doesn't marry."

"I thought so."

"Did you? I have only recently realized it myself."

"It isn't too hard to guess. You almost seem to glow when you start talking about Greek, but you have said nothing about a fiancé."

She smiled. "There is no fiancé, of course. He's hypothetical—like the scholarship. But I am fairly sure … " She stopped, embarrassed.

"You could get either of them if you wanted?" He grinned, and she could feel herself blushing.

"At any rate—it's odd, but you're the first person I've told about this. I suppose it was Harriet talking about marriage that made me think of it seriously. Everything with her is part of a plan and a pattern, you see. Even that silly novel—she brought it to the beach because it's the sort of thing you're supposed to read for relaxation, and the beach is a place to relax. She studies Political Economy because it'll be useful to her with her charity. She has a low opinion of men, but she needs a husband for the lifestyle she has planned, so recently she's set aside her disdain and begun looking methodically for the right man. She's very practical. And I realized that what she was planning for—the husband, the household, the children, the domesticity—it was a whole different life, for a different woman. I can't be both. It isn't that the thought of a domestic life repels me. In many ways it sounds very nice. But I must devote myself to whatever path I choose, and it's the life of study that draws me the more strongly. That is where I must place my allegiance. Besides, there is a freedom that a woman can only have when she remains unmarried—there is no use denying that. And there is a beauty in self-reliance."

"Doubtless. There is also a danger of self-reliance turning into pride," he said.

"Is that a danger?"

"I should say it was. But then I don't suppose we would agree."

"I don't suppose we would." After a moment she went on, with a passion that surprised her: "The life of the intellect should be lived, if not in solitude, at least in the absence of domestic concerns. That has often been remarked, but I believe it is doubly so for a woman, who would be expected to put her husband's success and career before her own, to say nothing of the care of her children and the upkeep of her house. She is already attempting something that many would call unnatural, venturing into a man's province, and she must give up a portion of her womanhood in order to do so."

"Is that how you see it?"

"Of course. I am a realist."

"No, I meant … does not marrying really mean giving up your womanhood, even partially? Does it make you less of a woman to lack a husband? Pardon me—I shouldn't phrase it as a question. I should simply say *I* don't think it's true. I think you'd just be a different kind of woman. Different from your mother and your sister, I mean, not different from what you are now."

She wasn't sure quite what kind of argument he was trying to make here; certainly it was not the one that she had expected.

"You think I can't escape the confines of my sex at all, then?"

He laughed. "I didn't mean that, either! I suppose I was trying to say that I—that I don't think you *need* to. It's 1925. The 'confines of your sex' aren't what they used to be—are they? I don't know. Admittedly it isn't really my field. But I would think you could be a woman and a scholar, and you don't need a husband for either of those things, so you should only have one if you *want* him. This other—if it's the life you feel called to, it's what you should live. If you'll pardon the expression."

"What expression?"

"'Called.'" He grinned up at her apologetically. "It implies there's Someone to do the calling."

"It's just a turn of phrase," she said sternly.

"If you like. But what will you be a scholar *of*? Greek, I know, and there's this dodgy pagan manuscript that you want to write your thesis on—but after that? Or is that about as much as I could understand of the whole thing?"

"No, I daresay I could make you understand more. It's not really very technical, not the part that I love. It's poetry that I love best, the way it can transport you straight to the heart of what someone thousands of years ago thought and believed. And … the way it sounds—much like what you appreciated about Anglo-Saxon. Poetry in any language has that beauty of sound, at least to some degree. To be honest—I don't wish to sound like Mr. Peacham, but if I *could* split myself into more than two people, I'd devote one self to Latin and another to Greek. There is awfully good stuff in Latin, too—and the Romans were a nation of farmers at heart, which gives me a feeling of kinship with them, coming from a farming family. And there's quite a lot in both languages that hasn't been decently edited—there's quite a bit of work to be done. I'd like to make translations, too. There are the Loeb Editions—you know them? The little green and red books, with translations on the facing page. Hesiod, now, he hasn't been brought out in a Loeb yet. If he had, you could read him for yourself, and plenty of others like you. I should feel I was doing a useful service helping to make that possible—I don't think that everyone ought to, or can be expected to learn Latin and Greek, but everyone *should* have the opportunity to read great poetry. That is much more important. Mind you, I should be happy to support myself teaching those who do want to learn Latin and Greek."

"I can see you would be good at it."

"Thank you—that's kind of you."

"Do you write your own poetry, too?" he asked.

"No. I've never … No."

He waited a moment to see if she was going to go on, but she was already embarrassed by how much she was talking.

"And your family in Saskatchewan—you said you haven't told anybody your ambition yet, aside from me, and I don't really count—but what do you think they will say when you do?"

She shrugged. "Who knows, really? I've given up trying to guess what they will think of anything I do. I'm only here now because my father had a dream which he … which he took to be a sign, or a prophecy, or something."

His eyebrows rose. "Of you getting your MA?"

"No, of someone I would meet if I came back to Toronto. A man—a servant of the Lord, dressed like a tomfool (his words, not mine) but a true man of God all the same. And smoke and fire, or maybe not fire, just smoke, and … I don't know, somebody is saved from something."

"Damnation, one would expect," he replied automatically. "Though perhaps that's too obvious." He was silent for a while, and looked thoughtful. "Your father, is he … when he's not prophesying—"

"He's a farmer," said Elsa repressively, aware that it wasn't the whole answer. "I've never told anybody about that dream, either. I don't know what it is about you that makes me tell you these things after having just met you."

"I think I do," he said. "Perhaps I'll tell you later."

He sat up and ran a hand through his hair, ridding it of sand and disordering it again. He must know, Elsa thought, how well that suited him. "On further reflection, I might come under the … Look, they've found the boat."

They had. Harriet was waving from the shoreline, while Peachy stood knee-deep in the water, talking to the father of the family that was piling out of the boat.

"I suppose we had better go join them," said Elsa.

Mr. Underhill was already getting to his feet. He looked down at her with a curious smile. "It was fun while it lasted, wasn't it?"

"Oh, indeed." She wondered why he put it like that.

"Look here," Peachy was saying, irritably, when they reached the group around the boat, "we *paid* for this boat, and you made off with it and have had a nice hour rowing about the lake in it, with our belongings under the seat all the while, and I think it's actually quite decent of me not to ask you to reimburse us for the rental fee."

"All I am saying, young man," the father resumed, while his wife jigged nervously in the background, glancing from Mr. Peacham to

Mr. Underhill as if wondering which of them was going to hit her husband first, "is that it was a reckless thing to do, and you ought to take better care of these young ladies than that."

"What? But—that—" Mr. Peacham gabbled, turning red with anger and embarrassment.

"You're quite right," Mr. Underhill cut in penitently. "We really ought. Thanks awfully."

"Not at all. Good day to you." And he herded his family away importantly.

"What a dreadful little snot," Mr. Peacham declared, watching him go.

"Rather," said Mr. Underhill, reaching over the side of the boat to dig among the garments folded up under the seat. "But one can extract a useful moral from him. We really *ought* to be more solicitous for our fellow man—and, as the case may be, woman—than for our worldly possessions. Also, he did bring the boat back. Without robbing us, apparently." He straightened up, pulling a wristwatch out of the pocket of a pair of grey trousers.

"So now that you've got your boat, are we all going to go for a ride?" Harriet inquired.

"I'm afraid it's nearly three o'clock," said Mr. Underhill, putting his watch back in its pocket, "and I had promised to have tea with the Dean at four."

"What? Can't he leave you alone on your birthday?" Peachy demanded.

"He invited me *because* it's my birthday, idiot."

"Well, there's no time for boating, in that case," said Harriet briskly. "It's probably just as well. My parents will be expecting us before long. Shall we all pack up our things and troop over to the pavilion for the dressing rooms, then?"

Mr. Peacham looked suddenly like a child about to burst into tears. "I can't believe it! I thought you had the day off!"

"I told you I had to be back by four. The man's trying to be friendly—it doesn't come easily to him. I can't in good conscience not go."

"It's really too bad of those people not to have kept your boat a little longer," said Harriet, "so that you would have been 'unavoidably detained.'" The men laughed.

"At any rate," said Mr. Underhill, "we can't leave without taking the boat back to the boathouse where we got it, which means a short trip, at least. And it's in the direction of the pavilion."

"An excellent thought!" Harriet exclaimed, beaming at him.

They returned to the girls' encampment to gather up blanket, sun-umbrella, and picnic basket—Harriet had to snatch *Sister Agatha* away from Mr. Peacham again—trooped back to stow everything in the men's boat, and dragged it out into the water. Mr. Underhill steered, and Mr. Peacham rowed and sang bits of Gilbert and Sullivan, with Harriet reminding him of the words when he forgot them, and joining in when he required an extra character. When Mr. Peacham nearly dropped his oars to hit a particularly prolonged high note—"*However plain she be I'll LOOOOOOOOOOVE her!*"— Mr. Underhill caught Elsa's eye and shook his head, and she laughed.

All too soon they had reached the boathouse, and the two men gathered their belongings from the floor of the boat. Mr. Peacham extracted a wad of white linen and dangling suspenders, Mr. Underhill an armload of black wool that Harriet said looked unseasonably warm for the August afternoon. He said it was. The men and women parted ways at the pavilion to head for their respective dressing rooms.

"Well!" said Harriet, looking at Elsa, when they had located their lockers and put down their things. "That was something, wasn't it?"

Elsa laughed. "I'm glad that I did let that family take the boat, after all. We would never have had occasion to talk to them otherwise, would we?" She sat down on the bench opposite the lockers and bent to unfasten her shoes.

"It was Providential," Harriet agreed fervently. "I am sorry, my dear, that I left you with the dull one. I just … well, I'm afraid I was being a little selfish."

"Oh, but he wasn't dull! He's lovely."

Harriet had been leaning inside the locker, but she popped back out to look at Elsa with arch surprise. "Why, I didn't know you even cared about such things!"

"No, I didn't mean … " Elsa felt herself blushing again. "He's a charming person. Enigmatic, perhaps, but not dull at all. It's just that he and Mr. Peacham have a sort of music-hall comic-duo friendship, and his role is the straight man." She shrugged. "I won't deny that he's handsome, too. I should like to remain friends with him."

"*Friends?*" Harriet repeated, more archly than ever.

"Friends! Do get moving—we don't want to keep them waiting or have them leave without us, do we?" She was halfway out of her own bathing suit, but Harriet hadn't yet made a move to undress.

"They *won't* leave without us, silly, and we *do* want to keep them waiting. Honestly, sometimes I think you really were born yesterday, Elsa. *Friends!*"

She wondered whether to say, "Harriet, it's a euphemism. Of course what I actually mean is that I want to sleep with him." She decided not to. It would have shaken her friend out of her ebullient mood; she knew Harriet didn't approve of that kind of thing.

"And what does he do for a living, your 'friend'?" Harriet asked, leisurely untying her flowered scarf and fluffing out her hair with her fingers. She added: "Peachy's a Bay Street lawyer, if you can believe it."

Elsa couldn't believe it, since it directly contradicted what Mr. Underhill had told her. "I don't know what Mr. Underhill does," she admitted. "I didn't ask. I know he studied Anglo-Saxon at one time, and Greek, but inattentively." And apparently he believes in God, though he used not to.

"You *didn't* interrogate him about his command of classical languages after I left you alone together?" Harriet paused in wriggling out of her bathing costume to look at Elsa despairingly over her shoulder. "*Tell* me you didn't."

"I didn't! And Anglo-Saxon isn't a classical language, for heaven's sake. It came up in the course of conversation."

"Conversation about school, I'll bet! You are just incorrigible. Oh, but Kit must be something at the university. He's having tea with a Dean of some sort, didn't he say?"

"That's true," said Elsa absently, buttoning her dress. "But he didn't strike me as an academic."

She looked at herself in the mirror at the end of the change room, while she waited for Harriet to sort out her complicated under-garments. Elsa had come to the beach in a frock from home, blue checked gingham with a no-longer-fashionable length of skirt and large pockets on the front. At school she made an effort, within her means, to dress a little more smartly, but at the moment she looked very much like a farmer's daughter. She looked at the pale face in the mirror, considering the irony of the fact that it had made her squirm a little when Harriet called Mr. Underhill 'Kit' just now. She wondered whether it was true that she both wanted to seduce the man and felt that she didn't know him well enough to call him by his nickname. She decided that it was. She was not entirely pleased with this lack of logic.

"Maybe not," said Harriet, still pursuing the question of Mr. Underhill's profession. "Come to think of it, Peachy said that he keeps livestock."

"Mr. Underhill? With those hands? Don't be absurd!" Though they weren't delicate hands; they looked strong, but well kept.

"Well, Peachy said something about it."

Peachy makes things up, Elsa thought; we've already established that. Aloud she said, "Let me help you with your dress."

"I've got it," said Harriet placidly, continuing her slow progress with her buttons. "Why don't you fix your hair or something?"

"What's wrong with my hair?"

"Nothing, my dear. Just comb it out and put it up again—or leave it down, which I always think looks more feminine and suits you. They won't *notice*, exactly, but there'll be an indefinable something about you that says you took some care, that you want to look your best in front of them. That's why we're taking our time—we don't want to look eager, but we want to look like we care. Or at any rate," she finished awkwardly, as Elsa had sat down on the bench, showing no inclination to do anything to her hair, "*I* care."

"I know, Harriet," said Elsa gently. "I can see that. We have different ambitions."

"Oh, I know that, too." Harriet finished buttoning her dress with surprising efficiency, and set to brushing her own hair, and was ready to go in only a few minutes.

"I wonder how *they* will look," Harriet said thoughtfully, as they gathered up their belongings. "With their clothes on."

"Shall we have a small wager?" Elsa suggested.

"Shocking! What do you propose?"

"Mine will be better dressed than yours."

"Oh! The nerve!"

"And—*and* you'll be willing to admit it. Or I'll buy that pink frock from Eaton's that you tried to talk me into."

"You must be very confident," Harriet said, wide-eyed. "You were so opposed to that frock."

"It made me look like a hollyhock. Just a moment." One of her stockings was slipping down, and she put down the umbrella and paused to pull it up, while Harriet stepped out into the sunlight beyond the dressing-room door.

"Oh, golly!" Harriet turned back and stared at Elsa. "He meant *metaphorical* sheep. How silly of me! You're not going to like this."

"What?" Elsa straightened up and brushed past Harriet through the doorway.

"That," said Harriet, nodding toward the door to the men's dressing room. "Look."

Mr. Peacham and Mr. Underhill were indeed waiting for them, although they seemed to have been distracted by some absorbing topic of conversation, and were not really keeping a watch on the dressing-room door. Elsa was seeing them from a distance again, as when she had first studied them across the beach, and the man she had sat in the sand talking to for the last hour appeared a stranger to her once more. Mr. Peacham's white linen was a thoroughly crumpled suit, which he wore with a straw boater pushed far back on his head, and a waistcoat in an appalling purple and red paisley. Mr. Underhill's armload of black wool was a priest's cassock.

"Metaphorical *Roman Catholic* sheep. Oh, Elsa! Were you telling the truth when you said you didn't know what he did?"

"Yes. The absolute truth."

"How on earth can you have talked to him for an hour and not found out a thing like that?"

"You don't understand, Harriet—*I* was talking for an hour. I hardly gave him the opportunity to say a word." This was perhaps an exaggeration—but more than anything, she was struck by the selfishness of her own behaviour. She hadn't made an effort to find out anything about him; she had just talked about herself. Of course, he had asked a lot of leading questions. That he was obviously used to listening to people talk about themselves didn't make it any better.

"I don't know," said Harriet. "If I know you, you brought up the subject of religion at least once—I think he could have found the opportunity to tell you that he's a priest."

"I'm sure he could have—no doubt he should have—but I didn't make it very desirable for him, and I don't really blame him. *Please* don't say anything about it, Harriet. Pretend that I guessed or something. Well, no, don't do that, but … " Really she wanted to suggest that they duck back into the dressing room before the two men saw them, and leave by the door onto the beach; but she couldn't ask Harriet to forgo another opportunity to talk to Mr. Peacham.

"I will say that you win the bet, though," Harriet remarked. "He does make it look good."

This was true, though Elsa wished it weren't. It wasn't just that anyone would have looked good next to Mr. Peacham in his wrinkled suit and paisley waistcoat. The stark black of Mr. Underhill's costume looked out of place by the beach pavilion, but it gave him a kind of remoteness and gravity, in spite of his youthful appearance, that was, Elsa had to admit, very priestly. And the cassock was exquisitely tailored, with a long row of neat buttons down the front, and a kind of wide belt that hung down on one side with a fringe—there was probably a name for it—and his toffee-coloured hair was no longer mussed. He was certainly what her father would have described as "dressed like a tomfool," and he was certainly a worse victim of superstition than Hesiod, but he did, as Harriet said, make it look good.

"You don't suppose they're both Roman Catholics?" said Harriet, abruptly worried. "I thought they said they were at Trinity—didn't they?"

"Yes," said Elsa wearily. "But people convert. Anyway, they're not necessarily both the same thing—look at us. Let's go, if we're going."

"Poor Elsa! I won't say anything, I promise, but I think it's too bad of him—particularly being so handsome."

Harriet's idea of not saying anything was to march up to Mr. Underhill (*Father* Underhill? Elsa thought despairingly) and say in a loud voice, "Reverend! I had no idea!" and begin to tell him about her plans for her charitable foundation. He took it in stride, only once glancing past her at Elsa, but with no particular expression. It was Mr. Peacham who looked dismayed.

"We're going to catch the streetcar," he said stiffly. "Are you ladies ... "

"Yes, that's where we're going, too," said Elsa, taking pity on him. In fact, Harriet would ordinarily have hailed a cab. "We'll walk with you."

"Here, you'd better let me take that," he said, hastily seizing the umbrella which she was carrying. He must have noticed that his friend had already taken the picnic basket from Harriet. His ill-concealed sulkiness made Elsa want to laugh, in spite of everything.

They walked behind Harriet and Mr. Underhill up the street of small, new houses that led up from Kew Beach to Queen Street, falling farther behind as Mr. Peacham, in spite of his long legs, slowed his pace to a disconsolate slouch.

"Disappointed?" he said.

"About what?"

He jerked his chin in the direction of his friend's retreating back. "I take it he didn't tell you."

"I didn't ask," said Elsa repressively.

"Well, he keeps his own counsel remarkably well, does Kit—but he doesn't lie."

Unlike some, Elsa thought. "I didn't suppose he did. But is it entirely appropriate for a man of his profession to be … Isn't the beach a bit … " Ought I even to know what he looks like in a bathing suit? she wanted to ask.

"Oh, I see! Decency, and all that. Well, he might not have come down of his own accord, though he isn't as strait-laced as all that. But that's the sort of friend he is, you see. I didn't tell him where we were going—I showed up at the Parish House and said, 'It's your birthday, I am taking you out, it's no good protesting,' or words to that effect. I didn't even let him change. He put up a token protest, but I know him too well. He's a good sport. I had the bathing suits in the basket with the picnic things. We always used to come to this beach with my parents when we were boys."

They walked on in silence for a few moments while Elsa thought about this. The lie that he had told Harriet about being a lawyer she didn't feel she could address—it would be easy for him to deny it, and it was also just possible that Harriet had misunderstood some reference to a shop on Bay Street, the way she had taken literally his reference to Mr. Underhill's flock. But here, she thought, was something that she could in all fairness take him to task for.

"Mr. Peacham," she said finally.

"Oh, please don't call me that," he protested off-handedly.

"Mr. Peacham. If you heard a girl boast about how she could get her lover to do things that went a little against his conscience because he was just that devoted, what would be your opinion of her?"

"Eh?"

"I think it would be a low opinion, don't you?"

"Well … yes, I suppose it would. Bit manipulative. Not quite nice."

"Well, I'd just take care, if I were you, not to use your friend the same way."

He gave her a glassy look. "Oh, you would, would you?"

"Yes. I'd buy him a birthday present, if I were you. Something he'd really like—not just something that you think is funny."

"Look here! This is a bit much. Especially from a girl. I'll bet you're just sore because clergymen aren't your cup of tea—and you rather thought you fancied him."

"Mr. *Peacham*!" This was so very close to—in fact so *precisely* the truth that she all but shouted at him. He seemed genuinely taken aback. "I realize I may have spoken boldly," she went on, "but I hope I have not given you the impression that I am really the sort of woman who would have designs on a celibate clergyman."

"Oh," he said, chastened. "No."

Her lack of logic had reached a real apex there, she thought miserably.

"That goes *double* for Harriet," she added, fiercely.

"Good. Good. Er—I mean, of course."

An idiot, Elsa thought, but decidedly a likeable idiot. She could see how if he showed up on your doorstep and told you that you were going out somewhere, you would go.

They reached Queen Street just in time to catch an approaching westbound streetcar. There were only a few empty seats, and none together. The women sat, Harriet immediately behind the centre doors, Elsa several rows back, and the men stood. Mr. Peacham lost little time in abandoning Elsa in order to stand in the aisle by Harriet. Mr. Underhill came back to stand near Elsa.

"Subtle again," Elsa observed, nodding towards Mr. Peacham and Harriet.

"It's his middle name," Mr. Underhill agreed. "I hope Miss Spencer will find it more flattering than annoying."

"Oh, I think so."

"I owe you an apology, Miss Nordqvist."

She looked up past his buttons and starched collar, and smiled. "No, you don't." It was fun while it lasted, she thought.

"I do apologize, though. You were kind enough to confide in me, and I was not similarly forthcoming. I was waiting for a … for the right moment, I think—which was silly."

But there wasn't really a right moment for what he'd had to say, Elsa thought. That he regretted some of what had gone on on the beach made her uncomfortable; she would have preferred to be the only one feeling ashamed.

"If anything," she said stiffly, "I'm the one who should apologize. I must really have been preaching to the choir with all my talk about … about not marrying, and … "

His expression was unreadable—almost a determined *non*-expression. After a moment, he said, in a thoughtful tone, "That's an odd phrase. It's been my experience that choristers need to hear sermons as much as anyone."

The streetcar filled up, and he moved back, so they had no further opportunity to talk for some time, even supposing they had had more to say, which Elsa wasn't sure of. His last remark puzzled her. As people cleared out, he came back to stand beside her, but he confined himself to asking where she and Harriet got off.

"Yonge."

"I'm one stop before you."

"What, Church Street? I thought you weren't going to work?"

He laughed slightly. "I live there as well. I'm curate at the Cathedral—I mean the old Cathedral, not … Anyway, I live in the Parish House." He looked as if he wanted to say more, but he didn't.

Mr. Peacham was the first to get off, at Parliament Street. He bounded through the sliding doors with his picnic basket and stood waving on the sidewalk as the streetcar rattled onward.

As they reached Church Street, Mr. Underhill returned Harriet's basket to Elsa, and said goodbye to both of them.

"Goodbye, Reverend," said Harriet. "Lovely to have met you!"

Elsa had got up to come sit in the now-empty seat beside Harriet. On impulse, she leaned around the rail just as Mr. Underhill was stepping down from the streetcar.

"Happy birthday," she said, through the open doors.

He looked back, smiling, as the doors slid shut. She saw, rather than heard him say "Thank you," before he ran for the curb.

"I wonder what he meant," she said aloud.

"By what?"

"I said … well, I'd been saying something about marriage, before, and … classic arguments against marriage, really … "

"Oh, Elsa," Harriet groaned.

"I didn't know I was talking to a Roman priest! Anyway, I said, just now, that I must have been preaching to the choir. And *he* said, 'sometimes the choir needs a good sermon,' or words to that effect."

"Well, he has a point. Just because they can sing doesn't mean they aren't sinners."

"No, Harriet—metaphorically. What did he mean metaphorically?"

"Was it a metaphor?"

"Yes, you know—'preaching to the choir,' you know what that means."

"I thought that was what you called a cliché, not a metaphor."

"Well—true. But all the same, what did he mean?"

"I don't know. But I'll tell you one thing you don't seem to have noticed."

"What?"

"He crossed Queen when he got off, and went south on Church."

"Is *that* a metaphor?"

"No … not that I know of. It just means the cathedral he was headed for is St. James, not St. Michael's."

"Which means *what*?"

"He isn't a Roman Catholic priest, you goose. St. James is the *Anglican* cathedral."

"*What*? You distinctly said RC sheep!"

Harriet shrugged. "It didn't occur to me. And it probably doesn't make any difference. If he goes about in his cassock on a weekday in August, he's probably so High Church that he might as well be a Roman Catholic, for your purposes."

"I don't have any purposes as far as that man is concerned," Elsa declared, a little shrilly. "I hope I never see him again. Anyway, I don't believe in God."

"We all know that, dear. I can lend you *Sister Agatha* if you like. Sir Roderick might have some tips for you."

"Oh, God!" said Elsa miserably and illogically.

"All I can say," said Harriet philosophically, "is that I think it's a shame they found their clothes after all. You'd never have found out that yours was a clergyman, and I'd never have known that mine had such terrible taste in waistcoats."

Chapter Two

THE REHABILITATION OF
DELINQUENT BOYS

A week later, on Sunday night after Evensong, Kit Underhill sat on a window-sill in a Cabbagetown rooming house, smoking and listening to a loud, profane discussion of modern art. The room was Peachy's, and Kit was on the window-sill because there was nowhere else to sit. A critic of some sort who lived up-stairs—a slight, twitchy young man with thinning hair, whose name Kit thought was either Riley or Wiley—had spread out a couple of large charcoal drawings on the unmade bed. He and Peachy, and two short-haired, artistic-looking young women who had wandered in from somewhere with mugs of coffee, were standing in the middle of the room, looking at the pictures. A dingy white cat belonging to the landlady had curled up on the piano stool, and the only other chair in the room was full of dirty dishes. The window-sill was not very wide, and Kit could only sit on it by wedging the heel of one shoe against the window frame and letting the other leg dangle—he looked (he thought) picturesque, but he was not comfortable. He was looking around the room unhopefully for an ashtray.

"But the sheer goddamned bourgeois *smugness* of his draftsman-ship!" Riley or Wiley groaned. "How can you *defend* it?"

"No, no!" one of the artistic young women protested. "Look at the looming form of the church steeple in this one—could there be a clearer indictment of middle-class values?"

"*Could* there?" cried Peachy. "I should certainly hope so! It isn't an indictment of anything—it's a study of light and shadow, that's why it's called 'Light and Shadow: Study #3,' not 'Bolshevist Rhapsody' or 'Composition with Looming Church.'"

"No, no! The 'shadow' signifies ignorance, surely! You see how it's cast *by* the church, across the pavement, here … "

"Well, but the house is casting a shadow in this one, and that can't mean the same thing, can it?" the other young woman objected doubtfully.

"Exactly!" cried Peachy. "It's just a picture of a church—sort of a dark, ugly-looking church, I'll grant you—"

"But it's all so goddamned *figural*!" Riley/Wiley howled. "His early works were sheer, savage outpourings—spontaneous, vital! This, this—well, it's just as you say, goddammit. *It's just a picture of a church.* It's a crushing disappointment, I tell you. We should never have agreed to exhibit his new work without seeing it first."

"You *would* defend it, Peacham," said the angrier of the two young women with an ironic laugh. She cast her eye around the room, taking in the crucifix that hung above the bed, the collection of candles and images of saints covering the top of the piano, the clergyman in a Roman cassock perched in the window—and she shook her head.

"And what do *you* think of the pictures, Father?" the other young woman inquired tentatively.

Kit had given up looking for an ashtray and tapped the ash off his cigarette into one of the dishes in the chair under the window. He was slightly dismayed at being appealed to, but he dutifully studied the pictures on the bed, unwedging himself from the window frame to turn and get a better look.

"I, um, have to agree with Peachy that it's an ugly church," he said finally. "And an ugly house, for that matter. And I think I also agree with Miss, er—"

"Cole," said the angry young woman, surprised.

"With Miss Cole—that that's probably rather the point. You know—squalid conditions of urban life, and … oppressive whatnot."

He shrugged diffidently. "Anyway, I'd *hope* that's what he means to convey."

"But it's so go—d—so *obvious!*" Riley/Wiley censored himself unexpectedly, with a sort of choking noise.

"It must be," said Kit, "if I could figure it out. I'm sure I couldn't have made head or tail of the savage outpourings."

Miss Cole laughed explosively. "Nobody could! That's what R.W. liked so much about them!"

"Yes, they were dreadful, really, R.W.," said Miss Cole's milder friend. "You didn't know whether you ought to be offended or just nauseated. I'm glad for his sake that he's started drawing *things*—it seems much healthier, somehow."

Kit resumed his former position on the window-sill and turned his attention back to his cigarette, wondering whether R.W. might actually stand for Riley/Wiley.

The cigarette was Turkish, an expensive brand that he liked but never bought for himself; Peachy had surprised him by presenting him with a box of them when he arrived. In fact, "presenting" was the wrong word—he had tossed the box to Kit across the room. "A late birthday present," he had said off-handedly. "Those are the ones you like, aren't they? Oh, and feel free to smoke, if you like. I know you're *deprived* at St. James." "Funny," Kit had replied, wondering what Peachy had not been able to afford for himself because he had spent money on those cigarettes. And what private guilt had impelled him to buy Kit a present, which was not his normal practice.

"But what we really came down here to ask is how Watson is doing," Miss Cole said.

"Back to normal," said Peachy. "Wrote a sonnet this afternoon. I looked in on him and he read it to me."

"Was it a depressing sonnet about suicide?" Miss Cole asked warily.

Peachy considered this. "I don't think so. It's hard to say what it was about, of course. I only say it was a sonnet because that's what he told me it was. I think there were fourteen lines in it, but one of them was 'ribald.'"

"What did it say?" R.W. looked interested.

"'Ribald.' That was the whole line. It was a description of … No, I don't know. Possibly something to do with transcendence—when in doubt, I think that's what most of Watson's stuff is meant to be about."

"Well, it does sound like he's back to normal," said Miss Cole's friend. "He's very lucky to have you as a neighbour, Peachy. I'm not sure anyone else around here would have actually stopped him taking all those tablets."

"I'm sure I wouldn't have," said R.W. Miss Cole glared at him. "Look, I'm not saying I think the man should have killed himself because he can't write. I just don't think I would have noticed, what with one thing and another. I've been da—dr—dreadfully busy."

"Well, fortunately he didn't have to depend on you," said Miss Cole, "because we've got Peachy the … Prodigal Samaritan or what-ever he is." She glanced at Kit, either seeking approval or hoping he was going to object. He smiled, and she looked away, beginning to blush.

Miss Cole and her friend left shortly after that, but not before offering Kit a cup of coffee ("though it's not very good"), which he politely declined. R.W. packed up the hated charcoal sketches in a portfolio with elaborate care, and took them away, still muttering about bourgeois draughtsmanship. Peachy shooed the white cat off the piano stool and sat down.

"I don't think that fellow Watson was really going to kill himself," he said.

"No?" Kit blew out a delicate thread of smoke and looked at him with an affectionate scepticism.

"No … I mean yes. He probably was, at some point. But he must have had some inkling that when he came to tell me all about it and ask me to be his literary executor, I was going to confiscate his precious tablets and talk some sense into him."

"I expect that's what he came to you for, really," Kit agreed.

"Whether he knew it or not."

"Yes."

"Are you happy strewing ashes all over my furniture, or would you like an ashtray?"

"Oh, you have an ashtray?"

"Somewhere."

He found it after a moment, on top of the piano, behind a statuette of the Blessed Virgin, and presented it to Kit. It was oddly clean. Peachy himself did not smoke.

"That was impressive, you know," Peachy remarked. "You had Miss Cole eating out of your hand—and she hates men, absolutely hates them. And isn't too terribly keen on the church, either, for that matter. What is your secret?"

Kit shrugged. "I don't know—I don't do it on purpose."

"Oh, doubtless it's a gift of the Holy Spirit," said Peachy without bitterness. "You got Ralph Wiley to stop swearing for five minutes, too—nearly as remarkable. Do you want to hear my new composition?"

"*Do* I?" Kit stubbed out his cigarette end in the clean ashtray and hopped down from the window-sill. He twitched a rumpled blanket across the end of the bed and sat down on it. "Play," he directed.

"It's a Nocturne of sorts," Peachy explained, spinning around on the stool to face the piano. "I don't know what you'll think of it."

But you do, thought Kit, as his friend bent over the keyboard and poised his long hands on the keys. Or you should, by now.

It began as a delicate, almost evanescent melody, built into a passage full of powerful chords, then trickled exquisitely away again. There was a poignancy to all of Peachy's compositions, even when he tried to be bombastic or modern, as if his essential good nature shone through in spite of himself. This one wasn't even trying to hide its tenderness.

"It's beautiful," Kit said inadequately, when the last note had faded and Peachy had spun around to face him again.

"Thanks … It's unfinished, of course. It needs something. I have a feeling it's just the first movement of a suite."

"That could be good," said Kit, but with an aching heart. It would be good if he thought the suite had any chance of ever being finished. It would be good if he thought it wouldn't languish like all of Peachy's other half-started projects, while Peachy moved on to a new idea for an opera or toyed for a while with an old idea for a jazz band.

Peachy had half turned away on the piano stool and was running a forefinger dreamily across the surface of the keys. "It's for Harriet," he said.

"Who?"

It wasn't Kit's finest moment; he knew even before Peachy turned an incredulous, glassy stare on him that he shouldn't have said that, but it had been a genuine question. He was sure he didn't know any Harriet.

"Harr-i-et," Peachy repeated slowly. "The woman I am going to marry."

"What?"

"Marry!" He leapt to his feet. "My future Wife! The partner of all my—"

"Yes, I'm familiar with the concept! Who is your future wife? When did you get engaged? It's the first I've heard of it."

"We're not *engaged*, you horrible realist. This is a private determination of my own. She is to become my wife. To that end are all my thoughts directed, all my—"

"Oh! Is it the girl from the beach—the other one, the pretty one?"

Peachy was giving him another glassy look. "The 'other one'? The '*pretty* one'? You don't remember her name."

"Spencer. I didn't remember her first name. It's been a long day. Anyway, I didn't talk to her very much, until—" Until she decided I might be useful to her, he thought, but he had just enough sense not to say that. "Well, at all, really."

Peachy sighed and sat back down on the piano stool. "Yes, well, since you have reduced the discussion to such a level, Harriet Spencer is indeed the woman I mean. Although I think you're too hard on her friend—she was pretty too."

"No, I think I'm being quite fair. Miss Spencer is pretty. Her friend is … something else. 'Pretty' is not the word I'd use."

"'What?' he cries in his turn. And what *is* the word you'd use?"

"I don't know … I don't think there's quite a word—you might need a phrase. Something-ly beautiful." He shrugged. "I'm not a poet. Anyway. You were saying. You plan to marry Miss Spencer. You have written part of a suite or something in her honour—which is very lovely, by the way, and bound to impress her."

Peachy closed the cover of the piano keyboard and leaned back dramatically against it, arms outflung. "She's everything I have ever wanted in a woman, Kit. Such sweetness, such vivacity, such … such a light, clear soprano tone—stop laughing! It's quite important—I couldn't possibly marry a woman who couldn't sing."

"No, I suppose you couldn't."

"Or couldn't appreciate music, at least. But that was what struck me immediately, you see—I mean apart from her obvious radiance, her *angelic* face, her breathtaking … " He noticed the shape he was sketching in the air and shoved his hands embarrassedly into his pockets. "Her—her figure, which the bathing costume did certainly show off to advantage, and which you must admit was, well, flawless. Not to say … "

"Breathtaking. You did."

"Yes, well, I stand by it. 'Pretty' indeed! But it was her knowledge of music *and Scripture*, you see—she said 'Psalm 55' even before she said 'Mendelssohn.' That was what impressed me. I grant you she seemed rather uninformed in other regards—couldn't quite picture her as a Political Economy major, to be honest, but—she probably just wants a little building up or something. Women often do, I'm told—the culture doesn't encourage them to develop their minds, and so they waste their potential. Well, I'm something of an expert on that—the irony is not lost on me, my lad. But … the point is, I love her. I just love her." Suddenly he looked genuinely desolated. "Oh, I know I sounded confident a moment ago, Kit, but really I haven't a hope. She can't possibly love me—how could she? I couldn't even advise it, from a rational perspective. If I were her brother or something, I'd probably forbid it."

"Take heart! She may not have a brother. And if I were her brother, I *would* advise it. Heartily."

"No doubt, but you're a fool—I've long known it. Kit, it's no good! Even if by some miracle I could win her love, what then? Could I look after a sweet, delicate creature like that?"

"Of course. You're not a brute. Anyway, are you absolutely sure she wants much looking after?" This was as close as he could comfortably get to saying: I think she misrepresented herself to you. The friend Miss Nordqvist had described so eloquently hadn't sounded to him like a particularly delicate creature. Which was to her credit, Kit thought, and would no doubt be better for Peachy, too.

"Oh, I don't mean … I know I'd be *nice* to her. I mean … well, this whole idea of settling down and marrying, you know, it makes one wish one had … I don't know, finished one's degree … done something with one's life. How can I offer her a husband who cobbles together an income at three or four precarious jobs, with no prospect of anything better on the horizon?"

"You could look for full-time work."

"We've been over this before, Kit. I can't leave old Doughty in the lurch—the shop would fail if I quit. And I'm not being self-important, I'm just stating the plain truth when I say Montano could not keep the band together without me. And we have to rehearse in the mornings because Sykes still works the night shift. I know the reviews don't bring in much money, but they don't take me long to write, either, and at least they get me free tickets to shows. I'm not qualified to do anything that pays real money—anything that I'm willing to do, I mean. I can't take handouts from my parents, it simply isn't right. I couldn't work in an office or anything like that and still have time for my music—and I can't give that up."

They *had* been over it before, many times, and it always ended the same way, with this recitation of things that Peachy couldn't and wouldn't do. Half of it—two thirds, maybe—was about not wanting to let other people down. The rest …

"But you do, actually," Kit said. "All the time."

"What?"

"Give it up. Not altogether, obviously, but piecemeal—and in the end, I'm afraid it'll amount to the same thing."

Peachy looked at him doubtfully. "You mean because I can't focus my energies and stick to one type of music? But I've explained to you—"

"I don't mean that. I mean because you never finish anything."

"But that's … that's just a symptom of … that's just because I can't devote myself to one form, it's—I haven't found—"

"Let me put it this way. *Why* do you want to make music?"

"Why?" Peachy slouched lower on the piano stool, arms folded, irritated. "Because it's what I'm good at."

"But why do you want to do the thing you're good at? I don't mean why does *one*—why do *you*?"

"To glorify God." He pushed himself upright on the stool and looked at Kit belligerently.

"Exactly."

"What do you mean, 'Exactly'? I thought I'd rather called your bluff there."

"Not at all. But suppose you wanted to build a cathedral. Would it be good enough, do you think, to scribble a plan on the back of an envelope and leave it in a drawer? Obviously not. The thing has to exist in the world. It's what we've been given the world *for*."

"I see what you mean," Peachy admitted grudgingly. "But there's so much I want to do—there aren't enough hours in the day, that's why … " He gestured hopelessly. "That's obviously a very poor excuse. But my music does exist in the world. You've heard it, for instance."

"Yes, but who am I, really? I'm like the drawer with the plan of the cathedral in it. It's *something*, but it's not enough."

"All right. I suppose I see that, too. But what are you suggesting?"

"You've got to finish something. Really finish it, and have it performed somewhere—let it out into the world. It doesn't matter what it is. You want … " You want somebody to knock you on the head so you forget about all the competitions you won as a child, everything your teachers and your parents' friends and the contest adjudicators said about how brilliant you were going to be, how the world was your oyster and you could do *anything you wanted* when you grew up. "I think you want to stop worrying about what form is the best, what the name of Peverell Peacham will be known for down the ages, and just see something through to the end. Because I don't think you're meant to do just one thing—you're meant to do a lot of things. And you have to start somewhere."

"Where? For instance."

"That suite—the thing that you're writing for Miss Spencer."

"It won't be worthy of her."

"Peachy!"

"Oh, all right, all right. I take your point. Better to give her something that falls short than not to have anything to give her at all, eh? But here's another complication! How am I to see her again? I don't know where she lives!"

"She lives at Victoria College, you nitwit—or will, in a week. She told us that herself."

"Oh, right you are! Perhaps—do you think?—it might be better to write her a song … "

"Mm."

Peachy smiled knowingly. "He shows great restraint—as usual. Now!" He pushed himself away from the piano and leaned forward, planting his hands on his knees. "To return to a much more *interesting* matter. 'Something-ly beautiful,' Kit? Please elaborate."

"I can't … I thought I made that clear."

"I tell you what," said Peachy with an air of magnanimity, "I'll look her up for you, shall I, when I'm hanging around Vic, pining for Harriet? Subtly arrange a reunion—give you the opportunity to expand your vocabulary a bit. Mm?"

"No, please don't do that. I'd prefer … I don't think it's a good idea."

"You don't think it's a good idea because I shouldn't be loitering around a girls' residence, or you don't think it's a good idea because you don't actually like the girl? Because it looked to me—not that I spared much attention for you, but it looked to me like you liked her."

"Actually, I'd go further than that," Kit said gloomily. For the past week he had dwelt on his memory of Elsa Nordqvist with an adolescent obsessiveness that he had rarely suffered when he actually was an adolescent.

"*Would* you?" said Peachy. "You don't say! But then why don't you want to see her?"

She's an atheist who is convinced she needs to lead a single life in order to fulfil her intellectual calling, he thought. "I don't really think I have anything to offer that she wants."

Peachy stood up again, apparently propelled upward by the strength of his perplexity. "Don't say that! It's not like you."

"No?" Kit had draped himself across the end of the bed by this time, his head resting on one arm. The idea of talking about this made him very tired. "What is like me, exactly?"

Peachy considered this a moment. "Well, frankly, you've usually been the pursued, not the pursuer. So it's natural that when faced with someone you want who doesn't seem to want you, you're a little out of your element. That's understandable. But all the same, it isn't like you to take such a defeatist attitude."

"I don't think it's a defeatist attitude."

"What do you think it is?"

"Respect."

"What?" Peachy brushed this aside. "No, I say it's plain inexperience. This Miss Nordquest—"

"-qvist."

Peachy rolled his eyes. "Miss *Thing* isn't the type of Sunday-School-teaching, aspiring missionary who usually falls for your particular air of slightly raffish saintliness, and you're just not sure how to proceed. But fear not, my lad, I am here to instruct you. What you lack in the experience of unrequited love I more than make up for, as you know. And I wouldn't despair, by any means. It's no great matter to—"

"Stop right there. If you begin using words such as 'conquer' and 'overcome' in connection with Miss Nordqvist, as I believe you were just about to, I shall knock you down." He said it without moving from the end of the bed, which may have made the threat unconvincing.

"I'm not advocating *violence!*"

"You're not advocating anything that I am going to do, at all. I'd be happy listening to her read Greek for hours at a time, even if I only understood one word in three—in fact, she makes me want to get my old *Introduction to New Testament Greek* out of the back of my cupboard, or wherever it is, and have another crack at it so I could dimly appreciate her brilliance. But I don't want to get into an argument about the existence of God with her—I hate arguments about the existence of God, I don't think they convince anybody—and I don't think she wants to have one with me, anyway. She's nicer than that. If I ever find that I can be of service to her—I mean, if she should want a dragon slain, or Masses said for the repose of somebody's soul, or anything like that—I'm her man. Otherwise, I think it's better for both of us if we keep our distance from one another."

Peachy sat on the bed and looked down at Kit. "I don't know about this. It sounds very noble, but it's a little weird. What if she likes you?"

"It's not the point, but she doesn't." Kit sat up. "I'm fairly certain she thinks I'm an idiot—and an idiot of questionable moral character at that. But what was I going to say? 'Actually, I think celibacy is rubbish, and I'm tired of trying to convince my bishop and everybody I know that I'm not absolutely wading into the Tiber just because I'm thirty and I've never been engaged. So, yes, I *was* flirting with you'?"

Peachy was laughing by this time. "Well, if you were tempted to say that to her, perhaps it is better that you do try to avoid her."

"Actually, I think she would have laughed," Kit said, feeling perversely defensive of Miss Nordqvist's sense of humour.

"If you say so. Do you want me to look her up, then?"

"I do not."

Peachy kindly abandoned the subject after that, and lapsed back into rhapsodizing about Miss Spencer and wondering how he could write any piece of music worthy of her perfection. He might have taken Kit's remarks about the plan of the cathedral to heart, or he might not; it was hard to tell.

They went down the hall by and by, to check on the suicidal poet, and found him toasting a cheese sandwich in his fireplace. He insisted they join him, fetched out more bread and cheese from a desk drawer, and wanted their help with an article that he was writing called "Transcendence: What Is It?" The answer seemed to be "I don't know, and neither shall you." Kit thought that was more or less all right. The cheese sandwiches were delicious.

It was well past midnight when Kit left. He walked through

perfectly empty, silent streets, hands in his pockets, feeling a certain detached amusement with himself.

It wasn't, when he considered it lucidly, at all surprising that the first time he saw Peachy after his birthday, Peachy should have mentioned those girls from the beach. Actually, it was ridiculous that this had taken Kit by surprise. It had been clear on the beach that Peachy was smitten with Miss Spencer, and though Peachy being smitten with girls was a regular occurrence, there had been something a little out of the ordinary—a certain shameless direct-ness—about his behaviour at the time that should have suggested to Kit that this infatuation would at least last out the week. But it hadn't suggested anything to him, because he had been too busy being infatuated himself.

That was not a regular occurrence. He was by nature—or maybe it was nurture—somewhat slow to form attachments. It was a trait closely related to his dislike of talking about himself. Then too, years of being Peachy's friend had made Kit reluctant to become attached to (or, worse, to attract to himself) any girl who might at any moment, in the dizzying vicissitudes of Peachy's heart, turn out to be the one, the only, the very person Peachy couldn't live without. He wasn't having any of that kind of nonsense.

Sometimes Kit felt that his real calling, his real assignment on Earth, was to be Peverell Peacham's friend, and all the rest was ei-ther window-dressing or just a means to an end. Sometimes, when he was feeling particularly uncharitable, he thought that Peachy would have agreed with this assessment. Not that Peachy was really self-centred. He had his moments, but they were more than balanced by his generous, affectionate nature, his huge capacity for worrying about other people. It was just that he moved at such a pace, flitting restlessly from one thing to another, in love, in art, in everything; it was work just to keep up. There were times when Kit's affection for Peachy consisted mainly of gratitude for the past; he never felt less than that. Most of the time he still felt considerably more. That was how it was supposed to be.

Peachy had coined the term "step-cousins" very early on, to emphasize that their relationship was absolutely unique—which of course it wasn't. They were not blood relations, but they had lived together from childhood. It was the kind of friendship, Kit thought, that must have been routine in the ages when noble families sent their sons to be brought up in each other's houses. The idea pleased him. It was easy to tally up the ways Peachy had changed his life, harder for him to tell how he had influenced Peachy. It went as far as their names: Peachy had been Peachy since time immemorial, but no one before Peachy had thought (or would have dared) to call Christopher Underhill "Kit."

At Trinity the two of them had been at the heart of a group of passionately opinionated men and women who argued about art and philosophy. Peachy was in his element with these people, but Kit would have been an outlier if he had not been inseparable from Peachy. So he was something of the quiet centre of the storm. People introducing him to one another would say things like, "This is Kit Underhill; he's an Anglo-Catholic like Peachy, only not so absurd."

That group of friends had been decimated by the Great War, but Kit and Peachy were left. For a while they had shared an untidy apartment in the West End, a place that Kit remembered like one of those Renaissance paintings full of dramatic light and shadow—not because that was what the apartment had been like, but because that was how he had felt during that period. But an undiscussed rift had developed between them, even before Kit was finally ordained and went to live at the cathedral. It was paper-thin and easy to forget, but when he remembered it, it was like having a dislocated soul.

It was when Miss Nordqvist had begun talking about her friendship with Miss Spencer that Kit had begun to find her really fascinating. Perhaps, he thought, this was because she reminded him of the way he wanted to be, the way he was at his best: diffident about himself, but enthusiastic about his friend.

Admittedly, it was her physical beauty that had first caught his attention. She was tall enough, in her shoes, to look him straight in the eye, and so slender that her figure was more angles than curves; but far from looking fragile, she had an air of poised and elegant strength. There was in fact nothing delicate about her. Her long fingers were reddened with work, her high cheekbones lightly freckled by the sun. Her hair in its slightly fuzzy plait was almost the colour of cream. She moved with a kind of casual grace, and spoke in a low, measured voice that became ecstatically musical when she talked about her studies. The thought of how neatly her breasts, which were very small, would have fit in the palms of his hands had kept him uncomfortably awake for part of one night, and he had woken the next morning not only disgusted with himself but almost sick of the thought of her. Then he had remembered her sitting in the shade translating Hesiod for him on sight (whatever she claimed, he was pretty sure that was what she had been doing) and he was as ashamed of his distaste as of his lust.

He really did feel that it was better that they not meet again. He *didn't* have anything to offer that she wanted—and he didn't know how to offer what he did have in any way that would not offend. His main evangelizing tactic, such as it was, was to try to make the whole business look good, but he had a feeling that with Elsa Nordqvist, given how he felt about her, that would have looked about the same as flirting. Would probably have been about the same. And that wouldn't get either of them anywhere. For his sake, he would have liked her to decide that she was wrong about the intellectual needing to live alone. For her sake he hoped she would realize that she was wrong about God. But he didn't think he had the wherewithal to make either of these arguments effectively. Of course, this might be a problem, and something that he ought to be worried about. He was not terribly given to worrying. Occasionally, by way of a private joke with himself, he worried about that.

Then there was the strange fact that Miss Nordqvist's father seemed to have had a prophetic dream about him. He had naturally not mentioned that to Peachy. He did not feel that the dream itself, or whether or not he believed it was about him, had any particular implications for his behaviour towards Miss Nordqvist. In her telling of it, the dream had only required that they meet—or that she meet someone who sounded suspiciously like him, anyway—and that had happened. Whether they were required to meet again … Well, he had to admit that, if the dream were really prophetic, it seemed more than likely that they would. He stopped on the sidewalk and smiled up into the glow of the nearby streetlamp. He could not remain really despondent for long, and since he was twelve years old he had known why. *After all, I hope that I'm wrong. If it is your will that I may be useful to her, I'm all for it.*

"I just don't see how," he admitted aloud.

A policeman on the opposite sidewalk was eyeing him with what looked like a mixture of professional suspicion and Protestant mistrust. He crossed himself imperturbably, nodded to the policeman, and walked on.

*

If his path was to cross Elsa Nordqvist's again, Kit saw no likelihood of its happening in the next week, before term started and Peachy could act on his plan of loitering around Victoria College. As far as that went, he was right; but on the Thursday afternoon following his conversation with Peachy, something else happened which, like Peachy's infatuation, he had not foreseen but probably should have.

He was at an Exhibition of Work at the newly opened St. Alban's Industrial School, an institution for rehabilitating delinquent boys by teaching them carpentry. He was carrying around a glass of syrupy lemonade which he did not wish to drink, gravely considering the collection of three-legged stools and squat tables that had been produced by the boys. He would have enjoyed talking to the boys themselves—or rather, as was his usual practice with people, getting them to talk to him—but they seemed to have been given strict instructions to confine their conversation to "Yes, Reverend," and "No, Reverend," and otherwise to stand beside their creations staring into the middle distance and looking uncomfortable.

He had stopped in front of the lopsided work of one particularly small and sad-looking delinquent, and catching the boy's eye, he held up his glass of lemonade between thumb and forefinger and said confidentially, "I don't suppose you know where I could get any gin?"

The boy flushed bright red with the effort of suppressing laughter, and just managed to squeak out, "No, Reverend!"

Kit sighed. "No, I thought not. Not that kind of a party, is it?"

"*No*, Reverend!"

Someone had come up behind him, and he hoped it was not one of the teachers.

"Hello, Pastor Kit!" said a slightly familiar voice.

He spun around. "Good Heavens, Miss Spencer—*please* don't call me that."

"I was joking. I never would."

"But you just did."

"Well, I won't do it again." She smiled prettily. "To tell you the absolute truth, I don't *quite* remember your surname. It's Under … something. Wood?"

"Hill," he supplied happily. This made him feel better about not remembering her Christian name earlier in the week.

"Underhill, of course. How silly of me. It did just cross my mind that I might meet you here, but then I wasn't sure if I would recognize you in trousers. I mean, I thought, if he's not wearing that nifty black frock … But then, you are."

"Miss Spencer, I feel bound to tell you that this conversation is becoming increasingly painful to my feelings."

She laughed. She had a charming laugh, both hearty and musical at the same time. It was one of the few things he had really noticed about her on the beach. She was dressed smartly in a pale green, tailored suit and a green hat with a dramatically swooping brim and a vast bow protruding from one side. She looked both very businesslike and very feminine. A calculated effect, he thought.

"You mustn't pay a *great* deal of attention to the things I say, Reverend."

"No? Well, I shall try to remember that, but it isn't my usual practice. What brings you here this morning? I didn't think that delinquent boys were part of your mission."

"No, they're not, really—at least I don't think that they are. Perhaps they should be—I'm sure they need help as much as the girls. I'm here with my mother. She's on the Board."

"They seem to do good work."

"Yes ... " Miss Spencer sipped her lemonade. She looked at the small delinquent who had not known where to get gin. He had been following their conversation with ill-disguised interest. "Do you like it here?" she asked.

"Yes, Miss."

"Oh, yes?" She cocked her head to one side, charmingly. "What do you like about it?"

"I ... I'm learning a useful trade, Miss," said the boy, after a moment's hesitation, but with obvious sincerity.

"Excellent," said Harriet, beaming at him. "Well, keep up the good work!"

She turned to walk on, but paused, obviously expecting Kit to accompany her; so he did.

"I really believe he meant it," she remarked. "He is awfully young, poor thing—I suppose his skill at furniture-making will improve."

"No doubt," said Kit. "And that's not entirely the point. Even if he doesn't turn out a first-class carpenter, it'll have done him good to feel that someone cared enough to teach him. You can see that already. It wouldn't be the case for all of them—a lot of them probably resent the interference, or think they do—but for that boy, I think this place has done very good work."

She looked at him curiously. "You sound as if you speak from experience."

"Me? I don't know the first thing about carpentry."

"That's not what I meant."

"No?"

She frowned at him, but decided to leave it at that. They passed down the row of workbenches, looking at a succession of more or less similar stools and tables and delinquents.

She said: "The Board has plans—perhaps you have heard about them—to open a matching place for delinquent girls. Of course they would teach the girls cooking and housekeeping, not carpentry. My mother thinks it's 'the perfect opportunity' for me."

"They need someone to run the girls' establishment?"

"No, they just need money."

"But you don't want simply to pour your money into something," he guessed. "You want to run it."

"Is it wrong? When you put it like that, it sounds wrong."

"It could be. If you just want to have things your own way, or to have a lot of people to order around, that I should say would be wrong—or at least that would be a wrong reason to withhold your money from a truly worthy venture that needs it. But if you're not absolutely convinced that the venture is worthy, that is something different. You told me on the beach that you had pretty specific ideas about girls' education. And if what you want is to be able to use your talents, quite apart from your wealth, to be of real service to mankind—well, womankind, I guess—that's not wrong at all."

She looked up at him from under her ridiculous hat, her gaze coolly thoughtful. "No, it's not, is it?" she said after a moment.

"Thank you for putting it in that perspective. I don't think my mother quite sees it like that."

"You could of course compromise by making a donation to this new school but explaining to your mother that you need to reserve the rest of your money to support your own initiative."

"I could. That's a good idea. Aren't you going to drink your lemonade?"

"Perhaps if I become very thirsty."

She looked at him archly. "I suppose you would rather it were tea, or something."

"Or something," he agreed.

They stopped in front of another work station, where a skinny, freckled boy was lounging beside a fine collection of stools with elaborately turned legs.

"These are handsome, don't you think, Miss Spencer?"

"They're very nice. Perhaps you should buy one for your vicarage."

"I don't have a vicarage. Perhaps you should buy one for your residence room."

"They ain't for sale," the stools' maker informed them languidly. "Not to the 'general public.' We make 'em for schools an' hospitals. Charity."

"That's a sound policy," said Kit. "I don't suppose you could show us how it's done?"

"What?" The boy looked faintly suspicious.

"The fancy legs," said Harriet. "How do you make them like that?"

"Oh, that's easy. It's just on the lathe." He gestured at the machine behind him.

"How does it work?" Kit persisted. "Can you show us?"

"Please?" Harriet added.

The boy shrugged, to show he didn't really care about it. Kit recognized the attitude well. But he was not surprised when the boy turned to pick up his chisel with the unmistakable air of a craftsman who enjoys his work. He started the motor of the lathe, and set the chisel to the wood. Kit and Harriet watched as the spinning wood took shape under the blade, the curled shavings falling away to the floor. The boy stopped abruptly and offered the chisel to Kit.

"It's easy. Try it."

"I'll make a mess of it," said Kit, and proceeded to prove himself right. The boy seemed amused. Harriet did a better job when he gave her a turn, but declared that it was hard work.

A couple of boys from neighbouring workbenches were discreetly watching by this time. One volunteered to show Kit how to use the bandsaw. "But it's not suitable for women," he warned Harriet gravely. When Kit had seen the saw demonstrated, and said he didn't think it was suitable for him, either, he returned to find a crowd of boys gathered around while one of their number was showing Harriet how to pick pockets.

"You're going to get us into trouble," he remarked, unsure whether he was talking to the boys or to Harriet.

"It's not my fault I have a natural aptitude," she said.

"Do you want to learn to make a smoke bomb?" a voice at Kit's elbow inquired sweetly.

"No, thank you. Kind of you, but—no."

"Charlie Boult could teach you something," another boy suggested.

"No, I couldn't," Charlie Boult, a big, dark-haired boy, protested gruffly.

"Sure he could—he could teach you to win a fight. Charlie knocked down a teacher one time."

"Did you?" Kit asked, interested.

"I did, Father," Charlie admitted, "but I would never do it again."

"Well, but—do you suppose you could knock *me* down, if you were to try?" Kit couldn't resist asking.

Charlie looked him up and down critically. "Yeah," he admitted. "How?"

"*You're* going to get us into trouble!" Harriet observed.

"Probably," said Kit, grinning.

Charlie, as Kit had expected, chose to explain himself in actions rather than words. But he hadn't been intending actually to hit a priest, and Kit had no difficulty dodging the slow-moving fist and tripping his assailant. Where he got into difficulties was when he put out an arm to catch the boy and prevent him actually falling; he stepped on the hem of his cassock, and both of them ended up on the floor. Neither of them fell hard, but Kit was decidedly on the bottom. Charlie was inclined to be horrified, until he saw that Kit was laughing; then he didn't seem to know what to do with himself. Finally a strangled laugh escaped him.

"You know," said another boy, "we got a gym, with mats and everything."

This was all that Kit needed to hear. When Harriet's mother and several of her colleagues on the Board found them later, it was because a crowd had collected in the gymnasium, where one of the teachers was intervening to help Charlie haul off a particularly fierce delinquent who had just succeeded in knocking Kit (collarless and in shirt-sleeves by this point) flat on his back with a painful and unsportsmanlike attack. Charlie himself, though more of a boxer than a wrestler, had made a respectable showing, taking Kit down a couple of times and then graciously ceding the mat to his smaller colleagues.

Somehow Kit didn't need to be told that the severe-looking woman staring down at him, flanked by two severe-looking United Church ministers, was Harriet's mother.

"I do hope you are all right, young man," she said, in a tone which suggested that this was perhaps not entirely true.

"More or less," said Kit with greater sincerity, picking himself up from the mat.

"Now, where has my daughter got to?" Mrs. Spencer wondered aloud, turning away from Kit. "Someone said that she had come this way in the company of a popish priest or something of the sort, but I don't see any sign of her."

Kit had no idea where Harriet was either, so after a moment he decided it was not necessary to admit that he was the "something of the sort."

He turned to Charlie, who was standing nearby looking rather anguished, and held out his hand.

"Thanks awfully."

"What?"

"For a good match. You know, and for saving me from a painful death at the hands of that last fellow."

Charlie shook his hand gravely. "I don't think I saved your life, Father," he said, "but, uh … " He struggled for a few moments with a thought that he couldn't put into words.

Kit smiled. "It's all right either way."

He found Harriet (not that he had been looking for her) sitting on the steps outside the back door to the gymnasium.

"Your mother was looking for you," he remarked, draping his cassock over the railing and sitting down a few steps below her, wincing slightly.

"Yes, I thought she might be. That's why I came out here. What happened to you?"

"Oh, my last opponent seemed to think that biting and … kicking were good ways to win a fight." He dusted off the knees of his trousers and ran a hand through his hair. "They *are* good ways to win a fight, if you really badly want to win—which apparently he did. Reformation is just a distant goal for some of these lads, I'm afraid. It's salutary to be reminded of that." He set about reattaching his collar.

"You seem to know rather a lot about it, actually," said Harriet musingly. "Were you by any chance a delinquent boy yourself?"

"No, I was on the varsity wrestling team."

"That's not what I meant."

"No?" He relented. "No, I wasn't a delinquent boy, not exactly. I wasn't very good, and I did live in an institution for a couple of years, but it was an orphanage."

She frowned. "But I thought … Never mind. You seemed to have some fellow-feeling for them, that's all. I suppose you're just empathic."

"I consider it part of my job," he said. He meant that quite seriously, although he was aware, and didn't mind, that it sounded flippant. "Oh, bother."

"What?"

"Someone's pinched my cigarette case." He had searched the pockets of both his cassock and his trousers without finding it. "Serves me right for being a bad influence, I suppose."

"Decidedly," said Harriet, producing something from her purse and offering it to him. It was a cigarette case—in fact, it was his. "I was practising my pocket-picking skills—and I wanted an excuse to talk to you again."

"I'm sure that wasn't necessary," said Kit. "Actually, I'm sure *neither* of those things was necessary." He opened the case and extracted a cigarette for himself. "Would you like one—or perhaps you have already helped yourself?"

"How shocking! I don't smoke!"

"But you do pick pockets—one can't assume anything anymore. Did you take my matches as well?"

"No, if you haven't got matches it's not my fault."

He found his matches and lit his cigarette, and looked up at her expectantly. She seemed to have fallen into silent thought. She really was very lovely, he noticed belatedly, with neat cupid's-bow lips and long eyelashes; but it was a sort of loveliness that didn't interest him very much. He thought that this would have been true even before he had heard Peachy's rhapsodies on Sunday night. This manufacturing an excuse to talk to him again made him a little uneasy.

She was looking at him now. "You know," she said, "you're really something."

"Am I?"

"You're very good-looking."

For a moment he was about to reply automatically with thanks, or to tell her that she was too kind—but something about her tone stopped him. He had a feeling it wasn't really a compliment. He nodded.

"And you know it, which I always think is a point in one's favour—these people who go about believing themselves plain when they're anything but just bore me. In fact, I think you're a little vain."

"Oh, no," he said seriously. "Colossally vain. But, you know, ashamed of it. So I suppose the net result is as if I were only a little vain."

She laughed. "And frank—when you want to be—which I also like. And amusing, and a perfect gentleman. You're altogether an attractive person. Yet you don't attract me. Not really, I mean. Not in any significant way. Not that I dislike you at all, but—you understand."

"I think I do."

She nodded. "I thought you would—because you don't particularly fancy me either. Do you?"

"Surely you wouldn't wish me to. Considering what you have just told me."

"Oh, I might. Just to gratify my own vanity, you know. Or if I thought you would make a good husband or something. I have always wanted to marry a minister, you know."

"Presumably not my kind."

"Oh, absolutely. It would vex my mother *terrifically*."

"I can see that it might."

"But I don't suppose you would marry me."

"Of course I would, if I approved of the groom. Wait, don't tell me, 'That's not what you meant.'"

She laughed. "That would probably do the trick as far as vexing my mother is concerned. All right then. Shall we say we have a deal?"

"Let's."

"Now I just have to supply the groom."

"I might be able to help you with that."

"Oh?"

"I mean, I know where to find him, if that's your concern. And for what it's worth, I can assure you that he's even more of a spike than I am."

Miss Spencer was silent for a few moments. "What does he do for a living?" she asked finally. "He's not a lawyer, is he?"

"A lawyer? No." Kit wondered if she had understood him; he had thought he was being reasonably transparent.

She nodded sadly. "Elsa said he wasn't—or said that you said he wasn't, and that she believed you. And I don't think she's inclined to let sentiment cloud her judgement where *you* are concerned. She thought maybe I had misunderstood something he said, which was charitable of her. But it wasn't like that. He told me positively he was a lawyer—he even told me the name of the firm, though I forgot it almost immediately. Perhaps he *used* to work there?"

Kit looked up at her, feeling almost winded with sorrow. He had been prepared for about half of that, it was true, but the other half was a sickening shock.

"He has … Mr. Peacham has two-thirds of a BA in history—perhaps less than that—one was never sure how many of his courses he passed before he gave up altogether. He used to talk about law, but only in the way that one talks about running away with the circus. He has certainly never worked for a law firm."

"Does he have … he must have a job of some sort. He isn't a professional musician—that much I gathered."

"He does play in a jazz band, but they're disorganized and don't make very much money. He writes reviews for a couple of journals, and he works, intermittently, for an old friend who runs a ridiculous and unprofitable music shop. He is a very good man, Miss Spencer—I would swear to that, I would stake my life on that in an instant. He only tells the sort of lie that can very easily be found out. He isn't trying to get away with anything."

She was silent for another little while. "You know, you could just have said, 'I'm sure he wanted very badly to impress you—it's so unlike him to lie.'"

"But *that* would have been a lie."

She sighed. "And even Elsa doesn't think that you tell lies. But *why* would he have lied to me about such a thing? I would be bound to find out the truth, if we were to continue … if … It would be bound to come out."

"Heaven knows. I rather think he secretly likes to represent himself as unreliable."

"Is he?"

"Not remotely." He could try to explain how he knew this; he could tell her about the neighbour who had tried to kill himself, about those years in the West End. Except that he couldn't really tell her about that. "When we were boys … he used to make up stories to … so that I'd have to explain the truth. So, you know, I'd not want to say how I lost my pocket money, and Peachy would make up some story about betting on horses so that I'd admit that I loaned it to someone. It was … honestly, it was charitable, at first."

"It's good of you to try to make excuses for him."

He flicked the ash off his cigarette and frowned. "I don't know—if that's what I'm doing, I'm not sure it is good of me. I ought to be straightforwardly singing his praises at this point—that's what I'd prefer to be doing."

"But he's made that awkward for you."

"Rather." After a moment, he asked, "What did you tell him about yourself?"

She looked at him sharply. "What do you mean? The ordinary sort of things."

He exhaled a mouthful of smoke. "That *is* what I mean, actually. Why only ordinary things?"

"One doesn't want to overwhelm a man. It doesn't seem kind."

He thought for a moment about Elsa Nordqvist, about the intensity with which she had presented herself to him, and the answering intensity of desire that she had roused in him. He thought Miss Spencer had a point. But Peachy saw things in people that they didn't know about themselves; Peachy didn't have to be blinded by your magnificence in order to love you.

"I don't think you need worry about overwhelming Peachy," he said.

She sighed. "I might have a cigarette after all."

He dug out the case again and offered it to her. "They're Turkish—you don't want to inhale them. You want to smoke it more like a pipe. Which … is not helpful, is it?"

"What?" She held the cigarette gingerly between thumb and forefinger. It was plain that she had never smoked anything before.

"Here—give it back. I can't be responsible for this."

She sighed, and ground the neat, curvaceous little heels of her shoes discontentedly against the edge of the step on which she was sitting. "It's not part of my plan for my life, Mr. Underhill. Falling in love with a … with a *difficult* man."

"No. I shouldn't imagine it would be."

She looked at him and sighed again, pouting a little. "It could be part of God's plan, though, couldn't it? That's what you were going to say, I guess."

"Not really," he admitted. "Sometimes I just have to sit around looking like I *might* say that type of thing, and it seems to work quite as well."

Chapter Three

THE ABSTRACT EURYDICE

Elsa went up the pink stone steps of Victoria College with a bounce in her walk, dodging through the stream of under-graduates pouring out under the high arch of the entrance. Inside, the hall was warm and slightly stuffy, and she paused to wriggle out of the cardigan which she had needed outside, before climbing the stairs to the second floor. A lecture was still going on in the classroom at the top of the stairs; a professor's voice rang out, declaiming poetry.

The door across from the chapel bearing the name "A. Gallagher" was open when she approached it, the office full of light and a breeze from the open window behind the desk. Professor Gallagher himself, standing by the bookshelf, looked up at her knock and seemed almost as pleased to see her as she was to be there.

"Miss Nordqvist, come in—come in!" As usual, he pronounced her name with precision but without exaggeration. He replaced the book he had been holding on the shelf, and gestured to the chair opposite his desk.

Elsa perched on the edge of the chair, her cardigan gathered into a bundle on her lap with her handbag, her eyes drawn inevitably to the thick brown rectangle of leather and vellum that lay casually on the blotter in the middle of the professor's desk. Last spring she had spent so many hours in this office, sitting in this chair, with that manuscript in her lap, reverently turning its ancient pages and reading the lines of tidy brown script while Professor Gallagher watched indulgently from across his desk.

"It's like seeing an old friend," she said.

He laughed. "Indeed, it has taken on that character for me as well. But here is something else that may interest you." Sitting down at his desk, he produced a heavy sheaf of typed pages from a drawer. "I have finished the notes for my edition."

"So fast!" Elsa cried, taking the papers as he handed them across the desk to her.

"Do you think so? Well, nothing else could be allowed to take precedence over this, naturally. So I suppose it has been completed quickly. I am not dissatisfied with my progress."

There was silence in the airy office while Elsa leafed through the pages of the typescript. There was a long introduction to the work, and the text that followed was embellished with dense footnotes.

The Bibliotheka, she read from the introduction, *is a compendium of the teachings of a hitherto unknown sect whose members seem to have referred to themselves as the New Orphics. Though the collection itself may be dated to the Hellenistic Era, the sect is undoubtedly older, as we see here ideas presented in a highly refined and cogent form indicative of considerable development. The work is divided into twelve books, with short hymns addressed to Orpheus and to various personified abstractions intercalated between the prose sections. Books 1 through 4 set out the basic allegorization of the Orphic myth. The individual soul, or Orpheus, descends to the Pure Plain, or the Underworld, in pursuit of its truth, or Eurydice. It is in this descent and reascent that the soul acquires the ability to manipulate the matter of the world in accordance with its own desires. The transformation begins with the physical self, remade in the image of truth glimpsed in the Underworld, and may extend, in time and with diligent practice, to other elements of impure matter. The initiate who has succeeded in effecting the first transformation, that of the physical self, is said to have restored the beloved: Eurydice, who represents the soul's truth.*

In the later books, as she recalled, the identification of Orpheus and Eurydice was teased out with greater precision. The rhapsodic tone of the early chapters receded, giving way to a series of exercises illustrating how an individual's will might be disciplined in order to approach the descent to the Pure Plain, where reality could be altered and the inner self and its "fleshly container" remade into the image of the soul's truth, the abstract Eurydice. There was a surprisingly clear, if subtle, organization to the work's ideas.

"Oh, I see you solved the problem of that ambiguous pronoun!" Elsa noted happily, as she arrived at a passage that they had discussed for some time last year.

"Yes—that was a crux that you brought to my attention, I believe," said Professor Gallagher, "and I must thank you for that. Though you'll see that ultimately you were mistaken as to the construction … "

"Yes," said Elsa absently, having moved on to the next chapter.

Finally she looked up from the pages of the professor's notes to Gallagher himself, watching her from the other side of his desk.

Arthur Gallagher was young for someone of his impressive reputation—perhaps forty-five, certainly not much more. He was a slight, elegant man. His greying dark hair was curly, but he kept it sleekly pomaded, not a lock out of place, as tidy as his textual criticism. His clothing was always spruce and well-kept, too—the work, as he was fond of telling people, of a valet, not a wife. Except for this slightly unnecessary attention to exteriors (which, however, produced a not unpleasant effect) he was in every way Elsa's ideal of the unattached, single-mindedly devoted scholar. His facility with Greek and Latin was dizzying, his knowledge of Classical literature encyclopedic. His theories were often audacious, but always rigorously supported and convincing. Elsa so passionately wanted to be like him that she had once or twice almost forgot herself so far as to tell him so, which would have crossed a line between admiration and intimacy which she wished to leave uncrossed. She found herself unintentionally imitating his patterns of speech, and adopting his opinions on subjects that had nothing to do with Greek philology. She would, she had once told Harriet, probably have dressed like him if she could.

She was careful not to tell anyone other than Harriet how much she admired Gallagher. She felt it would have been difficult for anyone else to understand that her idolization of him was something quite different from romantic love; and she had no desire to be thought of as a girl who was in love with her professor. Harriet believed her when she said that she was not in love with Professor Gallagher. But Harriet also thought that being in love with one's professor wasn't such a bad idea, provided the professor was a reasonable marriage prospect, and that Arthur Gallagher was probably the most marriageable faculty member in the School of Graduate Studies—and Elsa had had to tell her to shut up at that point.

"The notes are so thorough!" she said, looking back at the pages, a little embarrassed by her thoughts. "They're really very helpful—you clarified quite a number of things that I had difficulty with, just in the passages that I saw at a glance." She placed the typescript reverently back on the desk.

"Excellent," said Gallagher. "That was of course my chief aim."

"Do you know what I think, Professor?" Elsa said, perched on the edge of her chair. She had meant to tell him this last year, but the right opportunity had never arisen. Besides, it would have seemed presumptuous from an undergraduate; but she was an undergraduate no longer.

"Yes?"

"I thought this before, but seeing your edition makes me surer of it somehow. I think somebody wrote the *Bibliotheka* as a joke."

His eyebrows rose. "A bold claim. A hoax, you mean?"

"No, no—not to deceive, or not necessarily so. Just for … a lark, you know. A—a *jeu d'esprit*. Someone in the Hellenistic era, obviously. I don't pretend to doubt your dating of the manuscript—I certainly wouldn't have the hubris to do that." She laughed a little awkwardly. "It's just that I think the work isn't a compendium or a serious treatise on an actual occult system. I think it's one man's flight of fancy."

Gallagher smiled at her patiently. "And how, pray tell, do you arrive at that conclusion?"

"The style strikes me as too unified—there's a sense of personality behind it. There are certain turns of phrase that he likes, and certain images. Flight, for instance, and 'the soul's truth.' He likes sets of threes. And then the dual number, which is so useful—as I remember you pointing out in class—well, he uses it all over the place, but it is unusual in prose of this date, isn't it?"

"Yes, somewhat unusual. It would seem to point to one compiler, at least, who has put his stamp on the work. But you are going further than that in your claim, aren't you?"

"I—well, it's such wishful thinking, that's all." She was on shakier ground here and she knew it, but she went on. "It doesn't seem like a real cult—it's all too logical and straightforward. A real religious text would tell you that you need to sacrifice some animal, or … or burn incense or recite some nonsensical prayer a certain number of times before you can achieve what you desire. But he says: Discipline your will and you can transform your reality; nothing outside of yourself is necessary. It's a wonderful, a *seductive* idea. And … quite silly at the same time. But it's just because it's such a very good *idea*, not a messy, contradictory jumble of practices and teachings, that I think it was only ever one person's idea."

He smiled thoughtfully. "Well, it is an interesting interpretation. A little short on proof—one hopes, Miss Nordqvist, you are not relying on what they like to call 'feminine intuition,' as that would be a dangerous basis for serious scholarship. But you are merely speculating. I think you will find that you are mistaken, of course. Mistaken, I mean, in the capacity of this treatise to inspire belief. It is not just superstition and fancy that can attract devotees, you know."

"No," said Elsa, feeling her face heating up. "I suppose I did not mean to suggest that."

Gallagher looked down at his desk for a moment, while Elsa's mortification grew more and more intense.

He looked up abruptly. "How would you like to meet the owner of this manuscript, Miss Nordqvist?"

"The—the countess?"

"She goes by 'Mrs. Graves,'" he corrected her. "Her late husband's surname. Though I believe that in her native Russia she was indeed something in the nature of a countess."

"I—is she worth meeting?"

"*Worth* meeting?"

"Oh, I apologize. I'm afraid that sounded … It's just that you took me by surprise, Professor. I meant to ask whether you thought there were any particular reason why I should meet the countess—Mrs. Graves—but I suppose you must, or you would not have suggested it." She was now just gabbling idiotically.

"She is a fascinating woman," said Gallagher, a little reprovingly. "Well travelled, of course, and with a varied, though sad, history. She would be happy to meet you. And the experience would broaden your horizons."

"Oh. Would it?"

"Indeed, I think so. I have mentioned your name to her in the past, and she has expressed a desire to see you at one of her gatherings."

"Oh. That's … that's very kind of her—very kind of you."

"Indeed, it is very kind of Mrs. Graves. I have here an invitation." He produced a thick, cream-coloured card from a drawer and slid it across the desk toward her. "I believe the gathering is this coming weekend—I, alas, will not be able to attend. But now—we must turn our attention to the real reason you came here this afternoon. Your thesis topic for the coming year."

*

"The absolute *what*?" Harriet was indignant. "That doesn't sound right!"

"The genitive absolute," Elsa repeated leadenly, "in the works of Plato."

"Is it a philosophical thing?"

Elsa shook her head. "It's a grammatical thing. I hate to say so about any research topic, but … it's really not very interesting. It isn't at all what I was hoping for."

They were in Harriet's room, sitting on her bed. The breeze billowed the pink and green curtains with their stylized roses, with which Harriet had replaced the plain residence curtains. The bedspread under them matched the new curtains, as did the cloth covering the little round table that Harriet had brought with her, and the bowl of real roses on the table were almost the same shade of pink as the ones in the fabric. Harriet was like that; she improved on everything she touched, made it better, made it prettier. A package of expensive cookies was open on the table beside the bowl of roses. Elsa had eaten several without really tasting them.

"Of course it's not what you were hoping for," said Harriet, "and you had every reason to hope for better. Why did he make such a production of showing you that manuscript if he wasn't going to let you work on it?"

"I don't know," said Elsa wretchedly. "I feel as if he *was* going to let me work on it, only he changed his mind. I'm afraid it was because I told him my theory about how it was written by one person, and he thought I hadn't any proof—and of course he's right, it's just that … well, I *am* convinced of it, you know, but I hadn't any intention of trying to make anything of it. At least, if I did, of course I would be circumspect about it—I'm not … I mean, I think there are indications that point in that direction, I wouldn't say it was a flight of fancy, and … Oh!" She clenched her fists on the fabric of her skirt, miserably reliving the scene in the office. "He accused me of 'relying on feminine intuition'! It was humiliating."

"What's wrong with feminine intuition?" Harriet demanded, taking another cookie from the package. "He's just jealous because he hasn't got any."

Elsa shook her head, waving away both the cookies and the suggestion. "It isn't a basis for sound scholarship—he's quite right about that. But he wouldn't have needed to say it to a man. That was what was humiliating. To be taken for a silly woman with silly ideas. I *shouldn't* have mentioned my theory. I've destroyed his good opinion of me."

"Well, I don't know … he might not have liked your theory very much, but from what you say he seems to have come up with this Plato garbage pretty quickly—maybe he had it in mind from the beginning. He might have some man in line for the topic you thought he was going to give you, and didn't think he could give it to a girl after all. That is the sort of thing that happens, you know."

"Yes, I know, but it can't happen to me!" Elsa protested. "This is my chosen life, Harriet—this is what I have determined to devote my life to. My whole life. Not a husband and a family, not a household or … any of that—but scholarship."

"Well, you can't let something like that depend on the whim of a stupid professor," said Harriet rather crossly. "That would be like me letting my mother talk me into that delinquent girls' scheme. Worse, actually."

"What?"

"Oh, it wasn't you I was telling about that. Never mind—I meant that if it's really your ambition, you *can't* simply have been waiting for Gallagher to hand it to you on a platter. So you'd hoped he would make things easy for you, and he hasn't—it's too bad, but it isn't the end of the world."

This wasn't quite the reaction Elsa had been expecting to her (as she thought) dramatic revelation of her plan for her life. "What if it means I'm not good enough?" she demanded.

Harriet shrugged. "What if it doesn't? It's the first any of us have heard of it, if that *is* what it means. I think you're just getting worked up." After a moment, relenting slightly, she added, "Not that I blame you. I'd get worked up too, I expect."

"Thanks."

"Do you not *want* to get married, though? I never thought that of you."

"What do you mean?"

"Well ... I never thought of you as the spinster type. I suppose I've always pictured you in a big house with a lot of children."

"Really?" Elsa was startled. "Vividly pictured it, you mean, or just ... just thought about it?"

"That's a funny question. Pretty vividly, I guess. I mean, I hadn't worked out what wallpaper you would have in the living room or anything. It's just sometimes when I think about how I'll miss university life, I imagine visiting you when you have your own house, and that's what I picture. To tell you the truth, I've always found it comforting to think about. Funny that I never mentioned it until now."

This wasn't another prophetic vision, then. Elsa was relieved.

"Well, it would be hard for you to visit me in Saskatchewan."

"What, really? Oh, but I never thought you would go back to Saskatchewan, not for good! Would you really?"

"No, Harriet—but I'm not going to have a house full of children, either. That's the life I'm giving up. That's just what I've been trying to say—I'm giving up all that in order to devote myself to a life of study. That's why I was getting worked up, you see. It's my whole future—I have to know that it's worth doing, that I can make a real contribution."

Harriet was silent for a few moments, looking out at the grey sky beyond her cheerful curtains. "Well, if it's really what you want ... Elsa, *of course* you'll make a real contribution. To—to whatever it is that you want to contribute to—posterity, or the advancement of human knowledge, or whatever it is. Anyone who had ever met you could tell that. But ... I mean, *if that's what you're really asking*."

"What?"

"I mean … don't get mad, but I just mean that it's one thing to wonder if you can really do anything worthwhile—probably everyone who *does* worthwhile things wonders that—but it's another thing to wonder if you'll get the recognition you deserve for what you do. And you won't, you know. Probably. You're always going to be a woman."

The transformation begins with the physical self, Gallagher had written in his introduction. *The physical self, remade in the image of truth* … How stupid.

"Of course," Elsa said. "I'm not mad. You're right, you're absolutely right—I'm not really worried about whether I can be a great scholar, but about whether I can make Arthur Gallagher think me one. Which isn't the same thing at all. But one is supposed to do these things without thought of reward."

"I suppose so." Harriet wrinkled her nose. "No, no—that doesn't make sense. You can't give up the happiness of a married life for scholarship and then not expect any kind of reward. Not unless you believe in Heaven."

"I'm not necessarily giving up *all* the happiness of a married life. I could still have a lover."

Harriet gave her a sceptical look. Elsa was again disappointed by this reaction to her revelation.

"I could, you know! I would do it."

Harriet sighed. "I know you expect me to be shocked, Elsa, but I'm not. It's of a piece with all the things you say you don't believe in. And with what you've done in the past, I suppose. I mean, when you told me the story about your boyfriend that you had as a girl, I—well, I could tell that you didn't *regret* any of that, and that it was the sort of thing you might do again. Mind you, I don't agree. I think you want independence, and being somebody's mistress isn't any kind of independence, not in a respectable city like Toronto. It would mean all the encumbrance of marriage and none of the stability. Also," she added primly, "I think it's wrong, and I think you'll find it so yourself and won't actually do it. You're not really an immoral person."

"Oh, am I not! *Thank you.* I don't think I am either, and I don't think it would be immoral to have a lover. I don't think I did anything immoral when I was sixteen. I think when you talk about encumbrances and dependence, you're picturing some sort of dreadful kept-woman situation, and I shouldn't argue for a moment that there's anything desirable about that. But I'm not contemplating anything like that. I intend to earn my own living."

"Well, you're right, I suppose I was thinking of *La Dame aux camélias* or something wretched. But all the same, could you stand to live a life where the possibility of having a child would be something to dread, not something to look forward to?"

"That's still pretty melodramatic, Harriet."

She laughed. "Isn't it? I seem to be in that type of mood, somehow."

Elsa did not ask why. She thought she knew, but she didn't really blame Harriet for not confiding in her. She hadn't made herself seem like much of a confidante lately. She changed the subject to talk about Harriet's classes, the new freshies, safer subjects.

Later, as Elsa got up to return to her own room next door, Harriet, unfolding herself from the bed, said, "You know I would still invite you to dinner."

"What?"

"If you were somebody's mistress—I would still invite you to dinner."

"Oh, well—that's kind of you."

Harriet pursed her lips. "Sort of. I mean just private dinners, you know—*tête-à-tête*—not parties. I couldn't invite you to parties. And I'm not being melodramatic—that's just how it is."

"Oh, forget it, Harriet. I daresay I won't have time to have a lover—I'll be too busy being the foremost expert on the genitive absolute in Plato. But talking of parties—I almost forgot. I *was* invited to a party. It's a little odd." She dug in her handbag for the invitation. "Professor Gallagher gave this to me."

"Professor Gallagher? He invited you to a *party*?" Harriet did not reach for the invitation, as if even to touch it would be slightly improper. In spite of herself Elsa wondered whether she ought to have taken it.

"It's not his party—it's this woman, this countess or whatever she is, who owns the manuscript."

"Have you met her?" Harriet inquired, wide-eyed.

"No. That's the point—she wanted to meet me, and so she invited me to her party."

"What do you mean she wanted to meet you?"

"Professor Gallagher mentioned me … " Even as she said it she realized that this didn't sound good.

"He wouldn't give you a decent thesis topic, but he talks about you to countesses?" Harriet's voice rose in a crescendo of dismay. "And I suppose he expects you to go to this party?"

"I think—it sounded as if he does. But he said he wouldn't be there himself."

"He *said*. Elsa, my dear, I do hope you have more sense than to get involved in this. It's altogether inappropriate."

"Why?" said Elsa, suddenly belligerent. "If I were a man, there would be nothing wrong with it."

"But you're not a man!"

"And I'll never be treated like one if I don't act as though I deserve it."

"Elsa, I don't really understand why you would want to be treated like a man, but *that's not what this is*. Professor Gallagher—I *guarantee* you Professor Gallagher has not forgotten that you're a woman or decided to ignore the fact that you're a woman. He's being plain old inappropriate, inviting you to parties full of people you don't know, where he's supposedly 'not going to be there,' and all I can say is, you should be very, very careful. And *not go*. Definitely not go."

"And that's *exactly* what I'm talking about," Elsa snapped. "How you expect anyone to treat you like an equal—well, you don't, do you? And that may be all well and good for you, but I won't have it—I absolutely won't have it."

And she banged the door shut after her.

The trouble was, she reflected miserably as she sat in her own room, she didn't really disapprove of Harriet's viewpoint. Harriet's sense of high-society propriety, *for Harriet*, made perfect sense. But applied to Elsa, the country girl cum ivory tower scholar, it was like an absurd and disproportionate hat, ill-fitting, unnecessary, and awkward. The trouble was that when she refused the set of rules that made sense for Harriet, she had nothing in particular with which to replace them, and her frustration at that lack bubbled over into ungracious anger. She would have gone next door and apologized to Harriet right then, but she had no confidence that it would turn out any better; she might only make matters worse.

*

She went to Mrs. Graves's party, in the end, mostly because she couldn't quite pin down a good enough reason not to go. She imagined a conversation with Professor Gallagher in which he would ask her the reason for her absence, and she would stammer and say something unfortunate. She realized with some distress that she was in fact assuming that he would be there, even though he had said he would not. Her thoughts about this party were almost entirely distressing.

The invitation was cryptic, referring simply to "A Salon, 8:00," without telling her whether it would involve dinner or what to wear. Harriet could no doubt have given her a better idea, but she did not want to raise the subject again with Harriet. So she ate a small and early dinner in the dining hall and got out her best frock, which was a low-cut, dark blue thing of which she was secretly proud. She had only worn it once before, to a party at Harriet's grandparents' house. At the time, she and Harriet had contrived something rather out of the ordinary with her hair, but she was unable to replicate it on her own and didn't try very hard. This occasion did not really seem worth it. She snuck out of Annesley Hall in a long coat that was warmer than the evening required, more worried about hiding her telltale, out-past-curfew dress from Harriet than from the porter.

Mrs. Graves had a suite in a brand-new downtown "apartment-hotel." Elsa set off to walk there with only a general idea of where she was going. It began to rain before she had got far on her way, and she was grateful for her long coat after all, and glad that she had not succeeded in doing anything fancy to her hair. Her flimsy party shoes were beginning to hurt her feet, and she was almost ready to give up and turn back when she discovered that she had been about to walk past the building. She presented herself at the desk in the gleaming lobby, wet, tired, and bedraggled, and asked for Mrs. Graves's suite.

An attendant escorted her to the top of the building in a private elevator and pointed, when she stupidly seemed to need further direction, to an open door on the other side of the landing. Light and voices from inside indicated that the party was already underway, although she was precisely on time. She looked in on a florid Neoclassical foyer, full of palms and marble and gilt columns.

She had been standing awkwardly in the doorway for a few moments before a woman of about her own height and build, with short, marcel-waved hair of a bright, buttery yellow, detached herself from a group talking loudly beyond an inner doorway, and strode across the foyer towards her.

"Elsa Nordqvist! It must be!"

"Excuse me?" said Elsa, startled.

"Oh, it is only that dear Professor Gallagher has described you to me so clearly that I knew it must be you. How beautiful you are!"

The woman had extended her bare arms, wrists clanking with silver bangles, and cupped Elsa's face in her long, cool hands before Elsa knew what she was doing. Elsa took a step backwards out of mere surprise, pushing her hands away with a broad gesture. A look of outrage crossed her hostess's face briefly—but only briefly. Before Elsa had a chance to finish flushing with embarrassment, the woman was smiling again.

"You must not be offended, my dear Elsa! Where I come from, we are not so cold. But no! I do not call you cold—it is only that you want a little warming up, yes? My name is Anastasiya, and that is what you must call me. Titles and surnames we dispense with in my little circle—it is so much more intimate."

She spoke with only the ghost of a foreign accent, but that was the only thing about her that did not seem exaggerated. She was elaborately made up, and wore a startlingly décolleté dress, thick with silver sequins. A white ostrich feather bobbed above her sequinned headband. There was a kind of fragile, old-young girlishness about her that made her age hard to guess. She's like somebody playing a Russian countess in a film, Elsa thought—and doing it badly. But that might be what exile would do to you: make you into a sort of parody of yourself, disconnected from the places and people that made you real. She felt sorry for the woman.

"I—I am very pleased to meet you," she managed. "I hope I am not late."

"My dear Elsa—I may call you Elsa, may I not?—you are *intended* to be late! It is the done thing. But yet, I knew that you would come on time, so I invited you a little later than my other dear guests. I hope you will not be offended. I did not want you to feel out of place."

Well, that was a forlorn hope, Elsa thought.

Mrs. Graves waved up a servant who had been hovering somewhere and insisted on helping Elsa out of her coat herself, and solicitously patting her bedraggled hair. She wore a heavy, spicy perfume which seemed to linger in Elsa's nostrils even after her hostess had moved away—which she did not immediately do. Instead she shepherded Elsa into the large and lavish living room of her suite, twining an arm around her waist in a way that made it impossible to shake her off, and introduced her effusively to a series of intense and loud-talking people who tried not to look completely puzzled about who she was or why they should care. They were almost all men.

Finally, a fiery-eyed young man seized Anastasiya (they really did all call her that) by her free arm and dragged her away to his circle to settle a dispute about "the proper approach of the individual energy to the revelation of the soul's truth." It was then, left on her own to listen to the conversation going on around her, that Elsa realized what everyone in the room was talking about.

"It was not until our reading of Book Six that I truly began to feel ready to attempt the Descent," one languid man with a cigarette-holder was saying in a carrying voice. You could hear in the way he said it that he thought of the word "Descent" as capitalized.

"I don't think it's a thing you want most of the population to get their hands on," said a man sprawled on a couch. "Not that they'd be able to make anything of it, but all the same! The potential for abusing the teachings … "

"But"—from another corner—"what the *Bibliotheka* tells us, of course, is that such a choice is unnecessary because the whole system of morality is so utterly irrelevant."

"Such a freeing realization," a woman's voice agreed unctuously.

Every single one of them was talking about the *Bibliotheka Orphika*. And talking about it in such terms! The voices were those of impassioned believers: Harriet's cultists, whom Elsa had so breezily dismissed as fictional. The New Orphics. She was in a room full of them.

Someone had come up behind Elsa and was offering her a tumbler half full of clear liquid. By the time she realized that it wasn't likely to be water, it was already in her hand. She looked at the person who had handed it to her, hoping to give it back discreetly. It was a young man in grey tweed, sandy-haired, spectacled, and blandly handsome. This was what she saw after a moment; but by then her heart was already pounding and her hands shaking. When she first looked at him, for a fraction of a second she had the horrible impression that he was the wrong shape, as if his body were a garment worn by something of an entirely different outline. The nightmare vision was gone so quickly that she had no time even to guess what trick of his posture or the lighting of the room had created the impression.

She took a step backwards, clutching the glass of whatever it was, and murmured "Thank you." The spectacled young man smiled. There was certainly something unpleasant about his smile; it was the sort of sly smirk that made her want to grab at the straps of her gown to make sure one of them hadn't slipped off her shoulder. But the idea that rose in her mind—that he somehow knew what she had just seen—was clearly fanciful.

She made her way to a vacant seat on a sofa, seriously worried about her own sanity, and sat down, holding her glass in both shaking hands, and found herself in the midst of another conversation about the *Bibliotheka*.

"To my mind," a woman in a gold turban was saying, "the teachings in Book Seven confirm what I have always felt about the baseness of matter. It really is utterly, utterly base, isn't it?"

"But," said the young man beside her, "can it truly follow from that that one need not ... that one may truly be permitted to ... " He licked his lips nervously. "Er ... "

"Sexual licence," said a very fat man on the other side of Elsa, who proved, to her dismay, to be part of the same conversation. "Sexual licence," he repeated, enunciating each syllable juicily. "That is what you are trying to get at, *boy*—that is what is always on the minds of fellows like you, but you cannot *spit it out*." He leaned toward the turbaned woman and the young man, nearly putting his large elbow in Elsa's lap in the process. "And the answer is *of course*. How can it but follow from these teachings that *any* code, *any* stricture that attempts to regulate the conduct of the flesh, the material, our bodily *baseness*, is a simple waste of time? Eurydice—Spirit—is all that matters. Spirit shapes all to her own will."

I am in a den of iniquity, Elsa thought. That is what this is. And it isn't the least bit appealing.

"And what do *you* think?" the turbaned woman asked, turning to her.

"What do I think?" Elsa repeated miserably. I think this is what Harriet was trying to protect me from, and I just thought she was being *too proper*. I think I shouldn't be allowed out.

"About the teachings of Book Seven. The vileness of the material world, and the duty of the soul to transcend."

"I think ... the treatment of the ascetic theme is unusual. I think ... to be honest, I think that Book Seven might be a later interpolation. It doesn't really fit with the themes of the earlier books, and it isn't mentioned in the later ones."

The others stared at her.

"Do you mean to tell us," said the woman after a moment, "that you have read *all* of the *Bibliotheka*?"

"Um ... have you not?"

"*Where* did you read it?" demanded the fat man.

"In ... in the manuscript. At university. I haven't studied it thoroughly, certainly not so much as I would like—there are passages where the language is obscure, and my skill at Greek—"

"Greek?" cried the young man. "In the manuscript?"

She became, to her intense discomfort, the centre of attention in that half of the room. The situation, as far as she was able to piece it together from their hysterical explanations, was something like this: Professor Gallagher had produced a translation of the

Bibliotheka, at Mrs. Graves's request, which she was doling out, one chapter at a time, at readings in her monthly salons. They were to get the final chapter of Book Eight tonight, which meant they had four more to go. Professor Gallagher himself never attended the salons; upon revealing that she was the professor's student, Elsa was pressed for details of Gallagher's appearance and manner, and heard that he was "quite the mystery" to all of the others. She was not surprised that he never came here. At first she was disgusted at the idea that he had produced a translation for these people, but then she had to admit that there was no really logical reason why he shouldn't have. But why on earth had he sent her to this gathering? As a punishment, because she had suggested that no one could ever have believed in the manuscript's contents? As a joke? She was not sure which would be worse.

Anastasiya was summoned and made to explain *what she meant* by not telling them that this young woman had actually read the entire manuscript of the *Bibliotheka* in the original Greek. She gave a girlish laugh and said that she had been sure they would find out on their own. She then perched on the back of the sofa behind Elsa and petted Elsa's hair again and asked if she wanted another gin and tonic. Elsa said that she wasn't thirsty.

The woman in the turban tried to return the conversation again to the question of the baseness of matter.

"Don't you agree, Elsa,"—everyone called her Elsa, as their hostess had not mentioned her surname—"that in view of the utter vileness of the material, we ought not to allow ourselves to be concerned with rules that merely seek to control what we do with that base substance?"

"I don't know about the rules," said Elsa, sitting forward a little to try to move out of reach of Mrs. Graves's petting fingers, "but I don't, personally, agree with the premise. I don't think matter is base—I think it is the only relevant thing."

"What do you mean?"

"I mean I am a materialist. I don't believe in the supernatural. So naturally—"

They laughed, but Elsa winced; she hadn't meant to sound so precious. Was it possible, she thought, that Professor Gallagher had sent her to the party because he thought she would enjoy being fawned over by these stupid people?

Of course it wasn't all fawning. "You don't *believe* in the super-*natural*?" the fat man demanded, leaning over her again. "You have had the privilege of reading the entirety of our precious manuscript, and you don't believe in it? How has this been allowed to happen?"

Mrs. Graves came to her rescue here. "Dearest Elsa studies the manuscript as a scholar, Maurice. She must maintain an intellectual detachment. It is vital to her work."

"But aren't we being so careful," another man put in, more calmly, "to restrict our numbers, in view of the power that we know to be contained in these teachings? I hope we're not to understand that your professor, Anastasiya, is showing the manuscript to all sorts of people—uninitiated people?"

"But as I don't intend to try to use it—I mean use the doctrine— for anything, I don't see that you have any cause for alarm," said Elsa reasonably.

"You don't believe that our thoughts impress themselves on the vile matter of the world?"

"No, certainly I don't. Our thoughts are our thoughts, and I'm sure it is a fine idea to regulate them for our own comfort, but they are strictly inside our heads. They don't influence the outside world—except in the normal way, if we act on them. And the world isn't vile, either. It can be very lovely. People can be very lovely."

Rather to her surprise, she found when she said this that she had one particular person in mind. She had not thought about him much in the nearly three weeks since that meeting on the beach. And for some reason—more surprising still—the image that came to mind now was not of him in his bathing costume lounging in the sand, but of that last moment when he stood outside the closing streetcar doors, looking back at her, departing from her to return to his own world. People could be very lovely …

"I think if you're looking for an excuse to ignore conventional morality," she added, "saying that matter is vile is a particularly silly one. And if you ask me, a lot of the things that we think are a good deal worse than the things we think them *about*."

They were the sort of people who take anything at all pithy or persuasively phrased to be a pearl of wisdom, and so Elsa acquired, to her disgust, a reputation as a kind of interesting heretic, a person worth interrogating and arguing with, rather than a non-believer to be ignored. That their hostess was clearly enamoured of her did nothing to help.

She managed to extricate herself from the group when they began reciting favourite lines from the intercalated hymns of the manuscript, in an overwrought and embarrassing translation that she hoped was not Professor Gallagher's. But she was not feeling quite so kindly towards Professor Gallagher as usual. Another, really awful, idea about why he might have sent her to this party was hovering in the back of her mind. He wasn't—he *couldn't be*—a New Orphic himself?

She left her glass of gin behind a pseudo-classical statue on a small table, wiping her hands convulsively on her dress afterwards as if they were dirty, and ducked into an alcove half-screened by large potted plants. It was not the clever escape she had hoped for. At the end of the alcove was a couch and a pair of lovers embracing, apparently unconcerned by the fact that they were only half hidden from the rest of the room. Of course, why should they be concerned? Everyone knew that matter was vile, and that (somehow) this meant it was perfectly all right to … Elsa became hastily absorbed in studying a collection of photographs on a sideboard, to avoid looking at the couple. *I have got to get out of here*, she thought.

The photographs were obviously mementoes of Mrs. Graves's

travels. In one she stood in front of a pyramid, clasping an impractical hat to her head; in another she was perched on a camel. There were photographs of Mrs. Graves in an evening gown on a boat, Mrs. Graves in white furs at Stonehenge, Mrs. Graves with a stout, whiskered gentleman in front of what might have been the British Museum. They all seemed to have been taken recently; she looked the same age in each. And in each—lounging against a loose bit of pyramid, holding the bridle of Mrs. Graves's camel, standing behind the whiskered gentleman, and sitting on a fallen stone at Stonehenge, smoking a pipe—was the young man in grey tweed. If there had been only one picture, she would probably not have recognized him—he had a wholly unmemorable face—but there were a dozen of them, and there was no mistaking that it was the same person in each.

"Pretty fair likenesses, aren't they?"

He had come up behind her again, trapping her between himself and the couple in the alcove. He smiled his oddly unfriendly smile.

"Oh, yes," said Elsa noncommittally. "Mrs. Graves is obviously well travelled."

The young man in grey tweed reached around her, unnecessarily close, to pick up one of the photographs. He presented it to Elsa. It showed Mrs. Graves with a parasol at an archaeological dig, the young man in grey tweed leaning on a pickaxe in the background. (He *was* wearing a tweed suit, in fact, in all the photographs, although of course you couldn't tell whether it was always grey tweed.)

"Very interesting," said Elsa, shifting a little to one side so as not to stand so close to him.

"Is it?"

"I—yes, I suppose so. Is that the site where they found the manuscript?"

"Ask me why I'm in all the photographs."

"What?"

"Why am I in all the photographs? Ask me."

"Well, I suppose you are—an employee of Mrs. Graves." She hesitated for a moment, but this seemed the most likely explanation. Mrs. Graves might have been old enough to have an adult son, but it did not seem tactful to suggest it.

He set down the photograph coolly. "Her confidential secretary," he said. "Everywhere she goes—I go."

"That must be very interesting."

"'Interesting'—such a weak word, though well meant, I am sure. Oh yes, it is 'very interesting.'"

"I am sure there are many other words that would suit better," said Elsa.

"Oh, very many. Words have … such power—haven't they?"

Someone else had come up behind Elsa while they were speaking, and broke suddenly into their conversation.

"He's right," he said, in a husky, urgent voice, "but you mustn't listen to him. You'll forget the words, just as I did. The words and the signs. I can't remember any of it now."

Elsa looked up at the speaker, alarmed. He was a towering, white-haired man, with broad, stooped shoulders and huge hands. She had seen him before, standing in the corner of the room by himself. He fixed dazed blue eyes on her.

"It's all *his* doing." His gaze flicked past her to the young man in grey tweed. "Ask him what happens when you light the candle. Ask him what *really* happens!"

"Ought I to?"

"Not really," said the young man. "Indeed, you're safe to ignore anything he says."

He looked up at the huge man complacently for a moment, some obscure battle of wills apparently taking place between them. Elsa seized the opportunity to walk away, annoyed to find that her hands were shaking.

She sat down on a vacant seat at random. Someone soon joined her, but it was a harmless-looking woman, small and bright-eyed and loaded with lapis lazuli beads.

"You're new here," the woman observed. Elsa admitted that she was. "How exciting for you! Do you know the history of the manuscript? It is most interesting. Mrs. Graves found it in Egypt, you know, when she was traveling there after her poor husband's death. There was a pyramid, I think, that had never been looked into, and she paid for the archaeologists to investigate."

"It wasn't a pyramid," said Elsa. "It was a Roman bath that had been converted into a monastery in the Middle Ages."

"Oh, I see you know all about it!" The woman beamed; she was one of those equable souls who is always glad to be corrected by someone more knowledgeable.

"Well, I knew that part," said Elsa. "I didn't know—I had no idea—that so many people were interested in the manuscript."

"But of course we are! When the article about it came out in *Inquiry*, describing this new system of thought—not new, of course, I don't mean that, but very ancient, only new to *us*, you know—well, a great many people took notice. A great many eager inquirers. Mrs. Graves has said that she was quite inundated with requests to see the manuscript and learn from it, and of course it is very precious and very old, even considered in absolutely worldly terms, and so she couldn't let just anyone look at it. Besides, that wouldn't be right, considering what is in it. So she began offering her salons to a select few, to keep the knowledge within appropriate bounds, you know. It wouldn't be quite right for everyone to get to know about it, would it? The knowledge is so very powerful."

"Is it?" said Elsa dryly. "What does it do?"

"What do you mean?"

"I should have thought it was a straightforward question: What does it—the manuscript, the 'knowledge' in the manuscript—*do*?"

"It—it expands the horizons of your mind, it gives you a sense of your place in the order of things, what you are capable of—oh, it's wonderful! I am constantly forgetting, you know, constantly returning to the old way of thinking, I need so frequently to be reminded of the power of my own mind, the grandeur … oh, it's hard to believe that we are really so very *central* to things, but that is the truth that I have learned here."

"So," said Elsa, when it was clear that this was the extent of what she had to say, "it doesn't really do anything."

The little woman looked almost cross. "Well, I don't know why you say that. I mean, it's a book—I don't know what you would expect it to do. Of course I *have* descended to the Pure Plain, though only the once."

"You have."

"Oh yes. I lit the candle—Mrs. Graves has discovered that it's much easier if you light a candle that has been prepared in a special way—I don't know exactly how, but it focuses the energy so much more effectively. And then I … well, it took me a little while, because I'm so very used to thinking of myself as a small and humble person, you know, as I said, and so the mastery doesn't quite come naturally to me. But I found that after focusing for a little while on the *idea* that my mind might be powerful enough to alter the fabric of the world, well, then I was there."

"You were where?"

"The Pure Plain, my dear."

"Oh yes? And what was it like?"

"Well, it was … it was fascinating."

"But it was like a place?"

"Oh yes. You knew you were really there. I mean, there was no doubt … only it wasn't exactly comfortable—I wouldn't say it was exactly comfortable."

"And did you see a vision of your true self, or whatever it is you're supposed to see?"

"Not your true self, dear—the person that you need to become.

It's all about transformation—becoming someone entirely new. Oh yes, I did see that."

"And?"

"Well, I wished I could have done what needed doing—I could see how it could be done, but I just haven't the control, I'm afraid. But it was eye-opening. So very eye-opening."

"You'd do it again?"

"No … no, I think I learned enough from that one time. I think I had my perspective altered, you know, and that's really what counts."

"No doubt," said Elsa, trying to keep the laughter out of her voice.

The young man in grey tweed had reappeared. "I have been sent to collect you," he said. "Mrs. Graves does not want you to be left without a seat. We are about to have the reading, you see. Words, as we were saying earlier. Words … of a very special sort."

"Yes," said the little woman with the lapis lazuli. "Now you'll see what I mean."

They had arrived at the focal point of the evening: the reading of the next chapter from the *Bibliotheka*. The company was already moving from the living room into the library, a smaller, darker room where folding chairs had been arranged in a semi-circle around a table draped in a heavily patterned red cloth. In the middle of the table lay a familiar brown object. On either side of it were branched candlesticks full of lit candles. As people entered the room they formed a queue to pass by the table, each pausing to bend and kiss the cover of the manuscript.

Elsa had stopped inside the door, rooted with horror, but the young man in grey tweed was motioning her to join the queue herself. When she made no move, his eyebrows rose.

"Won't you join them in doing obeisance?" he inquired, in a perfectly neutral voice.

"Absolutely not," said Elsa. "For one thing, it's a sixteen-hundred-year-old manuscript—they shouldn't be … slobbering on it." *Also, it's clearly idolatry.* Rationally, she told herself, she was of course convinced that there was nothing wrong with that. There was no reason to feel—as she did feel—that she ought not to remain in the same room with it.

The smile of the young man in grey tweed became perceptibly more friendly. "They are very, very silly people," he said in an undertone. "Come." He touched her elbow. "You and I will find seats together at the back, and you can tell me what *is* a good excuse to ignore conventional morality."

*

In the light of morning, the empty lobby of the hotel looked almost shabby. Or perhaps that had more to do with how Elsa felt. She draped her coat over her shoulders and shook out her loose and hopelessly tousled hair, and set off on her way home.

She supposed that according to all logic she should be ashamed of how she had passed most of the previous night. But when she reflected on it, even in the calm and clarity of daylight, she could not say that she wished she had behaved any differently.

The morning was cool but bright, the streets deserted. She was not certain of the time, although from what she could see of the sky, between tall houses and trees that had not yet shed their flame-coloured leaves, she thought it was mid-morning. She was hungry, but even if any shops or restaurants would have been open, she didn't know where they were. She would have to give an account of what she had been doing, and face the consequences of being out all night, on an empty stomach. She slowed her pace, feeling a little less satisfied with herself. She wondered what would happen if she were to tell the Dean of Women the absolute truth.

She was crossing a tree-lined side street of genteel houses when she was stopped by a familiar voice, raised suddenly in song. Looking up, she saw the singer approaching, hands in his pockets, hat pushed back at a jaunty angle.

"*From Bantry Bay up to Derry Quay, from Galway to Dublin … Town …* " his voice faltered as he saw her too, and he stopped in his tracks. He finished the rest of the chorus in a more subdued tone: "*No maid I've seen like the fair colleen … that I met in the County Down*—Hello, Miss Nordquist."

"Hello, Mr. Peacham."

She could see him taking in the sight of her evening dress and untidy hair. "You really *are* a departure, aren't you?" He looked slightly pained.

"Am I? I don't know what you mean."

"You're not at *all* the sort of girl that usually—no, never mind," he corrected himself hastily. "I suppose you're on your way … home?"

"Yes." There didn't seem any point in denying it.

"Ah."

"And what are you doing in this part of town?"

"Walking through it on my way to church. It *is* a Sunday morning."

"So it is. Well, I won't keep you."

"Oddly enough, I'm early. Woke up with the dawn—well, woke up with the fistfight on the landing that happened at dawn. Choir practice doesn't start for another half an hour. I'll … walk you part of the way, at least," he offered awkwardly. "It's not much out of my way. My church is just on the other side of campus."

She gave him an amused look. "That's *clearly* not necessary—but if you like."

They walked on in Elsa's direction, and she wondered what to say to him. He was obviously a bit scandalized by her appearance, but it must have occurred to him that it would be a better idea to cultivate her acquaintance than to make an enemy of her. She was not inclined to make it easier for him, but she didn't altogether want to cut him dead, either. She thought of asking conversationally when was the last time *he* was out all night at a party and walked home in the morning in the clothes he'd worn the night before. She was pretty sure the answer wouldn't have been "What? Never!"

"I suppose," he said at last, "that you and Miss Spencer see a lot of one another?"

Well, that was refreshingly direct. "We live in adjoining rooms this year, so we do, indeed." Now are you going to ask me, like an imbecile, whether she confides in me the secrets of her heart, and whether she has talked about you? Please don't, Elsa thought, because the answer won't reflect well on either of us.

"That must be nice," was all Mr. Peacham said. After a moment he added, wistfully, "Kit and I used to live together. It was a good life. Oh—I bought him a birthday present, you know, as you suggested."

"Did you?" This change of topic took her by surprise.

"Mm. He was utterly puzzled, I could tell. Still, it was good advice—you were quite right. I could stand to be a better friend. I'd do anything for him really, in the ordinary way—you know, dying, and going to prison, and—oh, all that sort of thing. But one ought to be able to handle the small stuff too, eh?"

"Yes, one ought."

"I suppose women are better about that sort of thing. I mean, the little things come naturally to you—the domestic touches and so on." He stopped in his tracks and pushed his hat even farther back on his head. "Golly. You know, I quite see why you're giving me that look, Miss Nordqu-quist. That's patronizing Victorian rubbish, isn't it? Of course if you don't give women any more scope to express their devotion than the d-domestic, er, whatnot, then that's what they'd do, isn't it? I suppose that's what—or at least that's an idiotic paraphrase of what you were going to say, isn't it?"

She laughed. "Well, apparently I just have to look at you in a certain way, Mr. Peacham, and you come up with these things on your own."

"That's to my credit, I hope?"

"Oh yes."

He beamed. "Do you know what I should really like?" he said confidingly. "Talking of gestures, you know, and friendship, and that.

I write music, you see—I don't make a living at it, because one can't, really, but it's, it's what I do. And I've never written anything for Kit. In all the years we've been friends. You know, something that he would really approve of. I should like to, but I don't quite know where to start."

"I should have thought that would be the easy part," she said. "Couldn't you write a hymn?"

"A hymn?" He looked doubtful. "That's not really my style. Musically, I mean. Too simple. I did once try to write a Mass setting, but it was a disaster. Even Kit wasn't particularly kind about it. He said the acolytes would all have passed out by '*pleni sunt coeli et terra.*' He had a point. It's just that there was so much I wanted to put *in* it, you know, it was too important—I couldn't leave anything out." He looked at her. "Basically, it was too long to be of practical use in a church," he explained. "And that was just the part that I'd written—I didn't even start the *Agnus Dei.*"

"Well, I don't know," said Elsa. "I can't claim know much about church music, but I still think a hymn could be good. Maybe it would be salutary for you to have to write something simple."

He laughed. "That sounds like a thing he'd say. Maybe you're right."

"Mr. Peacham, why have we been talking all this time about Mr. Underhill?"

"What? No! No reason. I—I didn't mean anything, I mean … I don't know. Why shouldn't we? I don't know what you mean."

She stared at him. "I guess you don't. Why are we talking about Mr. Underhill and not Harriet, Mr. Peacham?"

"Oh! Oh, I see. What … what is there to be said about … Harriet? Anything?"

"Quite a lot. But I don't know whether you are the man to say it to, or not."

"Oh, I *am*! Miss Nordqui—sorry, Nord-qvist—I am most certainly the man to say it to! Anything you could have to say about her, about Miss Spencer, I do most ardently desire to hear!"

"Well, I don't want to make you late for your choir practice."

"Nonsense! I know all the music. Byrd for four voices—I could sing it in my sleep. Who knows? I probably do!"

"Be quiet for a moment, then, and listen." They had reached the corner by this point, and she stopped on the sidewalk and turned to face him. "I don't know what Harriet thinks of you—she hasn't told me. That's *not* a good sign, either for me as a friend or for you as a lover, because she certainly thinks something of you, and if it were unreservedly good, why wouldn't she tell me? And, on the other hand, if it's bad, why doesn't she ask my advice? But I will tell you this: I love Harriet very much, and I may not think in terms of whether I would die or go to prison or 'all that sort of thing'—maybe it's because I'm a woman, or maybe it's just because I'm a realist—but I would do anything I could to prevent her being treated shabbily." She wanted to say "having her heart broken," but that, she thought, might give him unnecessary hope. She wasn't at all sure that Harriet's heart was in danger.

"I see. Well, I … I'd try to treat her well, you know. The thing is, I expect you think she's worth at least ten of me, and I'd agree with you. I treat people shabbily all the time—I can't help it, I'm a shabby sort of fellow. But I *want* to do better. For what that's worth."

Elsa smiled slightly. "That depends on your world-view, I guess. It might be worth a lot."

"Or … basically nothing?"

"Or basically nothing."

"But—speaking candidly, Miss Nordquist, and I suppose this is what you expected me to say at the beginning—do I have a chance with her?"

"Well, I wouldn't let too much more time go by, if I were you. It's already been three weeks."

"Yes." He nodded grimly. "But … "

"Oh, to change the subject completely—there is a public lecture at the museum on Tuesday night that Harriet and I are planning to attend. I don't suppose you have an intense interest in methods of Neolithic flint-napping?"

"You don't suppose? Miss Nord*qvist*, you wrong me cruelly! I have an abiding passion for Neolithic flint. I *rave* about Neolithic flint—my friends frequently complain that I seem to talk of nothing else. What time is the lecture?"

"I don't remember. But I am sure there is a notice at the museum. You can easily pass by on your way home from church."

He nodded. "That seems more than fair."

He left her, to make his way to church and choir practice, and she walked on, past the new Trinity College, grey and ostentatiously pseudo-medieval, to arrive back at the familiar red brick front of Annesley Hall. Harriet was sitting on the stairs in the lobby when she came in, with her coat and hat on.

"So you did go to the party," she said.

Elsa sat down on the step beside her. "Yes, and it was absolutely ghastly, and you were very right to warn me not to."

"I gave an excuse for you, when you weren't in at curfew—they asked me whether I knew where you were, so I said yes, you were visiting a sick relative, and you'd told me to pass along the message, but I'd forgotten, and how silly of me, and I was so sorry—I think I did a decent job of making it seem like my fault, not yours. So you may have to pretend to have a relative who lives in Toronto—though I suppose you could say he died in the night, and that's why you were gone so long. You *were* out all night."

"I locked myself in the bathroom."

"What, and they couldn't let you out until morning?"

"No, no—I locked myself in the bathroom on purpose, Harriet. It was easier than trying to sneak out—I would have had to ask for my coat, and I didn't think Mrs. Graves would have let me go. Not to mention her secretary." She shuddered slightly, at the memory of the young man in grey tweed. "I did my best, I really did, to convince myself that there was no rational basis for objecting to any of it—I don't really believe that there is any such thing as blasphemy—how could I?—and I *agree* with these people that the moral code is outdated and unnecessary. I tried to be very clear-headed and reasonable and rational about it. And then I very reasonably and rationally went and locked myself in the bathroom and put all the towels in the bathtub and slept there. The maid found me in the morning when she came in to clean, and I managed to collect my coat and get out without seeing anyone else."

Harriet was staring at her in bewilderment, but she was also starting to smile.

"Elsa, I'm glad you're all right, and I want a proper explanation as soon as I get back from church. I *am* glad you're all right." She stood up. "Oh! There was one other thing. Your father telephoned, and I happened to answer it. I told him you were washing your hair, as I didn't think he'd believe the one about the sick relative. He asked me to give you a message—he didn't know if he'd be able to phone again later. I wrote it down, as it didn't make any sense to me." She produced a slip of paper from her handbag and unfolded it. "He said he had 'more information about the man you're to meet—his initials XP—entwined in gold.' I think he meant a monogram, and that this was how you would recognize the man. He seemed to think it was important. Elsa, is your father a spy?"

"He's a farmer."

"That's what I thought. Do you know what he's talking about?"

"Yes," said Elsa. "Rubbish and nonsense, that's what he's talking about." She got to her feet as well. "I'll tell you about that later, too."

She climbed the stairs after Harriet departed, feeling surprisingly relieved. She didn't know anyone with the initials X.P.

Chapter Four

YOUNG, ENERGETIC, MODERN, RELEVANT

Kit gave his cup of tea one more methodical stir and set the spoon down in the saucer. He bent to untie his shoes and curled up on his bed. He had had a tiring morning on the heels of a poor night's sleep, and he could feel a headache preparing itself, like an orchestra tuning its instruments before a long, loud symphony. His plan was to drink his tea, read his book until he fell asleep, and miss the whole show. He could still be tough when he needed to be, but he liked to pick his battles. He pulled the knitted counterpane up over his knees and folded his pillow into a comfortable shape. The curtains were half drawn over the window beside the bed, letting in just enough of the feeble, grey daylight to read by. He sipped his tea and found his place in his book.

"*From world to world one so-ong shall ring—*" Peachy's voice carried easily up from the foyer. He had obviously come through the front door singing. "*The Lo-ord omni-i-potent is King!*"

Kit pulled the pillow over his head with a groan.

"*The Lord is King! Da-du-um-da-dum*—Hello, Mrs. Richardson!" Peachy's voice carried pretty well even when he was not singing. "Beautiful day, isn't it?"

Kit couldn't hear the housekeeper's reply from under his pillow, but he imagined it expressed puzzlement. The morning was dull and overcast.

"Oh, well—*I* think it's a beautiful day, anyway. Is Kit—I mean Father Underhill—in?"

Kit lifted up the pillow enough to hear Mrs. Richardson say that she had seen *Mr.* Underhill come in and thought he was upstairs. He threw the pillow across the room and sat up.

Peachy got through another verse of "The Lord is King" coming up the stairs, and flung open the door of Kit's room without knocking. He was dressed in an almost tasteful Fair Isle jumper and plus-fours, and he carried a bag of golf clubs slung over his shoulder.

"Go away," said Kit. "Go away this instant."

"It's ten thirty!" Peachy exclaimed. "What are you doing in bed?"

"It's ten thirty *on a Saturday*—what are *you* doing out of bed? I've already been to Morning Prayer and a Chancel Guild meeting and had a long conversation with a madman who has pinpointed the date of the Eschaton and wants to know what I am going to do about it. And what I am going to do about it is drink my tea and read my book and take a nap."

"Nonsense—what you're going to do is come golfing with me! When is it, by the way?"

"What?"

"The end of the world."

"Some time in 1952. You've ages to repent. Now go away. I am not coming golfing with you. I am actually going to pretend you never mentioned the subject, as it makes me fear for your sanity."

Peachy had set down his bag of clubs. He picked up Kit's pillow from the floor and replaced it on the bed.

"What are you reading, anyway? Church Fathers or something, I suppose." He picked up the book and turned it over. "*The Inimitable Jeeves.* Very improving, I'm sure. I am loath to tear you away from it, but this is more or less a matter of life and death."

"I doubt that very much," said Kit, taking back his book with some violence. "I doubt the whole thing, as a matter of fact. You hate golf."

"'Hate?' Mm, I don't know, that's a strong word. I may at some time in the past have expressed a slight distaste for the sport, certainly, but it's only because I never gave it a fair chance."

"You used to follow me and Mac around the course every Saturday in our freshman year, howling about what a stupid game it was, plunking your ball down in every bunker you could find, and needing the rules explained to you every second hole. We had to beg you to stop coming with us."

"Ah, but that's just my point—I may be a rotten golfer, but you're not. That's why I have to bring you along, you see. I promised I would. You have a whatsisname—a handicap—of seven. Which is quite good, isn't it? You see, I remembered that."

"Peachy! Harold MacIntyre's handicap was seven. Mine was twice that, at my very best, for a few months in undergrad—*twelve years ago*. I haven't been on a golf course since 1914. Who exactly have you been telling that I have a handicap of seven?"

"Oh … Harriet. She quite likes golf, apparently. She's played it with her father since she was a little girl, in New York—did you know she used to live in New York? Apparently she won some sort of golf championship as a teenager. I, er, learned all this the other day, in conversation. I happened to run into her, you see … "

"While you were standing on the front lawn of her residence, trying to figure out which was her window?"

"No—I never actually did that. I thought about it, but … Anyway, as it turns out there wasn't any need. She came to Evensong at St. Thomas's last Sunday."

"Did she?" Kit was pleased.

"Yes—I saw her sitting in the nave a few verses into the first psalm—*Who layeth the thingigummies in the waters / and maketh the clouds his chariot, and walketh upon the wings of the wind,*" he chanted, "and there she was. I can't imagine what brought her there, and she wouldn't say, except that she'd heard it was interesting, and she'd decided to ditch the evening service at Timothy Eaton."

"So you spoke to her."

"Oh, yes. We had a long conversation about church music, and politics, and the Reformation—the Verger had to shoo us out eventually because he wanted to put out the lights. But Kit! I thought I was in love with her before, but I was a fool! I hadn't any idea what a mind she has, and what *opinions*! The opposite of my own in many regards, but that's not important. It was a sort of revelation. I had no idea a woman could be so attractive."

"That is all wonderful," said Kit sincerely, hugging his blanket-covered knees, "and I'm very glad to hear it. But how does golf enter into it?"

"Well, we went our separate ways, but then on Tuesday I ran into her at this public lecture I went to. Neolithic flint—dullest subject on earth, as it turns out, but there she was."

"And there you were—but why?"

"Oh, I don't know, it might have been interesting. That's not the point. The point is, I said 'Hello!' and we chatted a bit again, and she agreed that Neolithic flint wasn't really *all that*, and then, I forget how the topic came up, but she said that she was going golfing on the weekend with a friend who'd never played before, and she asked if I played."

"And you said you did."

"I was quite honest about it, as it happens," said Peachy loftily. "I said that I *had* played in university, but that I was never any good. Then I was just talking, you know, and I said that if I was a bad golfer it wasn't for lack of good examples, because I'd played with a couple of friends who knew what they were doing. And—I mean, I did remember that Mac was always the better golfer, I just got the numbers mixed up. So I said that you had a handicap of seven, and she said that was decent, and that if I would bring you, I could come with them on Saturday. So you do see why you have to come, don't you?"

The trouble was, he did. Peachy had apparently made an honest mistake, for once, and although it would no doubt be a point against him to show up with a friend who wasn't nearly as good a golfer as advertised, that would still be better than showing up alone. But Kit really did not want to go.

"I still don't understand what you were doing at a lecture on Neolithic flint," he said, stalling. "That is the oddest part of this story."

"It's no odder than Harriet Spencer coming to Evensong at St. Thomas's. But she seemed to know what she was in for. I don't know why you aren't perplexed about that."

Because I know exactly how that happened, Kit thought. "You're evading the question."

"No, I'm not. I had reason to believe that she might be at this Neolithic shindig, so I went along, intending to run into her. I hadn't the least idea what Neolithic flint was—I do now, by the way, having sat through the lecture, but it's extremely boring, so I won't burden you with it. *Will* you get up and get dressed? We're supposed to meet Harriet and her friend at Annesley Hall in forty-five minutes."

"That's all very well, but I don't have anything reasonable to wear on a golf course, not here. All of my things from university are at your parents' house. Besides, it looks like rain."

"Oh, I'm *counting* on rain. Nothing would please me more. We would have to sit in the clubhouse and talk about opera, or theology, or political economy, instead of trying to play that wretched game. And I don't care what you wear—you can come in your cassock and surplice, for all I care. But you *must* come."

"What were you going to do if I'd been busy? I might well have been—I was until half an hour ago."

"But you're not now! Why are you making feeble excuses?"

Kit rested his forehead on his knees. "I don't feel well. I have a headache—I got next to no sleep last night."

"What, really?" Peachy was suddenly dismayed. "You didn't sleep? Why didn't you say? I didn't know you still had that trouble—don't they look after you here? I mean, they know, don't they, that you've … that you … need looking after?"

Kit looked up at him and couldn't help smiling. "I don't, my dear. I could have slept very well if I'd had the opportunity. I was up all night with the family of a parishioner who'd tried to kill himself.

I spent most of my time in the kitchen, helping the sister make endless pots of tea … and rice pudding. I'm not sure why, but she was fixated on rice pudding. The only time she actually broke down and cried was when it looked as though we didn't have enough sugar. Fortunately I found some more in the back of the pantry. Then I don't think anyone ate the rice pudding in the end, except me … Which is a shame, because it was very good."

"Oh. I see. What a mess. Forget that I said anything about the other business—don't even know why I did, really. I know you're all right." But he sat there for a moment looking at Kit with an expression that completely belied his words. He *hoped* Kit was all right, clearly, but it would have made him happier to be able to *do* something to make sure. That was Peachy all over.

"Thanks. If you don't object to my wearing black trousers on the golf course, I've remembered I do have that grey waistcoat that your mother knit me. At least I won't look *quite* like I'm going to a funeral."

"Oh! You—you're going to come?"

"Of course."

"Hurrah! I'll help you by finding the waistcoat for you." He flung open the doors of Kit's wardrobe. "I do appreciate it, old man, really I do. If ever you make up your mind to let me help in a similar way, you know you've only to say the word. Here you are." He had found the waistcoat on an upper shelf, and held it out appraisingly. It was very conservative by his standards.

"Wait a minute," said Kit. "Peachy, this friend of Miss Spencer's who doesn't know how to play golf—it's not … "

"The atheist girl you're so afraid of?"

"I'm not afraid of her!"

"Well, split hairs if you like. No, it's not her. It's someone with a nickname—Muffy, or Miffy, or something like that. I know that sounds vague, but, really, I'm sure it's not Miss Nordquist. I wouldn't do that to you, Kit," he added seriously. "I mean, admittedly, it does sound like the sort of thing that I might do, but in this case I haven't—and won't. I … " He sat down on the chair beside Kit's bed, still holding the grey waistcoat. "I saw her last Sunday."

"Who?"

"Miss Thing! Norqvist. I was on my way to Mass, and I met her coming … going … home, I'm afraid. In an evening gown. On a Sunday morning. I'm not—I don't tell you this thinking that you'll be scandalized or heartbroken, obviously."

"Obviously," said Kit, a little icily. He was *surprised*, though, and he doubted that it meant what Peachy evidently thought it meant.

"It's just that I thought I *ought* to tell you, because it seems like the sort of thing you should know about a girl that … "

"That I've already said I have no intention of seeing again?"

"Yes, but the fact is, I think you should reconsider that."

"What?"

"Look, she's a dear friend of Harriet's, and any friend of Harriet's—and *such* a friend, Kit! You should have heard—no, you should have seen the way she looked at me when she said she'd do anything to keep a man (meaning *me*) from treating Harriet badly. It made my blood run cold. You couldn't have done a better job of it yourself. What I'm trying to say is that I think she's splendid. And I know she was out all night, and that doesn't quite make her seem like a nice girl, but honestly, who cares about that? In this day and age. And you of all people—I mean, if anyone could … Oh, I don't know. I like her, that's all. I think you should give her a second chance. She was the one who told me about the Neolithic flint lecture."

"Was she?" So she thought that Harriet and Peachy were a good pair too. Kit didn't really need any reason to think more highly of her.

"Yes, and not only that, but she told me that she and Harriet were planning on going—but then, when I went, Miss Nordquist wasn't there, and Harriet didn't seem to care very much about the flint herself. I think Miss Nordquist might just have told her to go to the lecture in order to meet me. Which was awfully nice of her. Actually, I wonder if it wasn't Miss Nordquist who sent her to Evensong, too. Don't you think it might have been?"

"It might have been," Kit agreed, magnanimously.

Peachy looked at him thoughtfully. "But was it?"

"No," said Kit. "That one was me."

"That makes more sense."

"Come on, Peachy," said Kit, getting up from the bed. "If we're going to go golfing, we'd better go."

"But when did you and Harriet … "

"We met at a charity function. I'll tell you about it on the way."

Canon Plumptre was in the front room when they came downstairs, talking to a big, silver-haired man in an expensive suit. Peachy stopped at the foot of the stairs to retie a shoelace, and Kit overheard their conversation through the open door.

"Alexander Britton is retiring," Canon Plumptre was saying, "so they are looking for someone to take over at St. John's in Earlscourt."

This was news to Kit, and it interested him.

"Ah! A breath of fresh air, eh?" said the other man. "That could be a great thing. Get someone new in there who could shake things up a bit."

"I don't know. I don't think they'd stand for much shaking up at St. John's. The parish is very … "

"Mired in the Dark Ages?"

"I was going to say that they have a particular way of doing things … It's a very strong parish in many ways—very active. Not a lot of money, but they do good works—according to their own lights. I mean—charitable, you know. Very Catholic, but … eccentric, too. They do a Corpus Christi procession down St. Clair Avenue that would make the Bishop of Rome blush—or so I've heard—but I've also heard Britton hold forth at great length about his objections to birettas."

"I suppose one of his assistants will take over from him."

"I doubt it. Sturgeon is ancient, and Baldassare—one assumes—is too busy writing unreadable books about the Holy Spirit. They have somebody or other as a curate, a middle-aged former bank teller—not exactly what you would call a rising young star. I doubt they'll be looking to install him in the rectory."

The canon had spotted Kit and Peachy in the hall, but evidently decided to ignore them. His interlocutor, however, was looking Kit up and down with interest, and the moment when Canon Plumptre could have let the two young men pass by without making an introduction had passed.

"This is Christopher Underhill, our curate." Plumptre was looking at him doubtfully, plainly wondering where the knitted waistcoat and the golf clubs had come from.

The silver-haired man identified himself; he had some absurd name, Bulger or something, that Kit forgot instantly.

"Glad to meet you!" he declared, shaking Kit's hand violently. "Golfing, eh? A man after my own heart! I hope the weather improves for you, but I have to admit I don't think it will." He shook Peachy's hand too, and repeated his absurd name. It *was* Bulger. "I admire your dedication to the game! I was just telling the Rector here how today's churchman needs to be more like the businessman."

"Oh?" said Kit, finding that his tiredness made it easier to conceal the horror and scorn that he would normally have struggled to keep to himself. "Does he?"

"He does indeed. Hard-headed, efficient, ambitious—we need to build up the Church the way I built up my company."

"Quite right," said Canon Plumptre faintly. His lips moved silently for a moment, as though he might be praying that Underhill would not say whatever it was he was going to say.

Bulger went on in the same vein for a little while, and Kit restricted himself to saying "Oh," and repeating the things the businessman said in the form of questions: "We need to take a pragmatic view, do we?" and "*Is* that the modern reality?"

Building to the climax of his argument, Bulger jabbed Kit in the chest with a large, bony finger. Kit had to make a physical effort not to hit him.

"You see, this is precisely what I have been talking about. You, son, are exactly the sort of man we need: young, energetic, modern, relevant!"

Plumptre gave a pained smile, as if he was thinking that he could have described Christopher Underhill perfectly well without using any of those words. Peachy, who was standing behind Bulger, opened his eyes very wide and nodded repeatedly. Kit had a sudden, horrible conviction that he was going to start laughing in a moment. Helplessly. Giggling, in fact. He could feel it building up inside him.

"That's very kind of you to say," he managed.

"Mr. Bulge," said Peachy suddenly and raptly, joining the conversation for the first time, "may I say how *utterly* I agree with everything you have been saying?"

"Bulger," the businessman corrected him. "Do you?"

"Oh, completely! Kit can tell you, it's a topic he and I always discuss. It's exactly as you say, it's the capitalistic spirit that the modern church is lacking. I've often thought that was something that the medievals had a better handle on than we, you know."

"The medievals?" Bulger was taken aback.

"Yes, selling indulgences and that sort of thing," said Peachy with impenetrable seriousness. "That's what you're talking about, isn't it? Then there's the pilgrim trade, of course. That's very good for business. If you're thinking capitalistically."

"Um … that's not quite … " Bulger looked hopefully at Kit, who was pressing his knuckles to his lips in what he hoped looked like serious thought but was actually a desperate attempt to swallow his laughter.

"That's not what you meant?" said Peachy, crestfallen.

"No," said Bulger. "Certainly not. The Dark Ages were—were … "

"Dark?" Kit suggested.

"Oh, but surely!" Peachy burst out. "I thought we saw eye to eye—I mean, *you* agree with me, don't you, Kit?"

"He probably does," said Canon Plumptre, who looked like he was himself trying hard not to laugh by this point. "But I think we can leave it at that. We won't keep you from your game any longer. The golf, I mean. To be honest, Mr. Bulger, Underhill is probably not the man you want."

Kit and Peachy walked to the streetcar cheerfully discussing the modern practicalities of pricing and distributing indulgences.

*

Annesley Hall was a handsome building of dark red brick, in style more domestic than collegiate Gothic, with a curved drive in front and female undergraduates buzzing in and out. By the time the two men arrived, the clouds had parted and the day was promising to be brilliantly sunny, in spite of Bulger's predictions. Kit's headache, apparently unimpressed with his altruism, was building to full strength.

Peachy approached the large main door of the residence tentatively. "She said to meet her here, but I don't know whether she meant this side of the door or the other. I don't know whether men are allowed in here."

"I'm pretty sure we're allowed to go through the front door," said Kit, and opened it.

Inside was a vestibule with leaded glass windows and another door through which even Kit thought they were not allowed to go. Beyond the windows they could see a large central staircase, and Harriet coming down it in a smart golfing outfit with her bag of clubs. She saw them and waved.

"Come in!" she said, holding the inner door open for them. "Oh, don't be silly—it isn't a nunnery! It's so nice to see you again, Mr. Peachy—Reverend Underhill. Oh, but Peachy tells me that I shouldn't call you that, as it's not correct. But it's what I've always

125

been used to, I mean with Methodist ministers. But he says you ought to put 'The Reverend Mister' on an envelope, but that 'Reverend' isn't a term of address—is that true? But then what am I to call you? He says 'Father,' but I *couldn't possibly.*"

Oh, but it might be a good idea, if you're going to carry on like this, Kit thought. He shrugged. "I leave it to your discretion. I'll answer to most things."

"Well, if you say so. Peachy also tells me that you're a pretty good golfer," she said. "But—"

"I was mistaken about that," Peachy cut in stiffly. "I, er, confused him with someone else. There were three of us, you see, who used to golf together in university—Kit and I and Mac, Harold Mac-Intyre. And I was never any good, as I told you, so it didn't mean anything to me whose handicap was what. I'm afraid I got them mixed up. Kit says his was fourteen or something. And he hasn't played in a long time."

"Well, that would explain why he hasn't brought any clubs and is wearing those shoes." She looked disapprovingly at Kit's black Oxfords. "But why didn't you bring your other friend, in that case?"

"Oh, he's … well, he's dead."

"I'm sorry," said Harriet, looking starkly mortified. "I really am very sorry."

There was an awkward silence. Kit wondered why it was that, even though he knew Mac was dead, had been dead for nearly ten years—even though he had been there when Mac died and seen it happen—the words should still feel like a blow, a dull shock, as if, after all this time, it might not actually be true while he wasn't reminded of it.

"I don't think he would have wished his memory to cast a pall over any group of friends," Kit said after a moment. "Especially not when they were on their way to the links. He was a man who wouldn't let anything interfere with his enjoyment of golf."

"That's a very sensible attitude," said Harriet, smiling gratefully.

"As it happens, I'm just as glad you're not a true proficient, Mr. Underhill, because I am sadly out of practice myself. I used to play nearly every weekend with my father, but he's got arthritis in his shoulder that prevents him enjoying it now, so I have got out of the habit too. We didn't have a single game all summer. But then I saw my old school-friend Milly Thorndike recently, and she has got engaged to a young man who golfs, and wants me to teach her the rudiments so that she can surprise him. I thought it was a sweet idea—don't you?"

"Utterly charming," Peachy agreed meekly.

"She said she would meet us here," Harriet added. "She lives in Forest Hill. She's bringing her car. Though come to think of it, I don't know whether that means a car and driver, or that *she's* driving. I don't think she drives. Of course, I hadn't seen her in years, but Milly never seemed like the sort of girl who would drive."

There was another awkward silence—this one, Kit thought, for no good reason. He could think of any number of conversational gambits: *How nice it must be to have a car and driver, and not to be reliant on the streetcar! Did Miss Spencer herself know how to drive? Did she think that Miss Thorndike's fiancé was a good golfer, or merely an enthusiastic one? Would she, Miss Spencer, have taken up golf in order to impress a man?* Yet Peachy stood there dumbly, saying none of this. (Peachy, who had proposed not long ago to instruct Kit in the ways of attracting women!) And at any moment now, Miss Spencer was going to give up and talk to Kit again. He wished he could fade discreetly into the background, but he was in a women's residence; there was nowhere he could safely go.

"Mr. Peacham," said Harriet suddenly, "have you written any more of your oratorio?"

"Oh! I've … well, no. Not written, as such. Though I have had a good idea for the initial dialogue between St. Æscwyn and the devil."

But it was apparently not the type of idea that could easily be explained. Conversation flagged again, and there was still no sign of Miss Thorndike and her car. Kit was beginning to feel hungry; his hasty breakfast had been too long ago, and too little to make up for an almost sleepless night on nothing but a bowl of rice pudding. He wondered if there were any plans for the party to eat lunch, or whether this was to be one of those outings where nobody got up the nerve to mention food until everyone was too hungry to think straight, and they all ended up crossly eating sandwiches in the street outside the first shop they came across. He decided that as he was not trying to impress anyone, he would be the one to broach the subject of food as soon as the whole party was assembled.

"There's Milly now," said Harriet finally. "But who has she got with her?"

She opened the inner door for the pair. Milly was a delicate, dark-haired girl in pink. She was followed by a large, balding, slightly pop-eyed young man in plus-fours and Fair Isle jumper and fringe-tongued Oxfords—unmistakably the golfer fiancé.

"Burt insisted on coming," Milly explained brightly, "when I let it slip that we were going golfing. Burt is so very fond of golfing. I'm afraid," she added, without the slightest trace of penitence, "that we are a little late."

"We've brought my car," Burt announced. "Milly had some idea of driving you there herself, but I don't like her driving. She hasn't got the brains for it."

"I haven't, really," said Milly, with apparent satisfaction. "And Burt's car is ever so much nicer than mine, anyway. He does all the work on the insides himself, you know."

At this, without waiting to be introduced to anyone, Burt launched into a long, jargony account of the things that he had needed to do to his car's engine that morning before they could leave. It gave one the impression that it was practically a miracle the thing ran at all, though that didn't seem to be the point he was trying to make. Milly beamed at him while the rest of the party stared uncomprehendingly, not even trying to look interested.

"This bunch doesn't know a thing about motor-cars," Burt observed angrily when they failed to laugh at some obscure, engine-related joke. "What a useless lot of friends you have, Milly!" And he repeated the punchline of his joke, very slowly and loudly, and groaned in disgust when they still didn't get it.

Burt was the last straw as far as that golfing party was concerned. Milly would probably have been bearable on her own, but the fact that she tolerated Burt—even seemed to be proud of him—made one dislike her, too. Kit had met his type before and had slight patience for it at the best of times. Harriet, it was clear, hated him on sight.

Sticking to his plan, Kit asked where they were going to eat lunch. Burt had already eaten lunch, but he objected, with loud groans and eye-rolling, to every restaurant proposed by the others.

"Look," said Kit finally, trying to sound jovial rather than vicious, "it doesn't matter whether you don't like their soup or think they're overpriced—*you've already eaten.* You don't get a vote."

Burt turned his pop-eyed stare on Kit. "I'm sorry to tell you, padre, but nobody put you in charge. *I'm* not part of your flock. My folks are Quakers from way back."

"Never mind that," said Harriet—also, Kit thought, trying to sound friendly, but failing horribly. "Why don't *you* tell us where *you're* willing to eat, and we'll go there?"

"I don't care where you go," said Burt, slowly and carefully, as if speaking to a dim-witted child. "I—have—already—eaten. Mm, sweetheart? I'd have thought university girls would be a bit quicker on the uptake." And he chuckled, to show that it was a joke and you would have to be a prig to object to it.

"Come on, old man," said Peachy, with a strained cheerfulness, "that's not quite nice. She's heard you say you've already eaten—we all have. Now what about that nice place on Yonge, with the cakes in the window? You know the one I'm talking about—what's it called?"

"Oh, I can't go in that place!" said Milly. "I take one look at those cakes and want to eat them all!"

"Yeah, she's not going near any cakes, let me tell you—I want her to fit into her dress on our wedding day!"

Milly giggled as if this were the most courtly of compliments.

Kit turned away from the group, wishing briefly that he were the sort of person who could just march out through the front door in a situation like this, without any explanation, and go home. Except that the people who could do that sort of thing were in danger of being as insufferable, in their own way, as Burt and Milly.

He looked up at the central stairway, and there on the landing was Elsa Nordqvist, leaning on the railing, looking down at him. He thought she probably hadn't known it was he until he looked up, so they became aware of each other at the same moment. Her hair was unbraided, and fell down over one shoulder in long, creamy curls. She wore a pale yellow blouse, the sleeves rolled up on her slender arms, and a dark skirt. She looked almost unbearably lovely. He couldn't believe it had been nearly a month since he saw her for the first time.

Neither of them smiled. He had the distinct impression that she was having a worse day than he was. In fact, she looked as though she had been crying. He wanted to run up the stairs, two at a time, and offer to do something for her, anything really, but especially something that involved taking her in his arms. And, on the other hand—since he wasn't going to do that—he wanted her to come down to the lobby and rescue him from Burt and his monologues about cars and his endless opinions about restaurants. He wondered what she wanted.

Chapter Five

PENS AND SPINDLES

Elsa wanted to forget the last twenty-four hours. But then again she didn't, because the things that she had learned yesterday she would not have wanted to go on not knowing. She felt like she had been a fool, but she could have been a worse fool. She wanted to talk to Harriet, who had been out all day yesterday with her parents and returned after Elsa had gone miserably to bed. Then when Elsa had roused herself this morning to come look for her, she found Harriet already up and out. Or not out, exactly, but standing in the lobby with a group evidently assembled to play golf.

"Personally, I like the cafeteria at Eaton's," a dainty girl in pink was saying.

"Aw, honey, why didn't you say so before?" groaned the large young man beside her. "Surely none of you people would object to going there?"

One member of the party had turned away and seemed to be trying to ignore the others. Elsa couldn't see his face, from this angle, past the brim of his hat, but she thought she knew who he was. Then he looked up, suddenly, straight at her, and he was indeed Christopher Underhill, extremely blue eyes and all. She wondered if she should have stepped back from the railing, gone back upstairs when she first thought it might be him, before he had seen her. She had told Harriet that she never wanted to see him again, and she had meant it. But that had been—or seemed to her to have been—so long ago now. The whole thing seemed unimportant. He would probably not remember her name.

He was looking at her now not with surprise or pleasure, but with a steady compassion. She realized it must have been obvious that she had been crying. This ought to have been mortifying, but somehow she couldn't summon the energy to feel it.

"Are you playing golf?" she asked.

"For my sins."

She should have started with "Hello," she thought, or said his name. He might think she didn't remember it.

"I expect you want to talk to Miss Spencer," he said.

"Thank you."

He turned and discreetly touched Harriet's sleeve. "Your friend Miss Nordqvist wants to talk to you."

Harriet looked up. "Elsa! The very person!" She seized Mr. Underhill's arm. "Elsa should come with us, don't you think?"

"If she wants to, though I can't imagine she has done anything to deserve it. But is there room in the car for six? If there isn't, I could … "

"What? Not come?"

"I would be willing to make that sacrifice. I am, as you know, extremely noble."

"Don't be silly. It's a Hudson Phaeton—weren't you listening?"

"Not really. And I don't know what that is."

"You're hopeless! It's a big car—it seats seven." She turned back toward the stairs. "Do you want to come golfing with us, Elsa? It doesn't matter if you've never played."

"I haven't."

"Oh, do come!"

"All right."

"Wonderful!" Harriet beamed. Perhaps she was too absorbed in her own affairs to pay much attention to Elsa's state of mind, but that was all right. Harriet's affairs were looking up; one of the golfing party was Mr. Peacham, dressed up (unlike Mr. Underhill) like a person who took the game seriously. "Go get your things—we've just about made up our minds where to have lunch."

Elsa hastened back upstairs to her room. She didn't really want to go golfing—any more than Mr. Underhill did, apparently. But to go out with people seemed a more sensible idea that to sit in her room alone, being miserable. It would take her mind off things. She snatched up a cardigan and her handbag. She looked at herself in the hall mirror as she hastily braided her hair and pinned on her hat. Actually, it was by no means obvious that she had been crying.

They piled into the car belonging to Mr. Butcher, the balding young man, with Harriet and Mr. Peacham in the back, Elsa and Mr. Underhill in the middle, and everyone hemmed in and poked and inconvenienced by golf clubs. Mr. Butcher proved to be a violent, angry driver. He sounded his horn at the least provocation, took corners at full speed, and jolted the car grudgingly to a halt only when he absolutely had to. This made the golf-club situation considerably worse.

"Steady on!" said Mr. Underhill when a particularly abrupt stop sent the golf bag that was wedged between him and Elsa careening painfully against her knees.

Mr. Butcher ignored him. Mr. Underhill crossly steadied the golf bag to keep it from hitting Elsa again.

He thinks I shouldn't have come, Elsa thought. *He's right. I've just exchanged one form of misery for another.*

They had not been a happy party to begin with, she realized, and her presence did nothing to help. Mr. Peacham made a few vague stabs at conversation with Harriet, but he was not his usual effervescent self; he seemed stifled or constrained by something. Harriet became impatient with this, and would periodically start talking to Mr. Underhill instead. Mr. Underhill himself was in something of a bad mood—indeed, Elsa suspected that he was unwell—and Mr. Butcher's driving seemed to make him nervous. He resisted, with a stiff politeness, all of Harriet's attempts to draw him out. Milly was the only really happy member of the party. As for her fiancé, he was a sort of social tyrant. He seemed to consider it a duty to insult everyone he was with as often as possible, with a strident, bullying jocularity, as if he was perpetually looking for a fight and at the same time perpetually surprised that nobody knew how to take a joke.

Lunch was expensive and took a long time coming. Mr. Underhill's food seemed not to be coming at all, but finally arrived when everyone else was almost done eating, so that he had to bolt it hurriedly. Mr. Butcher, having already eaten, treated them to a steady stream of talk throughout lunch, on topics ranging from the merely dull (his opinions on cars and politics) to the downright loathsome (his long, derisive account of his fiancée's interest in spiritualism). Everyone looked horrified by this, but only Mr. Underhill actually said anything.

"I am sure Miss Thorndike has more discrimination than you give her credit for," he said—very generously, Elsa thought. "It is easy to make fun of some of the ways that people seek meaning and purpose in their lives, but everyone feels that need to some extent."

This, of course, opened the floodgates of Mr. Butcher's scorn in his direction, which had probably been his intention. But it occupied Elsa's mind for the rest of the lunch as well. What else had she been doing in her studies but seeking a sense of purpose? And what was she supposed to do if, as it now seemed, that had been ridiculous all along, as laughable as Miss Thorndike holding a séance in her mother's living room to contact her dead cat?

Lunch finally over, they wedged themselves back into the car and set off for the golf course. The day had become surprisingly warm, and when they arrived, most of the party took off their sweaters, draped them about their shoulders, and rolled up their sleeves. They sorted out who would share clubs with whom (Mr. Butcher wouldn't share with anyone, not even Milly) and set out onto the first hole.

The men took their shots from their tee; the women, Harriet explained, started from another point farther up the green. Mr. Butcher whacked his ball mightily, sending it up in a great arc to land somewhere far in the distance.

"Damn!" he shouted inexplicably.

Harriet raised her eyebrows. "That wasn't so bad."

Mr. Butcher snorted.

"Poor lamb!" said Milly.

Mr. Underhill hit his ball about the same distance, but didn't swear. Mr. Peacham sent his ball shearing crazily sideways into a sand pit. He looked forlorn but not particularly surprised. Elsa realized that his convincing golf clothes were a bluff.

"Oh, dear," said Harriet. "That's bad luck."

"I told you I wasn't any good," he said mournfully.

The women walked up to their starting-point, and Harriet demonstrated the proper stance and how to swing the club, and hit her own ball straight down the fairway, farther than Mr. Butcher's. Milly gave her ball a pitiful little tap, and giggled, and Harriet went and fetched it back and made her try again. Elsa hit her ball as hard as she could, and managed to send it into the sand pit with Mr. Peacham's.

"What's the matter?" she asked, as she scrambled down into the sand beside him.

"What's the matter with what?"

"With you. Why aren't you talking to Harriet?"

She expected at least a token glare for being an interfering female again, but he only sighed.

"I'm not worthy of her. Of course I realized that before … " He took a pathetic swat at his ball, spraying sand around and accomplishing nothing. "But somehow this morning it hit me all at once, and I realized what an ass I've been. I suppose it was something Kit said on the streetcar coming over. He was telling me how he'd met Harriet at that home for junior criminals, or whatever it is, and about her plan for opening a girls' school, and he said that he admired her resolve. And I thought, she's a woman with a great mission in life—a sense of purpose. She doesn't need a man like me. She needs someone like Kit."

But don't you see that she didn't tell you any of this *because* she's attracted to you? Elsa thought. There was the fatal flaw in Harriet's strategy. What was the point of presenting yourself as an old-fashioned "sweet girl" to a man and then telling his best friend all about your ambitions behind his back? Unless it wasn't primarily Mr. Peacham that she was interested in after all.

"I don't think she does," she said aloud. "I think she *is* someone like Ki—like Mr. Underhill. At least in some ways. I don't think that necessarily means she needs to marry someone like him. Anyway, he's not available, is he?"

"Well, no, he's not," Peachy agreed absently, batting at his ball again. "But that's not my point."

Something else occurred to her. "He didn't want to come golfing, did he? You dragged him here the same way you dragged him to the beach on his birthday. It's clear that's how your friendship works. Peverell Peacham says jump, and Kit Underhill jumps. One day if you're not careful you'll drag him into something really awful."

At that he did glare at her, but it was not heartfelt. He succeeded finally in smacking his ball back up onto the fairway, and clambered out after it, leaving her in the sand trap in redoubled wretchedness. Seemingly she had accomplished nothing by sending Harriet and Mr. Peacham to the museum together. And why hadn't Harriet told her that she had seen Mr. Underhill after the day on the beach? Was it just because she thought Elsa didn't want to hear his name mentioned?

When she rejoined the others, Mr. Butcher was holding forth about airplane engines.

"I thought he was a Quaker," Mr. Underhill remarked to Harriet. "He can't have been in the RFC?"

"I think he was a mechanic. But maybe you should ask him how many planes he shot down."

But Mr. Peacham by this time was already explaining how he

and Mr. Underhill had waited until 1917 to enlist, and Mr. Butcher was shouting with derision.

"I think we'll let the topic go," said Mr. Underhill to Harriet. But Elsa saw the muscles of his forearm tense as he clenched the club he was holding in what must have been an uncomfortably tight grip. It wasn't hard to guess that the idea not to enlist had been Peachy's. Peverell Peacham said, "Let's not jump," and so they hadn't. And only one of them was ashamed of it.

Eventually they all made it onto the green, where Elsa managed to knock her ball into the hole rather neatly, and Milly missed several very easy putts.

"One would almost think you were doing it on purpose!" Harriet remarked, as they followed the men on to the next hole.

"Oh, I am," Milly said limpidly. "I don't want to be better than Burt."

"But you silly child—there's no danger of that! He's just swearing a lot, you know—he's not actually playing badly."

"Well, I don't know," said Milly with a bland obstinacy. "Better safe than sorry, I think. You might consider it yourself, you know. A man doesn't like to be shown up by the girl he admires."

Harriet opened her mouth to say something, then closed it again and was silent, frowning thoughtfully.

On the third hole, Milly hit her ball into a thicket, and Elsa went in with her to help her find it. Mr. Butcher's mocking laughter followed them in.

"If you don't mind my asking," Elsa said, "what is it that made you … made you fall in love with Mr. Butcher?"

"Only how wonderful he is!" Milly looked up at her with shining eyes. "In so many ways. He has so many opinions about so many things. Don't you think?"

"Oh, yes, of course." This was undeniably true. Mr. Butcher did have many opinions, about many things.

"And he is so very devoted, and so romantic," Milly went on, returning to her scrutiny of the undergrowth. "He brings me flowers nearly ever time he visits—big bunches, and so beautiful, he has *exquisite* taste. And he buys me jewellery for every occasion, and sometimes for none at all—it is almost embarrassing. But it is not just gifts—you mustn't think I'm materialistic. It is how he worries about me, and telephones every day when he can't visit, just to hear my voice—that's what he says, 'I just wanted to hear your voice'—and how *jealous* the dear boy gets when he sees me talking to another man. That's the real reason he came along today, because I mentioned there would be men in the party."

To be belittled in public but showered with affection and presents in private; to listen to all of his opinions but to have her own laughed at; to be unable to go out in mixed company without setting off a storm of jealousy: All this was romantic? Perhaps it was, Elsa thought; but then, who could want it? And yet it was better—or at least not much worse—than what she had got herself.

"And gosh," Milly went on, lowering her voice, "if I weren't so devoted to Burt, I would almost say he was right to worry. Mr. Peacham is all right, though he seems a bit stupid, but his friend is really *too* scrumptious, isn't he? I think Harriet could have her pick of them, but if I were her, I know who I'd choose. I wish we had him at our church. Oh, there's my ball, by that tree root!"

Was that just Milly being a featherbrain, Elsa wondered, or was it true—that Harriet had attracted Mr. Underhill as well as Mr. Peacham? The more she watched them now, the more she became convinced that it was true. While Mr. Peacham moped and shuffled miserably about the golf course, Harriet had succeeded in making Mr. Underhill laugh at what seemed to be some private joke about picking pockets. It might have been simple charity, since she could see that he was out of sorts, or it might have been flirtation, since she could see that he liked her. Either way, it annoyed Elsa; why wasn't Harriet trying to cheer *her* up? And when Harriet made a particularly good putt, and Mr. Underhill congratulated her on it,

Elsa saw him look at her with a smile of such clear, undisguised affection that she could feel the bottom dropping out of her heart with a thud.

It was all part of the general wrongness and painfulness of the world, in which none of them, apparently, could have what they wanted. Peachy couldn't because Peachy was an idiot. Mr. Underhill couldn't because he was the friend of an idiot and (apparently) because he was in thrall to an idiotic religion. Harriet couldn't because Harriet, for the first time in her life, didn't know what she wanted. Elsa couldn't because she was a woman, and had idiotically imagined that didn't matter.

Milly and Mr. Butcher might have had what they wanted in each other, but Elsa rather hoped for their sakes that they hadn't.

Harriet had begun valiantly trying to draw Peachy out again by recounting the plot of his oratorio to Milly.

"It's about an Anglo-Saxon nun named Æscwyn, an abbess, you know, the head of a convent."

"Oh, I could *never* be a nun!" said Milly.

"No, nor I, but that's not the point. This woman is, and she's very good at it—I mean she's a very holy person, a saint, as it turns out. And one night, as she's sitting in her cell, praying, she's visited by a devil in the guise of an angel, who tempts her to leave the convent and give up her holy life. He could perform a miracle for her, he says. He could change her appearance so that none of her nuns would know her, and she could start over and lead a worldly life as a whole new woman. And, oh my, he is *very* persuasive. He sings a gorgeous aria about how God doesn't *really* want her to waste her youth and her beauty—because she is quite young herself, you know—in this fruitless life, and how she should get out and see the world, and all that sort of thing. At least, I expect it will be a terrific aria—it's not written yet, is it, Mr. Peacham?"

"What? Oh, no."

"He'll be a tenor, though, won't he? The angel-devil. Quite a high tenor, I would think."

"Oh? I hadn't really thought about it."

Harriet frowned. "Well, that is what I should think. If he's meant to sound *really seductive*."

She couldn't speak much plainer than that, Elsa thought. But Mr. Peacham still affected not to understand her.

"He wouldn't seduce *me*, then," said Milly. "I like a man with a deep voice. Burt is a baritone, and—"

"But then what happens?" asked Elsa, trying to be helpful.

"She sees through him, of course," said Harriet. Mr. Peacham, who was taking his swing at that moment, missed the ball entirely. Harriet turned her back on him, and went on with the story, rather loudly. "She doesn't think for a minute that he's really an angel, and she grabs him by the hair and shakes him until he confesses. And then she banishes him, or exorcises him, or whatever, and he changes out of his angelic form, and goes and possesses a swarm of bees in one of the convent beehives. And then the bees all die, and so *that's the end of him*."

A woman with a great mission in life, this St. Æscwyn, Elsa thought. Just the sort of thing Peachy did not want to be reminded of.

"Ugh," said Milly absently. "I hate bees."

Harriet sighed and slammed her golf club angrily back into her bag, and Mr. Butcher said it all sounded like a lot of medieval superstition to him. They walked on down the course.

In the intervals between feeling sorry for herself and angry with the world, Elsa was somehow learning how to play golf. By the fourth hole, she was beginning to get the hang of the initial shot, or whatever it was called. She was good at following instructions, and Harriet's were clear and thorough. She hit her ball quite straight this time, a respectable distance down the fairway. Everyone congratulated her—even, after a fashion, Mr. Butcher.

"Not bad," he said. "Of course, that was from the ladies' tee. Quite a bit farther up, isn't it? Do they set it up like that for you at university, I wonder? Make the exams easier for the girls? They should, shouldn't they? I'd hate to think of any woman's brain tackling some of the stuff they threw at us." He whistled. "Seneca, and Cicero—it's just not natural."

"Burt has a BA in Classics," said Milly proudly.

"So do I," said Elsa. *I was going to have an MA and a PhD in it too. I had it all planned out.* And she realized that she was going to start to cry, right there on the golf course. It was the worst possible timing. It was going to confirm all of Mr. Butcher's opinions about women, and embarrass everyone, and put the seal on the whole miserable day. Or perhaps no one would notice, and that would be worse.

She managed to blink back her tears until they were walking to the next hole, and then hastily wiped away the few that escaped. She was shaking like a pot about to boil over. She couldn't go on with this. But she would create a scene if she tried to leave—someone would be sure to follow her—and where would she go? She couldn't get home on her own. She was trapped.

She looked up and realized that Mr. Underhill was walking beside her. He was definitely unwell, she thought. There were dark shadows under his eyes, and he was nursing his right arm as though it pained him.

"Are you all right?" she said.

His eyebrows went up.

"Oh," she said. "You were going to ask me that, weren't you?"

"I was thinking about it."

She smiled a little in spite of herself. "Well—no, not really."

"Me neither. I have a beastly splitting headache, my arm is sore, I'm hot, and I feel sick from eating my lunch too fast. I don't suppose you can top that."

She laughed weakly, wiping her eyes again.

"Never mind," he said. "Don't try. I've had an idea. You've just offered to take me back to the clubhouse in case I faint. Right?"

"What? Oh. Yes."

He stopped walking suddenly and bent over, putting his hands on his knees. Harriet and Milly, who had been walking behind them, hastened up.

"What's the matter?" Harriet asked.

"I don't feel at all well," he said. "I think I need to get out of the sun."

"What, really? You do look awful, Kit! Why don't we take you back to the clubhouse and find you a seat in the shade?"

"No, no—I don't want to interrupt your game. Miss Nordqvist already offered to come with me."

"Oh, that's good," said Harriet. "Elsa's by far the better person. She's much more maternal than I am, really." She looked at Elsa then, and started a little, but evidently realized in a moment what was going on. "Yes! Yes, that is a good idea."

Unfortunately, Burt had turned around and come striding back by this time to find out what the delay was about. He spotted Elsa's tears with the unerring instinct of the social ogre.

"What'd he do to make you cry, eh?" he asked, with a leering solicitude.

"Oh, grow up!" said Mr. Underhill and Harriet at the same time. A wry smile flashed between them.

"Aw, come on, then—let's just play golf," said Burt, evidently stung.

"Yes," said Harriet. "Let's. Mr. Underhill and Elsa are going back to the clubhouse—just leave them alone."

"Yeah?" said Burt acidly. "You're sure that's safe? You had him on the hook, I'd say—you're going to let him go off with another woman? I know her type, too, all—"

"That's *enough*," said Mr. Underhill. He didn't shout, but he didn't need to. He took a step toward Mr. Butcher, and Mr. Butcher, who was the bigger of the two men, took a step back. He fixed a pop-eyed stare on Mr. Underhill for a few moments.

Then he gave a kind of apologetic jerk of his head, and said, "Sorry. Uh. Father."

"Good," said Mr. Underhill, and turned away.

"Thanks," Elsa managed, as they walked back toward the clubhouse. She did not feel very maternal.

Mr. Underhill pushed back his hat and rubbed his eyes with the heel of his hand. "That was for the good of humanity—nothing to do with you." After a moment he added, "I'm just glad I didn't actually hit him."

"Why did you want to go and tell Mr. Peacham about Harriet's plans for her school?" Elsa asked suddenly.

"I'm sorry?"

"You told Mr. Peacham all about Harriet's plan to start a girls' school—which she'd told you, but she hadn't told him—and now it's made him despair of ever being worthy of her."

"Oh, is that what's the matter with him?" He sounded only slightly interested.

This annoyed her. "Yes, it's your fault—you should have left well enough alone."

"Should I? You told Miss Spencer that Peachy's not a lawyer."

"That's not the same! He *lied* about that."

"And you thought, I suppose, that there wasn't any future for the two of them that wasn't predicated on honesty. Well, I think so too."

"Don't take that—that *homiletic* tone with me," she snapped.

"Sorry," he said shortly. "But I'm not sure you quite understand Peachy. You seem to think it's a bad idea for him to know your friend's true character—but he was raving about Miss Spencer's brilliance after he talked to her at that prehistoric thingummy lecture. Which *you* sent him to, as I understand. So I really don't think you have the high ground when it comes to meddling in other people's love affairs."

She was a little stung by that, mostly because it was true. "I may be meddling, but at least I'm not sabotaging them."

He stopped walking and looked at her. "Are you suggesting that I am?"

"I suppose you know how you feel about Miss Spencer."

"I suppose I do," he said frostily.

"Well, she is very beautiful," Elsa went on reflexively. "And you're not inclined to be afraid of women, even if they have thoughts of their own. It's natural—I suppose when you met at the prison, or whatever it was—"

"It was a school for juvenile delinquents, and that is *terrifically* insulting. That's the sort of rubbish I would expect from that moron Butcher, not from you. Peachy is practically my brother. Do you think I'd pursue the woman I know he's in love with? Or do you just think I can't help myself because I'm a man and she's pretty, and God knows under those circumstances we can't possibly be friendly without *one* of us having an ulterior motive? Well, thanks either way. You're about the last person I expected to hear that kind of tripe from, but it's good to know where we stand."

She had made him furious with her, which was probably a feat, and the worst part was that he was angry because he was *disappointed* in her. He wasn't half as disappointed as she was. He was right; she had been led down a ridiculous path of antiquated antifeminist nonsense. At least he didn't seem to have noticed that there was also a large element of jealousy involved in it.

And now he really had made her cry.

"Oh, damn," he said quietly, but with feeling—as if that was the one blasphemy he was going to utter that year, and he was determined to make it count. "Elsa—Miss Nordqvist—I'm—"

"Don't! Don't you dare—don't say you're sorry—just—just—don't."

"Right. Here." He held out his handkerchief.

She took it, and they said nothing more for the rest of the walk.

Mercifully, they did not have to go all the way to the clubhouse. They came upon a couple of lawn chairs and a little table in the shade of a tree near the first tee, and managed to claim it before another approaching couple. Mr. Underhill flung himself down in one of the chairs, tipped his hat over his eyes, and proceeded to ignore Elsa, who sat down in the other chair and cried.

By this time she was crying mostly because she was crying, and a part of her recognized this. It didn't help. She would have resisted any attempt at comfort, and her only companion wasn't even offering any; he was ignoring her.

She looked at him through her tears. He was *studiously* ignoring her, actually. And it struck her suddenly that this was exactly what he would have done if the person crying had been, for instance, Peachy. And that this was almost certainly not his usual approach to dealing with a weeping woman. He was in fact treating her as if she were a man.

A few more tears trickled down her cheeks after that, but she didn't really feel like sobbing any more. She drew a shaky breath and dried her eyes and wiped her nose with Mr. Underhill's handkerchief. She folded the damp cloth in her lap. It was old and very soft, and embroidered with his initials, CU, in exquisite little blue stitches.

Mr. Underhill stirred and looked at her, smiled slightly, and looked away. He searched in his trousers' pockets for something, and subsided glumly in his chair when he couldn't find it.

"I'm afraid I don't smoke," Elsa said apologetically.

"What? No, nor should you. I've been meaning to stop. But this isn't *exactly* the moment I would have chosen." He leaned forward, resting his elbows on his knees, and looked up at her. "I know you don't want me to say it, but I am awfully sorry I got angry."

"You shouldn't be. You were absolutely right. I insulted you."

"But I don't think that was your primary intention. I think you misspoke. And I could have been a little slower to take offence. To be honest, I usually am."

"Can I … I'm sorry. Can you forgive me?"

"Of course." He held up a hand in a benedictory gesture. "I'm a professional." When she didn't appear to find that funny, he added, more soberly, "No, um … I, personally, am not angry with you, or insulted, or anything. I forgive you." He got to his feet. "I'm going to the canteen to get us some tea before I get too comfortable. Do you take milk or sugar?"

"I don't need any tea."

"Please don't be difficult, Miss Nordqvist. I'm an Anglican clergyman—I can't accept that anyone doesn't need tea. Milk, or sugar?"

She smiled. "Neither, thank you. Plain tea is fine."

He was not gone very long—just long enough to give Elsa a chance to blow her nose properly, tidy her hair a little, and put her cardigan back on. Before she had time to begin feeling sorry for herself again, he was back, with two cups of tea, one black and one milky. He hadn't, she noted, bought himself any cigarettes. He sank down into his chair and sipped his tea.

"How is your headache?" she asked.

"Going strong. How's your broken heart? I mean, besides being none of my business, obviously."

She snorted. "Clearly you don't really believe that. Anyway, it's not a broken heart."

"No?"

"No." She looked at him challengingly. "What do you think I was crying about?"

"Honestly? If I had to guess, I'd say you didn't get the thesis topic you were hoping for."

"Oh, I wish that were it! I didn't, you're right, but I'd almost forgotten about that now." She was silent for a moment, and blew on her tea. "I thought that you thought … "

"I know. But I didn't. Sorry—that sounded a bit piquey. I'm not trying to claim credit for great insight, it's just that I *was* listening to you the other day on the beach. Or … it wasn't the other day, was it?"

"No, it was nearly a month ago."

"It doesn't seem that long."

"Doesn't it?"

"Well, it's probably been a more interesting month for you. Starting a new degree and everything. The tail-end of Trinity-tide is a bit of a yawn by comparison."

They were silent for a little while.

"I do hope," she said finally, "that Harriet and Peachy … that … "

"Yes! I do too."

"You were right, of course—they can't go on misrepresenting themselves to one another."

"I think sending them both to that talk at the museum was a stroke of brilliance."

"That is kind of you," she said. "I thought he could use a little help."

"Quite frequently."

After another short silence, looking again at the monogram on his handkerchief, she said, "Do you remember the story I told you about my father's prophetic dream? I don't know if you'd remember that."

"Of course."

"Well, the man in it wasn't you."

"Oh. No? I did think it might have been."

"Yes, I expected that you did." She explained about the gold monogram of XP. "So I may need to look for a man named … I don't know, Xenophon?"

"Or Xavier, maybe—he could be a Roman Catholic after all." He grinned.

She could feel her face instantly flushing. She had not thought he had seen through her to that extent—or that he would have mentioned it if he had. "Oh, quite. I hope it goes without saying that I don't believe in this nonsense."

"Absolutely. I say, though, *do* tell me what's the matter. I mean, if you want to."

Elsa sighed. She had known, in a way, from the moment that he had looked up at her in the lobby at Annesley, that she was somehow going to end up telling him the whole story. She wanted badly to tell it to someone, in fact. She just felt obscurely that it was unfair—hard on him—that he should be the one to hear it. If he hadn't specifically asked her to tell him, she would have tried not to.

*

She had gone to see Gallagher on Friday afternoon, to discuss the details of the Platonic grammar project. She had been unenthusiastic about the meeting to begin with. The professor was certain to ask her about Mrs. Graves's party, she thought, and she didn't know what she could politely say about it. "Please don't ever try to send me there again—I will refuse to go," didn't seem very diplomatic.

Her interest in the *Bibliotheka Orphika* had remained undiminished after the party. If anything, it had become more intense. She was disgusted by Mrs. Graves and her friends and their absurd worship of the manuscript, but it made her only more fixated on her idea that the *Bibliotheka* was the work of one hand, more determined that this was a theory worth pursuing. Perhaps it was because the whole incident had lowered Arthur Gallagher ever so slightly in her estimation; or perhaps it was the thought of how satisfying it would be to prove to the modern New Orphics that their cult was entirely original to them, with no basis in any ancient practices. So she went to Gallagher's office determined to broach the subject directly.

"May I be quite frank with you, Professor?" she said, as she took her seat opposite his desk.

He looked at her with slightly raised eyebrows, but he said, "Certainly."

"I am probably out of order to mention this, but I hope you will forgive that. The truth is, I had been hoping, ever since last year, that a suitable thesis topic might be found for … well, that there might be something for me to do with the *Bibliotheka*. I realize it was presumptuous, but I'm afraid I had pinned my hopes on it—and I was

148

surprised when the topic you proposed last week was so different. I couldn't help wondering if it … if it reflected a lack of confidence in my abilities. I hope that I haven't done anything to make you think that I am unfit to work on the *Bibliotheka*. That is why I mention it now—not to protest at your decision, but to inquire as to its reasons, with the hope that I might correct my shortcomings."

Professor Gallagher was silent for some moments, rearranging the papers on his desk with a faint smile.

"I believe the time for me to be frank has also arrived," he said finally. He looked up at her. "Elsa. All of this—your thesis, the topic, the whole idea of my being your supervisor—it is quite irrelevant. There was a time when I thought of you as merely a student, but that time has long passed. For almost a year now I have been determined to make you my wife."

He paused, and sat there looking at her, with an expression less of affection than of triumph. Elsa thought, *This may be the worst moment of my life.*

"I'm sorry," she said finally. It was the only thing she could think to say.

It seemed to be a response that Gallagher had not considered possible. "What?"

"I said, 'I'm sorry.' You didn't phrase it as a question, so it didn't seem appropriate to say 'No.'"

He laughed. "You truly are maddeningly lovely, Elsa."

"Please don't call me that."

"Elsa!" He stood up behind his desk. "I am not sure you quite understand what I am offering you. You have just told me that your desire is to help me with my great work—and so you shall! But not as a student, certainly not as a student. Your passion is transparently obvious. You expressed yourself willing to accept the absurd alternate topic I offered you—what was it? I can't even recall. There could be no greater proof of your devotion. Accept it, by all means—finish your Master's degree, if that is the desire of your friends and family.

Then you can embark with me upon a far greater enterprise. You will be my partner in everything, by my side, the mother of my children. A nature such as yours will find its truest expression in wifely devotion. That is the opportunity I offer you."

"Thank you, I quite understood that. And no. My answer is no."

"There is someone else, I suppose."

"Of course there's someone else—there's *me*. I don't believe you have considered my feelings at all, but I have always been perfectly honest with you. I accepted the topic you gave me out of a sense of my duty as a student. I don't desire to help you with your work—my desire is to do my own work. I am very sorry if I have in any way misled you by expressing my admiration—I do feel tremendous admiration for your scholarship, but that is all I feel."

"Nonsense, my dear, you haven't misled me. You have merely mistaken your own womanly feelings for something absurdly masculine. You are placed in a unique position as a woman of more than ordinary intelligence. You can admire my intellect and appreciate my work—you do possess that capacity, remarkable among your sex—but your woman's heart need not stop there. Give in to your passion for the whole man, Elsa."

Elsa got up from her own chair. "Professor, please. You are making a fool of yourself."

"I beg your pardon?" he breathed.

"I am sorry that you seem to be in love with me. You've been rather insulting about it, which doesn't help your case, but that isn't really the point. The point is that I don't feel the same way, and I am not interested in marrying you. I'm not interested in marrying anyone, at all, as a matter of fact—if that makes you feel any better."

He stood looking at her with burning eyes. He really had made a fool of himself, and he must know it, she thought; and she truly wished he hadn't done it. She could not believe that this was a revelation of his true nature. If he apologized, she thought, if he admitted that he had been playing a ridiculous part, that someone had convinced him against his better judgement that this was the best way to court a woman—if he even said anything at all remotely loving—they might still have patched things up. They might have gone back to being student and teacher, like before. But she could see nothing in his expression other than outraged pride.

When he finally spoke, what he said was, "Clearly you are not as interested in furthering your academic career as you claim, either."

"I'm sorry?"

"I'd have thought that would have been obvious by now. I have offered you marriage, the status of a wife, and you have scoffed. Very well. You are a modern woman. You desire to do 'your own work.' How do you think you are going to do that, Elsa Nordqvist, if you make an enemy of me? Some of the unusual verb forms in the *Bibliotheka* could use investigation—a tedious task, but one that might suit you, after all. I could make that possible for you." He had come halfway around his desk toward her. His gaze was flinty, impossible to misinterpret.

"No, thank you," said Elsa evenly.

"Oh? *Oh?* You would give up so easily after all? Come! We two agree, I know, that earthly forms being what they are, chastity is an outmoded and absurd notion. A poisonous fruit. A soul-withering obsolescence. Come."

Elsa put her hand on the doorknob. She felt as if her blood had turned to ice water. He didn't believe in the *Bibliotheka*—how could he?—but he thought she did.

"Chastity," she said, her voice still level, "has nothing to do with it. What you are suggesting is prostitution—you are asking me to prostitute myself for a better thesis topic. I would rather die."

*

"Three cheers! And then you swept out of the room and banged the door behind you?"

"Well, I wasn't wearing a floor-length skirt, so I couldn't really *sweep*."

"What? You're *not* a character in a comedy of manners? Sorry, I have to completely rearrange my mental picture now. When you said, 'Of course there is someone else—there is me!' I sort of got the idea of you as a Jane Austen heroine."

"Thanks! I wish I were—it always turns out all right for them."

She had told the whole story, from the invitation to the party, through the night spent sleeping in Mrs. Graves's bathtub, to yesterday's conversation, which she remembered, much as she wished she didn't, almost word for word. In the course of her story, he had gone from reclining in his chair to sitting on the edge of it, looking progressively more outraged. She, on the other hand, had seen the ridiculous side of it as she had not before. Now he was looking at her with compassion again.

"It'll turn out all right for you, Miss Nordqvist. I think it will, anyway. But what happened after that?"

"Not much. I did try to … to sweep out and bang the door," Elsa admitted. "But the door stuck, and he got there before I could open it, and tried to stop me—oh, don't worry, it wasn't anything terrible. I got the door open eventually and got away."

"Good." From his expression, she thought she had scared him.

There had been a moment of physical struggle, of Gallagher touching her, and that had been rather horrible, but it had been over very quickly. When she stumbled out into the hall, she had nearly run into the young man in grey tweed. She had to push him out of her way, in fact, to get away from Gallagher's door. At first it had struck her as monstrous that he should have been there; but of course he must have been coming on some errand from Mrs. Graves.

For a moment she considered not going on, not finishing the story. This part he probably wouldn't understand.

"That wasn't … that wasn't even the worst of it," she said. After all, she had to go on. "The worst of it is what he said at the end—and not even what he said so much as *how he said it*. You see, he said, 'We two agree.' It's—English doesn't use the dual number, of course, but that's how you'd translate it. And 'a poisonous fruit,' and that list of three things … I don't know how he did it, and I don't know why I'm so sure that he did, but he wrote the *Bibliotheka Orphika*. I know he did. The personality behind it—you see, that was my theory, that it was the work of one man, because I thought it had a unified voice. It's *his* voice, his personality. His … his forgery. And that—and that—there isn't anything left to admire about him if he did that."

"No," said Mr. Underhill after a moment. "He's a toad. I'm so sorry."

"And you see … " She felt better already, she realized, to have told someone that, and to have had it taken seriously. "You see, that is what … why I am heart-broken—you were right about that. It isn't just the thesis topic, and it isn't just that I had to refuse an unwelcome proposal—it's that the whole thing is a sham. The manuscript I wanted to study is a fake, and the scholar I admired is a forger."

"Could you prove it, do you suppose?"

"Of course not."

"No, I mean—I understand that your conviction was based on what he said, and how it sounds like the style of the—the wretched thing. But if he did forge it, there must be some way of proving it, mustn't there? He must have made some mistakes."

"I suppose so."

"Or perhaps you just want to forget about the whole thing," he suggested.

She smiled. "Perhaps I do. The thing and the man."

"Perfectly understandable, and I'd say that was fine, except … "

"Except?" She looked at him in surprise.

"Well, except that he seems to have founded a cult around his forgery, and you found the whole thing sinister enough to want to spend the night in a bathtub, which frankly suggests to me that it was *very sinister indeed.*"

"But it's Mrs. Graves's cult. I don't think that Gallagher … "

"He could be her puppet, or she could be his, but it must be one or the other. Don't you think?"

"Or I could be wrong about the manuscript. There are any number of reasons why he might have said something that sounded like the style of the *Bibliotheka.* After all, he has spent months working on an edition."

"Well, if you are wrong, that's good, isn't it? Only … I'll bet you're right. And, mind you, even if you are wrong and the book is actually ancient, I still don't like the sound of people worshipping it."

"No, I suppose you wouldn't. It was all a bit unsettling. But," she added, a little archly, "isn't it just people seeking meaning in their lives?"

"You mean like Miss Thorndike's séance? Frankly, it sounds a lot worse than that. And you know I didn't really approve of the séance."

"No," she admitted. "You were just being nice, because Mr. Butcher was being so rude. I thought I could see a little battle being fought in your conscience between orthodoxy and chivalry, and chivalry winning."

"You're awfully perceptive."

"When I'm not being hopelessly naïve. I thought Professor Gallagher judged me on my own merits—I mean my work on its own merits. But that was stupid. Harriet tried to tell me so. I expected to be treated like a man, and I'm not entitled to that."

He frowned. "No, that won't wash. Even if we accept that proposition—and I don't think I'm prepared to, and I *know* you're not—if he thinks he doesn't owe you the respect due to a man, he still ought to have an idea of the respect due to a woman. Chivalry again, if you like. And he didn't even give you that. He behaved like a plain, old-fashioned cad. I mean, even before he offered to let you study the verbs in his fake manuscript as a reward for becoming his mistress—which, by the way, may be the shabbiest thing I have ever heard—the whole business about giving you a lousy thesis topic to test your devotion was pretty revolting. All of which is to say that you didn't deserve to be treated like that. But I'm pretty sure you knew that."

"I suppose I did. I did admire him, you know—I admired him tremendously. But I wanted to *be* him—I didn't want to marry him."

"Fair enough. There are plenty of people I'd like to—well, not to *be*, but to resemble, at least, and I don't want to marry any of them."

She laughed. "Well, you don't want to marry anyone—nor do I, only my reasons aren't so medieval."

"Yes, they are!" he retorted. "They're much *more* medieval. I'm an Anglo-Catholic, that's a Victorian invention—*you* were practically quoting Heloise at me on the beach. 'What agreement can there be between scholars and housemaids, writing desks and cradles, books and distaffs, pens and spindles?' I know that because it was one of my mother's favourites. Anyway, I don't know where you get the idea that I don't want to marry anyone. I've married six people already, as it happens."

Well, that was evasive, she thought. "If it were seven, that would make more of a difference. Do you think I'm foolish to take the view that I do of marriage?"

"No. I *like* medieval things." After a rather long silence, he said, reluctantly she thought, "I don't know that you're *right*. But I don't think you're foolish. I'll tell you something. My father is an academic—"

"A zoologist. I remember."

"Well, he was an Oxford don in the '70s, when they had only just been allowed to marry at all. But he was, for a long time—after that, I mean—very much of your opinion. He thought that scholarship and family life were incompatible, that he couldn't have done good work and been a husband and father at the same time. I don't think it was tradition that weighed particularly with him—neither of my parents was ever particularly keen on tradition. But he saw himself as having a responsibility to Science that he could not have combined with a responsibility to a family. Later, though, he came to believe that he had been mistaken—that he should have chosen a different life much sooner, and even that he had done wrong as a result of that conviction."

"Whom did he wrong? Science?"

"No. For the most part, me. I think you have heard Peachy refer to his aunt as my father's second wife? It's a polite lie—she's the only wife he's ever had."

"Oh! You're … "

"His illegitimate son. My mother was his mistress for nearly thirty years."

"And in all that time, he never married her?"

His eyebrows went up, and she felt herself flush; she knew what he was going to say next. "She didn't *want* to marry him."

"No. Of course not. She was the one who quoted Heloise."

"Yes. She didn't want a bastard son, either, but she was philosophical about it. She was forty when I was born—I was very unexpected. She kept me and raised me herself because she felt it was her duty. Also, I think, she couldn't stomach the idea of her son being raised by people who believed in rubbish—and her idea of rubbish was … pretty all-encompassing."

He was silent for a few moments. He spun his empty teacup around in its saucer with one finger.

"Anyway," he went on hastily, almost apologetically, "my father didn't feel the same sense of duty, and wouldn't acknowledge me as his son or, um, take any legal responsibility for me after my mother died. But that he subsequently regretted. Eventually he decided that he had been wrong to want to remain unattached in the first place. In fact, he … fell in love with one of his students, and she wanted children, and that reminded him that actually he had a son already. So they found me, and, in a spirit of penitence and something-or-other, brought me to Canada with them. But I don't—I don't tell you this because I think there's some clear moral in it for you. I know you're sufficiently different from my father. It just struck me that it might be relevant. Quite apart from anything, it's a circumstance about me that … well, it's why certain things don't shock me that you think might."

"Yes, I see. Thank you. I appreciate you taking me into your confidence." That sounded wooden and absurd. "I mean that … " She didn't know what she meant.

"Well, my mother was never ashamed of any of this, and my father, as I said, is now penitent. So it's not really a secret."

"I know … I just meant … "

"'Thanks for actually telling me something about yourself, even if it's really just a story about your immoral parents, you stupid secretive bast—I mean fellow'?"

She laughed. "Precisely!"

"But I know you secretly scorned me for being too tediously respectable—and you couldn't expect me to endure that when I had something like this up my sleeve."

"Isn't that what you would call being persecuted for righteousness' sake?"

"No," he said airily, "it isn't."

"I didn't think you tediously respectable, you know. I had the impression that you wore your halo at a bit of an angle."

"Hm. That is more or less the impression I try to give." He looked slightly dissatisfied.

It did explain certain things about him, she thought. It was no wonder he tended to veer off into vagueness or flippancy when presented with the possibility of talking about himself.

"What happened to you after you lost your mother? I mean before your father adopted you."

To her surprise, he didn't answer this question as succinctly as possible. He said, "She was killed in a motor accident. I was in the car too. She was driving, but it wasn't her fault—the brakes went on a hill, and we hit a tree. I was thrown out of the car, but I wasn't badly hurt. My mother died in the hospital afterwards—I was with her, and she knew I was all right. That's one of those things that doesn't register at the time, but afterwards it seemed very important. Sorry—that's not what you asked. After she died, I was put in an orphanage. None of her people were prepared to take me in, and my father's family was officially unaware of me—or *actually* unaware, I'm not sure. So … that was what happened."

She sat in silence for a few moments. "I'm trying," she said finally, "to think of anything to say except 'I'm sorry,' or 'You poor dear,' which isn't at all what you want, I'm sure."

He laughed. "I can't imagine you saying 'You poor dear' to anyone."

"What?"

"It's a compliment!"

"If you say so."

"I think it's churlish to refuse sympathy when anyone offers it. But you're right, I didn't tell you this so you could feel sorry for me. I'm not the same person I was then." After a moment he added, "My childhood wasn't devoid of love or anything—it was just always love *in spite of* something, or love offered against someone's will. It gave me a good understanding of love as suffering and duty, but it means that love as pure gift always takes me a little by surprise."

She didn't know what to say, but she thought calling attention to the fact again would be unhelpful, so she said nothing. He smiled, and she thought: How pitiful that when he is the one telling me all about his sad childhood, *I*'m still the one who needs to be comforted, and he's the one who has to do it.

Then she thought, suddenly: He can't talk to people about his mother, because even if they try to be nice, there's always the risk they'll betray their disapproval; and he *loved* her, he couldn't really disapprove of her even now. But he could talk to me, she thought. That was one thing she could do for him.

Slyly, she thought the best way to do it would be to make it seem as if she wanted to go back to talking about herself.

"I wonder," she said, after a moment, "whether I am 'sufficiently different' from your mother."

"Sufficiently different for what?" he asked, a little warily.

"You just said that I was different from your father … "

"Yes, although he's a university professor, and took the same view about scholarship and family life that you do. You're not like my mother—not at all. She wasn't a scholar. She met my father at a country house party, not at the university. She read a lot, but she wasn't a scholarly person really. She was more interested in gardening. She was also the sort of atheist that you're not—a proselytizer. She was passionate about a number of other causes, too, mostly to do with women's rights and education for the poor. She wasn't as much help to them as she might have been, because she wasn't respectable, and wouldn't pretend to be respectable—she would bring me places with her, and people would say, 'Oh, this must be your nephew,' you know, even if they probably suspected I wasn't, and she would say, 'No, he's my son,' and then they would try to call her 'Mrs.' and she would insist on 'Miss.' She wasn't very practical, but she was committed to truth. Sorry—I started off saying I didn't think you were anything like her, but I wandered from the point—I didn't mean to suggest you're not interested in truth."

"Oh! No, I didn't think you meant that. You were just telling me about your mother."

"Yes." He looked at her narrowly for a moment. "I won't say you're like her, because you're not—but I will say she would have liked you." He occupied himself for a few moments in thoughtfully squashing the crown of his hat, which sat on the table beside the teacups. "I didn't reject everything that my mother stood for, you know. I do believe in women's rights, for instance. She'd have been disgusted by what I've done with my life, but I said that she was committed to truth, and that was how she raised me, and I didn't reject that, either."

"That's fair," said Elsa.

"Maybe. It isn't really about being fair. But we're talking too much about me now—I don't know if you were finished telling me about what happened to you."

"Oh, I've talked about myself quite enough. In fact, it was starting to be like at the beach all over again—me babbling and you patiently listening."

"No! You needed to tell someone, and your best friend is preoccupied. I am happy if I can help you in any way. It pains me not to be able to challenge Gallagher to a duel, or … Well, let's be honest—just punching him in the face would be more my style, and that could still be arranged, if you wanted."

"Thanks! But you've been very helpful. I'd like to be able to return the favour some time." Belatedly she realized that this sounded sinister. "Not that I hope some horrible woman tries to blackmail you into … Gosh. That has a different meaning for a man, doesn't it? I *don't* think that would ever happen to you."

"Thanks."

"Or maybe that's not really a compliment for a man?"

"No no, it's a compliment. I don't think—by the way—that chastity is a … an outmoded and poisonous whatyoucall."

"No, I suppose you don't." She'd actually succeeded in embarrassing him, though not as badly as she had embarrassed herself. *I'm not very good for him*, she thought. *He's slow to anger and I make him angry; he doesn't embarrass easily, and I embarrass him.* After a moment she said, "You look like you're feeling better."

"I am. The tea helped—and sitting in the shade."

"Can I ask you something?"

She could see him subtly bracing himself. But he said, "Of course."

"How did you become a Christian?"

"Ah." He relaxed. "Somehow I always assume that people know that. It seems so obvious to me. I was evangelized by Peachy."

"What, really?"

"Of course. When we were boys. I lived with his family—I don't know if I explained that part. Polly—that's my father's wife—was all set to raise his poor dear illegitimate son, even though she's not remotely old enough to be my mother, and I was all set to turn into Edmund from *King Lear*. I confidently believe that I would have put somebody's eyes out by this time if I had actually been raised in her house. But, by God's grace, her sister, Mrs. Peacham, also thought that this whole *ménage* was a pretty bad idea. She talked it over with her husband, and he agreed, and they broached the subject with their son, but he'd already decided he liked me, and that was no problem. So Dr. Peacham took me aside one day when I was visiting, and asked what I thought of coming to live with them. He said, "We think it might be better for you." And I was sort of intrigued by the idea that anyone considered what might be better for me, and wasn't just interested in being sorry for me or telling me they loved me in spite of something-or-other, so I said yes. So that was how I ended up living with Peachy.

"Of course his parents suggested I come to church with them, but they were inclined to respect my wishes when I refused. Peachy, on the other hand, took this as a personal challenge and a gift from God: his first genuine opportunity to spread the Gospel to an actual heathen. It took him two weeks to get me through the church doors. There was the first Sunday when I said, 'No, thank you,' and the second Sunday I said, 'Maybe someday,' and the third Sunday I went. And the whole thing was kind of fascinating, and honestly, I could almost see why Peachy was so keen on it. I'd been to church services before, of a sort, at the orphanage, but this was completely different. And I sat in the pew by myself while everyone went up to take Communion—I wasn't baptized—and there was this inscription above the altar that said, 'God With Us,' and I thought, Well, maybe with *them*, and felt sorry for myself. And then it was as if with that thought—because I'd never even entertained a thought like that before—I had unbarred a door in my soul, and it burst open from the outside, and it was *terrifying*.

"So that was my conversion—I can't explain it any better than that, and believe me, I have tried. It didn't go particularly smoothly after that—I tried every way I could think of to get out of it, not out of conviction, or even loyalty to my mother, just because I was so scared. And I wasn't scared of things generally as a child. I was a little thug—I'd spent two years in the orphanage making the other children as scared of me as I could manage. But I was scared of this. It took all of Peachy's persuasive powers to get me to go the next Sunday, and for a couple of months it was like that—I kept desperately trying to close the door, until I got so tired that I couldn't keep it up. And that was when I started to notice that when I wasn't busy trying to fight off God, I was happier than I had ever been in my life. I liked this family that had taken me in. I liked Peachy, even when he was singing hymns outside my bedroom door while I was trying to sleep in, and reading me the 39 Articles over breakfast. I liked the school we went to. I liked Toronto—I didn't really miss Oxford, the way Polly kept saying I must. Probably *because* she kept saying I must. And I liked church. In fact, I loved it. So that was how that happened."

And this, Elsa thought, was a story that he *did* tell. Probably often. She wanted to find it rehearsed or unbelievable, but she had to admit that she didn't, and that it gave her at least as much insight into him as the sad childhood story.

"I see," she said.

After a moment he said, "Now may I ask you a question?"

"Yes." And she braced herself, too. Scenes from her own childhood crowded into her mind. She owed it to him, she thought, to explain herself, but she dreaded it.

"What are you going to do now? About your degree, I mean."

"Oh. I'm going to look for a new thesis supervisor, I suppose. It's a little awkward, but I suppose it's not the first time someone has had to switch supervisors. I'm sure the School of Graduate Studies will know how it ought to be handled. And I don't know what sort of a topic I may get … but honestly, it can hardly be much worse than that Plato nonsense. I might talk to Professor Kluge. He works on early saints' lives, I think, which doesn't interest me—not because they're religious, just because they're not very literary. But he was very encouraging when I took his Latin composition course last year, and he might be willing to take me on."

"You see, I knew that you were headed for a happy ending, Miss Nordqvist. You're too sensible not to be."

She smiled ruefully. "Thank you."

"Comfortingly," he said suddenly, apparently to himself.

"What?"

"Oh, it's a word I was trying to think of a while ago. To describe something."

"It's an adverb," she said. "It wouldn't describe a *thing*."

"Very well, a state of being. It's the right word, though. I don't know why."

They sat in silence for some time after that. A bird was singing in the tree overhead. Mr. Underhill had leaned back in his chair again and closed his eyes, and Elsa thought he might have fallen asleep. She fingered the embroidery on the handkerchief he had given her. She wondered who had done it: the unconventional mother, or the orthodox and ordinary Mrs. Peacham? She could picture him as a sturdy little boy in an orphanage, knocking down any other boy (and possibly girl—he'd had a radical upbringing) who spoke slightingly of his mother. Trying, for a few months, to take the same approach with God …

XP, entwined in gold, she thought. There was something about that … She traced out the shape in her mind.

Chi Rho, the monogram of Christ. Of course. How embarrassing—and her a Hellenist. But she had heard Harriet say the English letters, so she had not thought of the Greek ones. Her father must have seen the device in a church window somewhere, and it had worked its way into his dream. If there really had been a dream, and the whole thing wasn't just her father's bizarre way of giving her his blessing. This little detail made her wonder.

She looked out across the golf course, and saw a couple walking purposefully in their direction, hand in hand.

"Mr. Underhill," she said softly.

He opened his eyes.

"Look."

He looked in the direction she indicated, and his smile spread instantly.

"It's happened," he said.

"It looks like it has." She smiled back.

Harriet and Peachy arrived at the table under the trees, still holding hands.

"We've come to apologize," said Peachy.

"We're most terribly sorry," said Harriet. "We've been—"

"—terrible friends. At least—"

"At least I have."

"But I more so! I shouldn't have dragged you out here in the first place, Kit, it was the height of selfishness—I didn't give a thought to how you were feeling."

"Nor did I to Elsa's feelings! And I shouldn't have subjected *any* of you to Milly and her horrible fiancé!"

"But we were talking about it just now, you see, and—"

"And you're our dearest friends in the world."

"And we wouldn't hurt you *for* the world, and we're terribly afraid—"

"It's all right!" Elsa and Mr. Underhill were more or less shouting at them by this time.

"It's all right!"

"We're happy for you!"

"What happened, anyway? Explain yourselves—stop apologizing unnecessarily and tell us what happened."

"Peachy called Mr. Butcher a baboon on the eighth hole," said Harriet proudly.

"I'd had it with the way he was treating Miss Thorndike, that's all," said Peachy, poking at the grass with the toe of his shoe. "Actually, I'd just had it with him as a whole. And if you want the honest truth, I wasn't too impressed with the way she put up with him, either. I may have made a bit of a speech about how I thought you ought to behave towards the one you love, and I may have … " He looked a little dazed.

"Used me as an illustrative example," Harriet supplied.

"That's it, more or less. It just sort of popped out."

"It was very eloquent, actually."

"Thanks."

"But then I'm afraid he abandoned his didactic purpose, and they got fed up and went on to the next hole without us."

"We didn't care."

"No, we didn't."

Elsa looked across at Mr. Underhill and saw in his face how wrong she had been earlier. That wasn't the look of a man who had nobly decided to sacrifice his own hopes for the sake of his friend. Of course he knew how he felt about Harriet. He *approved* of her. He was transparently fond of her because he had decided that she was the woman for Peachy. It made Elsa surprisingly happy to know that he was not subject to the general, horrible unfairness of things. Indeed, she realized, the general unfairness of things seemed rather to have dissipated. She felt a sheepish, unfocused gratitude.

PART II

In Search of Peverell Peacham

Chapter Six

LIFT UP YOUR HEARTS

Close to, the statue of St. John was remarkable for its restraint. From a distance, you couldn't see the expression on his face; close to, you saw that there wasn't one. His eyes were upturned toward the Cross, but his face was a blank. There was no attempt to show his anguish; he looked numb. This struck Kit as displaying keen insight on the part of the sculptor.

"Does that look all right?" he called.

"Yes, Father! Much better!"

Most people did not see the statue of St. John close to, because he stood on the top of the church's rood screen. Kit was sitting beside him, at the top of a long ladder, on the edge of the screen's upper beam, in the space afforded by the row of Gothic pointy things that ran down the centre of it. He gave the folds of St. John's robes one final pass with his oily rag, and surveyed the chancel and the sanctuary from this novel vantage.

The sanctuary of the church named after the wooden saint was high-ceilinged and whitewashed. From his perch, Kit looked down at the stained-glass window above the altar, the only large figural window in the church, a beautiful, severe Christ as the Good Shepherd, flanked by a couple of endearingly silly-looking sheep. The High Altar was backed by bright blue curtains with *Holy Holy Holy* embroidered in gold around the top, their colour always almost-but-not-quite clashing with the altar frontal, no matter what the season. From here Kit had a discouraging bird's-eye view of the threadbare patches in the carpet on the altar steps, of which you became painfully aware every time you knelt on them. He looked down on the brass pavement candlesticks in the shape of grave but rather bosomy angels, divested of their purple Lenten veils in order to be polished. He studied the clean lines of the choir stalls, which had been designed by the same man who did the rood screen, and the bulging, Baroque pulpit, which had been made by somebody with very different ideas.

In the other direction, he looked out over the nave filled with huge, dark, old-fashioned pews. They had been salvaged from a much larger church that had been modernizing at the time St. John's was being restored. Faded banners embroidered with doves and grapevines hung between the clerestory windows. In the aisles, under the plain glass windows that betrayed the church's earlier, more Protestant, days, was an incomplete series of strange modern Stations of the Cross in brightly coloured ceramic. At the end of the centre alley was a stone font which had survived the fire that gutted the church in '82, and then been ineptly cleaned, so that it looked about a thousand years old. Two of the three small windows in the narthex had also been destroyed in the fire and replaced by plain glass, leaving only one of the original images, a very medieval red-haired angel in a cope, much more masculine than the candlesticks, grave and solitary and a little out of place. And to this collection of oddments, at Epiphany, 1926, after the retirement of the old rector, had been added the Rev. Christopher Underhill. It was halfway through Lent, and he still felt like a new and questionable piece of furniture that the parish hadn't quite decided whether or not to keep.

In the middle of the nave were Miss Finch and Mr. Oates, look-ing up at Kit, probably wondering what on earth he was doing.

"Anything else I should do while I'm up here, Mr. Oates?"

"Oh, do tell him to come down," said Miss Finch, who had been standing alternately on one foot and then on the other and looking agitated ever since Kit went up the ladder.

"I think that will do, Father," said Mr. Oates imperturbably. "Per-haps it would be as well if you came down now."

"Don't worry—I wasn't intending to stay up here all day. I was just enjoying the view. Mr. Boult, can you take the foot of the ladder again?"

Charlie Boult sprang to the task like one who had been waiting intently for those very words—as indeed, Kit thought, he probably had.

"One may not altogether approve of his views on rose-coloured vestments," said Mr. Oates, ostensibly to Miss Finch, as Kit was coming down the ladder, "but one cannot doubt his personal courage."

"Oh," said Miss Finch meekly. "No."

"One would not, perhaps, have thought the attribute altogether relevant to the work of the vicar of a suburban parish," Mr. Oates went on, "but then, one never knows, does one, Miss Finch?"

"Oh," said Miss Finch. "No, one never does."

Kit arrived at the bottom of the ladder, thanked Charlie, and looked Mr. Oates coolly in the eye to let him know that he had heard all that. Fulsome backhanded compliments were Mr. Oates's specialty.

"What *are* your views on rose-coloured vestments, Father?" Miss Finch asked, wide-eyed and obviously bracing herself to be alarmed.

Kit cupped a hand to his mouth and whispered stagily: "I *like* them. *Shh.*"

Miss Finch gaped for a moment, then squealed with laughter.

Mr. Oates followed Kit into the sacristy, where he went to wash his hands and dispose of the oily rag.

"Father, shall you be broaching the subject of *the Mattins incident* with young Henley, or would you prefer for me to take the matter in hand? I only mention it because of course it is properly your jurisdiction, but as you are new … "

"Oh, I'm sure if there is a subject to be broached, I can do it," said Kit, opening a cupboard and looking at a collection of brass vases, not because he had any interest in them, but because he found it helpful to have something to do when Mr. Oates was talking to him. "But I'm afraid I have no idea what you're referring to."

"Really? Well, perhaps young Henley's transgressions are more numerous than I thought! Nothing would surprise me less, of course. A fine fellow in his way, I am sure, but a little too inclined to *improvise*. You may perhaps not have observed it yet … "

Kit closed the vase cupboard, and opened another one full of candles. "Henley? My impression was that he's absent-minded."

"Ah? Well, no doubt that is one interpretation. No doubt. I was alluding to the speed with which he brought the choir in at Mattins on Sunday."

"Oh, that," said Kit, randomly rearranging candles. "I told him to do that."

"You … "

"Well, sort of. I told him to pick up the pace a little. Of course, he overdid it. I didn't mean for the trebles to end up running like that."

"I am sure you agree," said Mr. Oates after a moment, more stiffly than usual, "that it cannot be allowed to happen again."

"It's not my plan to have him do it that way every Sunday, no." Kit closed the cupboard and turned his back on it. He smiled in Mr. Oates's direction. "Mr. Cox spoke to Henley. He knew he was going too fast."

Mr. Oates looked grave. Very grave.

"It is of course not my place, Father … "

"No?"

Mr. Oates coughed, and looked graver still. "No."

"I should go help Charlie put the ladder away," said Kit, and headed for the sacristy door.

Mr. Oates was the person who was reported to have said, shortly after Kit's arrival, "He doesn't look like a priest—he looks like a matinee idol playing a priest in a melodrama." This had been relayed to Kit innocently by someone who thought it was funny, and it had caused him to spend a long time in front of the mirror in his bathroom the next morning, trying to slick back his hair in the most unbecoming way he could think of. (Ultimately he had calmed down enough to hear the whisper that suggested it would be ungrateful not to play to his strengths, such as they were, and had ruefully washed his hair, and been late and slightly damp for a meeting.)

"Why exactly was St. John the only statue that hadn't been cleaned?" Kit inquired as they walked back down the chancel. He had been told there was an elaborate story behind this, and he knew there was nothing Mr. Oates liked better than the opportunity to tell you an elaborate story.

"Oh, did no one tell you? I am surprised. It was a rather unfortunate affair. A difference of opinion between Mr. Trelawney and Mr. Harris was at the bottom of it, I am afraid. One does not wish to cast aspersions, of course … "

Doesn't one indeed? Kit thought. First I've heard of it.

"Mr. Trelawney, though a fine scholar and no doubt unimpeachable when it comes to translating Homer—you smile, but I assure you—"

"No, that just reminded me of someone I … " He stopped, because he realized he wasn't sure what he had been about to say. Mr. Oates went on with his story undaunted.

Someone I know? Used to know? Love …d?

Someone I pray for, and then try not to think about the rest of the time. But it was March, and he hadn't seen her since December—and then only fleetingly, at Peachy and Harriet's engagement party. He hadn't talked to her properly since September. And apparently he'd nearly stopped needing to *try* not to think about her.

" … so there was Perceval Trelawney, holding on for dear life to the Cross, and Mrs. Harris remarked quite aptly … "

Kit realized that he had missed a vital part of the story. He missed Mrs. Harris's apt remark, too, because now he was occupied in wondering how many of the people who had just watched him go up that ladder had expected him to fall to his death. He had thought it was just Miss Finch.

"But of course it wasn't funny—the man could well have been killed, or seriously injured. We retrieved the ladder and got him down safely, of course, but he would not be persuaded to go back up and finish cleaning the statues. Thus St. John remained untouched until today. And then of course the Trelawneys moved back to Montreal shortly after that. However, I don't believe that was related."

"I see," said Kit, relieved. That explained why he had never heard of Mr. Trelawney.

"Do you want me to put away the ladder, Father?" asked Charlie.

"Thanks—let's do that together, and then we need to get ready for Mass."

The two of them got the ladder down from the rood screen and carried it out of the nave by the choir door.

"I've got it from here," said Charlie firmly, setting down his end at the top of the basement stairs and taking hold of the middle of the ladder.

Kit smiled and let him take it. He sat on the top of the steps and waited for Charlie to return. His inability to go into the church basement was by now pretty well known in the parish, but poorly understood. Charlie Boult did not seek to understand, simply to help. Or perhaps he understood already; Charlie was a young man of hidden depths.

He was also, Kit thought, a sort of symbol of the very best of St. John's. He had returned to the parish a month before Kit's arrival. The fatted calf had been killed on his behalf very matter-of-factly and without fuss, but that only made the whole thing more beautiful. Mr. Oates had given him a job stocking shelves at his shop, and Mr. Cox had let him back into the Acolyte's Guild. There seemed to be a conspiracy not to mention Charlie's history to the new vicar, too; even the unhinged Miss Treep had only muttered darkly once or twice and rolled her eyes in a vague way. And Charlie was living up to all of this unforced charity gallantly. After Mass on Kit's first Sunday in the parish he had solemnly introduced himself, and said, "I'm not sure if you remember me, Father."

Kit did remember him. "Of course," he said. "You were the chap who wasn't really going to hit a priest."

Charlie smiled, torn between satisfaction and embarrassment. "Well, if there's ever anything I can do to help, then … you just say, okay? I know you're real tough. But sometimes it's hard when you're new and don't know the ropes."

This was very true, and Kit had been glad to take him up on the offer.

Charlie returned from the basement, Kit got up from the stairs, and they went back through the choir door together, tacitly preserving the illusion that they had both gone down into the basement.

"There's a meeting of the Mission Society this evening," said Kit, as he unlocked the vestry door. "That usually means a crowd at Low Mass, doesn't it?"

Charlie nodded. "I'll make sure there's enough stuff."

Mr. Oates was still hovering, with no particular task to do, but no particular reason to leave, either. He strolled into the vestry as Kit was putting on his alb, and stood critically watching Charlie flipping through the prayer book looking for the psalms. Kit wondered whether to ignore him or to ask pointedly if he wanted something. He opted for ignoring, and occupied himself in tying his cincture. Mr. Oates's shop was only on the other side of St. Clair, and he had a numerous staff, so he was able to pop into the church several times a day on slight pretexts. But probably he spent most of his time in the shop hovering, too, Kit thought, fussing and intimidating his clerks, being very important and yet rather in the way. If one could find some new project for him, something into which he could channel his energies productively, it would be a work of charity. And not just for Mr. Oates.

"Of course it more properly falls to Mr. Cox to correct such things, Charlie," said Mr. Oates, "but I could not help noting the last time you served Low Mass that you really ought to raise your voice in the responses. Remember that it is your responsibility to indicate to the congregation the proper points at which to join in."

"Mm," said Charlie, who was now busy filling the cruets. He looked up. "I mean, yes, Mr. Oates."

"Well, I will leave you to your work," said Mr. Oates finally, and strolled out.

"Did he ought to have said that, Father?" Charlie asked in an undertone, casting a sidelong look up at Kit.

"Well ... no, but he does have a point. You could speak up a bit. I know you know the words."

"Yeah ... I mean, yes, Father. I just get embarrassed sometimes because of my *r*'s."

"Your what?"

"*R*'s. You know. 'Ou*rr* Father*rr* who a*rrrr*t in Heaven ...'"

"Good Heavens, Mr. Boult—you don't say it like that."

"No, I know, but that's how I sound, you know, when I hear myself saying it next to you. You don't do the *r*'s."

"Don't I? 'Our Father who art—' no, I suppose I don't. I can do, if that would be helpful."

"Oh, no! Don't do that!" Charlie looked alarmed. "I mean, if—I mean, you shouldn't—because ..."

Kit raised his eyebrows. "I wonder if what you're trying to say is that my toffy accent is one of my saleable features, and I'd be a fool to lose it."

"No, Father," said Charlie, looking resolutely at the floor. "That doesn't sound like something I'd say."

Kit grinned. "It doesn't really, does it? You're too charitable."

Charlie rang the bell, and they processed out to the Lady Chapel in the north transept, where the pews were sprinkled with pensioners and housewives and members of the Mission Society dutifully turning up to attend Mass before their afternoon meeting.

There was a window in the back wall of the north transept that directed the late afternoon sun, at this time of year, straight at the altar in the Lady Chapel. It flashed on the chalice and dazzled Kit's eyes when he turned to pronounce the Absolution. When he raised his hand, the moment of cool shadow let him see to the back of the chapel, but dimly, like a vague dream image. A tall, elegant woman stood in the aisle behind the last pew, as if she had just come in and wasn't sure what to do. She wore a cherry-red dress and a white coat, a long string of pearls and a black cloche hat with a feather.

" … pardon and deliver you from all your sins … "

She disappeared into the blaze of sunlight; he had recognized her, but without pause, almost without surprise. She had looked different: better dressed, but also shyer, out of her element, a little bit less poised and strong. She was not someone he had loved. Just now, she was part of something he did love. It was magnificent in a way he could not have imagined. And it was true. She could resist it; she could remain standing at the back, thinking it wasn't true, but that didn't matter. Or it mattered, but not as much as she thought.

To say that he put her completely from his mind after this would not be quite accurate, but it was only because he didn't seem to need to. It was as if his love for her had bled out and mingled with his love for the whole congregation, the whole parish, Mr. Oates, Miss Treep, Charlie Boult, Henley who had led the choir in too fast, Mr. Harris who had done whatever it was that led to Mr. Trelawney dangling from the rood screen, Mrs. Harris who had made a joke about it. It was the first time he had recognized his desire for their approval as love.

As it turned out, she didn't remain standing at the back. By the end of Mass, the sun had moved enough that at the Blessing he could see where she was sitting, in a pew by herself, with a prayer book open in her lap.

In the vestry afterward, when he had got out of the purple chasuble, he said, "Could I ask a favour of you, Mr. Boult?"

"Of course."

"I have to talk to Mrs. Barrington about the charity sale. But there was a woman in a red dress, at the back of the chapel—not a parishioner. Did you see her?"

Charlie nodded slowly. "She didn't come up for Communion."

"No."

"I saw her."

"Do you think you could go talk to her?"

"*Talk* to her?" Charlie looked frankly startled.

"Just to tell her that I'll be along more or less directly. Don't worry—she won't think that's odd. We do know each other."

"Oh."

"But I'm afraid she'll leave if she thinks I'm busy or didn't see her."

"Oh."

Kit looked at Charlie and realized belatedly that he had asked him to do something that he liked slightly less than the prospect of being burned at the stake. He also had an uncomfortable insight into why. He had just been made aware of how much he loved the people of this parish; now he saw that, in an awkward, possessive, teenaged way, some of that love was returned. The moment in which he might have pretended that he hadn't seen this, or that Charlie had been wrong in his own insight, had passed.

"You'll like her," he said. He hoped it didn't sound like an order. "Her name's Miss Nordqvist. At least … it was the last time I saw her."

Charlie nodded gravely and went out of the vestry.

Mrs. Barrington was a businesslike woman, who didn't believe in wasting the vicar's time, but the charity sale, which she had recently taken over from Mrs. Gibbs, whose daughter had just had twins, was a shambles, and she came with a long list of thorny problems to discuss. Kit did his best to focus on her questions, but his mind kept wandering to the details of a conversation that had taken place nearly two months ago.

*

"She's lovely, of course, but it's more than that," Peachy had said musingly.

They had been hanging wallpaper—or Kit had been hanging wallpaper, and Peachy had been watching—in Kit's living room at the beginning of February. The faded Victorian roses that had covered the walls were giving way to bright Art Deco tulips. It was a satisfying transformation, but it was a lot of work.

"Oh, quite," Kit said distractedly.

"What? You haven't met her, have you?"

"Who? I thought you were talking about your fiancée." He thought Peachy had been talking about Elsa Nordqvist, actually, but if he hadn't, then Kit saw no reason to bring her into the conversation.

"Were you even listening to what I was saying?"

"No. I was hanging wallpaper."

Peachy heaved a huge sigh. "Soon enough, I shall be hanging wallpaper myself, I expect."

"You could do it now and get it over with," said Kit exasperatedly. "It'd be a help."

"I meant in the metaphorical sense—I don't suppose I will literally have to hang wallpaper, I would think Harriet could pay someone to do that. I meant everything that hanging wallpaper stands for."

"Which is what, in your scheme of nitwittery?"

"DOMESTICITY!" Peachy cried, bounding up from the radiator that he had been leaning on. "The house—the furniture! Tablecloths—tea-parties—children! All of it!"

"Oh, go boil your head!"

"Sorry, old man, I didn't mean—"

"Nor did I. I'm happy, Peachy—and—I've slopped wallpaper

paste all over my floor—and so are you happy when you stop to think about it. God has been awfully good to both of us. Don't find excuses to mope."

Peachy rolled his eyes. "I shouldn't, should I? I just can't shake the feeling of being … I suppose even you get the occasional thought that you might not be up to the job."

"Oh, quite. And, you know, I'm not, on my own, and neither are you. So *that's* all right."

They'd had this particular conversation about fifteen times since Christmas—sometimes it had even been Kit who had initiated it—and it had got to the point where they didn't need to go into the whole thing. It was just a sort of motif they had to allude to.

"Anyway," said Kit, "who's 'lovely of course'?"

"Oh." Peachy subsided against the radiator again. He frowned. "Well, it's more than that—that's what I was saying. She has a sort of magnetism about her."

"Who?"

"Anastasiya."

"Who's that?"

Peachy sighed. "Oh, never mind. A woman I met recently. At a party. I ended up talking to her for a long time, and she's a curious sort of person. Magnetic, you know, and very worldly, but … frightened."

"Frightened?" Kit had got himself tangled up in a length of wallpaper, and it took him a moment to add, "Of what?"

"Who knows, really," said Peachy. He said it in a way that suggested, to someone who knew him as well as Kit did, that actually, *he* knew. But Kit was presently too much occupied with trying not to tear his piece of wallpaper to put the necessary effort into drawing him out.

"But that wasn't what I was meaning to tell you."

"No?"

"It was something Anastasiya said. About … Oh, hell! You probably already know. I don't know why I've made such a production of telling you. About Elsa—about Miss N—and her professor. You know, I suppose."

"Mm-hm." He had got the length of paper onto the wall and was concentrating on lining it up with the adjacent strip.

"Is that all you have to say? For Heaven's sake, Kit, I know you have this weird idea about leaving her to her own devices, but isn't this taking it a bit far?"

"I don't quite know what you expect me to say. The man's a swine, obviously, but it isn't actually my place to knock his swinish teeth in."

"A swine? Who? Are we talking about the same person? The professor who translates this pagan rubbish—that's the one I mean. Anastasiya says he's a great man, and a bit of a catch. That was why she told me in the first place—not to warn me that Miss N. wasn't nice to know or anything, but to say how much she envied her."

Kit looked over his shoulder at Peachy. "What ... what do you mean 'not nice to know'?"

"You *don't* know. She's living with this professor, Kit."

"No she isn't."

"I'm sorry—but I'm afraid she is. Sleeping with him, anyway—but I think, to read between the lines, she's actually set up house with him. One of her friends at Vic told me she heard the professor say something that could only mean that. And Anastasiya ... more or less told me she knows it for a fact. I wish it weren't true as much as—well, almost as much as you, anyway. But you know it makes sense. She's stopped coming out with Harriet's friends—you know we've barely seen her since Christmas. I haven't brought it up with Harriet, and I don't intend to. If she wants to tell me herself, that's one thing. I know she *knows*—she still sees Elsa, but she doesn't talk about her the way she used to. You said yourself that she seemed worried about Elsa. It all fits together."

The last piece of wallpaper had flopped off at the top and slid glueily down the wall.

"It's bollocks," said Kit staunchly. "It's a story the toad Gallagher has put about because he *wishes* it were true."

He believed what he said, certainly, but he wished he didn't feel so much like a little boy refusing to take his medicine when he said it.

*

And now, after months of avoiding her friends—avoiding him too, although he didn't flatter himself that she had ever really considered him a friend—here she was, dressed in unusually smart clothes, looking as if something had changed for her, and not necessarily in a good way. *Oh, but let it be good! If that is what she's done, let it at least be because she wanted to, because she was wrong about him and realized she loves him after all. At least ...*

No. Scratch that. You're right of course. I was right. It hasn't happened. I don't believe it.

Still, he couldn't help feeling, as he went out into the church again to meet her, that the person he had to argue with, the person whose testimony he was doggedly refusing to believe, was her.

She was in the middle of the nave, deep in conversation with Charlie Boult. Of course she was; she was the sort of person who would take to Charlie instantly. He felt, as he had many times before, absurdly proud of her. As he came out of the vestry, Charlie was pointing toward the High Altar, and then pointing at something on a piece of paper in Miss Nordqvist's hand.

She had cut her hair, he realized as he approached. At least, he was pretty sure she had; pale strands peeked out from under her fashionable hat, framing her face. It had never occurred to him how well this could suit her, and he wished they were someplace where she might have taken off her hat. Though the hat suited her too. So did the dress, which had a discreet pattern of red glass beads down the front, shimmering under her opened coat. The coat was not new; he had seen her wearing that in the fall. He remembered how one of the buttons had popped off and she had tucked it carefully in her pocket to sew on later.

"Hello, Miss Nordqvist!" Automatically, he held out his hand, and she, less automatically, took it, and smiled.

"Mr. Underhill. It's nice to see you again." There was a moment, with Charlie still standing there, when the whole situation threatened to become awkward. Then she said, abruptly, "That bright purple suited you down to the ground!"

He laughed out loud. Charlie gave a surprised snort, not quite managing to slap his hand to his mouth in time. He muttered something and loped off to the vestry, grinning.

"I seem to have scandalized your henchman," said Elsa.

"He'll be all right," said Kit. "I think his problem is that he agrees with you."

"I see. He caught me on my way out the door and told me that you wanted to talk to me. He also gave me a leaflet with the service times and a tract about prayer." She showed him the papers she was holding. "I don't imagine you put him up to that."

"I didn't, but of course I approve."

She smiled again; indeed, she hadn't really stopped smiling. "So this place is all yours?" she said. "Or—it's the other way around, isn't it? You're all *its*."

"That's right."

"You look happy."

"Oh, well—I usually am. So I suppose I usually look it."

"No, I meant … when I first came in, there was a moment when you turned away from the Lord's Table, and it wasn't even that you were smiling, particularly, you just looked … well, happy is not quite the word. Radiant, I guess."

"Oh. Thanks. I daresay that didn't have much of anything to do with me, really." After a moment, feeling that something more was needed, he said, "I like my work."

"I expect you're wondering what I'm doing here."

"No," he admitted.

That took her a little by surprise. "I came to see you."

"I did think that was a possibility." But that wasn't really what he meant when he said he hadn't wondered.

"Yes, that's obvious, isn't it?"

"Do you want to sit down?" he suggested, indicating a pew.

"Thanks." She sat, and slid down the pew a little to make room for him. He sat next to her. "I had heard you became vicar of some place, but it took me a long time to find it. I didn't know whether it was John the Baptist or John the Apostle, and I think the first one I went to was the Baptist—but you're the Apostle, aren't you?"

"We are. Though when one of our wardens in the '90s commissioned a banner of the patron saint, the nuns who made it forgot to ask that question, so we have this oddly scruffy-looking Apostle John with a billowing red cloak appliquéd on to hide his raiment of camel's hair."

She laughed, which was what he had been hoping for. "What a shame. John the Apostle is usually such a fetching young specimen in all the Last Suppers, isn't he?"

"I don't know about 'fetching.' I think he'd have needed to be young at the Last Supper to have lived to write John's Gospel when John's Gospel was written. But that's more in your area of expertise than mine."

"Books that weren't written by the people who are supposed to have written them, you mean?"

"I just meant Greek manuscripts. But that's a fair point too."

Did that mean that she still believed Gallagher to be a forger? He tried not to feel too hopeful.

"Well, this place looks much more like you than that other St. John's, anyway. One can hardly move for candles—and those things on the wall are meant to be Stations of the Cross, aren't they?"

"I think that's the general idea." He went on, since this seemed a concrete and helpful subject to linger on. "To be honest, I think they're unfortunate. There aren't enough of them, and you can't tell what they are. No one likes them. They don't use them—when they do Stations in Holy Week I'm told they just go around the church and ignore them. But when I suggest that we take them down, they look at me as if I were a combination of a Viking raider and the French Revolution."

She laughed again, and then she was silent for a few moments, looking up at the rood screen.

"They've actually been very forbearing," he said, when it seemed she was not going to speak. "I've introduced some shocking liturgical innovations."

He tried to imagine explaining to her the battle of wills that had taken place between himself and Mr. Cox over the Gospel procession. He thought it would have made about as much sense to her as her explanations of Hesiod's grammar on the beach had made to him.

He went on: "And we're doing something the rector always wanted to do this year, and having the Holy Saturday liturgy at night, as it was done in the early church, and calling it the Easter Vigil and everything. I'm actually beside myself with excitement. I think we may even have a decent congregation, if only for the novelty of it."

She smiled tolerantly at him. Finally she said, "I don't know if coming to you is the right thing, Mr. Underhill."

"No?"

"No. I thought that almost as soon as I came in, and then I really was going to leave—but you must already have seen me, so I'm glad I didn't. I suppose you know … well, *do* you know that Mr. Peacham has broken off his engagement to Harriet?"

He had a feeling that was not unlike going up a flight of stairs in the dark and finding there was one step fewer than he had been expecting.

"No! At least, I knew that something had happened, but I thought she was the one who had broken it off."

"As you would. It's usually the girl who does it."

"Yes, that, and it's what I had heard from his parents. I haven't seen Peachy or spoken to him in a couple of weeks. But you knew that, I think."

She nodded. "Harriet said that you had quarrelled. She was quite upset about it. But she didn't know what it was about."

"*I* don't know what it was about, Miss Nordqvist. And I wouldn't have called it a quarrel. Is that what he told her?"

"It seems to be. What would you have called it?"

"Peachy being Peachy, I suppose. I thought he would cool off and I'd hear from him again in his own time. It's the sort of thing that has happened before. I was worried when I heard the engagement was on the rocks, and I did try to get in touch with him, but not as hard as I might have done. It's a bit difficult now we're living in opposite ends of the city—and I've been busy. So would he have been, I assumed—busy trying to win Harriet back. But what really happened with the engagement? I'm glad you told me, by the way. Were you worried that I wouldn't want to get involved, or take sides, or something?"

"No, not exactly." She looked down for a moment at her hands in her lap. *He* looked at her hands, finally. Her fingers were bare. In spite of everything he had been telling himself, his heart did an impromptu jig of relief.

"Here's what I know," she said, turning a little toward him, tucking one knee up on the pew and looking him in the eye. "Peachy told Harriet a few weeks ago that you and he had quarrelled, but wouldn't say what about. She had the impression that it had something to do with the wedding, and that Peachy had done something to offend you. That was how he made it sound—that you were the one offended, and you had stopped speaking to him. I didn't think that sounded likely, but I didn't say anything to her, because honestly, I hoped he had stopped lying, at least to her. And I couldn't see you quarrelling with him over the wedding. I'll admit I had more or less lost track of what was going on with that. My plan was to show up in a nice dress and hold Harriet's flowers and sign the register, and it didn't particularly matter to me where I had to go to do that. Not that I didn't care—I wanted them to have what they preferred, of course, and I thought that St. Thomas's sounded like more fun anyway. You and I talked about that at their engagement party, when we were hiding from Mrs. Spencer. Do you remember that?"

"Yes, I remember. You told me that Mrs. Spencer didn't approve of your dress." She had gone on, with that candour that delighted him but that she always seemed to regret moments later, to tell him how much she had paid for the dress, clearly implying that it had been more than she could afford. He wondered how much she had paid for the dress she had on now.

She smiled at the recollection. "And you said not to worry, she wouldn't have attention to spare for it because she'd be too busy being offended by what *you* were wearing."

"And I maintain that's true. Though there was a period after that when it looked like Timothy Eaton Memorial was going to prevail over St. Thomas's, and, as a matter of fact, I went out and bought a morning coat in the expectation of being relegated to a pew."

"I hope you at least bought off the rack and kept the bill."

"Naturally. And—since you don't seem to have kept track—it was back at St. Thomas's the last time I was consulted. The banns were supposed to be read first on Easter morning."

"Right. That was what I thought. Well, I *hoped* it might be true that Peachy had insisted on some hymn that you objected to, or something, but I really did think it was more likely he was lying. Anyway, Harriet's idea was to phone you, to get your side of the story, I guess, and I talked her out of that. I thought if Peachy was really lying, she shouldn't hear about it from you—and, in a general way, she oughtn't to need to ask around about things behind his back if he's going to be her husband."

"Agreed."

"I did think you'd approve of that, even though it cut you out of things a bit. And Harriet agreed, too. She told Peachy he didn't have to tell her what you had quarrelled about, but that he did have to make up with you, because they needed you for the wedding. Peachy said that there were lots of other priests in Toronto. I was actually there for most of this conversation—we were at a restaurant, and I was stuck in the back of a booth and couldn't get away. Harriet said, 'Don't be silly, that's not the point, he's your best friend, he should be the one to marry us.' Peachy said, 'Sometimes I think you care more about that than about who the groom is.' Harriet said of course not. Awkward silence. Elsa tries to finish her salad very quietly. Harriet breaks the silence first to say, 'You know you have to make up with Mr. Underhill'—or, actually, she says 'with Kit,' because that's what she calls you. 'Peverell, you know you have to make up with Kit.' I don't know if you noticed that she started to call him by his real name as soon as they got engaged? It's a sort of endearment, she says, because nobody else uses it.

"Anyway, at this point Peachy gets up without a word and leaves the restaurant. Harriet goes after him—first she didn't want to leave without paying for her meal, but I said, for Heaven's sake, go! and so she ran out. And I was about to order dessert for all of us, because I was sure they would be coming back in a bit, looking sheepish and perhaps wanting pie—and then Harriet came back by herself. She said he got on the streetcar and went off without a word—without even looking back at her. Then a week later, she told me that he had broken off their engagement. No explanation, just 'It won't work.' And something about his not being the man she thought he was.

"And the thing is … I didn't see the last bit, but I saw the rest of it, and it was play-acting. The whole business about being jealous, thinking she cares too much for you … it's just some old thing he brought up because it was convenient. It's vaguely plausible—he used to think she liked you better than him, back in the fall. But it didn't make him act like this, and it's not the real reason he thinks he can't marry her. I have *no idea* what the real reason is, but I know it's not that. I think Harriet knows it too, although she blames herself, and has been calling you a lot of names—which I didn't just tell you, by the way, because I know she's going to regret that. But she's completely heartbroken and can't—won't—do anything to help herself. It's as if … she came into her own when she met Peachy, and when he rejected her, she lost sight of who she'd become."

"I'm sorry," he said sincerely. He couldn't quite picture Miss Spencer heartbroken. Furious with Peachy, certainly, but not actually distraught. She was such a cheerful person; it was painful to imagine.

"So that is why I came looking for you, Mr. Underhill. It seemed to me that you might not know what had happened, but that if you did, you would want to do something to help. *I* want to do something to help, but I don't know how to find Mr. Peacham to berate him—or talk sense into him, or bail him out, or whatever it is that needs doing. If you can tell me, I could get on with it. I don't know what happened between him and you, and of course you don't have to tell me that. But I think that he did the breaking off there, too."

"Yes," said Kit. "You could put it that way. I was annoyed with him, but no more so than I have been in the past. I wasn't about to stop speaking to him. I don't mind telling you what happened, although it doesn't make very much sense. I'd offered him a job."

"A job?"

"Yes. Well, in a way. Or asked a favour of him. I might as well explain the whole thing. You may notice on your leaflet of service times, 'Choral Mattins' at 9:00 on Sundays."

"Yes, I see. I don't quite know what that is."

"Don't worry about it. Just note that it's one of four services on Sundays, and assume that's rather a lot. This particular one is the bane of the choirmaster's existence. He thinks it's 'not in keeping with the parish's Anglo-Catholic character,' and that not enough people come to justify getting together the choir and rehearsing and him getting out of bed that early on a Sunday. He was after the rector to get rid of it for years. But it's a part of the parish's traditions, and even if the congregation is small, they get something from it, and it's worth doing. Anyway, Betters, the choirmaster, never got anywhere with Father Britton on the subject, so he tried a different approach with me—he just said he wasn't going to do it any more. I said that was all right, that I would find someone else to take it on."

*

"Of course I was thinking of you all along," he had said, after offering this same story to Peachy.

They had been in Kit's living room again; they had established a pattern of Peachy dropping by the rectory after work. It wasn't remotely on his way home, but it was less of a detour than it would have been for Kit to travel out to Cabbagetown these days. Besides, Peachy had apparently received a specific directive from his mother to visit Kit, "who is going to get lonely rattling around in that huge house by himself."

"Me?" Peachy slouched lower in his chair, a glum sneer on his face. He had come over that day looking bleak, but Kit had depended on his news about Choral Mattins to lift his spirits. "I don't think I could get down to St. Thomas's in time to be cantor at 11:00 if I had to be out on St. Clair West at nine!"

"No, you couldn't."

"Well, there you go. I can't do it."

"But there's more to it than that, Peachy." This time Kit was the one on his feet, energetically pacing the room. There was a lot of scope for pacing, because the living room, although now freshly papered and with a rug on the floor, still had hardly any furniture in it. "Betters is ancient—he's always talking about retiring outright. If you took over Choral Mattins, the wardens would see how good you are, and it would only be a matter of time before I could get them to take you on as choirmaster. You've said yourself the choir is good already, and you could make them even better. And the organ is almost brand new. The stipend is laughable—everyone is always saying how lucky they are to have Betters for what they pay him—but that won't matter to you. You'll have a rich wife."

"I don't need you to find me a job."

"But that's not what this is. It's not as if I went looking for something for you to do. It's not a job, anyway, it's a situation. I'll admit it's not Westminster Abbey, but you'd have a choir you could write music for. It wouldn't prevent your doing any of the other things you were going to do—writing symphonies and giving recitals and all the things you talk about—it would just make them easier. It'd give you an answer when people ask 'What do you do?' that was really to the point—and that's not nothing. Besides … it's my church and I want you to be here. You and Harriet. And your kids, for that matter. I want St. John's to be known as the place where Peverell Peacham was choirmaster." He stopped in the door to the hall and looked back at Peachy, who was still slumped in his chair, apparently unmoved. He went on, more prosaically: "And Choral Mattins is the lynchpin of the whole thing. I can't just tell the wardens to hire some shiftless friend of mine to replace Betters. They still haven't made up their minds whether they want to keep me. But I can easily ask my friend to do me a favour by taking a job everyone wants done but nobody wants to do—it solves a problem for the parish, not just for me. Then all you have to do is be brilliant, and maybe be a little patient—and the thing will happen."

Peachy folded his arms and stared fixedly out the curtainless window. "And it all hinges on having a wealthy wife."

"Well, no. I mean, Betters doesn't have a wealthy wife—he teaches at the Conservatory of Music to make ends meet. You could do that sort of thing too, of course. But you wouldn't need to."

"It's no good, Kit. I can't do it. The answer is no."

Although what he really wanted to do at this point was pull Peachy out of the chair and shake him, Kit made himself walk across the room and sit down on the uncomfortable couch under the window. He looked at Peachy, and Peachy continued to stare out the window.

"At least think about it," Kit said. "I really do need someone to lead the Mattins choir. I know you don't want to give up singing at St. Thomas's, but I honestly think you would like this better. You wouldn't have to do it forever if you didn't want to. But you'd like it, once you got started, I know you would."

"No!" Peachy heaved himself up from the chair at last. "You can't rely on me, Kit. You ought to know that by now. And you don't want me at your church—not really. I'm not the kind of man you want to have around. I wish to God I was, but I'm not."

*

"And that was it?" said Elsa, when he had got to this point in the story. "He stalked out and you haven't heard from him since?"

"I had a note from him on the Monday following, cancelling plans we had for that night, but that's it. I have tried phoning, but it's not an awfully good way to reach him—the people who answer at his place are liable to have just taken cocaine, or to be in the middle of writing a masterpiece, or fighting with their mistresses, and don't pass on messages. Anyway, he hasn't stopped by or written—he can't ring, I'm not on the phone—and he hasn't been at his parents' when I've gone for dinner the last two Saturdays. I was down at the cathedral for something, and I dropped by his place, and one of his neighbours said he was in and another said he wasn't, and either of them could have been telling the truth, I suppose."

"So you weren't angry with him," she said—an observation rather than a question.

"No. A bit aggravated—I am in a pickle about Mattins, but I talked Betters into keeping it going until Easter, and I did think Peachy would come through in the end. I thought the whole thing was just a variation on his usual mania about not wanting to accept money that he hasn't earned. Honestly, I was waiting for that one to come up. It didn't make sense to me that a man who won't accept a loan from his parents to pay his rent would suddenly be reconciled to the idea of living off his wife. But he *had* seemed reconciled to it, and I thought Miss Spencer would talk him round again. I have enormous faith in her ability to talk Peachy round to things. She's better at it than I am, and I've had a lot of practice.

"But now I wonder if it wasn't something else to begin with. He seems to have been telling me a lame story about Harriet in order to quarrel with me, and then telling Harriet a lame story about me in order to quarrel with her. It's worrying."

"Yes," she said. "Even more so than I thought."

"I don't need to tell you, do I, that I think you did the right thing?"
 She nodded.

"I'll go round his place again and beat down his door and see if I can find out what's eating him. It may turn out to be something quite simple and concrete—or it may be a huge, vague, spiritual crisis. You never know with Peachy. Either way, I should have seen that something was wrong and tried to help before now. It's no good saying that I've been busy—true as that is. I'm so glad you came, Miss Nordqvist."

"I didn't mean to dump the whole thing in your lap."

"No, I didn't think that. If it turns out that we need to engineer a meeting, or … if Peachy has done something that Miss Spencer might need some convincing to forgive him for, then you will hear from me."

"I could give you my telephone number. You'll have to ask for me, but you shouldn't have any problem with drug fiends answering the phone."

"Delighted to hear it."

She dug in her handbag for a pen and hesitated a moment, looking at the papers in her lap. Finally she turned over the leaflet of service times and wrote her number on the back of it. She folded it and handed it to him.

"I will phone you," he said, "regardless."

"Thanks. Well … I suppose you have work to do."

"I do," he admitted. "But it is nothing pressing."

"I won't keep you from it. But I might sit in your church for a bit, if that's all right. Oh!" She laughed. "You are going to say, 'Of course!' and stare at me incredulously, I can tell."

"I was going to say 'Of course,'" he said gently, "but I wasn't going to stare."

"Ah. Well, it's a beautiful place."

"It is."

"Thank you," she said again.

He smiled, and got up and went back to the vestry. She had come to him not because of any need of her own but to ask him to help her friends. They were his friends, too; she could well have reproached him for not doing something to help off his own bat, but she hadn't.

He unfolded the leaflet and looked at the number she had written: *Midway 9413*. Who *would* answer the phone there? he wondered. It wouldn't be a Victoria College girl, anyway. He had heard Peachy ask for Harriet's number often enough to remember that the Vic exchange was Kingsdale, not Midway.

Chapter Seven

SAY "YES"

Elsa watched Mr. Underhill walk away up the aisle. Passing by the chapel, he paused to drop to one knee—not, as she stupidly thought for a moment, to pick something up from the floor. In front of the main altar he bowed, and turned and disappeared into some part of his church that she couldn't help but think of as "backstage." It *was* all very theatrical.

Now he looked just the way she had been picturing him in the months since she had seen him last. But when she had first come in, in the middle of the service, she had been startled by how different, how remote he looked at the front of the chapel. It wasn't that he had looked unlike himself, she thought, but that he had looked like more than himself. She had lamely tried to explain it by saying that he had looked happy, and then managed to embarrass him—how *did* she keep doing that? he wasn't exactly a shrinking violet—with the word "radiant." But she felt she had seen something about him that had always been true but that had never been obvious to her before. It was that his vocation was not primarily about austerity and joyless self-denial; that had always seemed at odds with his character and made her think him particularly deluded. But it was apparently about beauty and rejoicing as much as anything.

She did not know why she had said she wanted to sit in the church. Or rather, she knew why she had said it, but she did not know why it was true. The place seemed somehow both tranquil and fussily overdecorated at the same time. The woodwork was all in different colours that didn't match; the artwork represented all sorts of styles thrown together without any apparent concern for harmony or overall effect. But there was an overall effect, and it was of worship, of beautiful things heaped up and crammed in for the praise of God. Oh, it was certainly the place for Kit Underhill.

She had been struck by the way he had spoken in the service, his voice low and unassuming, addressing the emptiness that he believed to be filled with God: not trying to sway anyone with argument, not trying to be charismatic or impressive, but enacting his faith with a humble conviction. If it was theatre, he was very deeply immersed in his part.

The churches of her early childhood had been far more austere than St. John's, and even they had been ornate and prettified compared to the meeting halls and tents of the Revival. In a way, that had been a religion of the intellect, not pandering to the senses, not satisfying any craving for beauty. This, now, was surprisingly alien. The air smelled faintly, smokily sweet.

It was true that she had not been in a church in years—or it was probably true. She hadn't really thought about it. In any case, it didn't quite account for the way she felt now: like an interloper and apostate, as if she had been bold to come in here in the first place, and must now be sly and detached, must evaluate everything with a critical eye.

"So absurd, the things that they do in the name of worship … " Of course he hadn't been talking about Anglicans. But his words had a way of sticking in her mind and applying themselves to unexpected things; she had noticed this before. "What kind of a deity could desire this nonsense?"

She got up from the pew, annoyed to be thinking of this now, when she had meant to just sit and enjoy the exotically religious atmosphere. The tract with the title HOW TO PRAY slid off her lap and plopped onto the floor. She looked at it for a moment, then knelt to pick it up and tuck it in her purse. It would be rude to leave it lying there.

Straightening up, her eye fell on a statue of Mary in a corner of the church, with a lot of little candles in glass holders in front of it, many of them lit. She felt a sudden, ridiculous impulse to run and kneel on the cushiony thing in front of the candles and tell someone—Mary?—all the bits of nastiness she couldn't get out of her head. It wasn't a thing that would ever have occurred to her even in her churchgoing days—*especially* in her churchgoing days. She stood rooted to the spot with the silliness of it.

So absurd, the things … so absurd …

The acolyte who had talked to her before had come up the back stairs, in his street clothes, looking much less like something out of a painting and more like a manual labourer. For a moment she caught him looking at her unguardedly, as if he thought she was just about the most tedious thing in the world.

Well, a woman in a red dress, standing in the church by herself, clutching her handbag and staring at the statue of the Virgin? That was pretty tedious, Elsa thought. *I'm not a penitent prostitute or anything*, she wanted to tell the boy. *I'm cynically evaluating your simple faith. You've got me all wrong.*

He smiled at her: a warm, sincere smile that he seemed to have to drag up from somewhere far down inside himself.

"Take care," he said, with a brief nod, and went out of the church.

She shook herself a little, looking back up toward the front of the church, in case Mr. Underhill should happen to be about to come back out from the wings … But he wasn't; there was nothing there but a stained-glass Christ and the word *Holy* repeated above the altar. She turned away and went back out the door, down the broad steps onto Station Road.

She looked back at St. John's. It was a small, almost dainty-looking church, yellow brick decorated with bands of red. It must have occupied that corner since a time when it was surrounded by farms, long before streetcars rattled along St. Clair Avenue and Earlscourt was folded into the City of Toronto. A little churchyard fronted the street, with weathered headstones and some newer ones. Across St.

Clair were coal silos and a long row of billboards, but behind the church was a large park, preserving the illusion of a pastoral setting. She buttoned her coat against the chilly wind and headed for the streetcar stand.

She hadn't thought she would try to look for the church today, and she wasn't sure whether or not she wished she had been wearing a different dress. Once she would have thought this type of thing inappropriate to wear in a church. But then, those had been such different churches. She thought with a touch of amusement of what Mr. Underhill himself had on when she came in, the shimmering purple silk, figured and embroidered and gorgeous. She wondered whether he had noticed that she had cut her hair.

Waiting for the streetcar, she thought about their conversation, about what had been missing from it. It was really only the third conversation of any length that she had had with him, and the first in which she had not talked about herself. She had not wanted to. She didn't particularly want him to know how she was living now, how fully she had abandoned the plans for her life that she had described that day on the beach. And then if she did broach that subject with him, she knew she would want to tell him everything, so that he would know she had not given up on her dreams without a fight. And that would distract his attention from the important thing, which was reuniting Peachy and Harriet. It was as if the news of their broken engagement had woken her from the kind of stupor in which she had been moving for the last four months. It was all well and good to let your own life eddy aimlessly around your destroyed dreams, but you couldn't—*she* couldn't, she had realized suddenly—take the same approach when you saw it happening to someone you loved.

And Harriet had been marvellous in these last months: asking none of the questions that Elsa didn't want to answer; offering her own advice only in the most tactful and loving fashion. Falling in love with Peachy seemed to have taught Harriet something about relying on her own resources, and just how extensive those resources were. She had stepped into a role that had been waiting for her. The way she put it, it all had something to do with God: she'd had one idea of the man she had needed, but God had had another. Peachy, evidently, was God's idea. "I don't think you should tell him that," was all Elsa had said. Harriet had rolled her eyes and said that Kit Underhill had said that already.

She had seen him only a handful of times since the fall, but he came up in conversation all the time, entwined in stories about Peachy, in anecdotes about preparing for the wedding, in accounts of skating parties and church services and concerts that Elsa had not been at. She felt a kind of hypersensitivity to his name, as if people's voices got louder when they talked about him. She affected an elaborate indifference and made sure never to mention his name herself.

So it had taken her a while to make up her mind that she must involve him in all this, though she had thought of enlisting him immediately. But it had seemed a little unfair. He was so obviously the only one who had *not* had his hopes blighted just now. At Harriet and Peachy's engagement party he had looked almost incandescently happy. She remembered thinking: There's something in this besides happiness for his friends. Then a week or so later she had heard about his new church, and she guessed he must have had that news himself shortly before the party.

So he was happy; and maybe his friendship with Peachy was under some strain, but they were foster-brothers, basically family, and a brief period of not speaking to each other was not going to do them any real harm. Yet it was ill-timed. And the more she had thought about that, about the fact that Peachy seemed to have cut himself off from his fiancée and from his closest, most sensible friend at almost the same time, the more she became convinced that she had to involve Mr. Underhill after all.

She had tried to tell herself, in the past months, that it was better she not see him. They had nothing to offer each other that would not be counterproductive for both of them. But she had wanted to see him. Now, with an excuse to seek him out, she had been afraid she was going to start talking about herself as soon as she saw him. The last he had heard, she was headed for a happy ending with a new supervisor and a new thesis topic. That was how he must have thought of her in the intervening months. She was relieved that she had not said anything that could reveal to him how far that was from the truth.

In the streetcar, she got a seat in the back, and took her notebook out of her purse. She flipped to her unfinished translation. It was one of the poor, pedestrian hymns, and she had been trying hard to make something of it. She fiddled with the cap of her pen, no new inspiration coming to her aid. The problem was that the thing was too abstract. "The divine reason dwelling in our souls receives our adoration" was how Gallagher had rendered the first line. It was a good literal rendering, of course; that was what the line said. We adore a half-heartedly deified personification of our own faculty of reason. It was such a silly idea that there wasn't much you could do with it. *We adore the Goddess, Reason,* Elsa wrote, *Who finds her home in us.* That made two lines out of one, but she was trying to do this one in free verse anyway, so it didn't matter. It was a little better.

"Put in something really ridiculous," he had said, in that detestable, sniggering voice. She remembered him leaning on the couch beside her, looking at her over the top of his spectacles. His employer had been busy with her other guests, and he was taking the opportunity, as he so often did, to talk to Elsa. "Get them to do something— dance about naked, or sacrifice a goat—because they think it's in the hymn. Wouldn't it be satisfying?"

And it would have been. Of course, they had already read Gallagher's literal translations, so she would have to be somewhat subtle; she couldn't add lines about naked dancing or goats. But she could sneak in something: a new idea under the guise of a more accurate translation, a hint toward some new ritual. It would not be revolutionary, but it would plant thoughts in these credulous people's heads that had not been there before. She could, in small ways, shape their cult as she wished. The temptation was intriguing.

She turned over several more pages of the notebook. A few days ago she had made some notes towards a paper about poetry as a vehicle for doctrine, but had found it difficult to account for her own insights without going into detail about the Orphic hymns. And nobody would publish it if she did that.

"Why worry about them?" he had said, of the university establishment in general. She couldn't remember how the topic had come up, what in the world had compelled her to confide in him to this extent. It had probably been late at night. "They're a bunch of fools—no better than these morons … " He had gone on, into embarrassing details. He usually did. He wasn't like a real person, Elsa thought, just a collection of nasty suggestions and leering unpleasantness. She didn't even know his name. Occasionally it occurred to her that this was strange.

She turned back to the beginning of the notebook. These notes had been written when she was still working on the *Life of St. Eustacia*, the text that Professor Kluge had offered to let her edit. That seemed like a dream now: a bright, brief vision. But that was silly. At the time, she recalled, it hadn't seemed so crystalline and promising. The *Life* itself was not brilliantly written, its editorial problems more on the level of grammar than of style and sources. St. Eustacia had been aggressively courted by a pagan youth, and much of the *Life* was taken up with her long speech praising virginity and defending her intention never to marry. The thought had crossed her mind several times that she wanted to show that part to Mr. Underhill.

*

Anastasiya was waiting for her at the usual table at the usual café on Yonge Street. The place was Anastasiya's choice, but meeting at a café Elsa's idea. She had realized early on that she didn't like being alone with Mrs. Graves.

Elsa understood perfectly why she was keeping up this acquaintance—it was vital that she continue to be invited to Anastasiya's Orphic salons, and that meant staying on good terms with her hostess. She wasn't sure what Anastasiya got out of it herself. The older woman seemed to have convinced herself that they were friends, although they agreed about almost nothing, and their conversations consisted mostly of Mrs. Graves badgering Elsa about things. In her most charitable moods, Elsa felt sorry for Anastasiya—she was clearly to be pitied, in many ways. That was something, she supposed, but it wasn't friendship.

"My dear, what has happened to your hair?" Anastasiya exclaimed as Elsa sat down at the café table.

"Oh, I suppose you haven't seen me since I cut it all off," said Elsa, taking off her hat and running her fingers carelessly through the remnants. Actually, it was an expensive haircut, and she was pleased with it. She relished the feeling of the short hair slipping abruptly out of her fingers, where it used to carry on in tangles and frizziness. "I thought it might cheer me up. It did, you know. And it's much easier to look after—I don't have to braid it and put it up every morning, and I can wear these stylish little hats."

"But how sad! You had such beautiful hair, and the way you wore it suited your sweet, unspoilt nature, I always thought. I suppose some modern friend talked you into cutting it."

Elsa laughed, to cover her irritation. "Certainly not."

"But you will never take *my* advice," Anastasiya went on, ignoring the denial. "It is too bad."

"But I don't take anyone's advice. This 'modern friend' you think I have, who talks me into things, is my own self."

Anastasiya gave her a sulky look which suggested that she did not believe this. She was determined to regard Elsa as innocent and impressionable, "unspoiled" yet in need of loving improvement that only she, Anastasiya, could provide. *You would be even more beautiful if you would put on a little weight … You ought to dress in white, and use more rouge, it would suit you so well …* And the perennial favourite: *Arthur Gallagher loves you, Elsa; why do you go on stubbornly refusing him? You know you are only making yourself unhappy.* Curiously, Anastasiya talked little about the New Orphics when she and Elsa met like this. It was as if she grasped eagerly at the opportunity for an uncomplicated female friendship, all talk of clothes and hairstyles and men. Well, one man. Her choice of a friend to share all this with was a very poor one.

"Did you read the Professor's last letter?" she asked now, as Elsa had known she would.

"Yes."

"And?"

Elsa shrugged. "It was not much different from the two before it."

This was not quite true, though there was no need for Anastasiya to know it. There had been a penitent tone in the most recent letter, a hint that Gallagher would be willing to make all right if Elsa would forgive him—the first suggestion he had given that he might believe there was anything for her to forgive. Elsa didn't believe it; it was too vague, too likely to be merely lip-service to some idea that he thought she might like. ("I'll play the part of the supplicant if that will please her," she could imagine him saying to himself. "Such is my devotion!") And she didn't like it. She had no interest in forgiving Arthur Gallagher.

Mrs. Graves frowned. "And still his eloquence does not move you?"

"Not in the way he wants it to."

"He offends your modesty with the strength of his passion, I suppose," Anastasiya said with a sympathetic smirk.

This was the sort of thing it wasn't really safe to reply to, because anything she said would be taken as confirmation. Silence, too, for that matter. Much of Anastasiya Graves's conversation was like this.

Elsa attempted instead to change the subject. "What did you think of my translation of the hymn to the Divine Spark?"

"I thought it exquisite, my dear. But … I showed it to Professor Gallagher, and he told me that the phrase you translated as 'we know in our hearts' really means—"

"'Our minds will have comprehended'? I know that. But you couldn't expect me to put that in a poem, could you? More importantly, I asked you not to show my translations to Professor Gallagher."

"But they are such beautiful translations, and he is a highly respected man in his field—why would you not want him to see them?"

There was a ghost of a good point in this, Elsa thought. "It's only that I did not want Professor Gallagher to know I am translating the hymns for your salon. I am afraid he would misunderstand."

Actually, she was afraid he would understand all too well just what she was doing hanging around with the New Orphics, ingratiating herself with Mrs. Graves, finding excuses to be left alone with the *Bibliotheka*.

"But he doesn't misunderstand, my dear. He thinks it wonderful that you want to make such a contribution." She paused, looking at her ringed fingers for a moment, and then spoke confidingly. "The professor is quite sympathetic to our cause, Elsa, though I fear he does not quite admit it to himself. Perhaps … I had hoped that perhaps you yourself might be the means to bring him into a fuller sympathy. That is why I showed him your beautiful translation. Do you think that might not yet be so?"

"I really don't see how it could be."

Mrs. Graves was silent for a little longer. "They *are* beautiful, your translations. You have a genuine talent. Your economy of expression, your diction … the way that you transform the figures of the original into your own words … If I could write like that … "

For an instant her glance was rapaciously envious. She regained control of herself. "I think it a great credit to Arthur Gallagher that he looked favourably on your efforts, even though he realized that you were *redoing* his translations."

"That was very charitable of him."

"Not charitable—loving! Why will you not admit it?"

"Anastasiya, it doesn't matter what I admit about *his* feelings—mine remain the same. I don't love him. He had much better forget about me than keep writing to me, keep talking to you about me. Besides … isn't he being rather cruel to you?"

"Cruel?"

"Clearly you love him."

Mrs. Graves stared at her. "I? But … "

"Pardon me—I should not pretend to know your heart." She was embarrassed. She had been sucked into the atmosphere of feminine melodrama that Mrs. Graves was trying so hard to create. "But from the way that you praise him, from everything you say about him, it seems to me that you are asking me to conform to some model that you have in mind of how he ought to be loved, and … that you would not have thought so carefully about it if you didn't actually feel that way yourself. At the least, you think *very* highly of him. I can't believe he doesn't see that himself, unless you are much better at concealing it from him than from me. And how could a man who knows that you feel that way about him send you to court me on his behalf? Isn't that rather callous?"

"I—I don't … You are mistaken."

"I suppose I must be. But then, I don't really know you, do I?"

"Don't you? But surely we know each other quite well by now."

"What do you know about me, Mrs. Graves?"

"I know that you are spiritual, Elsa. You try to deny it, but that is only part of your greater denial, the denial of your feminine self. I see what you are trying to do, but it is futile. Your beauty and grace spring from that feminine essence—and you would not want to lose those. You are the real thing of which I can only ever be a pale shadow."

"That's absurd! I'm a bit younger than you, that's all. And I have been to university—it's a shame you never had that opportunity, because I think you would have liked it."

The way that Mrs. Graves glared at her for a moment after she said this was strange. But then, so much of what Mrs. Graves did was strange; Elsa had started to be bored by it.

*

She woke that night from a dream in which she had finally given in to the badgering of Mrs. Graves's friend Maurice, and agreed to model for him, only to find that everyone from the salon had come to watch him paint, and to look at her. At least, she thought it had been a dream; she was naked when she woke, so perhaps … She was alone in bed, and that wasn't right. She got up and walked through the house, looking for … Francis? But that wasn't right, either. That was years ago. This time it was someone different. Finally she woke up properly.

She sat in bed, hugging her knees, feeling betrayed and disgusted by her subconscious. She had a horrible suspicion that she knew whose house that was supposed to have been.

It was barely light, but there was no question of going back to sleep. She got up and wrapped herself in the blue silk kimono that she had bought with her last paycheque, and went out onto her balcony, which hung off the apartment house wall like a cage with its black metal railings. The whole side of the building overlooking the alley was covered in them, little perches where the inhabitants could put their heads out to test the weather, tend their potted plants, pin up their washing. Hers was in the lowest row of perches. She had no potted plants, and her laundry was still tumbled in a heap in her closet, but she liked the balcony.

It was bitterly cold; her old pink flannelette robe would have been more practical on a morning like this than the silk kimono. She looked up at the pale sky between the buildings, out at the curtained windows of the houses across the street. The building on the other side of the alley had an ornate wrought-iron cross on its brick wall, above the pair of modest Corinthian columns that decorated the entrance. She didn't know why the cross was there; it was just an apartment building, as far as she could tell.

It was quiet except for the sound of some city birds greeting the dawn. On the farm, this would not have been an early hour. She would already have been up and dressed, cooking breakfast, or helping her mother make bread or feed the chickens. She darted back inside, too cold to stand it any more, and shut the door behind her, wondering, as she did regularly, *Why are you not there? Why have you not given up and gone home?*

Her route that morning lay, as it always did now, back out St. Clair West on the streetcar. Not so far as St. John's this time, but nearly. She had been surprised to discover that Mr. Underhill's church was so near where she spent her days. She got off at Dufferin, and walked half a block to Fortini's Fine Jewellery. The door was already unlocked; Mr. Fortini had arrived before her, as he usually did. She hurried through the store to the back office, deposited her coat and hat, took a moment to tidy her hair in front of the mirror beside the file cabinet, and was back at work.

Since conceding defeat to Professor Gallagher (for that was how she thought of it) she had been living a sort of unreal third life, neither the scholar nor the farmer's wife of her imagination. Sometimes it struck her as amazing that only four months ago she had not known the names for different cuts of diamond, how to write out a receipt, or what type of customer was likely to be interested in the higher-end merchandise. Sometimes—more frequently—she was astonished that now she *did* know all of this, and she wished she could go back to not knowing it. She felt this trivia to be taking up valuable space in her brain, edging out the more important knowledge that she was no longer using. She made herself read Greek late at night, when all she wanted to do was sleep, sure that if she didn't, her skill would quickly erode. Yet she didn't know any longer what she was preserving that skill for. There was only one use she was putting it to now, and even she did not think that use was very noble.

No fewer than three men came in to buy engagement rings that morning. One seemed interested in buying the cheapest thing he could find; another left without making a purchase, because he wanted to spend more than the cost of Fortini's most expensive ring. The third man, who was really more of a boy, agonized for half an hour, and kept asking Elsa, "What about this one? If a man gave you this ring, would you say 'yes'?"

"It would depend on the man," she said patiently. It was not the first time she had been asked this question, although this young man was unusually persistent with it. "I like this ring—I think the band is very pretty, and even though the stone is quite small, the setting makes the most of it. So if a man offered me this, I would think he had good taste, or that he knew me well and knew what I would like. Do you think this is something your best girl would like?"

"Would you be able to tell that I only paid $27.50 for it, though?" the young man asked anxiously.

"*I* would be able to tell, yes, because I work in a jeweller's shop. But, you know, I wouldn't mind. I'd know that you bought what you could afford. And I think this ring is nicer than some of the more expensive ones."

"I'd spend five hundred dollars on her if I had it," the young man went on. "But I don't. I've got fifty dollars. What can I get for fifty dollars? Something that will make her say 'yes.'"

"Well," said Elsa, picking up the $27.50 ring from its cushion, "I think you keep coming back to this one, and maybe that's because it reminds you of your best girl. Do you think so?" She had decided that this was the ring for him.

"I don't know," he said helplessly. "It's pretty … "

"That's right. And she's pretty, too, I bet."

"She is so pretty! I know she could do much better than me. That's why I'm afraid to ask her. Do you think she'll say 'yes' if I get her this one?"

"I think that if you give her this ring and tell her that it made you think of her because it's pretty, that will give her the right sort of idea."

The young man frowned as if this was too abstract for him, but in the end he did buy the ring. Then Elsa had to endure a patronizing lecture from Gladys, the other clerk, who was younger than she but had been working at Fortini's for three years, about how to sell engagement rings.

"He was willing to spend more, you see, so you should have directed him to the fifty-five-dollar rings. Maybe even shown him the eighty-five-dollar one with the three diamonds. What I always do is say, 'Do you know what would make *me* say 'yes'?' and then I direct them to the more expensive rings. It's just a little trick I use."

"I see," said Elsa. "Thank you."

Gladys gave her a shrewd look, as though she suspected that Elsa was going to ignore her advice and go back to her own method of selling (or not selling) engagement rings.

There was a lull in custom after that. Mr. Fortini was out of the shop, meeting with a wholesaler. Gladys took the opportunity to go into the back office and telephone her fiancé at his workplace. (The ring that *had* made Gladys say 'yes' was not one of Fortini's, and Elsa guessed it was beyond the eighty-five-dollar range.) Elsa sat on a stool behind the display of cufflinks and wished she had brought some Greek to work with her.

If Arthur Gallagher had offered her that absurd little ring with its tiny diamond, she thought, she might well have accepted him. It would have seemed like a token of love, and she didn't know whether she would have been able to reject his genuine love.

She remembered Mr. Underhill telling her that he had married three couples. Probably more by now. She wondered what that must be like for him, if he really had no intention of ever being married himself. She didn't dislike selling engagement rings, but she felt a detachment from the whole process, much as the ring-buying men tried to implicate her in it.

She tried to imagine Mr. Underhill coming in here to buy a ring for some woman whom he had met in the last four months, some sweet little parishioner who would be thrilled with the idea of being the vicar's wife, who had overturned with her sweetness his intentions of remaining celibate. Fortini's was just down the street from his church—and, presumably, his vicarage. She tried to imagine his surprise at seeing her here, but she knew that he wouldn't show it, wouldn't say anything about it, would just treat her as he always did, not with tact but with charity. She imagined herself pulling out the most expensive ring in Fortini's, the sort of thing she was pretty sure vicars couldn't afford, putting it on the counter and telling him with deadly seriousness, "She won't say 'yes' unless you buy this one." She could picture him looking at her, blue eyes and boyish smile and buttons and everything, and saying, "Oh, really?" with his Oxford accent, and she felt so hollow with misery that she had to remind herself hastily that she had just made up the sweet little parishioner out of whole cloth. Her reaction surprised her, and she chose not to inquire too much into it. The last thing she needed was to add unrequited love to her other sources of unhappiness. She thought about Peachy and Harriet instead.

Peachy, when he asked Harriet to marry him, had given her an antique ring that had belonged to his grandmother. It was stunning: a large sapphire surrounded by diamonds, decidedly not the sort of thing you could buy at Fortini's. What no one had previously thought to mention about Peachy—including, especially, Peachy himself—was that he came from generations of wealth. He was not, in fact, the grossly unsuitable husband for Harriet that he had been at pains to appear. Eventually he had decided to admit it. Though Elsa thought most of the men who came into Fortini's for engagement rings placed too much importance on the role of the ring itself in securing a positive answer, she had to admit that when she had first seen that sapphire, it had been the beginning of a change in her opinion of Mr. Peacham.

He had proposed in December, months before anyone, including Harriet, expected him to, in the reading room at Annesley Hall, on his knees, but with a whimsical and Peachyesque speech. And the ring indicated not only that he had thought the thing out beforehand, but even that he must have told his parents what he was planning.

Up until that puzzling incident in the restaurant at the very end, he had been a model fiancé, and Harriet had been the envy of the other girls at Vic. Everyone agreed that it was hard to define his superiority. There were handsomer men, and more sensible men; there were definitely men with better career prospects. "It's just something about the way he treats her," one of their friends said at dinner one night. "Like he knows how lucky he is."

*

"Listen, Elsa," Harriet had said, one evening in January, when the subject came up in spite of Elsa's attempts to avoid it, "if you really are going to go to Mrs. Graves's again, I want Peachy to go with you."

"Peachy? Why?"

"Don't say *Why*! Because he's a man—and quite a tall, noticeable man at that. I want these people to get the idea that you have someone around who'll look out for you."

"I'll be fine, Harriet—they all loved me the last time, and this time I know what I'm getting into, so I won't end up locked in a bathroom. But if it would make you worry less, I don't mind Peachy coming. Just please don't tell him why I'm going, though. I don't … It's not that I don't want him to know, in particular, it's just that the fewer people who know, the better, and if he's actually going to be there, among these people … "

"Oh, absolutely! When he isn't lying, he's being indiscreet. I haven't told him any of your affairs, my dear. He doesn't need to know. Besides … No, he just doesn't need to know."

"Thanks." She thought she knew what Harriet had been about to say: "Besides, he'd just tell Kit, and Kit definitely doesn't need to know." And that was true; Mr. Underhill had already listened to more than enough of her troubles.

So Peachy had come with her. The whole thing had made her nervous in a number of contradictory ways. He was not the sort of person who could keep quiet when he saw things that he didn't approve of, and she pictured him overturning tables and making loud denouncements. Then, on the other hand, he was himself a superstitious person, and she wondered whether it was quite safe to let him in among the devotees of such a seductive brand of nonsense. A Catholic Peachy was bad enough; a New Orphic Peachy scarcely bore imagining.

She needn't have worried, though; he was very well behaved. He stuck close to her at first, even offering her his arm as they walked into the main room of Mrs. Graves's suite. She took it, laughingly, so that was how Mrs. Graves first saw them together. She stalked out of the group where she had been occupied, her gaze fixed on Peachy. He seemed surprised, but not in the way that Elsa would have expected.

"Is that Mrs. Graves?" he whispered.

Elsa nodded.

"I didn't think she would be so young."

"I don't know that she is," Elsa whispered back.

And Mrs. Graves was upon them, fawning on Elsa—"I feared

we would not see you again!"—but sparing a moment to unfurl a slow and artful smile in the direction of "your young man," as she was pleased to call Peachy. Elsa did not exactly tell her that she was mistaken, and neither did Peachy.

"I thought it might be a good idea for these people to think you had a man in your life," was what he said later.

"It was kind of you," she said. She did not add that she had been thinking something similar: that it might be as well for Mrs. Graves to get the idea that *he* had a woman already.

At first he had seemed intent on sticking by her side in the salon, which did not altogether suit her purposes, so when he had seen someone he knew and loped off across the room to speak to him, she was not sorry to see him go. Some time later she saw him in conversation with the giant, white-haired man who had told her on her first visit to ask what happened when you lit the candle. Or perhaps "conversation" wasn't the right word for it. He was backed up against the wall, clutching an empty glass, nodding with a kind of sick look on his face as the white-haired man talked. Elsa went to rescue him.

"He's mad," he said, when she had got him away on some pretext. "I need another drink. The man is completely insane."

"He's someone you know?"

"An old professor—well, not my professor, it was Kit who had a class with him. Anglo-Saxon. An expert and all that—but a bit eccentric, I think, even then. I knew he had retired, but I didn't realize it was because he'd gone completely round the twist. I've just been listening to a long account of how all his students have died and it's his fault."

"Dear me."

"I mean, many of his students are dead, there's no denying that— we were the class of 1916. But he was naming names—of people who I know for a fact are alive—and telling me how he'd killed them with his mind. I do really need another drink."

Mrs. Graves had come up behind them as they were talking, and took the opportunity of asking Mr. Peacham to tell her what he thought of Prohibition. This was clever, Elsa thought; it was a topic on which they were sure to agree. But Peachy surprised her.

"It's well intentioned," he said. "I suppose it's about protecting people from themselves, and that doesn't quite work—but it's a nice thought."

Mrs. Graves raised her eyebrows, and gave Peachy another carefully composed smile. Peachy, Elsa thought, was looking right through her. It couldn't have been comfortable.

When she left them, the conversation had turned, by a process that she couldn't remember, toward art—but she had a feeling it wouldn't stay there. She was summoned away by some of the people who had talked to her at the previous salon, who wanted to know her opinion of a passage from the first chapter of the *Bibliotheka*.

In the car on the way home—his parents' car, borrowed for the occasion—Peachy was quiet. Elsa was in a strange mood, satisfied with the outcome of the evening but also a little disgusted with herself. She watched his long hands on the steering wheel, his calm attention to the road, wishing he would talk.

"Where am I taking you?" he asked suddenly, at an intersection.

"Annesley Hall, of course."

"Ah. Right. I just wanted to make sure."

Her belongings were all packed, ready to be moved out on the following Monday, but she didn't think he knew that. Maybe Harriet had let something slip, she thought. No doubt Peachy would have been sympathetic; but the fewer people who knew, the better.

"Do you ever get … intimations about people, Miss N?" he asked, as he pulled the car into the drive in front of Annesley.

"Intimations?"

He stopped the car in front of the steps, and put on the parking brake. "Perhaps that's not the right word. Flashes of insight." He shook his head. "Don't mind me. I don't know why I thought you might … Sometimes it seems to me that we're alike, somehow."

"Is that your insight about me?"

"Maybe I'm missing the mark with that one."

"No … I think we are alike, in some ways. For instance, we both love Harriet."

He grinned. "Indeed we do. I'd do anything for her, you know."

"I know. But … don't come with me to Mrs. Graves's again, all right?"

"Harriet seems to think it's a good idea."

"I know, but … it really isn't necessary. She worries more than she needs to."

He frowned. "I don't know about that."

He *was* insightful, damn him. She couldn't very well tell him that it was she who was worried about him, suddenly—he would have been insulted by that, and she couldn't have blamed him.

"Oh, fine—come again, if you want to. But when you see that there's nothing to be worried about, do please tell Harriet."

"When I see that," he said gravely, "that's what I'll do."

Chapter Eight

SCONES FOR THE GLORY OF GOD

Kit sat at the prie-dieu in the Lady Chapel and stared at the open pages of the Bible and had to admit that he hadn't understood a word of the first lesson. Alone in the church, he was trying to read Mattins, but instead he had been thinking about Elsa Nordqvist, and not in a detached and charitable way.

She might be Arthur Gallagher's mistress. She might be in some trouble that as yet he couldn't guess at. But she was back in his life, and all he could feel was stupidly, feverishly glad.

Of course, he should have been too busy worrying about Peachy to think of her. He made himself reread the lesson and toil through the rest of the office before bolting from the empty church in a guilty effort to do something constructive.

He went first to Doughty's music shop. Doughty was alone behind the counter when Kit arrived, and obviously in something of a state. He had a bunch of boxes of guitar strings on the counter in front of him, and was trying to sort them while at the same time scribbling notes about a record of furious violin music that was playing on the gramophone, and making coffee in a saucepan in his untidy back room. He looked up at Kit's entry with a mixture of hopefulness and fear.

"Oh, Christopher. It's you, is it?" Doughty had a way of making perfectly uncontroversial things, such as one's own identity, seem a cause for distress.

"To the best of my knowledge. Is Peachy ... " The shopkeeper cast such a stricken look up at him that Kit couldn't quite finish the sentence.

"Is he?" Doughty repeated.

"Um … around? Expected? I'm sure he's told me what days he's working now, but I always forget. I guess I've got it wrong."

Doughty drew himself up behind the counter, in what would normally have struck Kit as a comical manner; he was a soft-faced, sloppy little man, and his attempts at dignity were usually rather pathetic. Now, however, Kit found himself presciently alarmed.

"Peverell Peacham no longer works here. I am surprised you did not know that. He left my employment a week ago."

"Oh," said Kit, trying to take this lightly. "Rotten luck for you—I expect you were counting on his sticking around until the wedding, at least."

"It was of course understood that Mr. Peacham would not continue on here after his marriage," Doughty went on with an even greater effort at dignity. "That arrangement had been discussed. However, it became necessary for him to terminate his employment earlier than planned."

"Why? Do you know why? He must have said something."

Doughty refused to meet Kit's eye for a minute, and shuffled out into the back room to pour his coffee out of its saucepan into a mug. He returned with the mug, which he set disconsolately on the counter. The violin skittered and squalled from the gramophone.

"I am not sure I should tell you what I know," he said finally, with a look of intense gravity. "If Peachy did not confide in you … "

"Don't be—don't worry about that. I'm sure it's something I know about. Was it to do with his engagement, with Miss Spencer?"

Doughty shook his head. "No, nothing like that. Really, I don't know much—in fact, I'm probably wrong. I shouldn't have spoken."

The bell over the door tinkled at the entry of a customer, a relatively rare occurrence, and Doughty rushed to serve the newcomer with unnecessary eagerness. Luckily for him, it was a regular whom he could easily draw into a long conversation about tuning pianos. By this time Kit was in danger of being late for a parish meeting.

He gave up, finally, and made his way back across town, wishing that he could afford a car, which was illogical since he didn't know how to drive.

Dr. and Mrs. Peacham came to the rectory that evening with a picnic hamper and the car laden with boxes. The visit had been planned weeks ago. "We'll come to dinner some time when you're settled," Dr. Peacham had said, adding, when his wife pointed out that this was not the way invitations to people's houses worked, "We'll bring the dinner with us, of course." Kit had been eagerly looking forward to it, even if it was a very modest introduction to entertaining in his own house. Now he met them on the verandah, and saw that it was just the two of them. He waited anxiously—while trying not to appear anxious—for some explanation of why their son was not with them. None seemed to be forthcoming. They were in the middle of a conversation when the car drew up on the dirt track between the church and the rectory, and they waved cheerfully to Kit and descended from the car still talking.

Dr. Gerald Peacham was like a grey-haired version of Peachy, with the same lanky build and the same intensity, though differently directed. Charlotte Peacham was a handsome, elegant woman of barely fifty, who gave a totally erroneous impression of serene and sarcastic detachment from the world. She asked Kit how he was, and he had to suppress a desire to tell her all about Elsa. She would certainly have been interested. And the next moment he was disgusted with himself again.

"I think these are the last of your books," said Dr. Peacham, coming up the steps with a large box. "Aside from the couple I set aside to read myself—you'll get those eventually. These are mostly novels. Do you want them upstairs or down?"

"Downstairs—in the living room. I can take them."

"Nonsense. There's more in the car." His tall figure disappeared into the hall with the box.

"These are curtains for your front windows," Mrs. Peacham explained, dumping vast mounds of green fabric into Kit's arms.

"They're lovely. I'd say 'You needn't have,' except, you know, I never do."

Mrs. Peacham laughed. "It's my favourite thing about you. I thought you ought to have curtains, even if you're never going to draw them. Not to have them at all would look eccentric. Besides, I think you'll find that fabric complements the wallpaper. I thought of your living room immediately when I saw it. I had Celia Weatherby help with the sewing—curtains are quite simple, but it gave her confidence to finish something almost on her own."

Kit had not heard of Celia Weatherby before, but he could guess who she was: another like himself, a young person somehow adrift in the world, whom the Peachams in their curiously undemonstrative charity had gathered up. They came and went through the big house on Walmer Road, sleeping in the spare room, or these days in Kit or Peachy's old bedrooms, storing the suitcases of their worldly goods or the stock from their failed businesses in the library, practising the piano in the parlour. They usually moved on, after a season, full of awkward gratitude. Kit, who had stayed for five years, moving out only to go to university, and leaving behind a bedroom that still bore his name, was an exceptional case. As a boy he had watched so many of the others struggle to accept the Peachams' charity with anything like grace that he had to wonder occasionally why it came so easily to him. It certainly wasn't because he thought he deserved it; but then, he didn't lie awake at night worrying that he didn't deserve it, either. "Deserving" wasn't a relevant category. Somehow he seemed always to have known that.

Dr. Peacham emerged in the doorway. "You need something on the walls in the front hall. You should look through those old engravings I have and pick out some that you like. I'll get them put into matching frames for you. I have too many to display properly."

"I'd like that—but there's no need for the frames to match. Not until I've had a chance to repaper the hall, anyway."

They brought in the other boxes, which were filled with things the Peachams were donating to the St. John's rummage sale, and they brought the picnic basket into the kitchen and unpacked it on the only table in the house. There was cold roast beef, beetroot salad, pickles, fresh bread.

"When it gets warmer, we'll have a proper picnic," said Mrs. Peacham. "You have a nice lawn for it, if it were cared for. I suppose you can talk to the wardens about that. Have they done anything about your poor housekeeper?"

"They don't quite know what to do. We have talked about it. They don't want to let her go, because it's quite true she couldn't find work anywhere else, considering how little she's able to do, and they can't afford—or claim they can't afford—to pay anyone to actually clean the entire house and do all the cooking. They make me begin to feel as though I'm being unreasonable to want to eat more than one meal every day and not live knee-deep in dust. Of course, they have a pretty clear idea what they think I could do to solve the problem."

"Did they have the gall to say so?"

"They hinted pretty broadly. I told them I'd pray for Mrs. Whittacker to make a miraculous recovery."

"I don't suppose they cared for that."

"Not really, no."

Kit took down three plates from the cupboard. Mrs. Peacham, holding four sets of cutlery, frowned.

"Peachy is not joining us?"

"I … don't know. Is he?"

"Well, is he here?" Dr. Peacham asked.

"No."

"Ah. Well, I expect not, then. But he knew we were coming, I suppose?"

Kit must have looked completely dismayed, because Mrs. Peacham intervened kindly: "Don't worry—if you forgot to tell him, it's all right."

"But I haven't seen Peachy in weeks."

"You mean he's not living here?"

"Living here? No!"

"He told us last week that he was moving in with you," said Dr. Peacham. "I mean he left a note to that effect—he came by when we were out to pick up some things, and left a note. Naturally I assumed it meant he had been evicted from that ridiculous rooming-house."

"No, I don't think it was that," said Mrs. Peacham. "The idea was just to keep Kit company in this vast place. I'd been telling him for months he ought to move in with Kit until the wedding. I was glad to find he'd finally decided to follow my advice."

"We talked to him about it on Sunday, but he said at that point he hadn't decided yet. We asked if he needed the car to move his things, but he said he had the use of his saxophonist friend's car while he's out of commission. Broke his ankle, poor fellow."

Mrs. Peacham was moving briskly around the table, laying out forks and knives, putting the extras back in the drawer, by all appearances unconcerned. Kit knew her better than to believe it.

"I don't know what he was planning on doing with the piano," she said.

"He told me he'd sold it," said her husband, pulling out a chair. "It wasn't a very good piano—not worth the trouble of moving across the city, not when … "

Not when he was about to be married to a woman who could afford to buy him a much better piano.

"But he wasn't," said Kit, answering the unspoken thought. "The engagement was off. And he wasn't planning on moving in here—he hadn't said a word to me about it."

They sat down at the table in an embarrassed silence. Kit could tell that the Peachams were annoyed, and not, as he thought they ought to have been, with him, for his failure to keep track of Peachy.

Kit knew they hadn't adopted him so that he could serve as a good influence on their son—indeed, it had been more the other way around. But he wished he could have offered that service now anyway, purely as a gift.

"Then the engagement is still off?" said Peachy's father. "We thought by this time he could have convinced Harriet to take him back."

"I'm afraid I don't know … He hasn't confided in me." *I've failed you.* "I should have made more of an effort to find out what was the matter."

"It's not your fault," said Mrs. Peacham, and Kit felt miserably both shut out of their private concern for their son and overindulged. He was annoyed with them for being more angry than worried. *He's your actual son; you have to love him more than me. That's understood.* He knew that they did. He wished they would show it a little more.

They got through the meal by talking about other things; the Peachams were better at this type of misdirection than Kit, and he couldn't guess what they were actually thinking. After they left, he went out to Mr. Oates's shop to use the telephone. The shop was closed, but he knew that he could usually find Mr. Oates there at this hour, working in his office. He disliked having to use Mr. Oates's phone, but there wasn't much he could do about it. To get a line put in the rectory would have required the wardens' permission, and Mr. Oates was one of the wardens.

As it turned out, Mr. Oates was not in, but Charlie Boult was locking the door just as Kit arrived.

"You want to use the phone, I guess, Father."

"If you don't mind. I won't keep you long."

"It's no trouble." He fumbled with the keys. "First time I've locked up—don't know which key is which yet."

The telephone was behind the counter. It wasn't a public instrument; Mr. Oates let the vicar use it as a favour. Charlie hesitated by the door, unsure how best to give Kit his privacy.

"It's all right," Kit said. "You can stay there."

A man answered at the rooming-house with a kind of grunt.

"I'm calling for Mr. Peacham, on the third floor."

"Peachy. Sure. Who's this?"

"Kit Underhill."

"The priest?"

"That's right. Do you know if Peachy is in?"

After pausing for a coughing fit, the man admitted, "I haven't seen him all week. It's Ralph Wiley—we met a while back, but you haven't been round in ages, have you?"

How all occasions do inform against me … "No, I'm afraid I haven't. Do you think you could knock on Peachy's door and see if he's in?"

"Oh sure. Won't be a minute."

He was many minutes, and someone else came through the hall and hung up the phone for him, muttering curses. Kit rang back. A woman answered this time, but before Kit could explain himself she was interrupted by a voice apparently shouting down the stairs.

"Well, how should I know?" the woman—Kit thought it was Miss Cole—shouted back. Then, speaking into the mouthpiece again, "*Are* you a priest?"

"Yes."

"Oh! Peachy's priest, right?"

"That's the general idea. I am looking for Peachy—is he in, do you know?"

"I thought he'd moved out. Someone told me they saw movers taking away his piano. Yes, all right, R.W.! Here's R.W., who's desperate to talk to you—I don't know if he has a confession to make, or what."

"Reverend? Ralph Wiley here—I knocked on Peachy's door for ages, and got no answer. And Mazursky from the basement says he saw men taking away his furniture—are you sure he hasn't moved?"

In the background he could hear Miss Cole saying something.

"Yes, I know, but it amounts to the same thing. Greta's telling me that it was just his piano, but the rest of the furniture belongs to Mrs. O'Reilly, after all. Funny that you wouldn't know if he'd moved, though, isn't it? I mean, I thought the two of you were like brothers."

"I don't think he has moved," said Kit, trying not to sound cross. "I think he sold the piano—but I'm not sure why. Anyway, thanks for your help."

He hung up the phone and hesitated for a moment before picking it up again. He had already kept Charlie waiting longer than he had intended. But he wouldn't talk long. He would suggest that they meet …

"Midway 9413," said a sonorous man's voice on the other end of the line.

"Uh—hello. Is … Miss Elsa Nordqvist at home?"

"Whom shall I say?"

"Underhill. Uh—Reverend." (*Really?*)

"Just a moment."

The wait this time was much shorter. The man came back on the line.

"I'm so sorry. It seems she's out."

"Thanks."

"Not at all. Good night."

He hung up the phone again and was overcome, suddenly, with a kind of furious grief. He wanted to ring the number again and shout at the sonorous man: *Who are you? What the hell are you doing in the place where Elsa Nordqvist lives? What gives you the right to know whether she's at home or not?* He also wanted to sink down on the floor and cry. It was some moments—much longer than usual—before he was able to be amused with himself, and even then it was only a bitter amusement.

He looked up and met Charlie's gaze.

"Bad luck," said the boy, tentatively sympathetic.

Kit smiled. "Bad luck."

He lay awake that night turning over all the recent conversations with Peachy that he could remember, looking for the places where he had ignored some warning, where he should have asked some question and had failed to. There had been a lot of overwrought Peachyness about Harriet's family not liking him, and Kit hoped he had been as sympathetic as possible to all that, but he had also felt it was the best policy not to encourage it too much. It didn't really matter what the Spencers thought of him; Harriet was over twenty-one, and there was nothing her family could do to prevent her marrying Peachy. Besides, it didn't seem to have come to that.

He had to admit that though he might have failed his friend, it looked as though Peachy was the one who had set him up to fail. This wasn't comforting, but it did suggest that self-pity might not be helpful.

Unfortunately, Peachy wasn't just then his main source of self-pity. When finally he started to slip into unconsciousness, he met the image of Elsa Nordqvist in her red dress, standing at the back of the Lady Chapel. But then she wasn't at the back of the Lady Chapel after all; she was standing by the side of his bed. She was sitting on the edge of it and taking off her shoes and stockings, and she was looking at him the way she had looked at him on the beach, coolly wanting him. And it was all right because … because … The dream logic broke down.

He woke on his back, with his left hand half under the waistband of his pyjama pants. He lay for a little while in a warm haze of arousal, feeling slightly sick, before he reached under the covers with his other hand to tug at the drawstring of the pants. The knot resisted just long enough for him to think better of this. He flung himself groggily out of bed and went to the bathroom to wash his hands and splash cold water on his face. This calmed him down, but it also woke him up.

He went downstairs to his kitchen; one of the few advantages of living alone was that he could do this kind of thing at all hours without worrying about waking anyone. He put on all the lights and made unnecessary noise getting out a pot to make cocoa. With his luck, he thought, Mr. Oates or somebody would be taking some sort of late-night stroll just now and would see the light, and he'd hear about it on Sunday. Second-hand, from the Altar Guild, after they'd all had a good discussion about it. He sat down at the table with his mug of cocoa, and looked around the kitchen, which was tidy because Mrs. Peacham had helped him wash up after dinner. He found himself remembering a different kitchen at a very different time, a little more than six years ago.

*

It was 1919. He'd been having a bad day, made worse by the depressing realization that he had become the sort of person who had "bad days." It was as degrading as the word "nerves." He tried to sleep, which should have been easy, as he hadn't slept at all that night, but the sun was hot on his bed, and people in the downstairs flat were loudly moving furniture. Nevertheless, he was still in bed when Polly and Vera "just dropped by" at noon. He unwisely answered the door in his dressing gown, looking, as the hall mirror informed him, like death warmed over and unshaven, which let him in for more than the usual amount of histrionic pity. Polly insisted on cooking something for him, and was so archly appalled by the state of their kitchen that she had to make a big show of washing dishes and putting things away in cupboards before she could so much as boil the kettle. Kit sat on the couch and tried to listen politely to Vera's amazingly undramatic account of the plot of a novel she had just read. "And then the heroine was abducted by a gang, and then the count rescued her, and then it turned out that the diamonds hadn't been stolen after all, and then … " By this time he had a blinding headache and wanted a cup of tea so badly he felt like an addict who had been deprived of his drugs by the idiotic fussing of his stepmother. Why, he wondered bitterly, could he not be allowed a little dignity in his suffering? Why did everything have to be such a bloody farce? Polly and Vera finally departed, leaving him with a bowl of too-sweet custard and a cup of too-weak tea. He tried unsuccessfully to read Augustine for a while, and fell into an unrestful sleep on the couch.

Peachy came home in the early evening with fish and chips and a bottle of contraband whisky.

"But you have to dress for dinner," he said. "Come on. You'll feel better."

And this was true. Dressed, and full of greasy fish, propped up on a pile of cushions in the window seat and nursing a glass of what turned out to be pretty terrible whisky, Kit felt exponentially better.

"Maybe we could move and not give her our new address," said Peachy from the kitchen. "I'm almost quite serious. I mean, what business is it of hers whether I want to leave a few dishes in the sink from time to time? It's not as if the place is overrun with rats. What in blazes did she do with the sugar?"

"I think she poured it into one of those jars on the counter. Possibly the one marked 'sugar.'"

"Oh. Well, it's a silly affectation, having things in matching jars on the counter. What's wrong with leaving it in the bag, I ask you?"

"I couldn't begin to say." He closed his eyes contentedly. He could have slept now; but he didn't really want to.

Peachy came back into the front room, picked up Kit's Church History textbook, and sat on the floor in front of the couch, stretching out his long legs across the rug.

"I suppose the things you've underlined in pencil are important? Tell me about Irenaeus."

"He was a bishop in—wait, why?"

"I'm helping you study for your exam."

"Oh." With the mood he'd been in all day, he ought to have said, "What's the point?" Instead, he took another drink of the insipid whisky and said: "Bishop in Gaul, in the second century—wrote a book against the Gnostics … You don't have to, you know."

"Nonsense. All part of the job, old man. You're not failing any of your courses on my watch. Now, what exactly was wrong with the Gnostics?"

"Um … they believed all kinds of twaddle. The world wasn't made by God so much as by his evil twin, which means matter's inherently rubbish, but the soul harbours a sort of divine spark, and you can do what you like in the world, by and large, with other people's wives and so on, but you're saved by the acquisition of special knowledge. *Gnosis*, in fact, hence the name."

Peachy was staring thoughtfully at the ceiling. "I find that quite depressing, actually. Maybe not the implications—I mean, I'm as much in favour of debauchery as the next man—but the fundamental idea. I like the world. And I was under the impression that God *loved* it. You know, to the extent of sending his only begotten Son … "

"You're safe there. You're orthodox—you're on the side of Irenaeus."

"Yeah … " He had transferred his thoughtful gaze from the ceiling to his friend, and it was touched with worry.

"So am I! You needn't look at me like that. Just because I'm—I'm having trouble being happy … it doesn't mean … " He felt choked, suddenly, by an immense, urgent love for everything: the sunset outside the window, the insipid whisky, the jars on the kitchen counter, Peachy. Especially Peachy.

"Oh, absolutely," said Peachy, frowning at the Church History textbook. "You're not yourself, that's all. Say no more."

"Thanks. B'lieve I shall."

They both laughed at that.

It had been another six months or so before he fully recovered his equilibrium, but that had been a turning point of sorts. He had seen that he must make an effort to show Peachy that his faith—and, more than that, his view of Creation—was intact. Never mind his college, and the archdeacon, and the diocese—*Peachy* needed to know. Kit passed his Church History exam, and began washing the dishes when Peachy was out of the house in the mornings. Then he borrowed a cookery book from Mrs. Peacham, and when one day Peachy came home to find him in the kitchen and asked what on earth he was doing, he said he was making scones for the glory of God.

"Of course you are," said Peachy, but as if he perfectly understood.

*

He took his mug of cocoa into the living room and sat in the comfortable chair by the fireplace, and eventually, for a couple of hours, fell asleep. He was woken by the sun blazing in at the curtainless south-facing windows, which was just as well, since he was not anxious for Miss Treep, who always came early on Fridays to return the vestry laundry, to peer in at his window and be alarmed by the sight of him in his pyjamas.

Immediately after Morning Prayer, he set off again for Doughty's, prepared, if necessary, to make a nuisance of himself.

It wasn't necessary; Doughty seemed almost relieved to see him, and Kit had merely to listen to a little whining about how hard it was to run the shop on his own before Doughty decided he was willing to explain what he knew about why Peachy had left.

"I will show you," he said. "I have it here somewhere. Of course he didn't know that I had it, and if he had asked about it, I would naturally have returned it. Indeed, I meant to return it, only it slipped my mind. You understand, he never told me himself that it had anything to do with his leaving. But it is quite obvious. He was even so good as to offer me some money—a loan, of course, which I fully intend to repay—by way of apology for quitting so suddenly." Kit had no doubt if he inquired he would find the amount of the "loan" was about the price of a second-hand piano. "Ah! Here it is." Doughty had been rummaging through a drawer in his desk, and produced a thickly folded sheet of paper. He spread it out on the desk and gazed down at it for a moment, then finally pushed it across the counter toward Kit. "You may draw your own conclusions. As I did. Though," he added, in a plaintive tone, "perhaps, as you said before, you already know all about it."

The page was filled with a sort of diagram full of overlapping circles and half-circles labelled things like *Mundane Consciousness* and *Intermediary Plain* and embellished with stars and moons and little human figures. One at the bottom of the page, with breasts, was labelled *Eurydice*. At the top was a sort of rubric: *Upon descending to the Pure Plain, the soul acquires the ability to re-enflesh itself as it returns.* Looking at it, Kit was filled with a sense of loathing so strong that he convulsively turned it face down on the counter.

"So you see … " said Doughty.

I don't, thought Kit. Not at all. "Where did you get this? How do you know it was Peachy's?"

"I saw him looking at it in the back room, last week. Then I found it on the desk as I was locking up. You will say that I should have left well enough alone, and I would have, only the drawing caught my eye. Naturally, when he resigned later the same week, I knew this must be behind it. After all, who would go on working in a humble shop like mine when he had important things like this in hand?"

"These aren't 'important things,'" said Kit, not quite able to keep the edge of stridency out of his voice. "They're—total rubbish. Peachy of all people would know that. He would never get mixed up in something like this."

Even as he said it he knew it wasn't true. Peachy would think the ugly diagram and the Pure Plain and the rest of it were nonsense, certainly. But that by no means meant he would leave it alone. He wouldn't laugh at it; he might be a little morbidly fascinated. He would, certainly, feel it his duty to *do* something about it.

Doughty would clearly have been happy to let Kit take the paper away with him, but Kit did not indulge him with the suggestion.

"You'd better keep it somewhere safe, in case he wants it," he said.

He returned to St. John's, attended to an accumulation of business that awaited him, and finally went into the church to pray for guidance. After a while, although no specific answer was forthcoming, he began to feel calmer. What he needed to do, he admitted to himself, apart from any personal considerations, was what he wanted to do anyway: ring Elsa Nordqvist.

He got up from the pew where he had been kneeling, and walked back down the nave toward the west door. Mr. Oates was coming in as he got there, with Charlie Boult behind him, carrying a large basket of rummage-sale items.

"Better bring that over to the rectory," Kit said. "We're keeping everything in the dining room for the time being."

Mr. Oates left Charlie to carry the basket and declared his intention to go home. Kit led the way to the rectory, remembering that he was supposed to go to a concert this evening, and thinking that he wasn't going to have the opportunity to ring Miss Nordqvist after all.

"I saw your friend this afternoon, Father," said Charlie, as Kit was unlocking the rectory door.

"Did you?" Kit gave him a puzzled look, but his heart leapt. He didn't think Peachy was widely known in the parish, but these people were always surprising him with the things they noticed.

Charlie nodded. "Miss Nord …qvist? In the shop. She was buying an apple, but then she was looking at the flowers we've got up by the cash register, and she almost bought some of those too. She took them out and then she put them back—maybe she thought they'd be too much trouble to carry on the streetcar."

"That seems likely."

"They were tulips." Charlie shrugged. "Red ones—kinda orangey red. Just thought … you know, you might be able to use that."

"Charlie … " He hesitated over how to suggest, kindly but clearly, that this was inappropriate, that this was none of Charlie's business, that there was a line that one ought not to cross … "Thanks," he said.

Chapter Nine

SOMEONE ELSE

Mrs. Bundt knocked on Elsa's door shortly after she got in from work on Friday.

"Phone for you, Miss Nordquest." Mrs. Bundt and her husband had one of the larger apartments on the first floor, near the telephone, and were usually the ones to answer it. "A Miss Spencer."

Elsa felt ashamed of her momentary disappointment. Harriet, it turned out, wanted her to come to an organ recital that evening.

"I'm sorry to spring it on you," she said, "but I'd forgot all about it, and I absolutely can't face going by myself. It's a benefit—orphans, or unwed mothers, or—oh, something terrifically deserving, and Mother expects me to go, and didn't understand when I tried to hint that it would be painful for me to sit through an organ recital. I mean, I don't suppose she even remembers that Peachy … plays the organ."

"Well, he does lots of things—it can be hard to keep track," said Elsa diplomatically. She was remembering Mr. Underhill's story about needing a choir director at St. John's; she wondered if Harriet knew about that.

"You're right, of course. But Mother never paid much attention in the first place." There was a desperate edge of misery in Harriet's voice.

"What time do you need me to be ready?" Elsa asked stoutly.

"I'll buy your ticket, of course—I mean, I would have bought one for Peachy, if … "

"But you needn't buy one for me—I've a full-time job, remember?

And I like organ music. Just tell me when and where. And how I ought to dress."

"Wear anything you like, it really doesn't matter. Only … can you meet me at Annesley at seven? I suppose that doesn't give you much time to get your dinner. If it's too much bother … "

"Nonsense! I'll be there."

It didn't give her much time for dinner. She made do with a hasty sandwich eaten in the little alcove that served as her kitchen. The new dress that she had worn to Mrs. Graves's the night before was draped over the back of a chair beside her bed, her shoes and stockings and artificial pearls flung about in various places close to hand. The whole was easily reassembled—the stockings, fortunately, were free of runs—and she was soon dressed again as she had been last night. The dress was black, sleeveless, with a low V neckline, the skirt just skimming past her knees, flaring gracefully from a dropped waist and a belt fastened in the middle with an elaborate silver clasp. She looked at herself as best she could in her small bathroom mirror and thought about what had happened last night.

*

The salon had been unremarkable, the same as always. Elsa's translation of the Hymn to the Divine Spark was received with swooning enthusiasm; Maurice repeated his attempt to cajole her into posing for him; Mrs. Graves's secretary said, "You're too good for these people—you know that, don't you?" and Elsa thought that yes, she did more or less know that, but was annoyed with him all the same.

She let herself be cajoled by the little woman with the turquoise jewellery into trying the Descent to the Pure Plain for the fifth or sixth time. Of course, "trying" was the wrong word. She lit the candle and read the designated passage from Book Two, and sat in the dark in the guest bedroom with the young man in grey tweed and a couple of earnest onlookers, thinking about nothing in particular, and as usual nothing in particular happened. Mrs. Graves, for some reason, was upset to find that they had talked her into it again. She cut the whole thing short when she walked in on them, and fretfully asked to talk to Elsa about something. Then she had nothing to say except to return to an old grievance.

"I don't understand why you continue to refuse Professor Gallagher. There is only one explanation I can think of. There must be someone else."

Elsa laughed, and even to her own ears it sounded unkind. She had lost patience with Mrs. Graves altogether. It felt dangerously freeing.

"You see, you are exactly the woman for him! Neither of you believes, for all your protestations of love and friendship, that I actually have a mind of my own. I must have been influenced by my 'modern friends,' I must be in love with another man, I must have got my ideas from my feminine intuition, my considered opinions must be reflexive Victorian prudery.

"Oh, but you know," she went on, only a little surprised at herself, "you are quite right, there is another man—or there *was*. His name is Francis Thorne. He edits a magazine in New York now, the last I heard, but he was a teacher in Saskatchewan when I knew him. He was my lover when I was sixteen and he was twenty. It wasn't for long, and I haven't seen him in years, but he's the man who came between me and Professor Gallagher, if you like. I learned from him to expect better than what Gallagher offers. You see, in spite of what Gallagher thinks, I know the difference between admiring a man's intellect and loving him. I admired Francis, certainly, but I also wanted him, and it wasn't because of any rubbish about the baseness of matter."

"You … you *consummated* this affair?"

Her tone was as startling as her choice of words; she spoke with distaste, almost with revulsion.

"We did," said Elsa, with a breezy defiance, "and it was lovely."

Mrs. Graves was white-faced, and looked strained and sick. "I suppose he was one of these vulgarly handsome, blue-eyed men, with artfully unkempt hair."

Elsa stared at her. "Why in the world would you say that?"

"Oh, I know the type."

But it wasn't a type, Elsa thought, so much as a satirical description of Kit Underhill. Francis, as it happened, was dark and tall and thin. She wondered whether it was possible that Mrs. Graves had been having her followed. But that didn't make sense of it; she hadn't seen Mr. Underhill for months, and their conversation the other day couldn't have looked very much like an assignation. Besides, she couldn't believe that Mrs. Graves, with her metaphysical preoccupations, would have been less concerned about the fact that she had gone into a church and talked to a priest than about what the priest had looked like.

She knew that she had done their spurious friendship irreparable harm with this revelation, and, though she had been annoyed with Mrs. Graves, that was not what she had intended. She pretended to have someone else that she needed to go talk to. Of course, as soon as she left Mrs. Graves's company, she found herself alone in a corner with the young man in grey tweed. This was what always happened. He proffered a glass of gin as if it were a private joke between them—which in a way it was, since he must have known she would refuse it.

"What would you become?" he asked.

"What?"

"If their silly religion were real, and you really could descend to the Pure Plain and change yourself into anyone—what would you become?"

"A man," said Elsa, not even bothering to pretend that this was something she had to think about. The trouble was, when she did think about it, she realized that it was not really true. She only wished it were as simple as that.

*

She pulled on her white coat but did not button it, as it was really too warm for the weather, and pinned on her only smart hat. She was down the stairs and halfway to College Street before it occurred to her that an organ recital would be in a church, and that when Harriet had said it didn't matter what she wore, she probably hadn't known that Elsa owned anything like this black dress. It was too late to go back and change, and she had nothing else clean to wear anyway. She walked on.

Harriet was waiting on the steps outside Annesley Hall. She made no comment on Elsa's dress. She was wearing something much more demure and pastel-coloured under her own coat. She seemed jittery and irritable. The sapphire that had belonged to Peachy's grandmother still glittered on the ring finger of her left hand.

"How did your exam go?" Elsa asked as they set off eastward along Bloor.

"It was gruelling, but I think I did all right. I studied like mad—honestly, it was a bit of a relief to have something to think about. I'm sick of everyone, Elsa! I know they mean well, half of them—except for the ones who obviously don't—but they keep coming round saying such trite, stupid things. *There's more fish in the sea*, and *You were too good for him anyway*, and *What a beast he must be to treat you like this, isn't it a blessing you found out in time?* That's Azalia Lewis's favourite: *Isn't it a blessing you found out in time?* I mean, is that supposed to be comforting?"

Elsa rolled her eyes. "Probably. Azalia Lewis is a nitwit."

"It's all such hypocrisy! They were perfectly nuts about Peachy before—before this—and nobody seems to be able to *fathom* that

I might still be in love with him. Nobody except you. And I hardly ever see you any more." She was starting to cry.

"I know," said Elsa. "It's so completely rotten." She put her arm around Harriet's shoulders and gave them a little squeeze.

Harriet snuffled and wiped her eyes with her handkerchief. "Did I tell you about the time that Peverell took me to St. Thomas's and played Bach's Fantasy and Fugue in G Minor on the organ, just for me?"

"You did, and I thought it was very sweet of him." After a moment, she clarified: "I still think so."

"Thanks."

They walked the rest of the way to the church in silence. It was a massive grey stone building, sleek and moneyed, quite unlike St. John's. (But why was she comparing it to St. John's? What was St. John's to her?) It was more than half full by the time they arrived, and Elsa hoped that in this crowd it might prove impossible to find Mrs. Spencer.

"I suppose your mother is here already, and is saving seats for us?"

"I told her not to—she likes to sit in the front, and I can't face it. I said we might get here late, and that we'd find her afterward at the reception. Let's sit down."

They found themselves a pew near the back, but no sooner had they sat down in it than a party slid into the pew in front of them, and one of its members turned to greet Harriet delightedly. It was Milly Thorndike, quick to explain that she *was* still Milly Thorndike, contrary to expectations. She was newly released from her engagement to Mr. Butcher, and had heard that Harriet's engagement was off too, and thought it was wonderful.

"Men are such *pigs*, aren't they? They're all absolutely the same! I've forgotten now, Elsie—you're not engaged to that minister, are you? Oh, good! Because otherwise you'd have to sit and listen to me and Harriet *abusing* them, and thinking all the while, 'But *my* fiancé isn't like that—is he?' when of course he *is*. Or … " She backtracked, illogically: "Anyway, he would be, if he were your fiancé."

"Then for the sake of his moral character, I'm glad he isn't," said Elsa. "Oh, look—I think the recital is about to start."

Milly giggled and turned back around on her pew. Elsa looked down at her program. The second item was "Fantasy & Fugue in G Minor—J.S. Bach." She stole a glance at Harriet but couldn't decide whether or not she had noticed.

The organist was a beefy blond man, as unlike Peachy as one could wish—but when he disappeared into his seat at the organ, that left nothing to focus on but the music and the empty front of the church. Elsa actually found this interesting, and lost herself in the huge chords of the first piece, something by Franck, her eyes tracing the stone saints in their architectural settings behind the altar.

The Bach piece began with a sort of crashing flourish. Harriet slipped out of the pew and walked quickly out to the back of the church. Elsa let her go without looking after her, wanting to let her be discreet. Milly turned around to look at Elsa.

"What's the matter?" she hissed. "Is she all right?"

"She's fine," said Elsa.

"I think something's the matter," Milly pursued. People around them were beginning to look at her. "I think I should go after her."

Elsa said nothing. Milly climbed over the rest of her party to get out of the pew and clicked noisily up the aisle after Harriet. Elsa stayed where she was.

The Bach finished, and Harriet and Milly returned, white-faced and obviously not on speaking terms. Elsa remained impassive.

They made it through the rest of the recital and joined the crowd funnelling out of the church into the hall, where cookies and little sandwiches and cups of punch were being served.

"I suppose it was childish of me to leave," said Harriet. "But I just couldn't stand to listen to the Bach. If you ask me, it was a rotten interpretation, much too bombastic, totally different from the way Peachy plays it."

"It was a little heavy-handed. What happened with Milly?"

"She cornered me in the ladies' cloakroom and was *so concerned*. I may have said a few unkind things about minding her own business. She had it coming. Oh, fantastic. Just what I need. Look who else is here."

She followed Harriet's gaze and saw a familiar figure in black.

"Well, it's an Anglican church, isn't it? Perhaps he knows people."

"You know, there was a time when I thought it would be a good thing for you to become fond of him. I'm so glad you didn't."

Elsa looked at her with surprise. "Are you? And—did you?"

"Yes, but that was before I realized what a … what he's like."

"And? What's he like?" She had known that Harriet was annoyed with him, but this sounded like something new.

"Never mind. It isn't anything you need worry about—it's not as if you have anything to do with him. Let's get some little sandwiches. I feel as if little sandwiches would do me good just now. They're so civilized."

Elsa followed her toward the refreshment table, perplexed and worried. She cast a glance back at Mr. Underhill, talking cheerfully with a couple of pink-frocked young women. She was going to have to find an opportunity to talk to him without Harriet knowing; or she was going to have forgo the opportunity altogether, which made her unhappier than she liked to admit. Her heart had done a little jump when she first saw him. Mostly because she wanted to ask how he had got on with Peachy. Mostly.

Mr. Underhill had seen her, and the smile which had been directed at the pink young women had drained away. She turned away from him toward the refreshment table.

They procured little sandwiches, and then decided that they were too warm in their coats, and took turns holding each other's piles of sandwiches while they hung their coats up on the rack by the door. Elsa's dress was now revealed in all its risqué glory. They went in quest of cups of punch. Mrs. Spencer passed by and stared disapprovingly at Elsa.

"I should have worn pink," Elsa remarked, sipping her punch.

Harriet looked at her. "You *never* wear pink."

"Good point. I believe your mother thinks I'm a flapper."

"Is she wrong?"

Elsa laughed.

"I am joking," said Harriet. "Sort of. But you do have your moments, Elsa. Oh, it's all right—I don't have to approve of everything you do, you know, I've never thought that. You're unconventional. I envy you that. But it isn't me—it isn't how I could ever be. I think that dress looks stunning on you, and it hurt my feelings when you went and cut your hair without telling me, because you know I wouldn't have tried to talk you out of it—I think it suits you."

"I'm glad!" said Elsa, struggling to keep up with the rapid flow of Harriet's thoughts. "I am sorry I didn't tell you, but honestly, it was such a sudden decision—I think I only made up my mind when I walked into the hairdresser's."

She wondered whether to pursue this theme further or to wait for Harriet to say more. Clearly the topic at hand was broader and deeper than dresses and haircuts. She had opened her mouth to say something when Harriet spoke:

"But it isn't me," she said again. "I don't mean just the short hair—I mean everything. Living on your own and doing what you like. I'm going to marry someone else."

"What? Harriet! Who?"

"I don't know. No one in particular. I just know that I am. Quite soon. Someone very conventional. It was a nice idea, my marrying someone like Peachy, but it was a bit silly, too."

"Harriet, don't be ridiculous. It wasn't an *idea*—it was you loving Peachy, and you just told me that you still do."

"I'm not being ridiculous, Elsa. I'm just going to do something that you won't approve of."

"Of course I don't approve of it—nobody would approve of it!"

"My mother would."

And there was really nothing Elsa could say to that. It was probably true; not only would Mrs. Spencer approve of the outcome, but she would probably follow and appreciate Harriet's reasoning. Mrs. Spencer had certainly thought of Peachy as a silly idea.

Some girls whom Elsa did not know were waving vigorously at Harriet from across the room.

"We'd better go see what they want," said Harriet. "Though I expect it's only to tell me how there are other fish in the sea, and all of them pigs. I suppose that's a mixed metaphor."

But the girls, friends from Harriet's school days, had not heard about her broken engagement, and innocently asked after "that musician that you're marrying." When Harriet admitted that she was not marrying him any more, they appeared to regard her as something of a skeleton at the feast, and didn't know what to say. They began reminiscing about things they had done at school, and Harriet entered wanly into it. Elsa, unable even to feign interest in this, said something about being hungry and walked off in the direction of the little sandwiches again.

She ran into Milly Thorndike on the way there, and, since she was genuinely curious about it, drew her into conversation long enough to be able to slip in the question, "What did Mr. Butcher do to make you break off your engagement?"

Milly was predictably eager to tell her all about it, but the explanation was not what Elsa had expected.

"He got some crazy idea about going into business for himself. He had a perfectly sensible job at his father's company, but he decided it wasn't fulfilling his potential, or some nonsense, and that really what he wanted was to get back into aeroplanes again—you know that's what he did during the War, not fly aeroplanes but just repair their engines, and he was wild about it. He wants to start a company that builds custom aeroplanes for people. I mean, have you ever heard of such a thing? It's perfectly idiotic. His father didn't like it, but his mother took his side, the horrible cow, and in the end they decided they would lend him some money so he could go ahead with it. But it meant he wasn't going to be able to afford the house he was set to buy me—he wanted to put all his savings into the business. He expected me to make do with some wretched little townhouse, and two servants, 'just until the business got going.' Which would have been bad enough, and it was a degradation that he would even think of asking it of me—and I told him so—but there's no guarantee the business ever *would* get going, is there? I mean, it could fail. He said so himself. 'I'm taking a risk,' he said, 'but I have to follow my passion. *I'll regret it if I don't.*' Well, I saw to it that he had plenty to regret anyway."

Elsa sipped her punch. "I suppose he expected you to be happy for him—to want him to do the thing that made him happy."

"I don't want a husband who can't provide for me—that's what I told him. I don't want to have to worry about money and do without new dresses and parties, and things that I want." She shrugged. "I'm not being materialistic, but, I mean, I did think he loved me more than that."

"You're being very materialistic," said Elsa, "but you may be right. Perhaps if he had loved you more, he would have been willing to sacrifice more of his own happiness for you. Perhaps if you had loved him more you would have put up with a townhouse and two servants."

Milly frowned and poked at her little sandwich, hiding her discomfiture in an attempt to figure out what the filling was. "You're probably right," she said after a moment. "I hadn't really thought about it that way. Oh, hello, Reverend!"

"Miss Thorndike, Miss Nordqvist."

"Mr. Underhill." So she was spared the effort of finding an opportunity to talk to him after all. She might have expected that.

"How extraordinarily sweet of you to remember my name," Milly was saying with a giggle. "And it *is* still my name, you know, even though by now I had expected … "

Elsa didn't say anything to excuse herself, just melted away into the crowd. She drifted aimlessly back to the refreshment table for some cookies and more punch, and thought that she had probably been a little unfair to Mr. Underhill. He had no doubt wanted to talk to her, not Milly. It shouldn't have bothered her to listen to Milly flirting with him a little bit. But maybe that wasn't why she had left, she argued academically, in her own defence. Maybe Milly had a hope of getting something out of her flirtation besides some polite conversation. You never knew. She ate her cookies and imagined Milly amusing her grandchildren with the story of the absurd man she had almost married as a girl. "Eyes like a fish, and nearly bald at thirty. And *this* is a photograph of your grandfather when he was young …"They would be duly impressed, but not shocked because of course he would have aged well. He would be a bishop or something by that time.

She was distracted by a more prosaic problem: she couldn't find Harriet. The school friends had disappeared too. She walked up and down the hall, wandered back into the deserted nave of the church, and finally down the stairs, following the sign for the women's cloakroom, where she found them giggling together in a little knot. They hid something as she approached.

"Harriet? Oh, she went looking for her friend. Oh! She must have meant you! Didn't she find you?"

She marched back up to the hall, now beginning to feel irritated. Harriet met her near the refreshment table, looking flushed and strange.

"Elsa, I've done something terrible," she murmured. "I've—I've *had too much to drink.*"

"Too much what?"

"Alcohol." She mouthed the word soundlessly, with a look of intense misery.

"Harriet! How on earth? At a church reception?"

"One of the girls from school had a flask of something—I don't remember her name, I kept trying to think of it but I wasn't even really friends with her at school—and they were putting it in their punch s-s-secretly, and said I should try some, and I did and I drank all of it, *straight*, not mixed with the punch, and quite fast, and she poured me some more, and now I'm—I'm—I know I'm going to start to cry, or I might be sick, I don't know which, but I feel awful."

"We'll get you out of here. I'll get our coats, and—is that … " She looked down at the punch cup that Harriet was holding. It was half full of something of quite a different colour than the punch.

"I should drink the rest of it, shouldn't I?" Harriet lifted the cup.

"No—no, you shouldn't. Here, give it to me."

She took the cup and set off in the direction of the coat rack. Mr. Underhill met her almost immediately.

"I consider that a dirty trick," he said. "Miss Thorndike indeed. I want to talk to *you*."

"Yes. I thought you might."

"I say—what's up?" She cursed his perceptiveness. He eyed the cup, which she realized she was holding as if it were filled with snakes.

"It's nothing," she said unconvincingly. She couldn't involve him, not after Harriet had made plain her current opinion of him. "Only— why is Harriet angry with you?"

"I didn't know she was."

"I see. But—you wanted to talk to me. What about?"

"Peachy is missing. Really missing. He's lied to his parents, quit his job—sold his piano. Nobody knows where he is. Least of all me. I feel responsible, and I have no idea what to do. I tried ringing you, but you weren't home. I can't tell you how glad I am you turned up tonight. You're the answer to a prayer." He shot her one of his half-smiles, apologetic.

"Why do you feel responsible?" she asked. "What did you do?"

"Nothing! Precisely nothing. Something must have been the matter, and I had no clue."

"It's not always possible to guess. We'll figure it out, though." She had no idea how; but she felt a sudden desire to comfort him. "I wonder … do you think Harriet has some suspicion?"

"You could ask her—she's coming this way."

But there was no time to ask Harriet anything. She was coming, fortified by the drink she had consumed, to confront Mr. Underhill.

"You!" she said grandly, and unnecessarily loudly. "Selfish, presumptuous, meddling bastard! You ruined my happiness. I hope you are satisfied."

Mr. Underhill stared at her. She should have looked comical, but she didn't; she looked magnificent.

"I'm afraid I have no idea what you mean," he said.

"Oh, *don't* you? It's not your fault, I suppose, that Peverell won't marry me? It wasn't your idea, selfish, meddling bastard, that he should break off our engagement?"

"Harriet!" Elsa hissed.

Heads were turning in their direction, punch cups and little sandwiches frozen on the way to mouths.

"I don't pretend to know why you did it," Harriet went on, "but I suppose you had your reasons. I suppose it wasn't convenient for you for your friend to marry the woman he loved. So you made sure it didn't happen."

"Miss Spencer, please believe that I have no idea what you're talking about. I would not have come between you and Peachy for the world."

"She's not feeling herself," said Elsa miserably.

"Yes, I twigged that, thanks."

"Right."

Harriet was now clearly making heroic efforts not to cry. "I know—I know it's no good blaming you really."

"It's not that I mind—I mean, if it helps—only I wonder if we could talk about it outside, while there are still a few people in here who don't think that I'm the father of your child, or … "

"I don't *have* a child!" Harriet almost wailed.

"No, no—I know that. I assumed that. It was a bad joke. What have you been drinking, anyway?" he asked as they shepherded Harriet toward the front door.

"Liquor."

"I'm shocked. Where did you get it?"

"Some school friends she met," Elsa supplied. "It's … " She held out the cup of snakes.

"I thought it might be," he said, taking it from her. "Did you have coats?"

"Oh, Lord—I'll go get them," said Elsa. "Or … Can you—will you be—"

"Miss Nordqvist, I was at Trinity College before the War."

"What?"

"This isn't the first time I've had to chaperone a drunk undergraduate. Get your coats. And my hat, if you'd be so kind."

"Is it one of those stupid-looking priest hats with a tassel?" Elsa asked, rallying.

He narrowed his eyes at her. "It's a black Homburg."

She found the coats and Mr. Underhill's (she had to admit) perfectly smart hat. When she returned with them, Harriet and Mr. Underhill were sitting on the church steps, friends again. He was still holding Harriet's punch cup, but it was empty.

"What was it?" Elsa asked, sitting down next to him.

"I have no idea," he said primly, handing her back the cup. "I should be ashamed to know what that was."

"Really?"

"Yes. How she contrived to get drunk on it I can't imagine."

Elsa laughed, and set the punch cup on the side of the steps for someone to find later. She got up and draped Harriet's coat around her shoulders.

"I should have told Mother I'm going," Harriet said, getting awkwardly to her feet.

"No!" said Elsa and Mr. Underhill at the same time.

"Okay, okay! I guess not."

They walked along Bloor in a soothing silence. Harriet took Mr. Underhill's arm, but she looked quite sober now. She could not really have been very drunk, and she had, Elsa thought, been rather magnificent confronting Mr. Underhill. But Elsa didn't believe for a minute that he had had anything to do with Peachy breaking his engagement. She would have to find out what put that idea into Harriet's head. As for Mr. Underhill, he had handled the situation with Harriet better than she had, of course, but she still felt that odd sense of protectiveness towards him.

When they reached Annesley, they left Mr. Underhill in the outer vestibule, and Elsa took Harriet upstairs. It wasn't until they had gained Harriet's room that she turned to Elsa and said, "I don't think I apologized properly. He's one of those people you don't apologize properly to, because he's so nice about things. He tried to turn it all into a joke, but I was really awful to him, wasn't I? I called him a—a—" She dropped her voice to a whisper: "*bastard*—didn't I?"

"Several times. You could certainly have chosen a better word."

"I don't really think he is a—a—"

"Harriet. You know he is, literally."

"What?"

"A bastard. Illegitimate."

"Oh, *no*! Of course I didn't know that! Oh, I must go apologize!"

"No, you absolutely mustn't, because if you didn't know that then I just told you, and you can't go tell him that now. Besides—he's probably left. I know *I* would have, if I were him." He doesn't know that I'm going to come back down those stairs, she thought. As far as he knows, I still live here.

"Oh, why is everything so miserable? I've made a fool of myself, Elsa."

"Do you know, I don't really think you did? I think you were just misled."

"Elsa, do you forgive me?" Harriet asked urgently. "I don't know what I'll do if you—if you don't!"

Elsa looked at her friend, her gold hair coming down around a face blotchy with crying, her eyes suddenly huge and frightened.

"My love, of course! There's very little to forgive, actually."

"Oh, Elsa!" Harriet seized her and hugged her awkwardly. "I *am* sorry," she said, stepping back.

"You should get some rest. This will all seem quite different in the morning, I expect."

Harriet nodded. She followed Elsa to the door, and when Elsa had walked through it she said suddenly, "I still love Peverell, Elsa, and he still loves me."

"Does he?" Elsa looked back at her.

"Yes. He told me so."

"When?"

"When he ... when he told me he couldn't marry me."

"I see."

"He wro—he said he 'had it on sound authority' that he was no good for me—naturally I thought that meant Kit. I thought Kit had been talking to him, trying to get him to ... mend his ways or something, and that it had backfired and made him decide that he just couldn't marry me after all. I didn't really think that Kit had *meant* to break us up. I mean, I do still think that must be what happened, but I realize Kit didn't mean anything by it."

"Well—if it was all a misunderstanding ... "

Harriet shook her head. "It's too late now. There's another woman."

"Don't assume just because—"

"I'm not assuming. He told me. This was later—just last Monday. At least that's when I got the letter. He—he wrote to me. I think he … was unfaithful, but he didn't really mean to be. And now he said he has to stand by the other woman. Of course I know what that means."

"Ah … yes, I see."

"That's why … That's what I meant. But of course I know that Kit isn't … I mean, it's absurd to think he's to blame. *I'm* to blame."

"That's absurd too, Harriet. Whatever Peachy did, *Peachy* did it. And, you know, he would be the first to say that himself."

"Yes. You're right. How are you getting home, Elsa? Hadn't you better stay here?"

"I'll walk—it isn't far. Don't worry about me. You just get some sleep."

She came slowly down the stairs, trailing her coat behind her. She felt drained by the whole episode, burdened by other people's sadness and unable to do anything about it.

Mr. Underhill was still standing in the vestibule where they had left him, hat in his hands, leaning one shoulder against the wall. He smiled faintly as he saw her approach. She pulled open the inner door eagerly.

"You're still here."

"I am. Your porter has been giving me funny looks."

"Well, you bring that on yourself."

"Do I?"

"Yes. Couldn't you try to look a little more … "

"A little more what?"

"Well, Protestant?"

"Certainly not."

She smiled. She was so glad he hadn't left. "Why didn't we tell Harriet just now about Peachy being missing?"

His eyebrows rose. "I did. While you were getting the coats."

"Oh."

"She said she didn't know where he was. She hadn't known he was missing, but the last time she saw him was the twelfth of March."

"And she got a letter from him this past Monday. Mr. Underhill, she just told me that Peachy cheated on her, that he told her so, by way of explaining why he couldn't marry her. *And* that he told her that, though it was apparently a moment of madness and he regrets it, he has to 'stand by' the other woman, which she, of course, takes to mean that the other woman is pregnant. And do you know what? Before you say anything—I don't believe it. Because if I were Peachy, and something like that had happened, I *know* I would have told you. So—unless of course you *do* know, and you can't tell me … "

"No! I can categorically assure you that I don't know that."

"Well, good. But you're not sure you disbelieve it."

"I—I find it very hard to believe. I think I lack your faith that Peachy would certainly have told me if it were true. I hope he would have told me, but … "

"It's not that it's so very implausible—you, as his friend, would wish to defend his character, of course, but he does lead a bohemian life, and I'm sure he knows a lot of people with … well, what you'd probably call loose morals."

"I never use phrases like that. But your point is sound."

"It's just that I don't think it's true. You know, I'm beginning to think it *is* feminine intuition after all. I'm brimming over with it, apparently."

He smiled wryly. "Isn't it just conviction?"

"You're too kind. The question is, was the whole thing a lie, or did he just mean something else by it?"

"Right. I don't know."

"We have to do something."

He nodded. "Do you have any idea what?"

"We could break into his apartment and look for clues. Unless, of course, you have a key—then we wouldn't need to break in."

"I don't. I used to, when he still lived at the old place in the West End. But he couldn't afford the rent on his own. He moved out a year ago—he lives in a rooming house in Cabbagetown." He pushed back his cuff to look at his watch. "It's only nine o'clock. Shall we go?"

"Really?"

"We have to do something. You said so yourself."

"You're not dressed for housebreaking."

He looked at her critically. "Neither are you."

"No, I suppose not. Let's go."

As they walked to the streetcar stand on Bloor it occurred to her to say, "Harriet apologized for what she called you."

"What did she call me? Oh! I saw you cringing. I'm not sensitive about that, you know."

"No, I suppose you're not. You've no reason to be."

"No. Kind of you, though."

"Oh, gosh. The thing that bothers you is when *other* people try to be sensitive about it."

He grinned ruefully. "I'm afraid that's true. But I'm aware it's unreasonable."

The streetcar was pulling up to the stop as they approached.

"Do we run?" he asked.

"Yes," she said, and they did.

"You know," she remarked, as they found seats, "a great advantage of the new short hemlines is not having to pick up your skirts when you run. Though I must say you manage it in a not effeminate way."

"Thanks. You'd be surprised how much thought has gone into that."

"No," she said, smiling very sweetly, "I don't think I would."

She looked out the window at the dark street for a few moments, as the car rattled on. She had realized on the way to the streetcar that she would have to tell him the whole story. She wished there were some way she could avoid it, even for a little longer, but the truth is that would only have made things worse.

"There is one other thing that I didn't mention the other day," she said finally. "I didn't think it relevant. I still don't—but you would be a better judge, so I ought to put you in possession of all the facts. Although I suppose you may know about this already. It's just that Peachy … Well, I should start at the beginning. I've … " She hesitated.

"Yes?"

"It's just a little awkward."

"It's all right."

"Easy for you to say. Arthur Gallagher threatened to bring my academic career to an end—you may remember I told you about that."

"Of course."

"Well, I didn't take him seriously, but he meant it. He began telling people that I had … that I was his … "

"Mm-hm."

"His mistress."

"That's what I meant by 'mm-hm.'"

"Yes. Thank you. It's so embarrassing—and at the same time, I'm embarrassed to *be* embarrassed, because I don't … I mean, if I *wanted* to be someone's mistress … "

"Mm-hm."

"Stop saying that. By this time, you see, I was working with Professor Kluge, who'd been very kind. He was going to let me edit the life of St. Eustacia on my own, which was … well, it's boring and Christian and full of nonsense about virginity, but, as a project, it was worlds better than the genitive absolute in Plato. To be honest, I was getting interested in it, in spite of myself, when Gallagher started spreading his rumours. It was clear that he meant to get me expelled, but he was going about it gradually. He was still hoping I would change my mind—in fact, he kindly offered to stop spreading the rumours if I would make them true. So I did the only thing I could think of, which was to drop out of school. He won, but at least I made an orderly retreat."

"Elsa! If all you did was drop out of school, Gallagher didn't *win*."

"I abandoned my career! I'm working in a shop!"

"And?"

"What do you mean, 'and'?" It had taken such an effort to admit all this to him; and this was his response? "I work at a jewellery shop. I'm a cashier at Fortini's Fine Jewellery. I've been working there for four months. It's not even a very *nice* jewellery shop."

"Is that what Gallagher wanted?"

"Oh. I see what you mean. No, obviously not. But it's not what I wanted, either. And I've been—I've devoted a lot of energy over the last four months to trying to get even. Not—not in a Count of Monte Cristo sort of way, don't worry. Honestly, I think it's something I'd probably have done anyway. I just … might not have gone about it with such single-mindedness. It was something you said, actually—that there must be a way of proving that the *Bibliotheka* was a forgery. Of course you were right. And, I mean, I was right. It *is* a forgery. But the reason I know this is because—the only way I could get to see it again, to look for clues, was to go back to Mrs. Graves's parties … to pretend to join her cult. I ran into her secretary at college, before I'd moved out, and swallowed my pride and asked him to get me another invitation. I haven't … I'm not involved in any serious way, I—I don't make a secret of my disbelief, and I think they look on me as a sort of project. But I offered to make verse translations of the hymns from the manuscript, so that they could sing them, or chant them, or something. Gallagher's translations are prose.

"Anyway, Peachy came with me a couple of times—three … four times, I think. He didn't know what I was doing there—at least, I never told him and neither did Harriet, but I suppose he might have guessed. It was Harriet's idea that he should come with me—she didn't like that I went by myself. I tried to talk him out of it after the first time. I didn't think it was … I didn't think it was good for him. I can't really explain it—I don't think he was drawn in, or starting to believe any of it, or anything like that, but … he was sort of fascinated, I think. Repelled and fascinated at the same time. He came a second time, and then I'm afraid Mrs. Graves had found out that he wrote music, and started trying to convince him to set my translations of the hymns. As far as I know she never succeeded—he claimed to object to it on musical grounds, but I think his real objection would have been theological."

Mr. Underhill nodded. "That all makes sense. Peachy said something that … I think he was talking about one of Mrs. Graves's parties, but I didn't know it at the time. I didn't know you had been forced to give up your studies, either, and I'm very sorry to hear it. I didn't mean to sound unsympathetic. I knew you weren't living in college any more—I … remembered the phone exchange for your dorm. And the other day when I phoned, a man answered. That's why I was hanging around. I thought there was at least an outside chance you might like someone to walk you home."

"That was very nice of you." And it was nice of him to refrain from commenting on her involvement with Mrs. Graves. She had been dreading the revelation.

Or maybe he was just preoccupied. "I'm afraid," he said, "that what you've just told me may be quite relevant. Peachy's employer showed me some papers he'd found … There was this weird diagram—something about the 'Pure Plain' and souls *re-enfleshing* themselves." He spoke with extreme distaste.

She nodded. "That's the *Bibliotheka* all right. At least, it's an embellishment on the *Bibliotheka*—there aren't any diagrams in the manuscript, but the cult has lots of them. And rituals—there's this thing they do with a candle, that's not in the manuscript either. So he was … involved somehow. I hadn't realized that."

"Neither had I."

They sat in silence for a little while, each of them (she supposed) digesting the unwelcome information they had just received. She studied his profile out of the corner of her eye. It was nice, but not his best feature; he was handsomer viewed straight on. There was perhaps something allegorical in that.

"So what do we actually know, then?" she said, rousing herself with a start. "We ought to be systematic about this. The last time anyone saw Peachy was March 12, correct?"

"Not quite. That was a Friday. His parents saw him last on the Sunday after that—I haven't seen him since the previous Thursday, when he turned down the Mattins job."

"No, but hang on—Harriet must have got that mixed up. If March 12 was a Friday, that was the day I was at the restaurant with them, when they quarrelled. And Harriet saw him after that, when he broke the engagement."

"That was shortly after, wasn't it?"

She nodded. "A couple of days later. Then a week after that he wrote a letter telling her he was leaving her for another woman, or *had* left her for another woman, or something. He told his parents he was moving in with you. He told his boss … well, he didn't tell him anything, but he gave him the impression that he was involved in something occult, which turns out to be Mrs. Graves's salon. That part seems to be true—whereas what he told his parents was an absolute lie. Suppose, for the sake of symmetry, we assume that what he told Harriet was somewhere in between: It doesn't mean quite what she thinks it means, but it's not completely untrue, either. Suppose there is some other woman—someone from the salon—and he's done something that makes him feel responsible for her. Her jealous husband saw them talking and threatened to kill her, say, and now he's promised to help her escape from him. Something like that. He doesn't want to get Harriet mixed up in it, whatever it is, and so he decides he has to break it off with her."

"That sounds like something he would do."

"It does, doesn't it? He didn't tell you about it, either, because you would have tried to talk some sense into him—or because he's trying to protect you too. But none of this quite answers the question of *where he is.* I wonder … ”

“Yes?” he said.

“I wonder if it isn’t somehow … ”

“What?”

“The Pure Plain.”

He looked at her for a moment. “You do recall that there’s no such thing.”

“Yes, obviously. Metaphysically, there’s no such thing. But I think that physically, there could be something … Several people at the salons have described very similar experiences—at least, when you strip away the mystical embellishments, they sound basically similar. I couldn’t help wondering if they don’t have an actual place where they take them.”

“Oh, I see.”

“Were you worried for a moment that I believed in it?”

“No.”

“Well, I don’t. Let’s be quite clear about that, just so that we know where we stand. I do not for one moment believe that there is anything supernatural about Mrs. Graves’s cult.”

“Truly, it didn’t cross my mind that you would. This is our stop.”

They got down from the streetcar and crossed the street to wait for another.

“Look here,” said Mr. Underhill, “I don’t want you to think … I mean, I do believe that you are suffering. I didn’t mean to suggest that just because working in a shop isn’t prostitution and slave labour, it mightn’t be really wretched for you. Or that I think you’re wrong to be unhappy about it.”

“No? But you made a good point—I didn’t actually give Gallagher what he wanted. I suppose I should take some satisfaction in that.”

“I don’t know,” he said thoughtfully. “It’s a kind of negative thing to take satisfaction in. After all, he did you more harm than you did him.”

“Do you think so?”

"I think so. He's prevented you, at least for the time being, from pursuing the work that you … that would make you happy. All you've done to him is put him through a spot of unrequited love."

"And that's not a species of exquisite torment?"

"Oh, rot."

"Well, don't forget that I have every intention of destroying his career, too."

He looked at her gravely. "I think I *had* forgotten."

"You're going to tell me not to!"

"No … But I'd tell you to ask yourself *why* you're going to do that. Would it be for the sake of revenge, or for the sake of telling the truth about the manuscript?"

"Couldn't it be both?"

"Oh, I absolutely believe that it could be both, that it probably is both. But if it is, you know you shouldn't do it."

"I don't know anything of the sort," she said, and that wasn't true.

They stood for some time in silence. She was bitterly angry with someone, but she wasn't sure that it was him.

"You were the one who told me I shouldn't let it go," she said at last.

"I know," he said ruefully. "But not because I thought you should get revenge on Gallagher."

"You do realize you've taken away my one comfort."

"Well, sort of. I've pointed out that your idea of comfort was wrong, according to a scheme of morality that may matter only to me. Whether you care about that or not is actually your affair." After a moment he added: "Obviously I hope and assume that you do. So … I am sorry."

He leaned out from the curb to look for the streetcar which was clearly not there. He turned back with a look as though he wanted to say something but had thought better of it. What he finally did say was, "It's not very far—would you rather walk?"

She set off so briskly that he had almost to run to catch up.

Chapter Ten

LET ME NEVER BE CONFOUNDED

K it dug his hands deeper into his pockets and tried desperately to think of a way to rescue the conversation without seeming to patronize her. Oddly, he thought of his father, who could be diverted from almost any grievance by a question about his research. Kit had seen his mother do it many times.

"You said you were sure the manuscript is a fake," he offered.

She smiled across at him as though she had seen the whole train of thought, complete with his childhood memories of his mother managing his father. He smiled readily back.

"I am," she said. "The weak link in the whole thing is the poetry. I had a … an intuition that it would be—that's why I offered to translate the hymns. Poetry is not really Gallagher's strong suit. He deals with it competently, but I don't think he has a poetic imagination. Most of the poetry in the *Bibliotheka* he didn't write himself. He was clever about this in his edition, of course, 'finding' the sources and analogues for most of the hymns, and then positing that the bad ones that he probably did write are 'very ancient.' Actually, there are little inconsistencies all through them. For instance, they use Homeric epithets, which makes them seem early, and some archaic grammar, but the meter also depends on a lot of words and constructions that are uncommon until much later. Well, you could explain all that away as deliberate archaizing by some Hellenistic poet.

"But he made one real mistake. He copied one of the later hymns from a published edition, and he included a conjectural emendation for an illegible line—that is, a line that was illegible in the only manuscript of the hymn known at the time that edition was published. That wouldn't necessarily be a problem—because, after all, the emendation could have been quite correct. Only it turns out that it wasn't. You see, another manuscript of the poem turned up and was published only last year, and the correct reading of the line is something quite different. So the only way someone could have got the version of the poem that's in the *Bibliotheka* is by copying it from Freiburg's 1885 edition in *Philologus*. Do you see?"

"Sort of."

"Well, trust me that it was a serious slip. Of course it was very sloppy of him to copy the emended line—he would have been much safer to have made up an entirely new line, then he could plausibly have claimed it was just a variant version. Probably he did the forgery before the new edition came out, and he may since have realized what he did wrong. I expect he has—he must have found the new version of the poem when he was preparing the notes for his edition. In other respects, it's a brilliant forgery. At least, as far as I'm able to tell. Obviously I'm only a student of literature … I don't know what an expert codicologist would say about the manuscript. It looks very convincing to me, and there's a convincing story about how it was found. Mrs. Graves was there, in fact. I have no idea how he managed that part."

But you've spent a lot of time thinking about it. And there was something disquieting in that. Kit wondered how truly displeased Gallagher would have been to learn that she had spent so long poring over his work, and could even express admiration for the skill with which he had fabricated it.

"Does he … do you think Gallagher knows that you have been going to Mrs. Graves's parties?"

"Oh—yes, he knows. He's given Mrs. Graves letters for me. She talks to him, of course—in fact, I think from the way she carries on that she's in love with him, although she claims not."

"Perhaps that's how he managed the finding of the manuscript," said Kit. "Do you think?"

"You mean that she's lying for him? Yes, I've thought of that. But it's not as if she found it on her own—she was with an archaeological team."

They arrived at the big, sad-looking grey house in which Peachy lived these days.

"What do we do now?" Miss Nordqvist asked in a whisper as they climbed the cracked and dirty steps to the door.

"Well, there's a drainpipe around the back," said Kit as he rang the bell with the faded word "Landlady" scrawled beside it. Miss Nordqvist looked at him with raised eyebrows.

"We're not going to waltz in and ask the landlady for the key to his room, are we?" she said archly.

"I thought we'd give it a try."

"Do you have some kind of plausible story for why we need it, at least?"

"I think so."

Mrs. O'Reilly answered the door in a cheap evening dress and threadbare bedroom slippers, an unlit cigarette in her hand.

"You're lucky you caught me, Father," she said, leaning in the doorway. "I've just got in. Something I can do for you?"

"We're friends of Peverell Peacham's," said Kit.

"Yes, I've seen you around." She looked Miss Nordqvist over appraisingly, and Kit felt a ridiculous impulse to defend Miss Nordqvist against whatever it was she might be imagining about her.

"Well, we're worried about Mr. Peacham," he said. "He hasn't been returning our phone calls, and neither his parents nor his fiancée have seen him in some time."

Mrs. O'Reilly considered for a moment, absent-mindedly tried to take a drag on the unlit cigarette, and then thought better of it. "I haven't seen him in a while myself, but there's nothing mysterious in that."

"No, I suppose not," said Kit. He found a box of matches in his pocket, struck one and offered the flame to Mrs. O'Reilly. "Actually, we were hoping you could let us into his room. We're afraid he might have become involved with some dangerous people, and we hoped we might find a clue as to where he's gone."

"Oh! Why didn't you say so at first, Father? If you think it would help. I'll get my keys."

When she was gone, Miss Nordqvist looked at him.

"So your 'plausible story' was just the truth."

"I'm surprised that you're surprised," he said loftily.

"I didn't say I was surprised. I'm glad it worked."

"Naturally it worked." He grinned.

"I see your plan to give up smoking hasn't been an unqualified success."

"Oh, but it has. I haven't had a cigarette since Ash Wednesday."

"What are the matches for?"

"Candles. Honestly."

They followed Mrs. O'Reilly up the filthily carpeted stairs and waited on the ill-lit landing while she found the key to Peachy's room. Accordion music and loud voices penetrated to the landing from somewhere above them. A door slammed below and footsteps pounded down the stairs.

"There you are," said the landlady, opening the door and stepping aside. She separated Peachy's key from the bunch. "Just lock up after yourselves and bring back the key, if you'd be so good."

"We can't thank you enough," said Kit.

Miss Nordqvist preceded him into the room. He switched on the light, and the chaos of the floor and furniture sprang vividly into view. There was sheet music on the bed, blown around over the rumpled sheets by the breeze from the wide-open window, and the room looked smaller without the piano in it.

"Is it … it isn't normally like this," Miss Nordqvist said. "Is it?"

Kit hung his hat automatically on a knob of the bedstead and considered the question. "There used to be a piano against the wall there, and a lot of this stuff was on top of the piano. Otherwise … yes, it's pretty much as normal."

"Oh, that's good. I mean, it looks like it could be the result of some cataclysm, but if it's how he normally lived, that's a good sign."

"When you put it like that, yes."

"You're tidier, I suppose," she said, looking at him.

He shrugged. "Marginally, I guess." He was much tidier, in fact, but for some reason he felt ashamed to say so. He had never been bothered by Peachy's mess.

Miss Nordqvist took off her coat and hat and hung them on the doorknob. She stood in the middle of the room, hands on her hips. He was distracted for a moment by the way her short hair curved around her face, and her dress skimmed and clung to her slender figure. Her eyes were delicately outlined with kohl. She could not have made much money as a shop clerk, he thought, but she had obviously chosen to spend her wages on making herself look lovely. Maybe it made her feel better, too. He could not say that he disapproved.

"What is it we're looking for, Mr. Underhill?" she asked. "Now that we know Mr. Peacham isn't lying dead on the floor, what is it we're most hoping not to find here?"

"I suppose … a perfumed letter in an unfamiliar hand, setting a time for an elopement?"

"Indeed. Or a demand for immediate repayment of a large sum, affixed to the wall with an Oriental dagger?"

"I suppose after what you've told me about Peachy's dealings with this cult, what I am most hoping we won't find is a pentagram painted on the floor in blood."

She laughed, then after a moment looked at him seriously.

"Really?" There was a touch of scorn in her voice which was unattractive. "You think Mr. Peacham has disappeared because he was dabbling in the Black Arts?"

"I think it's more or less a possibility."

"You do, do you?" The scorn had become more pronounced. It seemed unlike her, as if she were playing a part. "This is the sort of logic I am to expect from you."

"There's nothing wrong with it as logic," he said tartly. "He has disappeared; he evinced an interest in some half-baked occult non-sense before he disappeared. It's logical to suppose a connection. I'm not saying I think he's been bodily snatched away by the Devil."

"Oh, you're not. Good."

"That doesn't happen."

"I know that."

He thought half-heartedly of making some kind of joke about how they had found one metaphysical point about which they could agree, but he found he was too much annoyed with her. He pushed a heap of Peachy's clothes out of the way with the toe of his shoe and knelt to pull open the bottom drawer of the rickety dresser by the head of the bed.

"I've seen him put papers away in here," he said. "This is where I'd expect to find the perfumed letter."

He dug under several layers of gaudy waistcoats, perfunctorily folded, and pulled out everything he could find underneath. It did not amount to much. There was a diary with half a dozen entries at the beginning; a couple of unfinished letters in Peachy's hand, all with dates from last year; a long list headed "To Read," with only two items checked off; and another headed "General Improvements," on which Kit caught his own name as part of an unchecked but mercifully illegible item. Behind him, he was aware of Miss Nordqvist kneeling down—the hem of her short skirt brushing the floor—to pick up the statuette of Mary that used to stand on top of Peachy's piano. When he turned around she was kneeling there, studying it with apparent amusement.

"Nothing in there?" she asked, looking up. "No pentagrams or consecrated hosts or anything?"

"Not that I could find."

"Well, there are a lot of papers mixed in with his books up there," she said, gesturing to the shelf that had formerly hung above the piano. "I'll let you look at them—it seems less of an invasion."

He went to the shelf and began pulling out the papers that were shoved haphazardly in between the volumes.

"How are you as a palaeographer?" he asked Miss Nordqvist, who had taken a seat on the edge of Peachy's bed. He passed her a sheaf of particularly fevered scribbles. "I'm pretty sure it's nothing terribly private—it looks as though it might be notes for an opera."

"Impressive. Though not much worse than one would expect from the occupant of this room."

He began to recognize Harriet's writing among the items he pulled off the shelf, mostly in short notes that he had to make an effort not to read. Because the effort was not entirely successful, he gained a pleasing impression of her as an unsentimental and businesslike correspondent, even with her fiancé. There were also a couple of longer letters in her distinctive bold, looping hand.

"It seems to be a sort of Faust story," Miss Nordqvist said. "The opera. It's about a librarian who discovers a forbidden volume and sells his soul to the devil for the sake of … something he hasn't quite decided yet—Peachy hasn't decided yet, I mean, not the librarian. He's got several alternatives here with question marks: *Love? Beautiful woman? Knowledge?* 'Knowledge' is circled a couple of times, so that may be it. Very Faustian. There are also some marginal notes that say 'ravings' and 'doesn't make sense'—being a little hard on himself, but I suppose that's Peachy."

"It must be a new project I haven't heard about. Or an old one that died before it saw the light of day. I found these." He passed her the longer letters from Harriet. "I don't know if you feel our investigations should extend to reading them."

She held them still folded for a moment, biting her lower lip doubtfully.

"It would be easier, wouldn't it, if one's friends told one every-thing—if one could feel sure of that." She unfolded one of the letters. "This one is from last year. I think we can leave that alone." She set it aside and unfolded the second. "This is from just the other week." After a moment she set it down too and looked up. "I didn't know he broke up with Harriet in a *letter*."

"Did he?"

"It seems that way. That is the one she wrote him in response. I can't read it, of course, and I expect it wouldn't tell me any more than we already know—but why would he have done something like that in writing? Is he really … "

"So cowardly? Maybe. I'm not sure I would be able to face Miss Spencer with something like that myself. But he also wrote a note to his parents when it would have made more sense for him to telephone—or just to drop by the house. I remember thinking that was odd."

"So there's some other reason. He's gone somewhere. I don't sup-pose we could ask either Harriet or his parents about the postmarks on those letters without arousing suspicion."

"I don't suppose there is anything suspicious about the postmarks, or we'd have heard about it already. In fact, my impression was that the note to his parents wasn't posted, just left at the house. Come to think of it, the last communication I had with him was a note shoved in my mailbox. Here—you might as well help me look through this stuff. Peachy wouldn't mind. He has a high opinion of you."

"He does?"

"Mm."

He offered her a stack of odds and ends culled from the bookshelf. She had moved over on the bed, shifting some of the sheet music out of the way, unselfconsciously making room for him to sit down beside her. He hesitated, but there was nowhere else to sit in the room, the lone chair being filled, as always, with clutter, and the piano stool gone. He sat down on the bed, as close to the foot as he could manage without seeming absurd.

"He was composing something," she said, holding up some sheet music.

"He's always composing something. Just never from start to finish."

"This one seems like something you'd like. It's Latin—it's a hymn or something. I suppose I ought to know it, but my knowledge of this sort of thing is lacking. 'We praise you, God; we acknowledge you as Lord. You, Father Eternal, all the Earth worships. To you all angels … ' " She looked up at him. "You get the general idea."

"It's the *Te Deum*. Has he set all of it? How does it end?"

She turned over the pages of Peachy's notation. "*In te, Domine, speravi: non confundar in aeternum.*"

"'Let me never be confounded'?"

"Very good."

"Not my own translation."

"It's got all the parts for the choir, too. At least it looks like it to me. He seems to have finished it." She handed the pages to him. "I have a feeling, Mr. Underhill, that it's for you."

He looked through the pages, but the musical notation was little easier for him to decipher than the Latin. Peachy could look at sheet music and sing it for you at sight, the way Elsa Nordqvist could translate Greek (and Latin). Kit could only tell that it was a short, simple setting. He assumed that it was beautiful. He could have picked out the parts on the piano, but the piano was gone.

"It's one of the anthems from Mattins," he said.

She went back to sifting through the papers. He sat looking at the pages of music. Peachy's handwriting was terrible, barely decipherable, but he wrote musical notation almost tidily. Kit folded the pages carefully and put them into a pocket of his cassock.

"This might be relevant," he said, smoothing out a letter on thick blue stationery. "*My dearest Peverell*—this is not in Harriet's hand, by the way—*My dearest Peverell, A thousand thanks again for last night. I wish that I could write you the letter of pure friendship and gratitude that you deserve, but I am so frightened. I must beg you to come to me again, to help me get free from him. I know it is possible, just not in the way you imagine. The secret is in the Pure Plain. If you would only descend, just once, I know you would understand and would find the way to defeat him and free me. You understand and believe so much; why will you not believe this? I enclose the map which I showed to you before, in hopes that it will bring you to a better understanding of how you can help me.* And it's signed *Your grateful Anastasiya.*"

"That's Mrs. Graves."

"Yes, I thought it might be. Anastasiya Graves? That's quite a name." He remembered Peachy mentioning someone named Anastasiya.

"Isn't it? I don't think any part of it is her real one. But that's precisely what we were hoping not to find, isn't it? I mean, it's not perfumed, and it's not exactly a pentagram, but he was in deep with the cult, and there was another woman. At least Mrs. Graves is too old for his remark about having to stand by her to mean what Harriet thought it meant."

"I suppose that is a relief. Though I can't help thinking that what *has* happened—whatever that is—sounds a good deal less natural and more sinister."

She was silent for a few moments. "I never asked Harriet this, but had Peachy … for instance … been engaged before?"

He considered what this question was actually asking, and whether he could answer it frankly.

"He never even had what you could call a best girl," he said finally. "Unrequited love-from-afar was his speciality. He swooned and pined his way through undergrad, and then he calmed down for a while, and for a couple of years he became quite serious about a divorced older woman who was just sort of amused by him, and strung him along, and he kept making excuses for her—she's been hurt, she needs time, that sort of thing. There was never anything …

anything official between them, though I'm pretty sure they weren't just chums."

"Mm-hm."

"Yeah. He was the one who eventually saw that there was no future in it and stopped seeing her, but that left him very low for a while, and there really wasn't anyone much after that until Harriet. At least not as far as I know—and before this evening I would have told you that if there were anyone, I would have known. I still think that's true … But I have to admit that Harriet Spencer represented a real departure for Peachy. Mrs. Graves … Mrs. Graves is much more his type."

Miss Nordqvist nodded. "Do you know, I thought somehow that she might be. I don't see it myself—I suppose I wouldn't—but a lot of the men in the cult seem drawn to her, one way or another. I think she gives them the impression that she needs protecting."

"And do you think it's entirely false?" He had to admit that the pleading in her letter had given him pause.

She snorted. "What would she need protecting from? I think everything about her is entirely false, if you really want the truth. But that's just my feminine intuition again, and I daresay you're sick of hearing about that."

I don't think that's what it is, and I love hearing about it. He said nothing.

"What about the map that she says she included with the letter? I suppose that's the thing you found at the shop."

"Yes. Though there's also this. It was folded up with the letter." He held it out, feeling the same reluctance to touch it as he had about the diagram in Doughty's shop.

It was a typed page headed "Protocols for the Pure Offering."

"It's an incantation or something," she said, taking it from him. "'I offer up this pure soul …' Somebody else's soul, I take it, not one's own. A sacrificial virgin by the sound of it. How tedious. And, for that matter, how strange. There's nothing like this in the *Bibliotheka*."

"Well, naturally. They're making it up as they go along. Any half-baked supernatural nonsense they come across gets tossed in."

She looked at him humorously. "Do you know, I get the impression that what offends you most about this is not so much that it's evil as that it's lacking in theological rigour."

"I make no attempt to deny that. I like my supernatural nonsense to be very well thought out."

"There is quite a bit in Book 10 about how the pure soul can be manipulated by the Orphic initiate. I suppose this must be an extension of that. Here's something a bit more concrete, though" she said, setting the repellent "Pure Offering" page casually aside and picking up a folded pamphlet. "On the back of this theatre program—it looks like a note of an appointment, and it's for—well, it's for tonight, actually. *Purists' Meeting—8:00, Friday 26th, Hart House.* The play was on March 19 of this year—last Friday—so the 26th must be tonight. It's not in Peachy's hand … That's funny, though. It does look familiar."

He leaned over to look at the paper in her hand, and at the same moment she leaned back, and her white shoulder almost touched his sleeve, and he felt suddenly sick with desire. He also became abruptly conscious that their situation was inappropriate. Mrs. O'Reilly hadn't batted an eye, certainly, but that didn't signify; Mrs. O'Reilly ran a boarding-house where tenants routinely came home drunk and entertained their mistresses in their rooms.

"That looks like Mrs. Graves's handwriting," Kit said when he could concentrate on the note at all. "Here, see for yourself."

He handed her the blue letter and stood up, inadvertently dumping all the papers in his lap onto the floor. This required him to kneel at Miss Nordqvist's feet and gather them up. He tried to think of a way to introduce the idea of taking her home. He still did not know where she lived.

"Peachy!" boomed a voice from the landing, while Kit was still kneeling on the floor. "Ah! Not Peachy." A tousled head leaned in at the door, and the wild eyes of Watson the poet scanned the room. "Where is Peachy?"

"We wish we knew," said Kit, dropping some of the papers he had just picked up. "He seems to be missing. I don't suppose … "

"Missing? Peachy?" Watson seemed skeptical. "I expect he will turn up alive. I can't believe that he has enemies, not Peachy. By the way, Kit, I must thank you again for your help the other day. So kind of you, really it was. My publisher said he received the pages in time. I am most grateful. Most grateful. I'll have to do something to repay you. I don't suppose that you drink."

"No no—please think nothing of it."

"Did you just tell that man that you don't drink?" Miss Nordqvist asked when Watson had departed.

"I wouldn't risk drinking anything he had to offer—bathtub absinthe, for all I know."

"Ah. What did you do for him?"

"Absolutely nothing. At least, I have no idea what he was talking about. Not that I usually do know what Watson is talking about." He had finished gathering up the papers, but somehow he remained on the floor. "So does the handwriting match?"

"Oh. Yes, it's the same handwriting, all right. It's just that I was noticing something else. Either Mrs. Graves didn't write these things, or … or she did, and she wrote some other things, too. I don't know which would be worse—but, come to think of it, I do know which is more likely."

"I'm not sure I follow."

"No, of course not. I told you that Mrs. Graves gave me some letters—at different times—purporting to be from Arthur Gallagher. Pleading for my affection and so on. Only I think, looking at this, that she wrote them herself. The handwriting is basically the same."

"I see. Or … Arthur Gallagher wrote letters to Peachy pretending to be Mrs. Graves?"

"Which doesn't make any sense—he's never met Peachy and has

nothing to do with him. That Mrs. Graves would write fake letters from Gallagher … Well, it doesn't make a lot of sense, either, but she was terribly keen for me to make it up with him, for some reason. And the letters were … not suspicious, certainly, but some of them showed more humility than I expected from Gallagher."

"Have you seen anything," he said, trying hard to dismiss the implications of this last statement from his mind, "that you know was in Gallagher's hand?"

"I'm sure I must have—he was my professor. Yes, last year I saw some of his handwritten notes on the *Bibliotheka* … and certainly when I read his letters I didn't think that the handwriting was wrong, but then I don't know that I was paying particular attention to that."

"And you have only his word for it that they were *his* notes, I suppose, anyway."

"They can't have been Mrs. Graves's notes—she doesn't even read Greek. She's always moaning about it."

"So what do you make of this, then?"

"I wish I knew. One thing is clear, though. We ought to go to Hart House and find out what this 'Purists' meeting is about. Oughtn't we?"

"No. It's late—you can't go in there, and I can't leave you waiting outside unattended."

"It isn't that late. Besides, I'm not afraid of these people, if that's what you're thinking. I'm not worried about being made an offering of," she said amiably. "Apparently they only want virgins."

"Splendid. One of us has nothing to worry about."

It was one of those things that he didn't realize he was going to say until he had said it. And it was only after that, looking down at him (he was still at her feet), that she blushed. As far as he could tell, he didn't, though he couldn't imagine why. There was an absurd silence during which they avoided each other's eyes.

"One could hope," he said, getting up from the floor more awkwardly than he would have liked, "that 'purity' in this case might

271

mean something more than 'sexual inexperience.' But I don't suppose it does."

"Why would one hope that?"

"Oh, because there are more insidious and significant ways of being impure, I suppose." He didn't think "pure" was a particularly good word for himself. He neatened the bundle of papers he was holding, and dumped it back on top of Peachy's books. "But I don't somehow think that these people would recognize that. They seem unsubtle."

She was looking down at the floor, but she raised her eyes to him now. "If we're not going to the campus tonight, what do you think we should do?"

"I think we should go home."

"Oh."

"I don't think we can accomplish anything more tonight."

"Are you sure you don't mean that you think *I* should go home, and *you* should go to Hart House?"

"I'm sure I don't mean that. I have every intention of escorting you home—if you'll tell me where you live."

"Huron Street. Number 160. I've obviously got no inhibitions about telling you things. I'm not sure why you'd think I'd balk at my address. The building's the 'Lloyd George Apartments'—it's quite a lot nicer than this place."

"I should hope."

"Yes, I suppose I have a veneer of respectability, don't I?"

She rose from the bed and retrieved her coat and hat from the door.

"I'm sorry, Mr. Underhill," she said. "I feel responsible for Peachy's getting mixed up with these people, but of course that doesn't mean I get to salve my conscience by making a nuisance of myself trying to help. If you think I ought to go home, I will go home. I mean I'll let you take me home. We could walk down to College and take the westbound streetcar, and that would drop me almost at my door."

"Yes," he said. "I think I know the apartment house. It's down the street from my old church."

They returned the key to Mrs. O'Reilly and walked out into the night.

"The reason why you're not worried about being … sacrificed by the cultists," he began.

She looked up, ready to laugh at him, or at herself. "Yes?"

"I was wondering whether it was recent, or … or not. I'm being—I'm trying to be—pastoral, by the way, not prurient."

She smiled warmly instead of laughing. "Thanks. I suppose if I hadn't wanted to tell you about it I shouldn't have said anything. It was a long time ago. When I was sixteen. I had a boyfriend named Francis, of whom my father disapproved. He was a teacher—a very young teacher, only a few years older than me, and not *my* teacher. He taught History at the Catholic high school—hence, in part, my father's disapproval. He was unconventional, and I admired him for that. I had lost my faith not long before this, and I thought of him as a kindred spirit because he too struggled with disbelief—but he had lived with it for longer than I, and had clever things to say about it. He was experienced already when we became lovers—and he was very sweet, and it was, honestly, one of the best things I've known."

She said all this without belligerence or self-righteousness, but without reluctance either—just telling him.

"I miss it," she said. Not *him*. It. "We would meet in secret … we didn't think—even I at sixteen didn't think—that we had any real future together. It lasted about a year, and he left to move to New York, and there was never any real discussion about whether I might come with him—neither of us really thought it would be a good idea, although we *had* loved each other. It was just clear to us that we had different paths to travel. I thought I would go on to have other lovers … I thought once you crossed that bridge, it would happen quite naturally. But somehow it didn't happen. It hasn't happened yet, I mean. Once or twice I have almost—have at least made private plans to go to bed with a man, but, when it came down to it, realized it wasn't what I wanted. There was no genuine affection, as there had been between me and Francis, and without that, it's … I think you'd regret it afterward."

"I expect that's true," Kit said. And after a long silence: "I don't think I have anything wise or relevant to say about that. I'm sorry."

"That's all right," she said, smiling slightly. "I think … that may be part of why I gave up on marriage. I thought that if I couldn't even find a man I was willing to take as a lover, it wasn't likely I'd ever find one for whom it was worth giving up my freedom and my ambitions."

"I suppose that makes sense," he said sadly.

He was glad she had told him the story about her lover after they had left the intimacy of Peachy's room. It ought to have cooled his desire, but it had had the opposite effect; it gave her a new and uncomfortable fascination for him. She had known—she had grown to adulthood knowing—the pleasure of mutually satisfying sex. But he had always thought of her as a woman who knew a great deal more than he did. That had always been part of her attraction.

They reached College, and waited in silence for the streetcar. It was by now nearly nine o'clock, and the car was a while in coming. Miss Nordqvist buttoned her coat over her black dress and looked cold.

"Does it change your opinion of me?" she said suddenly.

"Only a very little."

She tipped her head to one side consideringly. "What does that mean?"

"I knew that you were set against marriage, but I never supposed you were particularly interested in chastity as an alternative. I thought that might be a purely ideological stance, but it doesn't surprise me very much to know that it isn't. You lived according to your convictions."

"I did, I suppose—I don't now."

"Maybe that's prudent, though. My mother had similar convictions and lived by them, and I know it wasn't particularly easy."

"I think you may just have made a convincing case for why I should have a lover."

"Did I? Bother."

She smiled at him, and the streetcar came. They climbed up into its light and warmth.

"Good evening, Father!" said a familiar voice. He looked down the half-empty car and saw Mrs. Barrington.

They had no choice but to sit next to her, since there were vacant seats, and he introduced the two women. Of all of the people from St. John's that they might have encountered on a Friday night on the streetcar, Mrs. Barrington was by no means the worst. Kit quite liked her. She was a widow in her sixties, from Yorkshire, had been married to a sea captain or something, and been very sanguine about it, like the woman in *Persuasion*. She had come to Toronto after his death, with her son, and lent her stately presence to many local charities and committees. She was now explaining that she was taking the streetcar home from a friend's house because her car was in the garage. It gave her a certain grandeur in the parish, the fact that she owned her own car.

"And how do you come to know Father Underhill?" she asked Miss Nordqvist.

"We have mutual friends," said Miss Nordqvist.

"Her best friend and mine were engaged to be married until recently," said Kit. Miss Nordqvist looked up at him doubtfully, but he went on with the story: Peachy's mysterious breaking of the engagement; Miss Nordqvist's quite natural suggestion that the two of them should do something to help; their mounting concern that something had actually happened to Peachy; their chance meeting tonight; and finally their visit to his apartment. By the end of it, Miss Nordqvist was clearly waiting with confidence for this disastrous and bizarre gambit to explode in his face.

"And did you find anything in the apartment?" Mrs. Barrington asked, directing the question to both of them. "Or are you now in search of further clues?"

Miss Nordqvist could not prevent her eyebrows from rising, but she managed to avoid actually saying, "Don't tell me you believe all that!"

"We found a lot of odd things," said Kit, "but nothing to quite explain where my friend has gone, or why."

"We did find one thing," said Miss Nordqvist, with a sudden mischievousness which was probably obvious only to Kit. "It was a note of an appointment made for this evening, at a place not far from here. But M–Mr. Underhill feels that it would be better for him to take me home rather than continuing to investigate."

"And very properly he feels that, I am sure," said Mrs. Barrington. "All the same, it may be a matter of your friend's safety, might it not? Have you informed the police of his disappearance?"

"He seems to have made himself scarce on purpose," said Kit. "I'm not sure it's a police matter."

Mrs. Barrington nodded. "Yes, I quite see. But are you sure, Father, that it would not be a good idea to look for your friend at this appointment which you say he has made? If he is not genuinely missing, it seems likely that he would keep it."

"You make a good point," Kit admitted.

"Where is the place?"

"Hart House—it's on the university campus. Women aren't allowed in," Miss Nordqvist explained. "And Mr. Underhill doesn't wish to leave me waiting outside by myself—"

"Quite properly! But it is on our way. We may stop there easily. I say 'we' because I would be happy to accompany you. There is no one waiting up for me. It would of course be as well not to lose any time, Father—you should not, for instance, take Miss Northquest home first, and then go to the university, as your friend might well be gone by then."

There was a certain amount of "But we couldn't think of inconveniencing you," and "If you're sure you don't mind," and "Nonsense, it's no trouble at all!" after this, but the thing was basically settled. This was Mrs. Barrington all over.

*

He left Mrs. Barrington and Miss Nordqvist on a bench outside Hart House, went up the flight of granite stairs inside, and asked the porter at the top for the meeting of Purists. He had to resist an impulse to add, "Also, who was fed with the Grail?" He felt as if he were on a slightly suspect quest, though maybe that was just the Gothic architecture. He was told that the Purists were meeting in the Music Room. He went upstairs and turned the wrong way down the quiet stone corridor, turned back, and finally found it. Through the glass panes of the door, he could see that the meeting was in progress. He eased the door open and slipped through. He knew as soon as he got the door shut behind him that his uneasiness had, somehow, been well founded. There was an oppressive atmosphere, more like a hospital waiting-room than a party.

There were perhaps a dozen men in the room, and, he noticed after a moment, a couple of women. One, a dark-eyed girl in an ill-fitting man's suit, looked around nervously at his entrance. Several of the men gave him puzzled looks, but no one asked who he was or challenged his right to be there. They were busy listening to the address of a man who sat near the fireplace, facing into the room.

"And we have found," he was saying, "that by bringing two, three, or even more, the effects may be doubled, tripled, and so on. It is of course not easy, but the rewards are significant."

Kit turned to a man near the door, and said in an undertone, "I'm looking for someone named Peacham. Peverell Peacham?"

The man laughed, rather mirthlessly. "Very funny. What are you dressed up like that for?"

"It annoys the bishop, and I think it's rather smart. I take it Mr. Peacham isn't here?"

The man shrugged and turned away from him. Kit scanned the room; Peachy was certainly not present.

"But you yourself have not seen fit to make the change," a member of the audience was challenging the speaker. "Or so you would have us believe."

The leader returned a smile that did not reach his eyes. "I have attained benefits compared to which a mere bodily alteration seems … trivial."

He was a man in his forties, grey-haired and dapper. There was a girl with him, lolling beside him but with an unpleasantly detached air, her clothing a provocative mixture of the demure and the revealing. Her chaste white blouse was unbuttoned over her breasts, her tight grey tweed skirt rucked up past the tops of her stockings. Having noticed her, Kit could not stop looking at her. She looked like Elsa Nordqvist reimagined by someone with poor taste: Elsa before she had cut her hair, and with fuller breasts and shorter, plumper legs. Elsa with horribly vacant blue eyes. (The real Elsa's eyes were a cooler grey, and emphatically tenanted.)

She must have felt Kit's gaze on her, because she looked up and met it, and her eyes were suddenly no longer vacant, only horrible. There was something wrong with her—no, not wrong *with* her, wrong *in* her. *She* was wrong, not only a poor copy but a copy made out of something ghastly. She should be—she should be—

God forgive me! he thought, backing away. To think such a thing about someone, just because she didn't so well satisfy his own irrelevant preferences—*that* was horrible. The poor girl could not possibly be what she had for an instant seemed.

Or perhaps she could. She stood up suddenly, her eyes still fastened on Kit. "Get out!" she cried in a harsh voice, accompanying the words with a violent gesture, a twisting and grabbing with her beautiful hand.

Kit got out. He stood in the hall outside the closed door for a moment, catching his breath, unable to escape the idea that he had just, in some upside-down way, been exorcised.

He had collected himself enough to start back down the passage when the door opened again and someone slipped out. It was a tall, white-haired man, hastily wrapping himself in a shapeless overcoat. Kit recognized him.

"You didn't listen," the man said, his voice a harsh whisper. "I told you not to come."

Kit decided to ignore this as nonsensical. "Professor Hallam," he said. "I didn't see you in there."

"But I saw you, Mr. Peacham."

"Ah, no. Underhill. But close—Peacham and I were always more or less inseparable."

The old man shook his head sadly. "I warned you not to come. Underhill is dead."

"Not this one, no. You're thinking of someone else. MacIntyre, maybe—he was the other one who usually hung out with us. He died in France."

"Do you want to know the truth, Peacham?"

"Underhill—but yes, very much, in general. And in this specific instance, especially."

"I know that you are not really a priest … "

"No? Maybe not from your point of view." He dimly recalled that Hallam might have been a Roman Catholic. He was colloquially—though unfairly, Kit had thought—known as a pagan, on account of his passion for tracing pre-Christian influences in Anglo-Saxon literature.

"So you can't make things right," Hallam continued. "Can you?"

"What things?"

"Everything. My soul. For a moment, when I saw you, I hoped—but of course it isn't true. Still … "

"I'd do what I can—I *will* do what I can, if you'll tell me what the trouble is."

"No … no. But I will tell you the truth. As I promised you. I will show you the book. If you will come with me, I will show you the book."

"That sounds good," said Kit. He felt that the conversation was getting away from him. "I've a couple of women waiting for me at the main entrance—we should just go collect them. Where is this book?"

"Not far. We can walk there. I will take you, but not the women."

"Then it's no go, I'm afraid—I can't just leave them."

The man looked stricken. "But I cannot show them—you cannot expect me to show them the truth. I should not even be speaking to you. He will know … " He glanced back at the door.

"Come along, and let's talk about it outside," Kit suggested.

He shepherded the big man down the hall toward the lobby and the main entrance. He remembered now that Peachy had said he'd seen old Hallam somewhere, and that he was off his rocker. It must have been at one of the cult gatherings that he had seen him. And he had not been exaggerating.

Miss Nordqvist and Mrs. Barrington were sitting on a bench in the porch. They had obviously been talking to pass the time, and had got quickly to the heart of some important subject—which, knowing the two of them, was not at all surprising.

"That," Mrs. Barrington was saying sternly, as Kit and Professor Hallam came through the heavy door into the porch, "is no doubt evidence of a commendable independence of thought. But it is still very wrong."

"Oh look," said Miss Nordqvist. "He's back."

"This is an old professor of mine," Kit explained. "Martin Hallam. I was in his Old English class some years ago."

"Were you?" said Hallam, frowning.

"Ah—yes, but I don't blame you for not particularly remembering. I wasn't a stellar pupil."

He introduced the two women. But of course Hallam had already met Miss Nordqvist.

"I have seen you talking to him," he said, looming over her. "I have seen you carelessly laughing. You are in grave danger."

"Am I? Well, I suppose you are too," she replied coolly.

Kit recalled her saying, "It would be easier if one's friends told one everything." Wouldn't it just?

But Hallam seemed to forget his intention not to bring the women with them now, in his eagerness to get away as quickly as possible.

"He hasn't followed us yet," he said, glancing behind him as they went down the outside steps. "Perhaps he hasn't noticed. Faint hope. He's playing some game. But we may outsmart him yet. Come on, come *on*. It's in the library, not far. He was an assistant librarian—the body that he uses, I mean. He was let go under suspicion of trying to set fire to some of the books, and killed himself. That was in '88."

"And then the library did burn in 1890," said Miss Nordqvist, who was managing to keep up with Hallam's long strides. Kit had fallen back to walk with Mrs. Barrington, who was having to scurry. "Though I suppose that couldn't have been your man, if he'd killed himself already."

"Of course not—of course not," said Hallam impatiently. "Because by then it wasn't *him* any more, only his body. He was trying to destroy the book that started it all, of course—though why he should want to destroy it … No, I know why he did it, all too well. I wouldn't try that—I know better than to try that."

"Is this gentleman … " Mrs. Barrington didn't know how to finish the sentence politely.

"He appears to be very confused," said Kit. "He said he has something important to show me."

A couple of students walked by, chatting on their way home past the War Memorial and under the newly finished Soldiers' Tower. Their voices faded with distance, and Kit caught himself trying to hear them, as though their voices vanishing into the night were somehow important, portentous. He looked up at the tower, gaunt and grey in the moonlight. He hadn't been down here, he realized, since the dedication ceremony.

They passed along under the blackened walls of University College, under the lit street lamps, moving from one pool of light to the next. The third light flickered and went out as Kit passed under it. Ahead of him, Hallam jangled something metallic in his pocket that sounded like more than keys.

They reached the library, cozy and ivy-covered, with a door like a castle or a church. Hallam looked around nervously, then produced a key with which he unlocked the door. For a moment he made no move to open it. Kit and Mrs. Barrington had arrived at the top of the steps.

"Mr. Peacham—"

"Underhill. Yes?"

"You do look very like him," said Hallam, gazing down at Kit. "He was always a pleasant young man, though his translations were frankly haphazard. I believe he did mean to take Holy Orders. But of course he was killed. They were all killed. Underhill, MacIntyre, Stephenson, Phillips, that librarian. Even Miss Peel, the girl that Underhill used to walk out with. All, all dead."

There was an awkward silence. Kit wondered whether to point out that several of the people he had named were alive. Since he was one of them, he doubted it would do any good.

"We lost so many young people," said Mrs. Barrington, with perfect dignity. "It was a very dark time."

Hallam looked at her. "You think that I am talking about the War."

"What else would you be talking about?" Kit retorted, suddenly angry. The thought of being subjected to mad ravings about the deaths of his friends sickened him.

Hallam looked chastened and said nothing more. He opened the door to the library.

"Do you remember the notes about the opera?" Miss Nordqvist whispered to Kit. "Or whatever it was. Ravings? About a librarian?"

"Yes."

"Well? It fits—doesn't it? And I know Peachy had talked with Professor Hallam, at Anastasiya's."

"Yes."

She's enjoying this, he thought. She was having fun trying to work out the mystery. So was Mrs. Barrington—well, he knew that was why she had offered to come along. He wished he could feel the same way.

The library was eerie in the dark, moonlight filtering through the skylights above the circulation desk, furniture bulking dark and unfamiliar in the shadows. In the men's reading room that opened off the lobby it was darker still, and the desks stood in ranks, the reading lamps standing up at attention. Hallam had blundered in among them, bent over, fumbling in the pockets of his shapeless overcoat.

Mrs. Barrington clicked across the floor in brisk little steps and bent to switch on a lamp. The ball of yellow light threw the rest of the room into deeper shadow.

"How do I know that one of you isn't him?" Hallam muttered, edging away from the light. "How do I know? It's her, isn't it? It's been her all along."

Hallam drew his hand out of his pocket, and Kit knew what was in it a moment before he saw it. He ran into the reading room, vaulted over the table between him and Hallam, and grabbed the man's wrist. The gun had come up, was pointed straight at his chest, but he wasn't the one Hallam wanted to shoot.

He twisted Hallam's wrist savagely and yanked the gun out of his hand. With a cry, Hallam lunged for him, and sent Kit spinning backward over the table, taking down a reading lamp—the glass shade and the bulb shattered, and sparks flew. Kit rolled out of the way.

Mrs. Barrington gave an uncharacteristic shriek of alarm, and Miss Nordqvist, from the entrance hall, shouted, "Kit!"

He got to his feet amid the wreckage of the lamp, and released the magazine from the gun. It was a German semi-automatic pistol; he had at one time known the name of it, but it was one of those things he had been happy to forget. Hallam was nursing his wrists and watching him silently from the other side of the table.

"Father, you could have been killed," Mrs. Barrington said in a strangled voice.

"Absolutely. So could you." Kit pulled back the toggle on the top of the pistol to check that there wasn't a cartridge in the chamber. There wasn't; Hallam had obviously not had occasion to fire it lately.

Elsa came into the reading room. "Are you all right?" she asked.

He looked up. "Yes, thanks. And, 'Of course you may.'"

"You're not Peacham at all, are you?" said Hallam, still on the other side of the table. "You *are* Underhill."

Kit glared at him. "Peachy could have done that, too." It was probably not true, but he felt bound to say it.

"What?"

"Yes, I'm Underhill—haven't I been trying to tell you that? No," when Hallam appeared about to come around from behind the desk, "better stay where you are and explain what you were planning to do with this pistol."

"You keep it," said Hallam. "You might want it ... if *he* comes after us. It wouldn't stop him, of course, but it might slow him down a little."

"Slow *who* down?" Kit demanded. He felt a strong desire to get rid of the gun.

The professor shook his head. "I don't know his name. I suppose he had one once, when he was a living person. But he let the Old One in, and He hollowed him out and uses him at His whim." You could pretty well hear the the capital "H." Hallam shuddered. "Uses him, and uses the rest of us through him. He makes us deliver him his victims. He made me send them all to their deaths, all those beautiful young people. Ask her." He looked at Miss Nordqvist. "She knows. She has been there."

"Where?"

"The thing they call the 'Pure Plain.' The mouth of Hell."

Elsa laughed out loud. "I have *not*, professor! And neither have you."

"I've seen you light the candle, and read from the book."

"Yes, and that's all you've seen, because that's all that happened. Even from my point of view. I'm sorry to disappoint, but I never pretended that it worked. That's why they kept getting me to try it over and over."

Kit looked at her. "When were you planning on telling me about this?" he snapped.

She shrugged. "I wasn't. It didn't seem important."

"You participated in their rituals? And that didn't seem important?" He was getting more wound up about this than he liked.

"Look. I've never thought a ritual you didn't believe in would be the slightest use to anyone. *Even* when I was a Christian."

"All right … " He took a deep breath. "That's a defensible theological position. I'm sorry."

Hallam was looking at the two of them as though they were the mad ones, and Mrs. Barrington looked sternly amused. Kit made an effort to calm himself.

In some corner of his mind he knew he shouldn't have told Elsa he was all right. He was not physically hurt. But he had faced, however momentarily, a man with a gun. He still had the stupid gun in his hand. And he knew the pattern. It was going to catch up to him. But he hated that this was what he had been reduced to, and he wasn't going to tell Elsa Nordqvist, of all people.

"Professor," said Mrs. Barrington, in the tone of reproof that had been known to bring even Mr. Oates to heel, "do you in fact have anything useful to show us? Because if not, I really think that we should forget all about this and go home. You have put us through quite enough unpleasantness for one night."

Hallam looked at Kit. "I'll take him—I'll show him."

"That might be the best idea, actually," said Kit. "The two of you can wait for us here. I think you might as well hang onto these, as well." He handed the gun to Mrs. Barrington, and the magazine to Elsa. "We won't be gone long."

"Very good, Father," said Mrs. Barrington, briskly pocketing the gun and switching on another light in the reading room. "Miss Northwest and I will occupy ourselves with cleaning up this mess."

Elsa gave her an incredulous look but said nothing.

Kit followed Hallam down the dim hallway. The professor was still talking, more or less to him.

"I know what it's like to let that power change you," he said. "I've felt it. I tried to do good with it, at first. I thought that here was something real at last, something that would let me be of use. I used it to make myself young, so I could … so I could fight. That was how I thought I could be of use. But it gave me back all my old desires, everything I thought I had conquered, it made me sick with them. In the end, I could do nothing, and you all died. *They* all died, I mean. I do see that you're not dead."

"Sure. And I feel guilty about that sometimes, too," Kit said lightly. Was that all this was? "I'm told that's common. Anyway. Where is this book you said you would show me?"

"I got out—at least part of me got out. I haven't let Him hollow me out like that other, not yet. I'll hold him off as long as I can. You'll help me—I know you will. In here."

They were heading towards the stacks, but Hallam had stopped and held open a door. In the dark, Kit had walked through it before he realized what was on the other side: a tiny, cramped lift.

"Oh—I'll take the stairs, thanks." He turned quickly, putting out a hand to the wall as if he could ward it off. But Hallam had followed him in and drawn closed the gate behind him. The door slammed and Hallam loomed over him in the darkness. Kit's heart had already begun to race.

"We're safer in here," Hallam breathed. "Safe from him."

"I'm sorry, but I—I'm not—I need to get out."

"Why?"

Damned if I'm going to spell it out for you. "Please just let me get out."

"You want to go throw yourself into his arms," said Hallam, half-laughing—entirely crazy. "But I can't let you do that. I have to save you from that."

He had pressed himself back against the gate, so that Kit would have had to drag him out of the way to open it. That would have been a challenge at the best of times. But now …

Panic was rising in him like the incoming tide, clutching at his chest, draining the warmth from his limbs. His hands were shaking, and he felt sick. He pressed his knuckles to his lips and swallowed convulsively. If there were any light in here, if the only other person present were not completely mad, he would have been ashamed to be seen like this; at least he was spared that.

"You think that you can stand up to him," Hallam was droning. "Like the blonde girl. I have seen you with her. I know what the two of you think you are doing—outsmarting Mrs. Graves. But you can't outsmart Mrs. Graves, because she's not real. No one knows that except me. And him, of course. I told you not to come tonight—I warned you not to come, I said I would show you the truth some other time, but now he'll follow us, and he'll find out. The truth is," his voice rose in a frantic crescendo, "I don't know where it is! The book—the real book, the one that started it all—it's in the library somewhere, that's how he found it, but I don't know where! I've forgotten the call numbers, you see. Along with everything else. I couldn't even recite the opening lines of *Beowulf*. It's all gone from my mind—that's the price I paid for defying him. You know, you understand—what would happen if you tried to sing? That is what he can do to you."

Kit tried to cling to the one part of this that seemed to offer some direction. "If you—don't remember the—the call number, why don't we … get out of the lift and—and look it up in the card catalogue?"

Hallam stood there, breathing noisily, a great big, stupid, noisily breathing madman, blocking the gate of the lift and trapping Kit inside it.

"Which are you?" he rasped finally. "Peacham or Underhill?"

"*Under*hill!"

"No … Underhill is dead."

The darkness was sparkling at the edges of his vision in a way that seemed familiar, and the air in the lift was—was—there wasn't much of it, or something. That was also familiar.

"For the love of God, Hallam—you're so convinced that I'm dead—do you not know how I was killed?" This seemed like a perfectly logical sentence, and at the same time it horrified him.

"How?" Hallam demanded urgently, breathing in Kit's face.

"I was buried alive, you goddamned stupid madman! *Open* the door!"

He pushed Hallam backward, but not with any remarkable strength. Hallam flailed and clutched at him, and they thumped against the wall of the lift. One of them—Kit thought it was Hallam—must have grabbed and tugged on the lever that operated the lift, and it began to rush downward. They had been on the ground floor; they were going to a basement, a sub-basement, down and down and down … Someone—and this was certainly not Hallam—screamed.

He was on his knees on the ground. It had stopped moving, but only because he was as far down as you could go, buried as deep as you could be buried.

It had happened so many times—but why? You'd think he would

have the sense by now not to volunteer, to let one of the other men go instead, let someone else be killed, or not killed, or whatever it was that had happened to him. You'd think that by now he would have got it right.

But no—that wasn't it either. It had only happened once, just now, and he knew what he had to do. Nothing—do nothing and it would be over. Don't try to get out. By now he could smell smoke, and under the hand pressed to his chest he could feel brass buttons.

His eyes must have been closed, because when he opened them the door—what door? there hadn't been a door—was open, and someone stood over him. The faint light glowed in her pale hair and on her bare arms. He realized with horror what had happened. He *had* let someone else go; it had been her. That was why, after all, he had known there wasn't any other way.

"No! Run! It'll come down! Can't you see it's on fire already? You still have time." But she didn't. He couldn't even make his voice sound convincing.

Her hand hit his forehead hard enough to rock his head back, he felt her fingers catching hold of his hair, and she shouted:

"In the name of Jesus, go out of him! Now! Let—him—go—*this instant!*"

She sounded like a combination of an Apostle filled with the Holy Ghost and a housewife shouting at a misbehaving dog.

"A-Amen," he gasped, on the edge of a huge, irresistible impulse to laugh.

Chapter Eleven

HIS GATES WITH PRAISE

Elsa switched on the light in the elevator. She knelt on the floor in front of Kit, holding him by the shoulders because she thought he might collapse if she didn't. He looked disoriented and spent, but nothing worse than that now. He had even laughed a little, although she thought that might have been hysterics—but he seemed to have regained control of himself.

"You're all right," she said gently. "You're safe." And why shouldn't he be? Already she was unsure what had happened in the last few moments. "You're safe." *That* she was sure of. Just let that idiotic Anglo-Saxonist try to get near him again.

He nodded. "Thank you."

"We don't need to talk about what just happened." That was as much for herself as for him.

"Splendid."

He drew a long breath and let it out, and for a moment seemed fixated on the cloth-covered buttons down the front of his cassock. He looked up at her again. She could feel that her hands on his shoulders were not actually supporting him, but she kept them there.

"Sorry for, um … " he started. "Sorry to be a bother."

"Don't be absurd," she said affectionately—so affectionately, in fact, that for a moment, until she realized that he hadn't noticed, she felt as if she had just told him she loved him.

"Do you think you can get up?" she asked, when this crisis was past.

"Yes. And get out of this wretched lift, even. What a good idea."

She let go of his shoulders and stood up, offering him her hands.

He took one, but didn't really need it. He still looked a little vague and vulnerable, but his hand in hers was warm and steady.

She managed to let go without any obvious show of reluctance. She wanted to tell him that she would stand between him and any harm in the world. She was aware of how absurd it would sound, but that was part of why she wanted to say it. She wanted to hear him laugh again.

Once outside the elevator door, he had revived enough to notice the way that she was limping.

"Are you all right?"

"A bit bruised. I fell on the stairs—I tried to run in these stupid shoes."

"Poor Elsa! I'm sorry."

"No no." *You were screaming. Of course I ran on the stairs.*

He raked his hand through his hair, looking more like himself.

"Where's Mrs. Barrington?"

"Upstairs, in the men's reading room. At least that's where I left her. She has Hallam's pistol, and she's put the bullets back in. Apparently her late husband taught her how to shoot. I'm not too worried about Mrs. Barrington, actually."

"No … but I'd just as soon Hallam didn't get shot."

"That's very Christian of you."

"Well, I'm—"

"A professional. I know." She grinned.

"What happened to Hallam, anyway?" Kit asked, looking around the dark little basement landing and through the fire doors into the stacks. "Was he gone by the time you got here?"

"Oh, no. When I opened the door—"

"You opened the door?"

"Yes." Clearly he had not been aware of his surroundings at that point. She didn't want to think about what he *had* been aware of. *The mouth of Hell*, Hallam had said. Which didn't exist. "Hallam was standing just inside the elevator, and I hauled him out of the way. I think he ran off into the stacks. At any rate, he didn't go up the stairs, so that must be where he went."

"You … hauled Hallam out of the way." He looked a little alarmed.

"Yes. I was worried about you."

"Thanks. I suppose the thing to do is to go back up through the stacks."

"So that we can run into Professor Crazy-Head in the dark?" she said doubtfully.

"I don't know that we can just leave him in here. He was making suggestive remarks about burning books."

"True."

They went into the stacks, down the aisle between the shelves. It was not so dark here—there were big windows that let in some moonlight. Their shoes were noisy on the concrete floor. The books felt like silent presences ranked on either side of them. The stacks were housed in a free-standing metal shelving unit five stories deep, with walkways of clouded glass tiles on each level. Elsa had only recently earned the right, as a graduate student, to go into them, but she didn't really care for the place; from the upper levels you could look down between the shelves and give yourself a good case of vertigo.

She tried to think rationally about what had happened. She posed it as a calm question to herself. When she heard Kit scream, when she ran down the stairs, had she been conscious of any other interpretation than the one to which she had succumbed? Certainly by the time she arrived at the elevator and saw him on the floor, and he had not known who she was or where he was—had not seemed to be present in the world with her at all—certainly by then she had been sure. The powers of darkness were real, they had laid hold on him, and it was her fault. It was at least partly her fault. He could be destroyed—everything that he was could be obliterated. And—this part followed as naturally as taking a breath—there was nothing, *nothing* she would not do to prevent that.

By now the first certainty had dissolved into confusion, because if she believed in the powers of darkness then she had to believe in what she had done in the elevator, and that was impossible. But the second certainty remained, a weight in her soul (which didn't exist), but a weight like a keystone, holding the whole precarious arch together. The continued existence of Kit, just as he was, mattered more to her than almost anything else.

He had paused for a moment, and looked up at the glass floor of the level above with a curious expression.

"Of course," he said, "we're not really even underground, are we?"

"No, the building's on a hill. The basements are all above ground." She wasn't sure what that had to do with anything.

There was a noise of footsteps above their heads.

"Professor Hallam!" Kit shouted. His voice drew an answering ring from the metal and glass of the stack shelves. "Where are you?"

The footsteps above broke into a run, and they heard the sound of someone coming down the stairs by the elevator. And there was a rustling along the outer edge of the stack shelves, and Professor Hallam loomed up quite suddenly behind them, between the two of them and the fire door where they had come in.

"He's coming," Hallam hissed, apparently talking to himself. "The girl's no good to him, but Underhill, now, he'd like Underhill. I never liked him, not really. Self-righteously Christian, always wanted to write papers comparing things to the Psalms. Which would have been all very well if he could have conjugated a verb to save his life. Besides, he was always very straight-laced. He walked out with these prim little butter-wouldn't-melt-in-their-mouths girls. Yes, Underhill would be a wonderful prize for him."

Elsa stood between the professor and Kit. In the shadows she could not see Hallam's face, only his white hair standing up wildly, his overcoat hanging askew, and the feral way he hunched his shoulders, ready to pounce. She took a step forward.

"You stay away from him," she said.

Kit seized her by the shoulders, lifted her bodily and swung her out of the way. He marched forward to face Hallam. The big man fell on him, and Kit put him on the ground as efficiently as he had thrown Peachy in the sand the day Elsa met him. He was himself again, the same man who had taken the gun out of Hallam's hand downstairs. Whoever he had been in the elevator, that was gone.

Kneeling in the aisle, pinning Hallam's arm behind his back to keep him down, he looked up at Elsa with a kind of amused exasperation.

"Look, I won't say it isn't sort of flattering, you wanting to defend me from giant madmen, but *what exactly* were you planning to do there?"

I want to protect you from everything: madmen, the powers of darkness, girls like me …

"Believe me," she said, "there was no planning involved in that."

Hallam slumped on the floor, limp and defeated. Kit got to his feet and dusted himself off.

"I'm sorry," he said seriously. "It was heroic and beautiful. I didn't mean to make fun of it. Or I did, but I shouldn't have." To Hallam he added, "You can get up if you'll behave yourself."

The professor rolled over with a groan and began laboriously to gather himself up.

"Kit," said Elsa, "you don't have to treat me like a man all the time."

"I don't."

"No. But you try to pretty often, and—really—that's good enough."

He frowned as if he didn't quite understand that.

"Oh, professor!" a laughing, familiar voice sang out from the direction of the elevator. "I need to talk to you, professor! It's about this extension that I need—*you* know. I'm afraid I simply can't turn in the assignment yet."

"Who's there?" Kit demanded.

There was no answer. Hallam staggered to his feet and began to back away from Kit.

"Wait a minute, Professor," said Elsa.

"I have to go," Hallam mumbled.

"No, you don't," she said. "What has he threatened you with? You're safe here. Don't go to him. We'll help you."

"You're not a real woman," Hallam mumbled. "None of them are."

"Steady on," said Kit. "That's not what we're talking about."

"Pro-*fess*-or!" the voice of the young man in grey tweed sang out again.

"Show yourself!" Kit shouted.

"Ah, that's more your style than mine," the voice replied with a laugh.

Hallam's shambling figure was almost at the fire doors leading to the landing. Suddenly Kit strode forward, and the professor, frightened, backed through the doors and slammed them shut. A second crash a moment later signalled that he had barred the doors. Kit stopped and turned back.

"Good," said the voice, muffled now by the door. "Leave them for a while. They're both … problems."

"Who was that?" asked Kit.

"I don't know his name either. I think he's the person Hallam was afraid of. Of course, there are doors like that on every level. I wonder if he'd realize … "

"If he's the person Hallam's afraid of, he used to be a librarian." He took off at a run for the back stairs. They reached the next level up before they heard the doors on that floor banging shut. By this time Kit was breathing hard and leaning on the railing, obviously tired.

"Go two levels up," said Elsa. "No—let me."

She kicked off her shoes and scampered past him up the stairs. But she was still limping; she wasn't much faster than he. She ran painfully up two levels, and was pelting down the aisle between the shelves when the young man in grey tweed got to the doors on that level. He paused a moment before swinging them shut, looking in at her, then past her, and his expression froze into a kind of snarl before he slammed the doors together. The bars that held them closed clanged into place, and Elsa slid to a stop on the glass floor. She turned to look back at the stairs. Kit had reached the top and stood hanging onto the railing, looking exhausted.

"Up, or down?" she asked.

"Neither—there are two of them. It's no use." Even as he said it, she could hear another set of doors clanging shut.

"You're right."

He hung off the railing and draped himself dramatically on the stairs, his head thrown back on the top step. She came and leaned over the rail to look down at him.

"Comfortable?" she asked.

"Not really." He smiled.

For the sake of saying something, she said, "What now?" But the answer was obvious: now they waited in the locked library until someone came to open it in the morning. Or until Hallam and the young man in grey tweed set it on fire, or whatever. Kit said nothing.

A cloud moved away from the moon, and a faint, silver light filled the stacks and fell obliquely through the railings and over Kit on the stairs.

"You look like a painting," she said.

She remembered the moment on the beach when he had become aware that she was admiring him, and hadn't looked pleased about it. That had puzzled her at the time, but it didn't now. She was not surprised when he sat up and mumbled something about finding her shoes.

She leant on the railing while he clattered down two flights and searched in the dark—the moon went behind a cloud again—for the shoes. She wished that she had not told him about Francis. But he had said it hadn't surprised him, and it wasn't telling him that made the difference. It was the fact that it had happened. For the first time she found herself wishing—passionately wishing—that it hadn't. She wished she were the sort of girl who could be just a little bit frightened of the prospect of spending a night in the library stacks with a man, even such a gentleman as Kit Underhill. That seemed somehow preferable to being the sort of girl with whom a gentleman would not want to be found in the morning by the librarians.

Below her she could faintly hear Kit humming to himself, something familiar—something old and churchy. Then, to her surprise, he started to sing:

"All people that on earth do dwell,
Sing to the Lord with cheerful voice.
Him gladly serve, his praise forth tell;
Come ye before him and rejoice."

She had never heard Kit sing before. She remembered that Peachy had once described his voice as "a serviceable baritone." She remembered too how Peachy had said this: with mingled affection and pity, as if he felt he had compromised his musical standards in the name of friendship, but was proud of having done so. To her ears, Kit's voice was beautiful.

"The Lord ye know is God indeed," she joined in the second verse. She was a serviceable contralto. *"Without our aid he did us make ... "*

He returned with her shoes, and handed them up to her while he was still below her on the stairs. *He's not worried*, she thought. *Not worried about the young man in grey tweed, or Hallam, or spending the night in the library stacks with me. He's happy.* He looked so tired that he hadn't the energy for more than one straightforward emotion—and it was joy. She tried to pretend she couldn't guess what he was happy about. (But being rescued from the powers of darkness, if such a thing were possible, surely *would* make you happy.)

"I was trying," he said, sitting down on the stairs "to think of a hymn that you would know."

"I know lots of hymns."

"Yes, I suppose so." He shifted over and gathered up the skirt of his cassock so that there was room for her to sit beside him. She did. "I just thought they might be a bit outside my repertoire."

"That's probably true. Do you know 'Soldiers of Christ, Arise'?"

"Ouch. Appropriate, I guess. But yes."

"*Come to the Saviour, make no delay?*"

"Um ... I think that's one of the ones in the back of the hymn book that they liked to sing at St. James." He hummed the melody experimentally. "Is that right? I thought so. They're very Evangelical there—I wasn't entirely at home."

"What about ... *Called to the heavenly banquet, brothers, Called to the heavenly feast—Washed in the blood of the precious Lamb and ...* something something—there's usually a lot of hand-clapping, it doesn't sound quite the same without it."

"Never heard of it! Happily."

"Tsk, tsk. It's popular in certain circles."

"*Let all mortal flesh keep silence, And with fear and trembling stand ...* No, I didn't think so."

"It's beautiful, though. Go on."

He sang some more, self-consciously now, his voice a little rough.

"How about this? *O what their joy and their glory must be, Those endless Sabbaths the blessèd ones see ...* "

"No, I don't like that one as well. Oh, I've thought of another one—you'll know the tune, but I doubt you've heard these words ... "

When they had sufficiently exhausted this game they sat in silence for a little while. "My dad's a lay preacher in the Tree of Life Revival," Elsa said by and by. "He got saved when I was eight. It was quite sudden—he went to one of their meetings, and came back a new man. We had been Christmas-and-Easter Lutherans before that. Mum was afraid at first he was going to neglect the farm because he was so zealous for the Lord. But he didn't. He says that God gave him the homestead and the land for a reason, and that's a sacred duty too, like his preaching.

"I used to go with him to all the meetings. I used to love it. I felt like I was part of something very grand, something building, you know, like a tide, like a revolution. Dad just preached, but there were others who healed people, and … cast out demons and things." *That's where I got that idea from, obviously.* "And there was always lots of singing. I used to love it," she said again. "Then after a while I started to see that nobody had answers to the questions I was beginning to ask—it wasn't just that I hadn't learned the answers, it was that most of the others hadn't thought to ask the questions, weren't bothered by the things that bothered me. I was hoping for some mystery beneath the surface that would make sense of the inconsistent doctrines, the hard Scripture readings—but there was no mystery. They hadn't overcome their doubt—they had no doubt to overcome. That was when I began to make up my mind that I wasn't a believer after all. It's funny, but I think that if I believed again, if I ever started believing again, I might rather go to a church like yours."

She waited, willing him to say, "*If* you believed? But you do believe—haven't you just proved it?" so that she could say, "No, but I don't."

But all he said, very quietly, was, "Thank you for telling me that."

"You look awfully tired," she said. "Do you want me to fetch you a few volumes of Donne's sermons to use as a pillow, so you can try to sleep?"

He laughed. "Very kind. No. What about you? Aren't you cold?"

She had left her coat in the men's reading room, where she had taken it off to humour Mrs. Barrington in her attempt to sweep up the broken lampshade, and she was cold. If he'd had a jacket to offer her, she would have taken it.

"No," she said brightly. "I'm fine."

He seemed to have woken up a little. "Don't be silly," he said, getting to his feet. "You don't even have sleeves."

He had unfastened his belt and got nearly a dozen buttons undone when they heard noises on the level above: a clang of doors and multiple voices.

"Father Underhill!" called one voice which Elsa recognized as Mrs. Barrington's.

"Hello!" Kit called back, after a moment's hesitation. "We're down here!"

Footsteps clicked and clomped overhead. Elsa retreated down the stairs instead of up, and Kit followed her.

"Who's she got with her?" Elsa whispered. "They can't have taken her hostage, not with—" Not when the woman was armed.

"I have brought the police, Father," Mrs. Barrington's voice rang out again. "It's quite all right."

Elsa gasped. "Kit! It's a rescue—get your stupid tomfool clothes back on!"

This, unfortunately, caused him to break down in helpless laughter and not to be able to negotiate his buttons at all.

"Stop giggling! I mean it! Mrs. Barrington will never let me near you again—you look *exactly* like someone who was interrupted in the middle of being seduced."

And that caused her to blush and to be unable to help him with the buttons. They went up the stairs to meet Mrs. Barrington and the campus police officers who had let her in, with Kit still substantially unbuttoned and trailing his belt. He brazened it out seraphically, taking his time with the buttons and offering no comment or excuse, which was really no more than she should have expected.

The campus police had offered—or been shamed by Mrs. Barrington into offering—to drive them all home. It was not entirely clear what story she had told them, and Elsa kept discreetly quiet. Kit, fortunately, was simply too tired to begin telling everyone the truth. He quickly fell asleep in the back of the police car. One of the officers had to shake him awake when they pulled up in the dark driveway beside St. John's.

"Why are you … " He blinked sleepily at Elsa. "They should have dropped you off first. You're much closer to campus."

She tucked her arm through his and drew him away from the car. "They think that I live here," she said.

"But you don't."

"Yes, but Mrs. Barrington saw fit to tell them that I'm your wife."

"What? Why?" He looked more dismayed about this than was entirely flattering. "But that's a lie. And—and not remotely plausible. I mean look at us."

Mrs. Barrington had finished speaking to the police and joined them.

"Mrs. Barrington, Miss Nordqvist has an apartment downtown—"

"No doubt, Father, but I felt it unnecessary for the officers to know that you are not a married couple."

"We're not an *unmarried* couple either, Mrs. Barrington. We're two people—who live in quite different parts of the city." The police car pulled away into the street and drove off. "You know that I don't have a car?"

"Ah. Yes, now that you mention it, I *did* know that. I remember it being mentioned at a charity sale meeting that you don't drive. But we can telephone—"

"Or a telephone."

"No. Of course. I recall that, too." Mrs. Barrington looked restrainedly distressed. "I should have thought."

Kit laughed suddenly. "It's all right. Really, it's fine. I have a spare bed, and a couch, and—it's fine. I am very grateful for your looking out for us and fetching the police. Let's go in."

He led the way around the south side of the church. There was a lawn here, with a couple of large trees, one with a child's swing hanging from it. Past the trees, a mass of Victorian Gothic Revival gables rose up in the dark behind an immense white verandah.

"What is it?" Elsa asked.

Kit gave her a baleful look. "It's my house."

"Good Heavens."

The front door, which, like the verandah, badly needed a coat of paint, opened onto a large, empty hall, with a flight of stairs on one side covered in threadbare carpet, and bright patches in the faded wallpaper showing where pictures used to hang. It was cold and smelled a little musty. Beyond the stairs were French doors leading into what looked like it might have been a dining room, but was currently being used to store a lot of boxes and baskets of junk.

"You can put your coats and things in the closet, and then this room's habitable," said Kit, opening another set of doors and flicking on the electric lights.

It was more than habitable; it was charming, and it was obvious that he had taken trouble over it. There was colourful modern wallpaper and a large oriental rug. The furniture was all second-hand, some of it shabby, but it had been artfully arranged in order to divide up the big room comfortably. A number of long green curtains were draped over one of the couches, waiting to be hung. There were pictures on the walls, and candles on the mantelpiece, a bookcase full of books, a record player and a large stack of records. There was a cheerful orange afghan thrown across a wing-back chair near the fireplace, and a mystery novel open face-down over the arm of the chair, so that you couldn't help but picture Kit curled up there reading.

Elsa turned from looking at the room to smile at him. His answering smile, oddly shy, broke through the weariness in his face.

It was another side of him, this one unexpected. She realized that without giving it much thought she had imagined him in some austere and semi-monastic bed-sitting-room attached to the church. Apparently that was more or less how he had lived at the Cathedral. That he should now be installed in a big, dilapidated Victorian place, and have made efforts at decorating—that was something of a shock.

"I'll make some tea," said Mrs. Barrington. "Shall I?"

Kit passed a hand across his eyes. "If you like. You know where the kitchen is, and you are welcome to it. I don't, personally, think I need tea."

"Is that possible?" asked Elsa, sinking down onto one of the couches, in case Mrs. Barrington expected her to come bustle in the kitchen with her. "I thought everyone who had been through any trauma always needed tea."

"Only," said Kit, "if they don't have port. But I do."

Mrs. Barrington, to Elsa's surprise, turned back from the doorway and said, "If that is the case, perhaps I won't make tea. Shall I fetch glasses?"

"I don't have port glasses—I, um, don't have curtains on the windows. But there are teacups."

"Excellent."

He opened a door at the bottom of one of the bookcases, and extracted a dark bottle.

"That's illegal," Elsa remarked.

"It isn't," he said, drawing the cork. "It's just old. Father Britton bought it before Prohibition and thoughtfully left it in the cellar for me. It's very good—a world apart from that fruity substance Harriet was drinking last … " He paused and shook his head, laughing. "This evening. That was just this evening."

"Surely not."

Mrs. Barrington returned from the kitchen with three mismatched teacups.

"I should have asked if you would in fact like tea," said Kit, filling one of the cups moderately and the other almost to the brim. "I don't suppose you want this."

"I'll try some," said Elsa. "Just a small amount."

He passed her the third teacup with a few teaspoons of port in the bottom of it, and said, "You can always have more." He piled up cushions on a faded chaise by the window, and sat down with his own brimming cup, kicking off his shoes and nestling back against the cushions with an almost feline contentment. After all, she thought, she should have known him better than to be surprised by this cozy room.

Mrs. Barrington meanwhile had taken the wing-back chair by the fireplace, folding up the draped afghan and picking up the mystery novel to look at it critically.

"It really was very good of you to fetch the police, Mrs. Barrington," said Elsa. "This is much more pleasant than spending the night in the library stacks."

"Well, I hardly know what else I could have done." Mrs. Barrington managed to sound both pleased and reproving. "A very sinister-looking young man came in shortly after—shortly after Miss Northwest went to look for you, Father. I hid behind the circulation desk when I heard him unlocking the door, so he did not see me, but I caught a glimpse of him, and—" She shuddered slightly at the memory. "He had left the front door unlocked, so it was easy for me to slip out after he had gone in. I was, as you may imagine, extremely concerned. Then when I returned with the police, we found the doors locked again, so it took us some time to gain entry. I do not know if the sinister young man had gone by that time … "

"Yes, we think so," said Kit. "He was after Professor Hallam, but they felt the need to lock us into the stacks before they went."

Mrs. Barrington shook her head, and took a sip of her port. "Well, it is all very unsettling, Father. I don't need to tell you that I fear for your friend, if he is mixed up with people like that."

"I think he will be all right," said Kit slowly. "He's more resourceful than most people realize."

"And he wasn't actually at the meeting," Elsa pointed out. The evening's adventure had, from one point of view, been a waste of time.

Kit set his empty teacup on the floor and rearranged his cushions. Elsa sat looking at the dark liquid in her cup. Finally she raised it to her lips and tasted it.

Once, when she was sixteen, she had made sandwiches for herself and Francis, which they had eaten together in a field, and he had brought a bottle of cheap white wine—still legal at the time, though only just—which she had dutifully tried to drink. He had been disappointed when she hadn't really liked it. Father Britton's port must have been bought at around that time, but she thought it hadn't been cheap. It tasted complicated: simultaneously sweet and acidic, and smoothly potent. She sipped again, gingerly.

She looked up, wondering if she were making a fool of herself. Mrs. Barrington had fallen asleep in her chair, her hands tidily folded, her grey head nodding forward. Kit lay curled up on his side on the chaise, likewise asleep.

Elsa slipped off her shoes and padded across the room to turn off the light. She sat on the couch in the dark for a little while, sipping her port, until the cup was empty. Then she pulled the green curtains over herself and fell asleep in her turn.

*

When she woke, she was alone in the room. The morning sun from the window behind her blazed on the jaunty modern wallpaper with its stylized tulips. She sat up into the heat of it, pushing aside the curtains under which she had slept, and riffled her fingers through her hair.

In the morning light the room looked a little shabbier, more obviously a bachelor's dwelling. She got up and walked around on stockinged feet, looking at the records—an eccentric assortment, obviously Peachy-influenced—and the pictures, a mixture of tasteful religious prints and family photographs. There was one of Kit and Peachy as boys, at the beach, arms thrown across each other's shoulders, identical teeth missing from their broad grins, Peachy already taller and skinnier, Kit already handsome, confident, strong.

A photograph in an oval frame hung alone over the mantelpiece. It was a candid picture of a woman in turn-of-the-century clothes working in her garden. She sat in the grass, hatless, a basket half full of flowers in front of her, shears in her hand, reaching up to clip a rose, but looking at the camera with surprised delight. You could tell (for the photograph was clear and crisply printed) that she had not been young when the picture was taken, but her smile was like a girl's. It was also amazingly familiar.

She poked along the bookshelves, assessing his taste in books. There were Bible commentaries and books on theology, but there were also a lot of novels: Dickens, Austen, Wodehouse, and a whole shelf of paperback mysteries. At the end of another shelf, lying on its side, was a battered and misshapen blue prayer book. She picked it up, and it fell open in the middle of the Litany, at a place where something had been stuck between the pages: a silver medal with a bust of the king, attached to a blue and red ribbon. On the opposite page, the words repeated in italics caught her eye: *Good Lord, deliver us. Good Lord, deliver us.* "For Distinguished Conduct in the Field" the medal said on the other side. Elsa's brother had briefly had in his possession a medal like this, awarded posthumously to a friend and entrusted to Sven to deliver to the man's widow. It was the highest award given to enlisted men and non-commissioned officers; he had explained that. She also remembered that the recipient's name was engraved around the rim of the medal. She held it between her thumb and forefinger and read: SERGEANT C. J. UNDERHILL.

There were other things stuffed into the prayer book, which must have been the one that he'd had with him at the Front: some folded, official-looking papers, and a collection of amateur photographs. These—she had got them out and was looking at them without stopping to ask whether she should—were all scenes from the trenches, pictures of men she had never met, probably never could meet, most of them. They were grinning at the camera or laughing among themselves. He was not a good photographer; the pictures were poorly composed and often out of focus. It was not a journalist's record; it was a carefully curated personal exhibit, a record of friendships, passages of happiness in the midst of an ordeal.

And there, finally, was one shot of the owner of the camera. He had clearly not expected or wanted to be photographed; he was sitting on a crate, looking up at the camera with an expression that said, "Oh really, must you?"—but also, of course, with a tolerant half-smile. Whoever took this one had known how to use the camera, and it was a brutally good portrait. His left arm was in a sling, and the other hand held a cigarette. He looked haggard and pale, and alarmingly young—and, at the same time, so beautiful.

She unfolded the papers and stood reading through them. When she had finished, she slipped the photographs and the papers back inside the book and set it gently in its place on the shelf, unsure what to do about this discovery. He had deliberately kept a secret of it; but she couldn't pretend not to know. It changed too much. And there was something else, hovering on the edge of her mind, not yet in focus …

"Miss Northwest," said Mrs. Barrington from the doorway.

"Oh, good morning!"

"I am glad to see you are awake. I have found a dress for you." She held up something large and pinkly floral. "It was among the articles donated for the charity sale."

"That's very kind of you, but I'm afraid it's not really my style."

Mrs. Barrington frowned, as if she thought this a joke in poor taste. "Miss Northwest, I obviously cannot allow you to leave the rectory in what you have on."

Elsa laughed. "I'm sure *that's* kind of you too, but I don't think my reputation will really suffer much from my being seen walking home on a Saturday morning in an evening dress."

"Miss Northwest, please do not imagine that I am concerned for *your* reputation."

This, though both amusing and irritating, did put a different complexion on the thing. She could have loved Kit less, she thought, and still not wished to subject him to malicious gossip. She was ashamed of herself for not having been the one to think of it. She took the dress from Mrs. Barrington without a word, picked up her shoes, and stalked upstairs to blunder about looking for the bathroom. It was a big house.

The bathroom was warm, the mirror still fogged from someone else's bath. She washed hastily, combed her hair with her fingers, and put on the large floral dress. It had a full skirt with a flounce, and a high lace collar of the sort that nobody had worn in a decade, and it was several sizes too big. Her black stockings and pumps did little to add to the effect.

There was no sign of Mrs. Barrington when she came downstairs, but she found Kit in the kitchen, barefoot and in shirtsleeves and suspenders, frying bacon on the stove. He looked up as she came in. He was obviously the one who had fogged up the bathroom; he was immaculately shaved and had apparently washed his hair.

"What *are* you wearing?" he asked, taking a step back from the stove to survey her.

"It's a rummage-sale dress that Mrs. Barrington found for me. I must look a fright."

"No," he said thoughtfully. "You look lovely. Like a lovely girl from about fifteen years ago."

She laughed. "That's very kind of you."

"It's nothing of the sort," he said gravely. "I know whereof I speak, too. Fifteen years ago I was very interested in girls who dressed like that."

"I'll bet you were." But she was pleased by the compliment.

The kitchen table was laid for three, and there was a bowl in the middle of it covered in a napkin. She peeked inside.

"Mrs. Barrington made biscuits!" She seized one and took a bite. It was warm and buttery and delicious.

"Mrs. Barrington has gone out to telephone her son. I made those."

"You're joking!"

He looked embarrassed. "It's not completely unheard-of, is it? I learned to bake a few things after the War, as a kind of therapy.

Readjusting to civilian life and all that." He flipped a couple of piece of bacon. "Actually it was to prove that I believed in the goodness of Creation. I don't have any talents—I mean I can't paint or write poetry or anything, and I'm not good with my hands—but I wanted to do something, make something material. Something good. So … it seemed like the thing to do."

She wanted to pursue this question of the goodness of Creation, which interested her; but she was also acutely aware that this was the first time he had said anything to indicate that he had served in the Great War. He wasn't keeping a secret of it, or not any more.

What she said was, "They're very good biscuits."

"I would call them scones, but I'm glad you like them."

"Kit, I was looking at some of your books, and I … I found your Distinguished Conduct medal."

He didn't look up from the frying pan. "Did you? Where?"

"You mean you lost it? Inside a prayer book."

"Oh, is that what I did with it? Yes, I remember that now. Bit disgraceful, I guess—but I am a civilian. It's not as if I need it for anything."

"There were some photographs in there as well. I looked at them."

"Did you?" He smiled faintly. "If you're apologizing, you don't need to. I'd have shown you those if you wanted. I could tell you the names of the men. I think there's also a clipping from the *London Gazette* explaining—roughly—what the medal was for, if you're interested in that. It's not my favourite subject."

"I read that. It said you were 'contemptuous of danger' and saved a lot of men's lives. That was the least surprising part of the whole thing."

"Well." His voice had become clipped and emotionless. He poked the bacon around unnecessarily in the pan. "Thanks."

"Why do you tell people you didn't fight?"

"I don't."

"You told us that you didn't enlist until '17. No … you didn't. Peachy told us that."

"Yes."

There was a long silence. The bacon was done, but he made no move to take it out of the pan.

Finally he said, "I think it's true, as far as he's concerned. I mean I think he really did wait until 1917 to enlist. Or possibly he was drafted. I'm not really sure. I'm also not sure why he started telling people that I didn't fight. I don't even know why I let him. Of course it was easier to have an excuse not to talk about it—but I wasn't going to talk about it anyway, and I've never needed an excuse to keep my own counsel. And then … it was such a monstrous thing to lie about, I didn't quite know how to say anything about it without turning it into some sort of pistols-at-dawn situation. Or a Kit-breaks-Peachy's-nose situation. I can't help thinking it's somehow my fault, because I never confided in him. But, my God! What would have been the point in that? He was well out of it. I didn't want to involve him, even like that, even after the fact."

He turned off the gas and dumped the bacon hastily out of the pan onto a plate. He banged the frying pan back down on the stove and turned away suddenly in a way that made her think for a moment he was about to be sick. She realized that he was crying.

It had clearly taken him by surprise, and he had no plan at all for coping with it. He clung to the corner of the stove and tried to control himself, but his tears were childlike in their intensity. She stood paralyzed with uncertainty. *Pretend you didn't notice,* she told herself; *get another biscuit—scone—thing—and go find milk for the tea.* And another part of her protested that she *had* noticed, that she didn't take milk in her tea, that she couldn't leave him weeping, because he needed something else from her. Instead of moving away from him she moved toward him. She put out a hand and it had almost come to rest on his shoulder when he turned toward her, looking for the comfort that she had been about to offer. For a long moment they stood frozen like that. Then she pulled out a chair from the table and drew him gently by his sleeve.

"Sit," she said.

He sat, and she sat opposite him. She reached out and stroked his hair. It was soft and thick and slightly damp. She pushed it back gently from his forehead. He had covered his eyes with his right hand, and for the first time she looked closely at the signet ring that he wore on that hand. It was plain gold, without a stone; it would sell for something between seven and twelve dollars, depending on the quality of the gold and whether it had been specially engraved for him, which it likely had. Probably as a gift from his foster-parents for his ordination. The device was not his initials, but an intricate Chi-Rho.

Her heart beat a little faster. *I hope it goes without saying that I don't believe in this nonsense.* Surely he made the connection on the golf course, when she told him about XP. But he hadn't attempted to make anything of it. He must have known that it wouldn't impress her. And it wouldn't have then. But now?

He looked up at her, his eyes still swimming, unhappy in a slightly different way. She withdrew her hand. She wasn't sure when she had gone from trying to comfort him to just enjoying the feeling of running her fingers through his hair, but it had been pretty early on.

"I'm sorry," he said. "I don't cry—I mean, in the normal course of events. It's not really my style."

"I don't know about that."

That made him smile a little. He leaned back in his chair. "It just hit me suddenly how unsupportable it would be if he were killed, or if somehow I never saw him again—and this thing were unresolved between us."

"Yes," she said. "I guess it would be."

To her surprise, he went on. "He looked after me for a couple of years after the War, while I was trying to finish my degree. I had about energy enough to pass my courses—not always that, actually.

He rented a place in the West End—he'd been living in a dark little ground-floor flat when I came back, but he found us this high-ceilinged place with huge windows and a balcony. It wasn't strictly necessary—even at my worst, I could have coped in an ordinary-sized apartment—but it helped, and that was the kind of care he took over everything. He worked regular hours at Doughty's and even accepted money from his parents, and paid more than his share of things. He never gave me the impression he did any of it out of guilt. I'm sure he felt ashamed of not fighting, but everything he did for me after the War was just out of friendship, because he was glad I'd made it through more or less okay. I can't begin to tell you how grateful I am that he didn't fight.

"Even when he does idiotic things, I can't forget what a good friend he has been to me. And we still have no idea where he is. Last night, all that business with Hallam, that didn't help at all."

"No … I can't see that it did. Though if you did actually serve, some of what Professor Bats-in-his-belfry was saying makes a little more sense. And I suppose that's why you objected to 'Soldiers of Christ, Arise.'"

"Just poor timing. It's a good hymn."

Poor timing. Because not only had he been reminded of the War just then, he had been back in it. The thing that had been eluding her in the living room had come sharply into focus. What was clearest was that she had made a fool of herself.

"Kit, what happened to you in the elevator … You're claustro-phobic."

"Mm." He had got out his handkerchief and was drying his eyes. "It's very dignified, isn't it?"

"I didn't realize. What happened to you last night was a … was a nervous reaction brought on by being trapped in the elevator with Hallam."

He gave her a sidelong look, puzzled. "What did you think it was?"

"I don't … " To say that she didn't know would be a lie. "Kit, I watched you take a gun away from the man as if it were something you did every day—'contemptuous of danger' doesn't even cover it. And then a few minutes later something had terrified you, and you didn't even know where you were. I thought that the powers of darkness … " She couldn't finish the sentence. "I don't know."

"Oh." He looked ever so slightly embarrassed.

"If I'd known that you were in the War, I would have figured out what was wrong—I know all about shell-shock and how it … I mean, it's a perfectly well-understood sickness with rational causes, and … But I'd heard Peachy say repeatedly that neither of you served. It didn't cross my mind. What did *you* think I was doing? When I—when I—What did you think I was trying to do?"

"Heal me."

"Oh." She had been prepared, for a moment, to be deflected into anger with him. If he had known that there was nothing supernatural at work, and let her go on thinking … But it wasn't as simple as that. To him, there was *always* something supernatural at work.

And did it work? she wanted to ask. But that would have been stupid. Even if such a thing could work, he wouldn't know. The hallucination had dissipated, but that would have happened in due course.

"Well, it helped a bit, didn't it?" she said. "It made you laugh, anyway."

"It did."

Mrs. Barrington came into the kitchen, and Elsa popped up from the table with comical haste and began pouring tea. She glanced at Kit. It was very obvious that he had been crying, and by now she knew what to expect: either he would explain the whole thing in detail, or he would say absolutely nothing.

He said, "What would you call those, Mrs. Barrington? Scones or biscuits?"

Mrs. Barrington studied the bowl for a minute. "Tea cakes," she said. "They look very good. Did Mrs. Whittacker bake them? I didn't think she had been in yet."

"No, she can't usually get here before noon."

"I see," said Mrs. Barrington. She sat down opposite Elsa, and favoured her with a look which said very clearly that her interpretation of events was that Miss Northwest had done something to make Father Underhill cry—perhaps something involving tea cakes—and it was her intention to prevent it happening again. Elsa thought that on the whole she had to respect that.

They ate their breakfast, and Kit and Mrs. Barrington discussed regional terms for baked goods. Elsa was silent. *There had been nothing supernatural going on.* Finally Mrs. Barrington rose from the table.

"Miss Northwest," she said, putting her breakfast dishes in the sink, "there is an Altar Guild work party beginning at ten o'clock in the sacristy. You shall join me there, and afterwards my son will be arriving with the car and can drive you home. That is, when I have managed to get through to him. His line was engaged when I telephoned, but I will try again."

"I don't mind taking the streetcar," Elsa attempted.

"This will be much more suitable," said Mrs. Barrington.

"I expect Miss Nordqvist has to go to work," said Kit, picking up his own plate and Elsa's, "and that she would like to go home first and get a more … um, a different dress—fetching as that one is."

"I have the day off," Elsa admitted, gathering up the teacups. "Let me help you with the dishes, Mrs. Barrington."

"Better yet," said Kit, "let me and Elsa do the dishes, and you go telephone your son again."

Mrs. Barrington gave Elsa a look that suggested she doubted whether she knew how to wash dishes, but stepped away from the sink and went to put on her hat.

"I'm surprised she left us alone together," Elsa said, when she was gone.

"I know, it's entirely shocking. Look, if you want to go and catch the streetcar … "

She shook her head decidedly. "Mrs. Barrington would be disappointed in both of us. I couldn't do that to you. Besides, I can't leave you to do all the dishes by yourself." She had rolled up the demure, buttoned sleeves of the rummage-sale dress and begun to fill the sink. "For that matter, why do you have to do your own dishes, when you have a housekeeper?"

"Well, I have sort of half a housekeeper. I mean she only does half the work. She's not well. Father Britton had a wife and three unmarried daughters who did most of the housework themselves. He retired, and they moved to the countryside, and didn't take Mrs. Whittacker with them. She didn't want to go, I suppose—she's attached to the parish. I want the wardens to arrange a pension for her and hire me an able-bodied housekeeper. They think if they delay long enough, I'll marry and that will solve the problem."

She stacked the dishes in the sink. "But you don't want to marry."

He was digging in one of the lower drawers for a dish towel. "I don't want my wife to have to spend all day doing housework," he said. He looked up at her apologetically. "I know why you thought that, but it was never actually true."

"I suppose I had guessed that," she said.

She looked around his kitchen. It was large and spartan, with old fixtures, inconveniently laid out, but it was tidy, and that, she supposed, was because he cleaned up after himself. It must be lonesome, living in a big empty place like this on your own, but he was making the best of it. Several different things to say marched through her mind and were rejected. Did he expect his wife to sit on a cushion and embroider and look pretty all day? But that would be merely baiting him. She knew he didn't. Were there enough parish committees and guilds and archdeacons to invite to dinner to keep her busy? There probably were, but she couldn't see him insisting on any of that, either. Or was it just that raising his twelve children would be enough work by itself? He would probably settle for two or three children, and any woman remotely worthy of him would want him to have the whole dozen, anyway.

She admitted to herself that what she really wanted to ask was whether he wished his wife to have time to translate Hesiod and teach Greek at the university.

"It was wrong of me to be so coy about it," he said. He was sitting on the floor now, the dish towel in his lap, and she wasn't washing dishes, just standing in front of the sink. "I made up my mind a long time ago. I'm just not in the habit of telling people.

"I have to admit I'd been fascinated with the idea of begetting children for as long as I've known how it worked—and it was explained to me at an early age. So there was that. But then I met the Peachams, and saw how they had created this home that was a place of such love—*on purpose* they had done that. Not that it was difficult or anything, because at the heart of it was their marriage and their faith, which are both very strong ... You wouldn't find it anything particularly out of the way, I daresay. They're just a happy family. But I remember the first time I thought, *I could do that.*

"We were about sixteen. They'd had some argument with Peachy—I don't remember ... no, I do remember what it was about, but it was complicated and doesn't matter. They were in the right, though, and they were very cool about it, and after he'd stormed upstairs and sulked in his room for a while he came down and said—not with the best grace in the world, but you could see he was making an effort—he said, 'You're right, and I know you only have my best interests at heart because you *love* me.' And then all three of them laughed about it—'Yes, we *love* you, isn't it tiresome?'—and it was like ... seeing inside of a car, how the engine works or something. That might not be a very good analogy—I don't know the first thing about cars. Anyway, it was a revelation: They work at it. They try, they do the right things, most of the time, and the result is this beautiful place where love presides even over stupid arguments.

"And it flashed into my mind that I was probably capable of doing the same thing, that this could be one of the things I was for. You know how if you learn a language later in life, you might never pass for a native, but if you work at it, just because you have to make that extra effort, your grammar and your vocabulary and everything can be *excellent* … It's like that." He got to his feet and shook out the dishtowel. "I'm afraid I stopped making sense some time ago. I should just have said, 'I never really felt called to a celibate life. I've always wanted children.'"

"I'm glad you didn't just say that."

"I know. Sorry."

She scrubbed dishes for a minute. She thought about her own family, whom she had so easily dismissed from her life to pursue a career in another province, another world. She thought about the smoky, dark house made of sod that was the setting of her earliest memories. She had been born in that house: conceived in Sweden, and born in the winter of her parents' first year in Canada. She thought about her mother, who had made red-and-white chequered curtains for the two small windows of that house, which hadn't had any glass in them. Her mother would love the dress she had on now, would think it impossibly smart.

The sod house had been replaced by a timber-frame one, built by her father and his friends. It was much smaller than Kit's rectory, but her mother was so proud of it, filled it with guests at every holiday, fed all the brothers and sisters from the Revival every week, even though she didn't go to the meetings herself. But she adjusted; she always had. Her husband got saved, and she adjusted. Her son went to fight in France, and she adjusted; he came back an invalid, his lungs ruined by poison gas, and she adjusted again. Her eldest daughter wanted a life completely incomprehensible to her; of course she adjusted. Kit was right, Elsa thought; the Peachams would not have struck her as extraordinary. She had been raised in a place of deliberate love herself.

"How much of what Professor Hallam said last night is true?" she asked. "About his students, I mean. I thought it was all ravings, but if you did fight … "

"Some of it was true. Harold MacIntyre died in 1916. You would have liked him. He was your type—a scholar, and a skeptic about everything. He would be in those pictures you found. I could show you. And Stephenson, I think he was one of the others Hallam mentioned—his plane was shot down. Phillips was wounded pretty badly, but survived."

"And the girl Hallam mentioned?" This was what she really wanted to know.

"Peel? Well—she's something else now. She has a different sur-name, I mean. She married a military chaplain."

"I see."

"She did go to France as a nurse, but we had gone our separate ways before the War. I should rather say she threw me over."

"For the chaplain?"

"No. For my own defects. I'm not like Peachy. I don't—I never fell very hard for anyone. I didn't particularly need to." He said it apologetically. "I'm afraid I was one of those undergraduate men who is only ever without a girl friend for about fifteen minutes at a time. I walked out with three different girls in undergrad, and it was the same thing with each of them—they were more interested than I was. I *liked* them, but I couldn't see it lasting indefinitely. So it would go on for a while, and then they'd get the idea that I wasn't going to propose any time soon, and they'd break it off. They were the sorts of girls who were very clearly only in it for a proposal, and didn't have a lot of time to waste waiting for one. I do tremendously like girls like that—no nonsense, full steam ahead, everything part of their plan. You know—a bit like Harriet. But they don't really … start my engine, all the same. Besides, when you scratch the surface, I'm not the complete package they were looking for: it's not just the Anglo-Catholicism, which they always hoped was a phase, but there's also the complicated family, the illegitimacy, the fact that I wasn't baptized until I was twelve … I think each of them had a moment where they imagined explaining all that to their mother's friends or the women on their charity committees, and deciding, 'You know, he isn't all *that* handsome.'

"And so … I haven't had a girl friend at all since the War. I was sick, and then I got better—or thought I did—but then I was just busy."

She had noted the way he revised the verb in that one sentence: not *I don't fall*, but *I never fell* … It might not mean anything, but the imaginary parishioner-fiancée floated into her mind once more. Some perverse part of her hoped that she did exist: a nice girl whom he didn't have to try to treat like a man, who had never slept in his living room in an evening dress, or made him cry while he was cooking her breakfast.

He went on talking while he dried dishes. "I hadn't had an attack like that, like what happened last night, in years—I just avoided basements and lifts and things, and I was fine. I sleep well now, I don't have nightmares any more. So it took me by surprise. I didn't think I was still so … so fragile. I can't tell you how hard it was to accept that, at first. I made it through the War without, honestly, being much afraid of death—and my reward is to become terrified of *basements*?"

"It lacks a certain heroic something. Why basements, in particular?"

He gave her a look. "Trying to get me to talk about it? Okay. I've been doing pretty well so far. I was buried under a … a building that collapsed. I was doing some stupidly dangerous reconnaissance—it was obvious that the whole thing was coming down, it had been nearly shot to pieces. I had been leading a raid that ran into trouble, and I was trying to get the men back before dawn. I did—they all made it back safely. Only I didn't quite make it back with them, because the building … " He shook his head. "You shouldn't let me get away with not saying what the building was, you know."

"No?"

"It was a church—a medieval parish church. It had probably been beautiful at one time. Apparently it was spectacular coming down—it was hit by a shell and the roof caught fire, and no one was inclined to go back and try digging for me, because it didn't look like the sort of thing you survive. In fact, I'd fallen through into the crypt when the floor gave way, so I wasn't just … I was underground.

"The funny thing is, when I was trapped under the rubble, I wasn't frightened. I mean it's funny that's the thing I developed a phobia about afterward, because it didn't really scare me at the time. The whole thing was so simple: either I was going to suffocate and die very soon, and it would be such an easy death, compared to the things I'd watched other men go through—or it wasn't, because I was going to get out. I suppose that was how I was able to get out—if I'd panicked, I don't suppose I would have been able to think clearly enough about what to do. But there wasn't any point in panicking.

"Making my way back to our trenches was actually much worse. I was shot three times. The first bullet broke my arm—the other two didn't do much damage, but I was within an ace of standing up and presenting a clear target and getting it over with. Whenever I'd have nightmares, afterward, I'd be trapped in something, but I'd know that I had to get out, and that as soon as I was out it would get worse."

"Did you pray?"

He thought about this for longer than she expected. "At first," he said finally. "And at the end, after the third bullet, when I needed something to occupy my mind just to keep from passing out. But in the middle … Do you know what it's like when you are on the phone with someone and you have both run out of things to say, and there's silence on the line? It was like that."

"Oh."

"Afterward I used to pray that the other men I'd seen die—and the men I'd killed—might have experienced something like that toward the end. I don't know that I believe they would have, but at least praying for it seemed like something definite I could do."

"And you never talked to Peachy about any of this?"

He shook his head. "Nor to anyone else. I suppose I should have. Not talking about it—I guess that would supply one convincing psychological reason why I should have had to relive it occasionally. But it's not as if … I mean, Peachy never asked for any details. I was grateful to him for that. And I'll tell you something else. I know it's appalling arrogance, but I wouldn't have let anyone but Peachy take care of me the way he did—I mean, I could have accepted it if I'd had to, but I wouldn't have been able to stay friends afterward with anyone else who'd seen me that way." He paused in the middle of drying the teapot, and looked up at her. "Yourself excepted, obviously."

"Ah." She must have looked sceptical because he insisted:

"No, obviously! I've just told you a lot of stuff that I never told Peachy, and I wasn't lying when I said I don't normally cry. I can't even remember the last time … maybe my mother's funeral. But I'm not planning on showing you the door and—and pretending I don't know you in future, or anything. In fact I … wouldn't dream of it." He finished with the teapot and put it away in the cupboard. "You are very comforting."

She stifled a laugh. "*Comforting?*"

"Yes, absolutely. Like you could stand up to anything, like nothing in the world could get by you. Comforting like that."

She pulled the plug in the sink and watched the dirty water drain away. "Oh. I don't think that's true."

"I didn't imagine that you did. That doesn't really matter. *I* think it's true."

From the front of the house they could hear the door opening, signalling the return of Mrs. Barrington.

"What will I have to do at this Altar Guild affair?" Elsa asked, drying her hands on the front of the floral dress.

He looked at her apprehensively. *He thinks I could stand up to anything in the world, but he's not sure I can cope with an ordinary thing like an Altar Guild work party. I think he barely even remembers that I'm a woman.*

"They'll be making up bundles of willow or whatever it is that they use as an appropriate substitute for palm branches. There was a debate about it—there are factions, of course—but we finally came down on the side of whichever was least expensive, and I can't honestly remember what that was."

"Is it Palm Sunday tomorrow, then?"

He grinned, as if he found it quaint that there should be anyone who didn't know that. "It is. It shouldn't be too ghastly—the work party, I mean. I'll stop by when I'm dressed, and see how you're getting on, but then I have a funeral to be at."

"Okay, well—I'd better not keep Mrs. B. waiting." She headed for the door.

"Elsa." He caught her hand.

She turned, and he kissed her very fleetingly on the forehead. She was wearing heels, and he was barefoot, so he had to stand slightly on tiptoe to do this, and they both dissolved into embarrassed laughter afterward.

"Thanks," he said, letting go of her hand. "For everything."

"I'd do it again in a shot. Any time. You … you'll be all right?"

"I'll be *fine*. I'm going to a funeral—I'll fit right in."

Not smiling like that you won't, she thought.

"And you?" he said.

She knew that he was asking—or coming as close as he would ever come to asking—how she felt now about what she had done in the elevator last night. She wanted to tell him how grateful she was that he had not made anything of it, had not triumphed over her spectacular loss of rationality, not even archly or sweetly remarked on it. That must have taken some effort, and it was among the nicest things he had yet done for her.

"I'll be fine too," she said.

She put on her hat in the hall, adding the final touch of absurdity to her outfit. She followed Mrs. Barrington out of the rectory and across to the church, still feeling that momentary touch of Kit's lips on her forehead.

"Miss Northquest," said Mrs. Barrington, as they approached a back door of the church, "would you prefer that I introduce you to the ladies of the Altar Guild as my cousin, or as Father Underhill's cousin? Of course if you think you are likely inadvertently to refer to Father Underhill as 'Kit,' then certainly it would be preferable that you be *his* cousin."

"I think I can restrain myself," said Elsa smoothly. "But I don't see why it's necessary for me to be anyone's cousin. I mean to pretend to be anyone's cousin." She opened the door for Mrs. Barrington, who walked through with pursed lips.

They entered through the church hall, a large, barn-like space, and went down a little flight of stairs, through a door, down a narrow passage full of stacking chairs, up another little flight of stairs, through another door and down another passage, to come out, unexpectedly, in sunlit splendour, in front of the altar with its blue curtains and candles and gaudy angels swathed in purple veils, under the great, lit-up window of the Good Shepherd. Mrs. Barrington had crossed to an open door on the opposite side of the church before she noticed that she had left Elsa behind.

What had happened last night? For an instant, for a few moments, she had believed—not just in supernatural evil, which had seemed the rational, reasonable explanation for events, but in the power that could lay that evil low. It had been ridiculous, all a mistake. There had been no supernatural evil, just human frailty, the product of human evil. And the power, the Name that she had invoked in that moment of certainty in the elevator? Well. There hadn't needed to be any such thing, after all. There had been nothing supernatural going on.

And why, she thought, squinting up at the blazing window, why would that happen? Why would she see something that had seemed so obviously to point to the supernatural, only to have it disproven the next morning? And, at the same time, why should that stupid, panic-stricken misconception have made so many things better? The question formed itself in her mind: *Why would You do that?* It was as illogical as the child Kit's truculent thought, *Well, maybe with them.* There was no answer; but then, there wouldn't be.

There were half a dozen women in the sacristy when she entered with Mrs. Barrington. She was too dazed to register the names as Mrs. Barrington rhymed them off. There was an ancient, white-haired Mrs. Something, and three sylph-like Misses Something, much younger than Elsa, and two middle-aged women in aprons. She allowed herself to be introduced to all of them as Miss North-west.

"I'm afraid you may have to bear with me at first," she said, before Mrs. Barrington could explain whose cousin she was. "I've never been in an Altar Guild."

"And what brings you here this morning?" asked one of the middle-aged women.

"I'm a friend of Mr. Underhill's. I was at the rectory—well, it's a funny story. I'll tell you about it while we work."

And she did, leaving out the more incredible and private passages—which left only the bare skeleton of a story, but a true one. The members of the Altar Guild expressed amazement and sympathy, worried what could have become of Mr. Peacham, and advanced their own implausible theories. Mrs. Barrington was silent, but looked, when Elsa glanced at her, slightly chastened.

Elsa was surprised to feel herself at home among these women. The sylphs' dresses looked homemade, and the older women all had work-reddened hands. Mrs. Barrington, it turned out, was a very grand person by St. John's standards. The rest of them were the wives and daughters of factory workers and builders and bus drivers.

All of them were English immigrants. All had lost brothers or sons or nephews in the War. They talked about "Father Underhill" as if they had recently bought him, on sale, and couldn't believe their good luck.

Kit sailed in after about an hour, en route to the funeral, looking extraordinarily dashing in a black cloak. The sylphs wafted around him, inquiring about the deceased and trying to look appropriately but not unbecomingly sad. Elsa, arranging ersatz palm fronds, watched them without judgement or jealousy. They were not predatory; they were just coping, a little ineptly, with the difficulty of being young and female and talking to Kit Underhill without giggling. *I daresay you don't get that a lot*, she had said to him at the beach.

She followed him to the door of the sacristy on his way out. He looked back at her questioningly: *Are you coping all right?* She smiled.

She said, without realizing that she was going to, "Maybe I'll see you tomorrow."

"Tomorrow's Sunday—I'll be working."

"I know. I might come see what you do."

"That would—that would be lovely," he said, surprised. "Oh. Yes. Do please come." And he made a face, apparently aware of how much he had just sounded like a child hoping that she would come to his birthday party.

He left, and she went back into the sacristy. There had been nothing supernatural going on. Either that … either that, or what was supernatural was so large, so intricate and leisurely in its unfolding, that its details looked unremarkable from close to. She went in to polish candlesticks with the Altar Guild in a world that had not changed after all, that was just, illogically, as beautiful as it had always been.

Chapter Twelve

FOR HIS MERCY ENDURETH FOREVER

On the afternoon after the miracle, Kit sat on the floor of the deserted sacristy, trying to pull himself together. He had made it through Mr. Whittingham-Tweed's burial dry-eyed, which was not, perhaps, altogether required. But then, when he got home from the graveyard, he had found Peachy's setting of the *Te Deum* in his bedroom, where he had left it after taking it out of the pocket of his cassock that morning, crumpled and creased from having been slept on. He had taken it over to the church, where Betters was practising the organ, and showed it to him, hoping that he would catch him in a good mood and that he would be intrigued enough by the composition to play it through. He had, and it had been too much to bear. Kit had shut himself in the sacristy and sat on the floor and cried again.

In a strange way it felt good to be so unhinged. In a strange way *everything* felt good. He did not quite dare to know exactly why that was. Everything was just the same and completely different. He had become so good at pretending that he wasn't ill that the possibility of finally being well felt both like business as usual and like a kind of reeling drunkenness. But it was surely more than a possibility? He knew, he felt, that something had changed. He had known it at the time; there was no sense pretending he hadn't.

He was discovered sitting on the floor in the sacristy half an hour later—not actively weeping but still embarrassingly teary—by Charlie Boult.

For a moment Charlie stood in the doorway paralyzed with horror. Finally he held out an envelope bearing his employer's handwriting, and mumbled something about a message. Then, looking Kit urgently in the eye, and speaking in a much clearer voice, he said, "Father, is there anything I can do?"

It occurred to Kit that it would be a significant kindness to Charlie at least to seem to give this offer serious consideration. He wiped his eyes with his knuckles and looked at the floor for a moment and finally shook his head.

"No, thank you, Charlie," he said. "I'm all right really. But thank you. Is … is Mr. Oates expecting an answer to that?"

"Yes, but I can tell him that you were out and I left it with some-one," Charlie suggested eagerly.

"Could you? That would be very kind."

"No problem," said Charlie. He laid the letter on the counter and shut the door quietly behind him, clearly glad to be doing something of service after all.

Kit sat looking at the closed door for a moment. Then he got up, splashed water on his face at the sink in the corner of the sacristy, and stood looking out the window into the dark branches of a tree. He wondered whether he should have tried to explain to Charlie Boult what had really happened to him. Of course Charlie hadn't asked. But he should tell someone.

He went back to the rectory, changed into some old clothes, and went to work in his garden.

The rectory garden was a soggy brown mess, clogged with dead leaves, the stalks of desiccated perennials standing in pitiful clumps in overgrown beds. The plan of the garden had been old-fashioned in England by the time Kit was born; he hated to admit it, but the word that came to mind was "provincial." And it had obviously been half-heartedly tended for years before the rector retired. Kit had been looking forward to tackling it since he first spotted the snow-covered mounds of its formal beds at Epiphany.

He had been working happily for almost an hour, pulling out dried stems, clearing away the sodden leaves, kneeling to admire the earliest arrivals of snowdrops and crocuses under the trees, when he stopped to stand up and stretch, and felt for the first time that something was lacking. He looked toward the rectory and realized what it was. It was the first time he had ever worked in a garden without someone sitting on the porch reading a book, or knitting, or at least practising the piano in the front room with the windows open. Two choristers had walked by while he was working, it was true, and they had stopped to greet him and to be impressed by how much of the garden he had already dug up. It wasn't even technically true that the house was empty; Mrs. Whittacker was in there somewhere, working at her slow and painful pace, and would certainly have brought him a cup of tea if he had asked. He wouldn't have asked; he would have made tea for himself. Tea wasn't the problem. The problem was that the only people who were going to admire this garden, once he had finished with it, were people who didn't live in his house.

He went back inside, cleaned himself up, and did make tea. He took out all the photographs that were stuffed in his old prayer book, and spread them out on the living-room rug to look at them. He wished they were better pictures; the only one that was any good, as a picture, was the one that Mac had taken of him, the day after he'd returned from the field hospital. He had given Mac the camera because he couldn't use it with his arm in a sling, but that was the only picture Mac had ever taken with it. He had kept it for that reason, even though he tried, as a general rule, not to have pictures of himself unless there was someone else in them.

This time he was not surprised when the tears came.

*

Walking from the streetcar to the Whitmores' house at dusk, he thought that he might well make it through the evening without another breakdown. He hoped so. His stepmother had a tendency to refer to him as "poor Christopher" as it was. The sight of him helplessly weeping for no apparent reason would just have added needless fuel to her fire. And he didn't think she believed in miracles.

Vera opened the door when he rang. She was wearing a strange, shapeless, sack-like brown dress, which he had a terrible suspicion he was going to be asked to admire before long. She looked glum.

"Hello, Christopher," she said, drooping against the door by way of holding it open for him.

"Vera. What's up?"

"Nothing much." She peered at him. "Do you have a cold?"

"No, I'm quite well."

"Your eyes are red," she remarked, but without interest.

One wall of the front hall was entirely covered in mirrors—a new development since the last time he had visited—so he was able to study his reflection briefly, against the backdrop of the pink-and-pale-green striped paper on the opposite wall. His eyes weren't red, but they were puffy; in fact, his whole face was a little sketchy-looking, as if it had got soggy and hadn't quite dried out. It didn't really look like a cold.

It didn't really look that bad, either. He could see why Elsa had disagreed with him when he said crying wasn't his style.

"Well, hopefully no one else will notice."

Vera gave him a wry look. "Mother will notice. She always notices things, especially when you don't want her to."

"She does a bit, doesn't she? How's school?"

"Oh, boring. How do you like my dress?" she asked finally, but wanly, as if she knew he was going to have to lie in order to say something nice. Without giving him time to reply, she added, "I designed it myself."

He could have kissed her. "Did you really? How clever of you!"

"It's a prototype. I'm thinking of becoming a dress designer. As soon as I'm old enough to leave school." She tossed the last sentence aggressively over her shoulder into the house.

It had the desired effect.

"No you're not!" her mother's voice called out from the passage a moment before her mother appeared in person, taking off an apron and casting it aside onto a chair as she came. "Christopher, dear! Vera, how many times? Don't leave your poor brother standing in the hall—invite him in to sit down."

Vera gave an expressive shrug of disgust. She was fifteen, and sometimes acted like a young woman, but never around her mother.

"Moth–*er*. Last time I *did* that, and you told me 'not to treat him like a guest because he's your own brother.'" She produced a nasal and not-very-accurate impression of her mother.

"Vera! Is that any way to behave?"

On a rational basis, Kit thought, you couldn't really pick a side in this conflict. He did invariably side with Vera, but only on principle—though he wasn't altogether sure what that principle was.

Polly was looking at him closely now, and correctly interpreted his puffy face. Sort of. "Christopher! Has something happened?"

"Yes, Polly—something's always happened. It's the way of the world. I see you've had the decorators in. Or did you do this yourself? It's very striking."

Besides the mirrors and the wallpaper there was a glass table, a huge green geometric vase filled with pussy willows, and a bench upholstered in pink leather. It would have been decorators, he thought; Polly believed in paying people to do things for her.

"Do you like it? I'd been wanting something quite modern, and they did up some sketches for me, but it was hard to picture how it would all come out."

So she didn't like it, in fact.

"The mirrors make the space look bigger," Kit offered.

He was about to say something about the black-and-white linoleum, and how he had thought of doing something like that in his kitchen; it wasn't strictly true, but he was feeling pleased at the prospect of a topic that they could discuss like adults.

Then Polly said, "Yes, I made up my mind to do it now on purpose, even though it was a little more money than I like to spend at this time of year—but I wanted to get it done for your sake, so that you can take the old stuff that we had in here."

Kit stared at her bleakly. To Polly this no doubt looked like him being speechless with gratitude. That was the sort of thing that happened in Polly Whitmore's world.

"You see," she said, obviously pleased with herself, "we are always thinking of you, Christopher."

Yes, except when it came to thinking to ask whether he actually wanted her cast-off furniture. He tried to remember what had been in the front hall before. All that he could call to mind was a bulging Neoclassical sideboard with gilt columns and unconvincing busts of Roman emperors. And surely there had been some sort of artificial leopard skin on the floor? Vera was making a silly face at him from behind her mother's back.

"Everything is in the shed right now," Polly went on. "We thought the Peachams could help you transport it with their car. Ours is so small, and we don't want to risk the upholstery. Only it needs to be done quite soon because the roof of the shed leaks a little, and some of the chairs and things might get mildew. There were the gold ones with blue velvet, and the striped settee thing that never really matched, to my mind. The grandfather clock doesn't work any more, but it's quite handsome all the same. Of course I know it's all rather out of date, but nobody expects a bachelor to have nice things. Besides, I still have faith that you are going to find some lovely girl to marry, and she will of course want to make everything pretty according to her own taste. She'll probably want to do it all herself, too—I know you'll find a sweet, domestic girl, not at all like me."

It was typical of Polly that she could manage to patronize him, insult his taste in women, and fish for a compliment all at the same time.

"It's very kind of you," he said hollowly.

He promised to arrange with the Peachams to cart the furniture away. He would put it in the rummage sale, and then tell Polly how much money it had raised for the church. She ought to approve. It was exactly the kind of spurious sacrifice that she was always making.

Vera reminded her mother that now *she* was making Christopher stand in the hall, and she herded him into the living room, where Professor Whitmore had been sitting the whole time, engrossed in a magazine. He looked up over the top of his reading glasses, saw Kit, and stood up and shook his hand, which was what he did every time he and his son met. He sat back down, and clearly wanted to go back to his magazine, but was trying to be polite. Kit gave a nod in the direction of the magazine, offering him permission, and he took it.

"You really are looking a little … unwell, Christopher," Polly tried again. "Don't you think so, Laurence? Laurence!"

"Mm?"

"Don't you think Christopher is looking a little unwell?"

"What? No, not a bit." He glanced up at Kit to give colour to the statement.

Polly gave up. "I hope you are not working too hard, that's all."

"I'm fine," he said. He lowered himself into one of her odd, modern leather chairs, and smiled beatifically up at her. "Much, *much* better. Please don't worry about me."

She looked at him as if this was the most worrying thing she had ever heard.

"I wish you would have a talk with Vera about school," she said, sitting down and then getting up again to pluck the magazine out of her husband's hands, fold it up, and take it back to the couch with her. He looked resigned.

"What about school?" Kit asked.

"Why it is important—why an education is important to a modern woman. I think she would appreciate your perspective. She has begun to say that she doesn't want to go to university, but I am so determined that she must."

Vera was sitting on the hearth rug, trying to rouse the family's small, sleepy dog to play with her. The dog, whose gender had never been clear to Kit, was named Beagle, after Darwin's ship, though it was not in fact a beagle.

"I don't know that I have a particularly convincing perspective on that," said Kit, "as I'm not a modern woman."

Vera looked up at him. "You do wear a dress."

"Vera!" Polly squealed. Vera rolled her eyes, and Kit stuck out his tongue at her.

He slid out of his chair and joined Vera on the hearth rug. He picked up Beagle, removing it from the reach of Vera's teasing, and for a moment, in an access of affection, buried his face in its soft fur. Then he remembered why he didn't normally do this. It didn't smell very good.

"I know someone you should meet," he said recklessly, setting down the dog.

"A 'modern woman'?" said Vera sceptically.

"A very nice one."

"Oh, Christopher, really?" Polly cried. You could see her daughter's career ceding its place in her interest to her stepson's love-life. "We should be delighted to meet her! Wouldn't we, Laurence? Laurence!"

The conversation got out of hand after that, as things with these people always did. Only the necessity of getting out of the house finally put paid to the discussion of "Christopher's new young woman" and how and where and how soon they (meaning Polly) might meet her. The family was having dinner with the Peachams; Kit had come early in order to walk over with them. They set off finally, later than intended, but not later than usual. They were the sort of family that never arrives anywhere on time but always seems surprised about it. When the hour struck at which they should have been out the door, Professor Whitmore had just roused himself from his chair and asked the maid what she had done with his cane, Polly had decided to pick a fight with her daughter about the suitability of the brown dress for wearing in public, and Kit—who knew that the Peachams never expected the Whitmores to be on time for anything—was trying to teach the dog to fetch a piece of kindling when he tossed it across the living room.

The Peachams lived only a few blocks away. Kit walked beside his father, while Polly and Vera marched on ahead, now apparently arguing about hats.

"Sometimes," said Professor Whitmore, "I feel as if we are all acting parts in a third-rate drama about a ridiculous family, and you, Christopher, are the only one who doesn't seem to know his lines."

Kit laughed. "That may only be because my part, as written, is by far the most ridiculous."

"You know, if you do marry—sadly that is not altogether a non sequitur, as you know—but if you do, when you do, I should like to do something for you. Financially, I mean. Whatever is appropriate. Pay for a banquet or something—whatever fathers of the groom do. I mention it only because otherwise I should neither expect nor advise you to make us aware of your engagement until the last possible moment. Only I should appreciate the opportunity to make some gesture. I daresay you understand."

"I do, sir. It's kind of you. I will keep it in mind, but the situation, at the moment, is remote."

Professor Whitmore nodded. "Yes, I thought it probably was." He changed the subject and they walked on to the Peachams' discussing the aesthetic merits of the new Bank of Commerce building.

This was how the two of them got on: a general casual friendliness punctuated by occasional stilted gestures. Kit had never in his life asked his father for advice or offered him any kind of confidence, and Professor Whitmore had never sought to change this state of affairs. In fact, he seemed grateful for it.

The Peachams lived in a comfortably rambling, red-brick house with a turret. Kit had felt at home there since the first time he walked through the door, although he had at first resisted the feeling.

He vividly remembered that first day. He had been sick and ill at ease, weary of his father and new stepmother's awkward attempts at affection, and a little annoyed with himself for not being able to scrape up at least a token show of gratitude. Of course they didn't expect him to be grateful; they expected him to be traumatized and difficult, but they also seemed to feel that, if he couldn't give vent to his true feelings, that was somehow their fault. They were like two people who had read about love in a book and were earnestly trying to follow the instructions. They behaved like that with each other, which was just pitiable, but when they tried it on with him, it made him want to scream. He was neither grateful nor traumatized; he was just not interested in feeling things for other people or being told what they felt for him.

So it was balm to his spirit to sit in Mrs. Peacham's elegant and comfortable living room and watch her get angry with her sister about him. Mrs. Peacham clearly did not think he was a "dear boy." She did not go so far as to say so in front of him, but she was not very good at concealing her thoughts, and she thought the twelve-year-old Christopher Underhill was a reprobate and the son of a reprobate. She didn't approve of her sister's marriage, but that was nothing compared to her disapproval of her sister's adopted son, whose existence she had only discovered that moment when he was presented on her doorstep. When Polly said, "What would you have had us do, Charlotte, leave him in that ghastly orphanage?" she retorted, "Why was he *in* a ghastly orphanage? Couldn't his father have found someone to take him? An orphanage! No wonder he's sick. You'll be lucky if he doesn't have tuberculosis." Except for the part about probably having tuberculosis—which, however, didn't much scare him—it was all enormously satisfying. He appreciated being rated at his actual worth instead of fawned over and called a poor thing. Mrs. Peacham, unlike his father and Polly, obviously had a pretty good idea of what he was really like.

They had left him alone in the living room, supposedly to check on the preparations for lunch, but actually so that they could argue about him more openly elsewhere. He had prowled around and found a box of Dr. Peacham's cigarettes on a sideboard, and was helping himself to a large handful when the door from the dining room burst open, and a skinny, black-haired boy shot through, yelling over his shoulder, "No, you numskull! That was Augustine, and it wasn't a hippo*potamus*!" He slammed the door, and saw Christopher.

"Hey! Who are you? Wait—more importantly, why are you stealing my father's cigarettes?"

Christopher tapped his handful of cigarettes on the sideboard to tidy them, and coolly dropped them into his jacket pocket. He shrugged. It wasn't really a question that deserved an answer.

"Oka-ay." The black-haired boy seemed to see this. He changed tack. "Where can I hide? I need to hide. Guppy is coming after me."

Christopher shrugged again. "No idea. I don't hide."

This seemed to strike the other boy as a *bon mot* worthy of the Spartans, and it inspired him to turn and face his adversary when he appeared. "Guppy" was not aptly named; he proved to be a huge teenager who flattened the black-haired boy when he tried to offer violence. Christopher was briefly incapacitated by a fit of coughing, but when he recovered, he shrugged off his jacket and dove into the fray. He had given Guppy a bloody nose and made him cry by the time the adults discovered them.

They were all punished equally, which struck Christopher as fair. But Peachy (he had introduced himself by this time, and explained that *nobody ever* called him "Peverell") considered it a gross injustice that Christopher should be punished at all. He flung an arm around the stranger and tried to explain to his mother, in high-flown language, that this gallant had come to his aid in the heat of battle. It must have been Christopher's look of surprise—he hadn't intended to come to anyone's aid, he just liked to fight—that convinced Mrs. Peacham that this was a fantasy of her son's invention.

On the way out of the house, Christopher was quietly waylaid by Peachy, who offered to return the stolen cigarettes for him, "And we'll say no more about it." He gave the offer a moment's thought, and finally did give Peachy the whole handful of cigarettes. He was probably too sick to smoke them enjoyably anyway. But mostly he was thinking that, if he didn't give them back, this boy would tell his father that it was he himself who had stolen them. Christopher had no resources for dealing with that sort of thing.

He hadn't had tuberculosis, as it turned out; he'd had bronchitis, and he had given it to Peachy, who had gone on to become much sicker with it than he. Nobody blamed Christopher for this, but—probably because nobody blamed him—he felt bad about it. He took to visiting the Peachams, letting himself out of the house without asking his stepmother's permission, to inquire about his cousin. Peachy's parents had seemed to appreciate the intention behind this. Mrs. Peacham had surprised him by seeming to like him when he wasn't behaving like a delinquent, and it was on one of these visits, when Peachy was recovering, that Dr. Peacham had sat Kit down and said, "We've been thinking it might be a good idea for you to come live with us. What do you think?"

*

The Peachams' dining room was much the same as it had been on that first day, with the same combination of elegant furnishings and comforting, unpretentious food on the table, but the boy who had run in shouting about St. Augustine was not there for dinner. Kit had not really held out much hope that he would be. It was Polly, of course, who asked some over-solicitous question about Peachy's absence. Mrs. Peacham said that he was out of town with friends. Kit wondered whether this was a deliberate lie, which would have been unlike her.

After dinner, Dr. Peacham joined Kit on the porch. They had

both recently given up smoking, which made sitting on the porch seem somewhat pointless; but it was a nice evening for it.

"Have you heard from Peachy?" Dr. Peacham asked, and without waiting for an answer went on: "He seems to be doing all right. He wrote to us." He produced the letter from a pocket and unfolded it.

"He did? I haven't heard from him. Where is he? And why couldn't he telephone like a normal person?"

"Because, as it transpires, he is staying at a cabin in the woods with no telephone for miles."

Kit gave him an incredulous look. "Peachy? A cabin in the woods?"

"I know—it's implausible. But he addresses that in the letter."

This was true. Looking down at it finally, Kit saw that the first words of the letter were, *"You won't believe this, but …"* Peachy—and it was certainly Peachy's handwriting, even more sprawling than usual—went on to explain that he had been invited on the spur of the moment to come with his neighbour Mazursky to stay with some painters who had a place in Muskoka, and had gone because he felt desperate to get out of the city and forget about Harriet. It was superficially plausible; Peachy was exactly the sort of person to accept a last-minute invitation to do something that he didn't enjoy just because a friend wanted his company.

"He ought to have written to you," Dr. Peacham remarked. "I think you have been worried about him."

"Well, he must have known you'd show me this," Kit said, refolding the letter. "Saved himself the cost of a stamp."

He thought, in fact, that he had taken care of Kit in the same way he thought he had taken care of Harriet: by quarrelling with them. He thought that he could make people who loved him stop caring, for weeks at a time, whether he lived or died, just by behaving like an ass. It was a wonder he hadn't tried the same technique with his parents. What Kit felt worst about was that with him it had so nearly worked.

They sat on the porch for a little while longer in an unsatisfactory silence. Kit wondered if Dr. Peacham recognized it as unsatisfactory, and knew that this was because he, Kit, was for once not being honest with him. He found he still had a little anger to spare for Peachy, who had placed him in this situation.

Dr. Peacham was the first person Kit had talked to when he began thinking about the priesthood at thirteen, the only person he had talked to before going to the recruitment office in 1914. To ask Dr. Peacham for advice came very naturally to him by now. Indeed, it was the whole rationale behind their involvement in each other's lives. "We think it might be better for you," Dr. Peacham had said when he suggested to the twelve-year-old Christopher that he come live with them. "And let me be quite clear what I mean by that. I mean partly that we think you would be happier in our house, but also, and chiefly, that we think you would grow up to be a better man." Hardly a week had gone by in the last eighteen years when he had not thought about that, about how much he wanted that to be true.

"Have you made a start on your garden?" Dr. Peacham asked.

Kit smiled, but his heart sank a little. This was a good and safe subject. They could talk about it with every appearance of candour and easily avoid all the more difficult topics.

"Just this afternoon. I pulled everything out of the bed on the north side."

And they talked about gardening until Mrs. Peacham called them in to join in a game of cards with the others.

*

Palm Sunday went off without a hitch. It was one of those services with a lot of fiddly bits: baskets of palms and extra Gospel books and everybody just a little off-balance because things were not quite the way they were used to having them. Kit was deacon, and was complimented on his chanting of the Gospel of the Palms by a chorister's wife. Elsa came to the eleven o'clock Mass. He didn't see her there at first; the nave was crowded and, as he discovered later, she sat at the back. But she came up to take one of the bundles of palms that she had helped prepare the day before, knelt very gracefully, and flashed him an altogether indiscreet smile as she was getting up. She was wearing a smart dark-blue suit, very becoming and very appropriate. She did not come up for Communion, but he had not expected her to. On the way out of the church she was talking with Miss Finch about Saskatchewan, and paused just long enough to greet him, smiling again but showing no inclination to linger. He wondered whether this haste was meant to be for his sake or for hers. He found himself intensely aware that the last time they had been alone together he had kissed her. Awkwardly and unromantically.

Monday in Holy Week wasn't what you could call a day off, but he had a list of household chores he wanted to accomplish. The first was to take most of his clothes to the cleaner's; laundry was one of the things Mrs. Whittacker was wholly unable to manage, and he was running out of clean shirts and collars, and had been sitting on floors and sleeping on couches and wrestling with a madman in his cassock, and it was starting to look like it. He spent a truly disgraceful amount of time standing in front of his wardrobe considering what to wear instead, because his second destination, after the cleaner's, was Fortini's Fine Jewellery. In fact, he was considering the merits of two different pullovers when the doorbell rang. He went down to answer it in his vest, assuming it would be Mr. Oates wanting something annoying. He thought that for him to open the door incompletely dressed might provide an opening for a discussion of his need for a proper housekeeper.

It was Harriet Spencer. She looked strained and tired, and as though she had intended to be grave, but at the moment couldn't quite manage it.

"Did you just slide down the banister?" she demanded.

"Please come in. Yes, I did. How on earth could you tell that?"

"I don't know—I heard you jumping off at the bottom, I think. It's a good banister for sliding down—it hasn't got a knobby post to slam into at the end."

"That's right. How can I help you? And … can I finish dressing first?"

"Absolutely you can finish dressing."

"Thanks. I thought you were someone else."

"Yes, I suppose you did." She looked grim. What was that about?

He left her in the living room—she had been in the house a number of times before with Peachy, and had in fact helped him move in—and ran upstairs to grab the nearest of the two pullovers he had been debating. He went back downstairs, on the steps this time.

She was sitting on the couch where Elsa had slept on Friday night, which was now free of curtains (he'd hung them, finally, on Sunday afternoon, with the help of the sexton). She was looking very, very businesslike, even for Harriet. He felt a surge of affection for her; she was such a fine person, she didn't deserve to be tormented this way. This was about Peachy, of course, damn him.

"It's about Elsa," she said.

"What?" (Oh, Kit, do *try* not to sound like a moron.)

"I found out something that she doesn't realize I know, and I decided not to ask her about it. I love her very much, but there are some things we just can't talk about comfortably. So I decided I'd ask you."

"Ask me what?" He had been about to sit down in the chair by the fireplace, but he felt now as if he were about to be interrogated, and should remain standing.

"What happened on Friday night."

"Oh. She didn't tell you anything?"

"She doesn't think she told me anything."

"I see. I'm … inclined to think she might know best about that. I'm not sure it makes very much sense."

"*Sense?*"

"The whole thing. It was complicated." Now he was beginning to be annoyed with Elsa for putting him in this situation. If she wanted to keep things from her friend, she ought to do a better job of it.

Harriet gave him a severe and pitying look. "These things always are complicated, Reverend. And, you know, they're also quite simple. She didn't tell me anything because we haven't talked. I saw the two of you leaving Annesley together Friday night, after you'd seen me home, and when I phoned her Saturday morning, she wasn't in. I phoned back later—I was worried, which was silly, because I could easily have figured out then what happened. But I phoned back, and her busybody neighbour told me that yes, she'd just got in, wearing some strange dress, and that she'd said something flippant about having been at church. I hung up while the woman was fetching Elsa, because I didn't know what I could say to her after that.

"So I'm still worried, Kit—but I don't really know who I'm worried about. No, that's not quite true. I don't think you seduced her, because I don't think Elsa's seducible, and I certainly don't think she seduced you—because why would she have to, for one thing? and for another thing, she's much too decent, whatever she thinks of herself. So I think it just happened, and in the kind of world she really sometimes thinks she lives in, it wouldn't matter, it wouldn't change your opinion of her. It's a nice thought. But we don't live in that world—I don't live in that world, and I'm sure you don't either. I'm sure it will change your opinion of her, whether you want it to or not. Oh, I know this is well beyond 'none of my business.' But in spite of everything I said at that recital, I really like you. I don't want her to have destroyed her chance of a future with you."

He sat down finally. He almost wanted to ask what she thought she, personally, could hope to do about all this. Either she was just trying to make herself more unhappy—a possibility, certainly—or she did, on some level, also believe they lived in Elsa's ideal world, and she could talk a man out of centuries of ingrained rubbish about feminine purity with a little stern common sense.

"Can we go back to the part where I said this was complicated? Because I really meant that."

He told her the whole story, interrupted only when he went to the kitchen to make tea. When he got to the part about the lift, it was surprisingly easy to say, "I had an attack of nerves. I've suffered from crippling claustrophobia since the War." It was also easy to leave it at that. What Elsa had done was Elsa's business.

"I'm sorry for making you tell me all that," she said finally, cradling her empty teacup. "I knew some of it already. I knew about the War—that you fought, I mean, and that Peachy lied about it. He told me, just shortly before … whatever happened. Before he chucked me. He told me he did enlist in 1917, like he said, and that it was entirely because you had gone, and he couldn't stand it any more. He said he knew he would be a hopeless soldier—he's not exactly good at following orders—and that you and he had talked about it once before you left, and you'd agreed with him."

"Yes, I do remember that."

"And then there was his lady friend … his—his—mistress, is what he called her, actually. He was being very honest at this point."

"You don't have to tell me all this, Harriet."

"No, it's all right. I'm sure you know the worst of it. He'd told me about her—Mrs. Caruso—a long time ago. Apparently she wouldn't hear of him enlisting either, and it wasn't until he'd—almost—broken it off with her that he made up his mind. And then of course the War was over before he had finished his basic training—which he was quite hopeless at, as predicted. I just wanted you to know that he had told me all of that."

"I am glad."

"He didn't tell me that you were in love with Elsa." She set the teacup down and looked up at him. "You are, aren't you?"

He nodded. "I was trying not to be—he may have thought that I'd succeeded. *I* thought I'd succeeded, for a little while."

"But you didn't."

"Not in the least, no."

"I shouldn't have said what I said before. I didn't mean to … to … "

"No, please don't. I'm not insulted, I'm not shocked, and you didn't tell me anything about Elsa that I didn't already know."

"Oh." She picked up the teacup again, remembered that it was empty, and set it back down. "You know the funny thing about you, Kit? You're completely unconventional, and you just *don't care* that nobody can tell."

He laughed. "That's not strictly true. I'm just not very forthcoming. I'd be disappointed if some people couldn't figure out what I'm like."

"Well, I am sorry that I misjudged you. And here you and Elsa have been running around getting locked in libraries and things looking for Peachy, and all I've been doing is moping."

"Oh, Harriet. If it makes you feel any better, I've no idea what to do now. And I've done my fair share of moping too."

She laughed. "It shouldn't, but that *does* make me feel better. Maybe I'll take over now and do something useful. In fact, I think I will. I haven't decided what yet, but it will come to me."

*

He did manage to take his clothes to the cleaner's that morning, but he did not go to Fortini's. In the afternoon, when the church was empty, he let himself in and went down the stairs to the basement. He had no particular object, but he found he was too impatient to wait for one. He wandered through the shelves where the choir music was stored, past the wooden figures for the crèche, kneeling haphazardly behind a collection of cast-iron urns, and opened the door of a little back room, scarcely more than a cupboard, filled with candles and paper and baskets for the harvest display.

He closed the door, leaned back against it, and slid down to sit on the floor of the cluttered storeroom. There was a small window near the ceiling—he could just see a corner of the frame—but it was entirely covered up by boxes. As an experiment, he thought about the church above him, picturing the bulk of it, the weight, piling up its timbers and bricks in his mind. He pressed his fingertips clinically to the side of his throat, but he knew that he would feel his pulse to be perfectly steady.

"The question is," he said aloud, "how am I ever to tell her?"

But he thought that quite possibly she already knew.

He got up finally and dusted himself off. On the way out he spotted something shoved far back on a shelf behind the donkey from the crèche: a glass candle holder in a tasteful, fluted silver stand. It was the old presence lamp, the one that had been replaced in the former rector's time by a gaudy donation with brass cherub heads sticking bulbously out of the sides. Nobody had seemed to know where the old one was, or to be willing to look for it. He pulled it out of its not-very-convincing hiding place. The glass was slightly chipped, the silver tarnished, but it was otherwise sound and beautiful. He carried it with him as he went upstairs, humming "Soldiers of Christ, Arise."

Mr. Oates met him at the top of the stairs.

"Hallo, Mr. Oates!" Kit said brightly. Mr. Oates looked slightly confused. "I've been poking around in the basement—am I covered in cobwebs?"

"No, Father. I, er, understood that you suffered from claustrophobia or something of that nature, which prevented your going into the basement."

"Something like that. It was a species of what they call shell-shock. But I've recently been feeling much better. Look what I found." He held up the presence lamp.

"Yes."

"I thought we could get this one repaired to use on ordinary days and keep your father's gift for feast days. It would be nice to have some distinction."

"Oh! Yes—yes, certainly." And in a surprising burst of candour, he added, "I never really liked that thing my father donated. A very good and pious man, my father, but with little aesthetic sense. I didn't know you were a veteran."

"No. I didn't talk about it." Kit leaned on the railing and smiled up at Mr. Oates. The new truth was, in its way, even more difficult to talk about—he certainly hadn't managed it with his family, or even with Harriet—but this was a difficulty which he realized he could joyfully overcome. And Mr. Oates, for all his faults, was the sort of man to believe in miracles. "I shouldn't have said that I just started to feel better. It wasn't like that. A friend prayed for me, and I was healed. It's—at least—one of the best things that has ever happened to me."

A smile of startling sweetness spread over Mr. Oates's broad face. "I am so glad, Father. So glad."

*

It was Tuesday, and he had collected his cassock from the cleaner's, by the time he made it to Fortini's Fine Jewellery. Signs in the window of the small shop offered discounts and payment plans above displays of gold bangles and watches. On the doorstep it occurred to him to wonder whether an employee would get in trouble for talking to acquaintances when she was supposed to be working. But it was 1:00 on a weekday, and the shop would surely not be busy.

It was empty, in fact, except for a pretty dark-haired girl behind the counter, dusting a display of earrings with desultory flicks of a cloth. She glanced up with a professional smile which changed into a look of genuine appreciation when she saw Kit.

"I'm looking for Elsa Nordqvist—is she working today?"

"Well, isn't she popular! There was a tall foreign gentleman asking for her not more than a couple of minutes ago. She's on her lunch break, as I told him."

"Ah."

"You're welcome to wait, though. She should be back any moment. She's always very prompt."

He wondered whether he should leave. Did he want to be here when the other man came back? As a matter of curiosity, he thought that he did. He thanked the girl and wandered down the counter to look at a box of gaudy cufflinks.

The girl followed him, but she was more interested in finding out facts about Elsa than in trying to sell him cufflinks. "I didn't know she was Catholic," she said.

"She isn't."

"Oh. She must be religious, though. The other gentleman said he was going to go read his Bible while he waited for her."

"Did he? I thought I'd look at cufflinks."

She frowned as though trying to figure out whether this was a joke or just an inappropriate thing for him to say.

The bell over the door tinkled, and Kit looked up, but it was not Elsa. It was, clearly, the man who had been reading his Bible. He was an extremely tall, extremely blond, man in his fifties, wearing an ill-fitting blue suit and carrying a battered suitcase. He stopped just inside the door when he saw Kit, and stood staring at him with an incredible intensity. If it hadn't already been obvious who he was, that look would have clinched it.

"Mr. Nordqvist! How d'you do? My name's Christopher Underhill—we haven't actually met, but ... " He held out his hand.

Mr. Nordqvist did not take it. He went on staring at Kit, and when he finally spoke, what he said, in heavily accented English, was, "O give thanks unto the Lord, for he is good: for his mercy endureth forever!"

"I couldn't agree more," said Kit.

And then the sound of a door closing behind the counter, and Elsa, in astonishment: "Pappa!"

And Kit started forward just in time to catch Mr. Nordqvist as he crumpled toward the floor in a dead faint.

Chapter Thirteen

HOME, REJOICING

"He was just hungry—he'd been on the train all day and hadn't had anything to eat since breakfast. That's why he fainted. He'll be fine. Kit—Mr. Underhill—just happened to be here. It's not even related. He's a friend of mine."

Mr. Fortini still looked as though he thought this was a thin story to account for the presence of a huge, prostrate Swede and a priest in his office. As far as he was concerned, the priest could only be involved because the other man was dying, and since both of them seemed to have something to do with Elsa, the whole regrettable situation had to be her fault. Elsa left him to his perplexity and ducked back into the office. She didn't want to leave Kit and her father alone together.

I'm the one who should have fainted, she thought. She hadn't had the slightest warning of her father's arrival, and then to come in and find him quoting Psalms at the last person in Toronto she would have wanted him to meet …

"But why did you cut your hair off, Elsa?" Lars Nordqvist asked as she closed the door behind her, as if this were a topic they had been discussing.

He was sitting on the floor of the office, his long legs bent because there was not enough space between the desk and the wall to stretch them out, cradling a mug of cocoa in his huge hands. Kit, who had made the cocoa, was perched on the edge of the desk, displaying an air of calm and compassionate detachment that seemed at the same time very natural to him and very deliberate. She wished she could analyze the effect a little less and just appreciate it. She supposed that she knew him too well.

"I wanted to. I thought it would look nice. And speak English, Pappa. It isn't polite," she switched to English herself for the last sentence only, then realized that this made it sound as if what he had been saying in Swedish might have been rude.

"'But if a woman have long hair, it is a glory to her: for her hair is given to her for a covering.'" She needn't have bothered; her father always quoted Scripture in English. He'd been saved in that language, after all.

"Oh, stop it. Are you feeling better?"

He sipped his cocoa. "You work in this place? This shop?"

"You know I do. I told you so in my letter. That's how you knew to come here."

"But what about your studies?"

"I told you that too. I've given them up. Temporarily. There was a misunderstanding with one of my professors. You know all this."

"I do not know what I know," he said mysteriously in Swedish.

Elsa sighed and folded her arms. Kit, catching her eye, pointed at himself and then at the door, and raised his eyebrows. *Did she want him to go?* She wished he had not been there in the first place, but since he was, no, she didn't want him to go. But perhaps it would be kinder to him.

"Pappa, would you like Kit to go fetch you some sandwiches or something else to eat?"

Lars Nordqvist tipped back his head to look up at Kit, and put out a hand to touch him, for some reason. Because of their relative positions, he ended up seizing him by the ankle. If Kit found this disconcerting, he did not show it.

"Pappa … " Elsa tried feebly to protest.

"Who are you?" Mr. Nordqvist asked Kit. "You told me your name—Oonderhill—but who *are* you? How did you know my name?"

"I'm the vicar of an Anglican church not far from here. I guessed your name because I thought you looked like your daughter. And because it looked to me, when you walked in the door, as if you recognized me. But we've never met."

"I saw you in a dream."

"That's what I thought."

"You saw a man who was *dressed* like him," said Elsa.

Her father looked up at her. "No," he said. "I saw this man. It was his face that I remembered. He was dressed in white. Truly, God is great, and we are miserable sinners who cannot save ourselves! I thought that I had faith, but if I truly had faith, why would this surprise me?"

Kit looked down at him. "Oh, quite. 'For all have sinned, and come short of the glory of God.'"

Mr. Nordqvist nodded approvingly.

"What sort of white?" Elsa asked. *Washed in the blood of the Lamb? That sort of white?* For the first time, the thought of her father's vision frightened her.

"Popish tomfoolery," said Mr. Nordqvist, but without vehemence.

"Tell us about it," said Kit. "What else did you see?"

"It was a dream—what I mean is that it took the form of a dream. I seemed to know several things at once."

"The way you do in a dream," Kit agreed.

"I knew you to be a good man and a true servant of the Lord," Mr. Nordqvist said, patting Kit's shoe with a sort of absent approval. "I saw you dressed in white, in a white … thing, with gold … " He gestured vaguely up and down.

"Orphreys," Kit supplied.

"What?"

"Never mind. What else?"

"There was smoke, and … bells ringing."

"No doubt."

"And I knew, I felt in my mind, that you were going toward a great trial. I felt … that you would offer yourself for someone's sake, to save someone."

Kit looked down at him, expressionless.

"And—and I was involved somehow, Pappa?"

He shook his head. "No, I didn't see you in the dream. I knew that the place was Toronto. That is why I felt it was right for you to come here."

"That was all? But it's a big city, Pappa—we might not even have met!" Elsa protested illogically.

"But you did, didn't you?"

"We did," said Kit. "We met last fall on the beach."

"We became very good friends," said Elsa. *I don't want him to sacrifice himself for someone. Even if the someone might be me.*

Then she saw the way that Kit was looking at her: surprised, his calm detachment momentarily breached. She realized that he hadn't thought she would describe him that way.

"I'll go get sandwiches," he said suddenly. "You need something more than cocoa and biscuits, sir."

Rather than climbing over the desk chair and Mr. Nordqvist's legs, he gathered himself up onto the desk and scooted down to the far end of it, where he hopped off. Mr. Nordqvist watched this display with startled amusement. Kit picked up some papers that he had dislodged and put them back on the desk.

"Is that place across the street any good?" he asked Elsa, who stood aside to let him through the office door.

"Oh, yes, perfectly decent."

She stood in the doorway. He looked at her, then past her, and suddenly he laughed.

"Elsa! Look." He held out his right hand, palm down. She looked at it, unsure what she was supposed to be seeing, other than Kit's neat, strong hand. The signet ring winked at her.

"Oh, that. I figured that out—XP being Chi-Rho really. Silly of me not to have seen it immediately. You did, I think."

"I didn't mean that," he said, turning his hand over, and then taking it away self-consciously and putting it in his pocket. "It's nothing. I'd better go."

She went back into the office and closed the door behind her again. She didn't try to pursue his train of thought; there was too much else to think about.

"You didn't mention about the letters you saw," she said, leaning back against the door and speaking Swedish again. It put her at a disadvantage; she didn't use it often enough, and was rusty. But it seemed a necessary filial gesture now that they were alone.

Her father was occupied with getting to his feet in the small space available on the office floor. He dusted off his trousers and shook his head.

"I must have been mistaken about that. I thought they were the man's initials, but they're not."

"They're not anybody's initials. It's a …" She searched for the Swedish word. "A monogram, the first two letters of 'Christ' in Greek."

"Ah!"

"He has a ring with that device on it. And his given name is Christopher. It's the beginning of his name too. So you weren't far wrong."

"Ah! I see. I like him," he added, after a moment. "And I have remembered where I saw him before. It was seeing him smile that brought it to mind. Of course he was not smiling in that dream."

"What do you mean, where you saw him before? He said quite clearly he'd never met you."

"Not met him. Seen him. Drawings of him. Do you remember Brother Virgil Tucker from the Tree of Life? His son was an artist, and he was killed in France at the very end of the War. He used to send sketches home with his letters. I think your little priest must have been in his regiment."

"He's not *little*, and he's not mine. How can you be sure it was him? That was years ago."

"He doesn't seem to have aged much. Some men don't. But it wasn't years ago that I saw the pictures—it was last summer. Brother Virgil was going through his son's things and showed them to us. There were several of your friend—Isaac must have liked him as a subject."

"Of course. He was beautiful. He still is. Pappa, if you saw pictures of him … "

She waited for him to complete her sentence, but he didn't.

"If you saw pictures of him, you didn't have a vision. You dreamt about somebody you had seen pictures of. It doesn't mean anything." And it didn't matter that the idea of Kit sacrificing himself to save someone sounded so painfully in character.

"Of course it means something, Elsa," her father said patiently. This was his usual manner: patient, implacable, totally without logic. "It means that Almighty God wanted me to know something about this man. Something that was going to happen."

She shook her head. "It was just a memorable dream. You must have heard details about him from Virgil Tucker. His son probably wrote that Kit was an Anglo-Catholic and had been training for the priesthood in Toronto. That's how you knew all that in your dream. It was just a coincidence that he and I met."

Her father looked as if none of this was getting through to him. Elsa decided that she shouldn't have expected it to. It was enough that it had got through to her.

"Why did you come, Pappa? Why now?"

"God was telling me that you needed help."

She sighed. "What does that mean, exactly?"

"I don't know. That you might be in danger, or in need."

"No, what does it mean that God was telling you that? Doesn't it actually mean that you found yourself *thinking* that, that you found the thought in your head, for no obvious reason, and you decided it came from God?"

"Yes … No … God was telling me."

"How? How was God telling you? How does God tell you things?"

"Just … as you said. I find the thought in my head. From God, who has put it there."

"You *think* that God has put it there."

"God has put it there."

"Okay."

"Who else would have put it there?"

"Nobody. You. Your own subconscious. Nobody else. What if— what if you came up with it all on your own?"

"Then it is sin. Was it wrong? This thought, that you were in danger."

"Yes! Yes, it was wrong! I'm not in danger, I don't need help! And this is *not helpful*! Showing up at my work like this, embarrassing me in front of—in front of my friend. Carrying on about your stupid vision when it was really just a senseless dream. You've—you've made him think he's going to die."

"Should I have kept quiet about that?"

The worst part of it was that he asked these things with an air of genuine questioning; he was absolutely sure of what he believed, but he also truly wanted to hear his daughter's view. Since her childhood he had always been proud of her intelligence, and would have been the first to say that it surpassed his own. Since she had stopped believing the things that he believed, this attitude had begun to seem to her like a tragedy.

"No," she said wearily, "no, according to your own lights you did the right thing. I just wish you hadn't."

She heard the bell from the shop, and opened the office door to see Kit returning with sandwiches and pastries. The pastries he offered to Gladys and Mr. Fortini before bringing the sandwiches in to Mr. Nordqvist.

"The sun's out now," he reported. "When you've finished those, sir, why don't we walk over to my church? It's not far, and I'd like to show it to you. Besides, I think Elsa has work to do. You can come back and meet her at closing."

So Mr. Nordqvist ate his sandwiches, and Kit sat in the desk chair and chatted inconsequentially while he waited. This also seemed strategic, but was very deftly done. When they got up to go, Elsa finally said, "Did you know an artist named Isaac Tucker?"

"Yes. He was in my regiment."

"Did he ever draw a picture of you?"

"He might have done. He was always drawing pictures of everything." He looked uncertain for a moment, like a child unsure what behaviour will please his elders. *I can talk about this sort of thing now; is that what you want?* "I didn't know him well," he admitted.

"Pappa knows his father. He showed him Isaac's pictures, and there were several of you. He just remembered that now. That's where he'd seen you before. That's why you found your way into his dream."

"Oh, that's a relief, isn't it?" said Kit. "So it's not quite so uncanny as it seemed, then. You must be a bit relieved, sir." This was much less deft.

For a moment Mr. Nordqvist looked down at Kit (who really was almost short next to him) as if he could not understand why he would say this.

Finally, frowning, he said, "Yes."

They were almost out the shop door when Kit turned back.

"I nearly forgot. The whole reason I came here. Are you busy on Friday night? Late? It would have to be rather late—I can't get away until after Way of the Cross."

"Am I ... No, I don't think so." Could this possibly be what it sounded like? "I was invited to a party at Mrs. Graves's, but I wasn't really thinking of going."

"Can I talk you into it? Because it's a long story, but I've been invited too, and I'd much rather you came with me than not."

"Oh, I see." So it wasn't. "Of course."

"Splendid! I'll pick you up at nine?"

"Or we could just meet there, if that would be … No, forget I said that. I'll expect you at nine o'clock. You remember my address? And if Professor Hallam is there and tries to attack you, I promise to get out of his way."

He left with her father to walk to St. John's, and she went back to the office to tidy up. It had been a grey and bleak morning, but he had said the sun was out now. She hadn't noticed, back here. The office had no window.

She came back out into the shop and, because there were no customers to be helped, began very assiduously polishing rings, to make up for all the time she had just spent not working, and in the hope that Mr. Fortini would leave her alone. She looked out the window as she polished, at the sun gleaming on parked cars on St. Clair. She dropped the ring she had been working on, and it clicked and spun on the counter.

The office had no window, and was so crowded with furniture that her father couldn't stretch out his legs and Kit had had to slide across the desk to get out. But he had sat in there looking perfectly at ease. What he had been trying to show Elsa when he held out his hand was that it had been steady. He hadn't even noticed the confined space until he was out of it.

Did he think that she had something to do with this? He must. And maybe, in an indirect way, she did; maybe if he believed that her invocation in the elevator could have some effect, it *did* have some effect. That was, after all, how these psychological things worked.

But he had not persisted in his explanation. He had stopped and put his hand in his pocket. He had not said anything about the ring, either, back when he must first have put the thing together. He hadn't thought it would convince her. He hadn't thought either of these things would convince her. And he'd been right, of course; they hadn't. But why had that mattered to him?

*

The week went downhill. Even though Elsa's father had walked out of the office alive, Mr. Fortini seemed to have taken against her after the incident, and began finding fault with everything she did in the shop. Gladys had decided that she was scheming to entrap a Catholic priest, and treated her with a mixture of scorn and superstitious awe. Elsa had realized that if Sunday had been Palm Sunday, then Friday must be Good Friday, and felt mortified that she had for a few moments thought Kit was asking her on a date.

Her father returned to the shop at closing time on Tuesday with the news that Kit had invited him to stay at the St. John's rectory. Knowing her father, she could imagine how this had come about; he had probably come to Toronto without any plan of where to stay, and had started innocently asking Kit about hotels. He had taken to referring to Kit as "Brother Christopher," which made Elsa cringe. She could only imagine what Kit thought of it. Speculating what might be going on in that house with the two of them under the same roof occupied an uncomfortable proportion of her thoughts all that week. After a while it occurred to her that Kit, sensitive as he was to other people's feelings, must have had some inkling of how this arrangement would affect her, and she began to wonder what he was playing at. By Thursday she thought she had figured it out.

"I try to talk about you," her father explained as they ate dinner together that night, at a restaurant near her work. Having decided that he approved of "Brother Christopher," he had embarrassingly taken it upon himself to sing Elsa's praises to him. "I try to talk about you, and he does listen politely, but he always wants to change the subject to theology. Are you *sure* they're allowed to marry?"

"I'm sure! What do you think that stupid gigantic house is for?

He's just being a—just teasing you. When did you even learn the word 'theology'? And Pappa, please don't keep trying to talk about me. It's not going to look very subtle."

"I am only trying to help," he said innocently. And then, as he was paying the bill, the bombshell: "I must get back. The service starts at eight."

"The what?"

"The church service. Maundy Thursday."

"You're not going to a—a Mass at St. John's?"

"Of course I am. How could I stay under the man's roof and refuse to worship with him? Besides, he made it sound very interesting."

"But Pappa, you know it's not your kind of church. Obviously you know that." He'd seen the place; he'd been there three days. "But you can't get up and testify or start preaching, or—there won't even be any hymns that you know." Probably untrue; she thought back to that night in the library. "I think you'll find it very odd. And Maundy Thursday—I mean, it's likely to be *very* odd, even by these people's standards. I don't think you'll like it."

"Perhaps I won't. But I shall know what to do in that case."

"Which is what?"

"Sit through it with patience, and explain my thoughts afterward to Brother Christopher."

"*Do* you have to keep calling him that?"

In the end Elsa decided she had to go with him. There was no time to go home, so she had to go in what she was wearing: the same red dress in which she had first visited St. John's. Her father had called it "very modern" when he first saw it, but he made no comment on its appropriateness now.

When they arrived at the church, she tried unsuccessfully to convince him to sit at the back.

"I want to see what goes on," he protested, standing stubbornly in the aisle as she tried to edge into the last pew.

"You can see all right from back here, and you won't—we won't make spectacles of ourselves. There's all sorts of kneeling and bowing and—and—things, and everybody will know what to do except us. We don't want to be at the front."

He stared at her with what looked like puzzled concern, and didn't move from the aisle. "It does not trouble me to make a spectacle of myself in the name of righteousness. When did you begin to worry about such things?"

She slipped back out of the pew and marched miserably down the aisle to the very front.

The choir processed in, and there was a very medieval hymn that referred to the Cross as a Tree. Elsa was distracted by wondering what exactly the Latin phrase was that had been rendered as "shines forth in mystic glow," and how that could have been avoided. Her father nudged her and said in his idea of a whisper, "It's not exactly what he was wearing in my dream, but it's the same *type* of thing."

"Shh."

She was annoyed to realize that she had missed seeing Kit come in. They were up at the altar now, and there was some business with a censer. The choir began to sing the Kyrie in Greek, and Elsa realized that they should be sitting—no, kneeling, but they were not going to do that. Her father had taken out of his pocket a stub of a pencil and the dog-eared little notebook in which he wrote down sermon ideas that came to him while he was working on the farm. He licked the tip of the pencil and began scribbling something, murmuring under his breath. Elsa stared at the pages of her prayer book and decided that she would try to ignore this.

On Palm Sunday she had sat at the back, enjoying her detachment from the proceedings but feeling it to be precarious. She had gone up to receive a palm mostly in order to surprise Kit, who had been looking excessively gorgeous in his red dalmatic. But kneeling at the altar rail she had felt a powerful desire actually to be part of all this. It was a spurious and superficial desire, based on the aesthetics of the thing, like a desire to dance when you watched a ballet, or to sing when you listened to a choir. It didn't really have anything to do with God. But it had been powerful all the same.

During the Scripture readings her father contented himself with nodding gravely. During the sermon—delivered by an elderly assistant priest whose name Elsa did not know—he scribbled in his notebook and muttered. She was scarcely able to follow the old priest's words herself, although her father was clearly doing his best not to distract her. He sang along enthusiastically in the hymns, but when the congregation rose to sing the Creed he was too busy editorializing in an undertone about Faith and Scripture to notice, presumably, that she wasn't singing any of it. She realized that she wanted him to notice; she wanted to talk to him properly about this.

She needn't have worried about how he would behave during the Consecration, the part that most interested her. He was, she supposed, critical of the whole thing, but he was able to show respect. She was left wondering how much worse was her improper interest than his respectful detachment. She was watching Kit, listening to his voice, admiring again the way that he seemed himself and yet more than himself, clothed in the Power in which he believed; she was interested, certainly, but she was not worshipping.

If this is wrong, she thought, *if this is not the right way, or at least the right way for me at this moment ... please let me stop.* And she went on hearing not just the words but the voice that spoke them. And instead of a denial, what came to her—the thought that she found in her mind—was that perhaps wanting to be part of a beautiful thing unfolding, a thing in which he was just one beautiful part, was not after all a spurious and superficial desire. Maybe it was meaningless to suggest that it had "nothing to do with God."

Her father rose to go up for Communion, and, because there were other people in the pew and she was afraid of making a scene, she got up too. This threw her into a kind of panic, because then there was no sitting back down again, but she wasn't ready, she hadn't done whatever it was she should have done, the time—if there was ever going to be a time—was not now. She was so busy worrying about what she was going to do that she didn't notice whether her father knelt or not, whether he tried to take the chalice away from the assistant priest, or what kind of fool he made of himself. She knelt, and kept her hands firmly clasped on the altar rail, and she didn't know exactly what sort of calamity she expected—a thunderbolt from the church ceiling, or just a moment of awkwardness—but it didn't come. She realized that she had done exactly what she had been praying for—forgotten for a moment that the priest was Kit. He laid his hand lightly on her head, and blessed her, and that was it. It was not even a strange situation. She followed her father back to their pew feeling giddy with relief—feeling, in fact, *blessed*. The choir was singing a lilting paraphrase of Psalm 23; she fumbled through the hymn book and quietly joined in.

Perverse and foolish oft I strayed,
But yet in love he sought me,
And on his shoulder gently laid,
And home, rejoicing, brought me.

Communion was over, and then something else began happening, something she hadn't been prepared for, although she had warned her father that the service would be strange. There was a solemn procession down the aisle to the little chapel where she had first seen Kit celebrate Mass, which was now full of candles and flowers. Then the acolytes began gravely and systematically dismantling the sanctuary. They covered the great candlesticks again, this time in black shrouds; they carried all the little candles away, and all the flowers that had been behind the altar. They took down the blue curtains, and pulled the drapery off the altar itself, exposing the dark wood underneath, and Kit, who had himself taken off his chasuble and was in a plain white robe, washed the bare surface of the altar. And all the while the choir chanted the 22nd Psalm.

"What are they doing?" her father whispered.

She shook her head.

"What?"

"I *don't know.*"

Kit and his assistants left the sanctuary and knelt on the step outside the rail, and the acolytes extinguished the remaining candles and left as well. The electric lights in the sanctuary were turned off.

"On the Mount of Olives, I prayed to the Father: Father, if it be possible, let this cup pass from me; the spirit is willing but the flesh is weak. Thy will be done."

"Nevertheless," the congregation replied, "not as I will, but as thou wilt. Thy will be done."

The ministers moved down and knelt on the bare tiled floor in the middle of the choir.

"Behold the hour is at hand, and the Son of Man shall be delivered into the hands of sinners: ye shall flee, but I go to be sacrificed for you."

"Nevertheless, not as I will, but as thou wilt. Thy will be done."

It was like nothing she had seen before, this orchestrated bleakness and mourning. An unmoved part of her mind pronounced it silly. *You believe that he died, but not that he stayed dead. Surely it is ridiculous to pretend to be sad.*

But she was contradicting herself now. The unrelenting rejoicing of the Revival had come to seem to her thin and stifling. This wasn't ridiculous; it was honest. This is the way it unfolds: through pain and death and illogic. Through ugly things, and little things, unremarkable in themselves. Whatever it is that is happening, this, anyway, is how it happens.

All of the lights were off now, and the church was quite dark. The choir was filing out quietly, without ceremony. Kit must have left too; there would be no friendly chatting with people at the door. She felt stupidly desolated.

"What do we do now?" her father whispered.

Some members of the congregation were getting up and leaving.

Some were going over to the chapel where the candles were still lit. Some remained in their pews.

"We sit and pray."

"In the *dark*?"

Yes, in the dark. With no proof—no actual proof—that the light exists at all.

"You don't have to if you don't want to."

"Of course I want to. 'Rejoice evermore. Pray without ceasing. In everything give thanks: for this is—'"

"Yes, but quietly, Pappa."

It was not so dark that she could not see his teasing smile. He bowed his head over his joined hands.

"Dear Lord Jesus, please bless Elsa. Help her to love your word and your truth, wherever she finds them."

She didn't have to shush him again. After that they sat in silence. The light from the chapel in the corner glowed like a star, like a warm hearth beckoning a traveller in from the cold.

Pray without ceasing. It was work. She had thought of it as a thing you possessed or didn't possess, but the truth was that it was work, and she had not wanted to do it.

She could tell that her father was getting restless and would have liked to leave, although he was trying not to show it. He wasn't really one to sit still, even when he prayed; he liked to stride about and shout ecstatically at God. She had come here trying to humour him, but it had ended up the other way around. He looked up at a dark figure that had appeared in the aisle.

"Brother Christopher."

Kit slid into the pew beside them. "I thought you might like to go back to the house, sir," he whispered. "I brought you the key."

"What will you be doing?"

"Keeping vigil at the Altar of Repose—in the chapel over there."

"Doing what?"

"Praying."

Mr. Nordqvist nodded approvingly. "Without ceasing. I will go read my Bible." He took the offered key. "It was very interesting, Brother. Very interesting. I am glad I came."

Kit smiled. "So am I, sir. Elsa, Mrs. Barrington has offered to drive you home, if you like."

"Oh, that's … very kind."

It was—Mrs. Barrington could easily have cut her dead, and Elsa wouldn't really have blamed her. And it was late, and she hadn't been looking forward to the cold wait for the streetcar at an unfamiliar stop. She couldn't very well say that she wanted to stay, to approach that little glittering altar in the corner, when she wasn't even sure what it was about.

"I'll see you tomorrow," said Kit, as they parted ways in the aisle.

"Tomorrow? Oh, yes. Of course."

He meant the party they were going to in the evening. For a moment she had imagined he expected to see her at church in the morning. For another moment, as she watched him walk away toward the warm hearth beckoning in the darkness, she wanted to ask what time the service was.

*

Kit arrived exactly on time to pick her up on Friday night. When she came to the front door, he was walking down the street, looking at the numbers of the buildings.

It was a warm night for the beginning of April, and she had decided to wear only a shawl instead of her coat. She thought that the shawl, which was patterned in grey and blue, softened and changed the effect of the black dress—which, after all, he had seen before. She was ashamed of how much time she had spent after she got home from work considering this. Doubly ashamed when she saw that, of course, he hadn't changed for the party, but had come in his cassock and smart hat as usual. Though to tell the truth she wouldn't have wanted him to show up on Mrs. Graves's doorstep dressed any differently.

He had, however, done one thing that surprised her. He had brought her flowers.

"These are by way of an apology," he said, handing over the paper-wrapped sheaf without ceremony.

"For what?"

"For inviting your father to stay with me."

"But that was terribly nice of you! He was so grateful—and not just to be spared the expense of a hotel. He really likes you. I hope you don't think—"

"No, I'm not apologizing to *him*. And don't worry—he's a model house guest. The first I've ever had, incidentally, which is rather special. It just occurred to me that if our situations could be reversed—if my mother were still alive, and you invited her to stay with you—I'd be pretty well prostrated with embarrassment. Notwithstanding how much I loved my mother, and how well I'm sure the two of you would have got on. So on the off-chance that you might feel similarly—and I've no proof that you do, of course—I thought I should apologize." He gave her a look that was partly innocent and partly sly.

"I see. And I most fervently accept."

He laughed.

"I should put these in water. Do you … Would you … Come up."

"Okay."

As he followed her up the stairs, she tried to remember how much of a mess her apartment was. She thought she might have left her discarded stockings on the floor when she was searching for a pair without runs, and she knew she hadn't washed her dishes from dinner, but she couldn't remember whether she had made the bed. She was not well prepared for guests.

The bed was made, though sloppily, and the stockings were indeed crumpled on the floor, but the dishes were at least in the sink. Her books were lined up neatly on her desk, and piled neatly on the floor (she had yet to buy a shelf), and above the desk were a number of coloured postcards of ruins that she had recently stuck up with drawing pins, her only attempt at decorating. She was a little ashamed of this. He was a person who put pictures on the walls and had enough dishes to accommodate extra people for breakfast, even if they didn't all match. A person who thought it was "rather special" to have a house guest.

"Oh, you have a balcony," he observed, remaining politely just inside the door of the apartment and leaning in the door-frame. "I love balconies."

"There's not much of a view. We're only on the second floor." She set the wrapped flowers on the counter and pretended to look in the cupboards for a vase. She didn't have a vase.

"Still, you could sit out there in the summer evenings and read, I expect."

She hadn't thought that far ahead; she hadn't imagined herself living in this apartment for that long. But she didn't have any other plan.

"It's rather cozy," he said. "The apartment, I mean."

"Do you think so?"

"Well, I have a renewed appreciation for small spaces. I could be bounded in a nutshell and … all that. And there's nothing cozy about my house. Do you like living by yourself?"

She gave this some thought. "I suppose … when I think about it in isolation from all the things I *don't* like about my life right now, yes, I do. Not so much being by myself, but having my own place. I do like that."

"Me too. And at the same time I get lonely. Do you *have* a vase, or are you hoping that one will miraculously appear if you look in the cupboards long enough?"

"I don't have a vase."

"Is there flour in that jar on the counter marked 'flour'?"

"Of *course* not. How clever you are."

She filled the jar with water and carefully opened the paper surrounding the flowers. They were tulips: red, yellow, and purple: sturdy, stunning flowers, full of life and colour. She stood them in the flour jar and set it in the only clear spot on her desk.

"They're so beautiful. Where did you manage to buy flowers on Good Friday?"

"I didn't precisely buy them. One of my wardens is a greengrocer, and he was sending over a wagonload of lilies for Sunday—I asked if I could have some tulips at the same time, as a favour."

She thought he was trying to make the whole thing sound as unromantic as possible, but in fact a really flattering amount of planning had gone into it. She didn't somehow think that he had chosen tulips at random, either.

"We should get going," he said. "I thought we could pick up a taxi on College."

"Oh, no! Let's just take the streetcar. It isn't far, and—"That had been one word too many. He obviously had not taken a taxi to get here, but it was hard to say what that meant. In any case, she should have pretended not to notice.

"Thanks, but I'm afraid it does have to be a taxi. I'll explain on the way."

They left her apartment and went back down the stairs and out the front door. "There were two things I meant to tell you when I called at your shop on Tuesday," he said as they walked up to College Street. "The first is that Peachy wrote his parents another letter, claiming to be in Muskoka with some painters."

"Oh. That would explain things, I suppose."

"If we believed it."

"Which we don't."

"No, on the whole, I think we don't."

She nodded. "What about his parents? Do they believe it?"

"They do. But they still think it was Harriet who broke up with him, not the other way around. So it seems plausible to them that he might be in the mood to flee from civilization. That's certainly what the letter made it sound like he was doing."

"And … you haven't told them the whole story about Harriet, and Mrs. Graves, and the mad professor in the library?"

"Well, no. It's all a bit involved. And they seemed very relieved by the letter. I didn't really have the heart."

"Dear me. Positively a web of deceit by your standards."

"Yes."

"And the second thing? You said you had two things to tell me."

"It's slightly more complicated. I happened to mention you to my sister—"

"You have a sister?"

"Half-sister."

"Obviously. Continue."

"She's fifteen years younger than I, and we've never lived under the same roof—she's more like a cousin or a niece or something, but, in fact, she's my sister. And I spasmodically try to act like a brother, which is what this is about, I suppose. Anyway, Vera—that's her name—has recently decided that she wants to make her living designing dresses, which sounds pretty innocent to me, but her parents have their hearts set on her going to university, and are quite upset about it. They don't offer particularly convincing arguments, because they're her parents, and so naturally I thought of you. I told her she should meet you."

"Did you tell her that I dropped out of university and work in a jeweller's shop?"

"No. I thought you could tell her that, if you want, and how much you'd rather be back in school—or not. That isn't really the point."

"And what is the point?

"The point is I talked about you in front of my stepmother."

"Yes?"

"And now she thinks you're 'a woman in my life.'"

"I am, you know."

"And she's *so looking forward to meeting you.*"

She laughed.

"So, you know," he said, "I wouldn't subject you to that for the world, but—"

"You're trying to be a good brother."

"Even then. No, the thing is, Polly's idea was that I should bring you along to this party tonight."

"Oh, I see!"

"Yes. A friend invited her. Of course my first inclination was to say, 'Are you mad? I'm not going to a party on Good Friday.' Actually I think I may have said that—I'm not very diplomatic with my stepmother. But then two things occurred to me. First, we still think Peachy is mixed up with these people, and if he's not actually getting drunk in the woods with painters, he may be there. And second, Polly's a featherbrain and Vera's fifteen, and a very young fifteen, and I don't trust either of them not to get into some kind of trouble with these people." He spotted a taxi and stepped off the curb to hail it.

"So," she said, as he took his seat in the back of the taxi beside her, "we're doing this because you don't want your stepmother to think you're too cheap to pay for a taxi when you take a girl out."

"Admiral Road," he told the driver. "That's about it, yes."

Like the business with the tulips, this offhand invitation to meet his family was oddly flattering. He obviously had a strained and peculiar relationship with these people, and would have preferred not to expose her to them. But she couldn't help thinking that if he had liked her less he would have been more likely to give in to that preference. And at the same time, he clearly didn't think that she would care particularly about meeting his people, or he would have prepared her for it sooner.

His right hand lay on the car seat between them, and she was tempted to touch it. In fact, she sat thinking that she was going to, but she didn't.

"Did you tell my father that we were going to a party?"

"No. I told him I had to go out, but not where. He was going to a prayer meeting downtown that I found out for him."

"So have you given up trying to convert him?"

He grinned. "It's not like that. We're having great fun trying to convert each other."

"What? But you're not—you wouldn't … "

"Take him seriously? Of course I do. We have some major theological differences, but we also agree about a lot. As far as I can make out, the Tree of Life Revival is a pretty orthodox affair. Doctrinally, anyway."

"And their practices?"

"You mean the faith healing and so on? You won't hear me speak a word against that."

"No," she said, looking down at his hands, which were both in his lap now. "No, I suppose not."

The taxi stopped, at Kit's instruction, in front of a huge pink Neo-Romanesque building that alarmed Elsa until she realized it was not a mansion but a duplex. Kit paid the driver and opened Elsa's door. On the path to the left-hand door of the monstrous house, he stopped suddenly.

"Elsa. I've been trying to think how to say this—whether to say this. I know you find it very hard to believe that what happened in the lift last Friday … that anything happened. I don't know if you realize that I do too."

She looked at him in surprise for a moment, then she nodded. "I think so. Yes. I think I was just beginning to realize that."

"I'm sorry—this was obviously a ridiculous moment to bring it up."

"No. Thank you. I'm glad you did."

They stood for a moment longer on the path. She was picturing him kneeling on the church floor in that strange movement of choreographed sadness. *Not as I will, but as Thou wilt.*

"We should go ring the bell," he said finally.

They rang the bell, and the door was answered, after some sounds of running and shouting, by a small, beautiful, dark-haired woman in a kind of stagey Ancient Greek outfit, all diaphanous drapery and elaborate makeup. She stood aside to usher them into a violently modern hallway, and she and Elsa stared at one another.

You only needed to take one look at her to understand why the Peachams had adopted Kit. The woman could not have been much more than thirty-five. The ersatz Greek outfit was perversely fitting. Edmund from *King Lear* wasn't the literary precedent that Elsa thought Kit ought to have worried about.

"Polly, this is my friend Elsa Nordqvist," said Kit finally. Had he forgotten that it was a costume party, or had he just never known? If he'd forgotten, she decided, he would have said so. He hadn't known.

"Hello, Mrs. Underhill," said Elsa, too hastily, holding out her hand.

"Oh … dear … no," said the woman with a kind of delicate shock. "It's Whitmore, dear—Polly Whitmore."

"Of course," Elsa cut off the embarrassed, patronizing explanation that she saw coming. "I wasn't thinking. Silly of me."

"Not at *all*!" Mrs. Whitmore breathed. "It is a little unusual, isn't it?"

She glanced between Kit and Elsa with an obvious and unnecessary solicitude, tinged with reproof. Elsa felt she now knew everything she needed to know about Kit's stepmother.

"It's a costume party, then, is it?" she said conversationally.

"Oh, dear. Christopher didn't tell you, did he?"

"It must have slipped my mind," said Kit bleakly.

"It's all right," said Elsa. "We'll just go as ourselves."

"Well, that will be all right for Christopher—everyone will think that *is* a costume, won't they? But it's a shame for you, my dear. I'm sure I have something for you to borrow. Let me just go upstairs and have a look. I won't be a moment—and Vera isn't finished changing anyway."

She pattered up the stairs in her Ancient Greek sandals, leaving Kit and Elsa alone in the hall.

"I'm so sorry," Kit whispered, looking wretched.

"You cannot make me believe you knew at any time that it was a costume party," Elsa whispered back.

"No. But I did forget that I hadn't told you their name."

Elsa shook her head. "That's not your fault either. I should have waited to be introduced, and I should have thought that Underhill would be your mother's surname, not your father's."

It absolutely fit with everything she knew about him that he would have kept his mother's name even after his father had acknowledged him. All the same, it couldn't have been the path of least resistance; she felt oddly proud of him for standing by his mother to that extent.

A sliding door in the mirrored wall behind Kit opened to reveal a white-haired man in a smoking jacket, looking absurdly out of keeping with the modern decor.

"Ah. Christopher. I thought it was you." He shook his son's hand gravely.

"Sir, this is Elsa Nordqvist. Elsa, my father, Laurence Whitmore."

"I am delighted to meet you," he said. He didn't look delighted; he looked nervous, and Elsa realized that this made her rather like him.

"So am I," she said warmly, and she could see him realizing with relief that he liked her.

"Come in and sit down," he suggested. "They won't be ready to leave for at least a half hour. Will you take any coffee? I was just about to have some myself."

He ushered them into a room on the other side of the hall, which proved to be his study, a haven of unregenerate Victorian manhood, complete with button-studded leather chairs and a collection of taxidermized animals and specimens in glass jars. Elsa peered with fascination into the jars, and Kit said that he would take a coffee, *faute de mieux*, and offered to go fetch it. Elsa got the impression that the maid was unreliable. Of course. This sort of household always had an unreliable maid.

Left alone with Kit's father, she turned from her inspection of the specimens to smile at him. She caught him subjecting her to an anxious scrutiny, and then looking momentarily alarmed to be caught at it.

Finally he said: "I saw you looking at my collection. Would you care to hear about it? It is organized according to very specific principles."

"Of course, I'd be delighted!"

"It illustrates the similarities of various organisms at the early stages of development. Here, I will show you."

When Kit returned with the pot of coffee and cups, Professor Whitmore was showing Elsa the similarities between the embryonic chicken in one jar and the embryonic pig in another.

"I like your Miss Lindqvist, Christopher. She has that gift of being able to take a genuine interest in other people's subjects—not like these modern specialists that one encounters. You must bring her to dinner some time so that she may tell me about her own research."

"It's Nordqvist, sir," said Kit, pouring coffee and keeping his distance from the embryos in jars. "Not Lindqvist."

"Did I say that? I beg your pardon. I knew a fellow named Lindqvist once, that must be why. A physician aboard the *Lark* when we sailed to South America. A very fine fellow." He noticed that Elsa was still holding the jar with the pig embryo, and set down his coffee cup in order to take it from her and replace it in its case. "Do please sit down, Miss … "

"Nordqvist," Kit supplied again, moving some books from one of the button-backed chairs to the other so that there was room for her to sit.

Elsa sat, and sipped her coffee. Kit perched on the arm of the other chair. She looked at the books which he had added to the stack already occupying the seat of that chair. Augustine's *Confessions* and *Molly Marchant: A Servant-Girl's Saga* ("A thrilling tale of love and mystery in Old England!")

"I see you are puzzling over my eclectic reading list," said Professor Whitmore, sinking into his desk chair and trying to find space on the surface of the desk for his coffee cup. "Well, you see, what I do is I ask my son and my daughter to recommend books to me, and I alternate between them. I try in this way to manifest an interest in their lives. I had a great deal of catching up to do with Christopher, as perhaps you may know, but I don't wish to fall behind with Vera, and of course he understands. There you see one of his recommendations, which I am halfway through, and the next on my list, one of Vera's favourites, which promises—at least if you believe its advertising copy—to be equally gripping."

"So it's field research into the subject of your offspring," Elsa suggested.

Professor Whitmore shouted with laughter. "That is what it is! I have often thought that Christopher, in his relation to myself, is one of the strangest subjects I have encountered."

"Have you really?" said Kit, looking up with amusement from his inspection of the pile of books.

"Oh, indeed. I don't think I ever told you about the paper on little brown bats. I was writing a paper, Miss Nordqvist, on *Myotis lucifugus*, their mating habits and migration. This was in the year '19. It was just around the time that Christopher returned from France. I had not actually expected him to return, though I couldn't have said why. I had felt quite convinced, when he took his leave of us, that he was going to his death. So to hear—not from him, of course, but from his commanding officer, when I had occasion to speak to him—how very nearly and how willingly he had done just that … well, I am glad I only heard about it after he came back. But, as you may imagine, I thought to myself: Here is a young man whose hand I would be honoured to shake, were he a stranger. And he is not a stranger—he is my own son. I cannot claim to have had anything to do with making him the man he is, but I had something crucial to do with the mere fact that he exists. It is profoundly odd. As a geneticist, I found it profoundly odd. It put the little brown bats in a wholly peculiar perspective, and I never finished that paper. Although I do think that my conclusions, as regarded the bats, were sound. North American bats have not been adequately studied."

"You certainly never told me that, sir," said Kit. "I would have insisted that you publish the paper."

By the time Mrs. Whitmore came into the study and found them, Professor Whitmore had gone back to explaining the finer points of the embryos, and Kit was flipping critically through the thrilling tale of love and mystery in Old England.

"*There* you are!" Mrs. Whitmore exclaimed. "Laurence, I hope you are not horrifying poor Miss Nord-ke-vist! Most people find your specimens *just a little* distasteful, you know."

"She was interested, my dear. She tells me that she grew up on a farm and has seen much more 'distasteful' things. At any rate," he turned back to Elsa, "that is of course only a general précis of the matter, but I think you will begin to see why it repays study."

"Yes, it's fascinating. I wish we didn't have to go, but I'm afraid … " She looked up at Mrs. Whitmore, and caught her giving her a curiously critical look, as if Elsa were somehow failing to live up to her expectations.

"Vera thinks she has found something for you to wear, Miss Nord-ke-vist. She is upstairs putting the finishing touches on her own costume. Shall I show you up?"

She followed Mrs. Whitmore out of the study and up the stairs. Mrs. Whitmore went on talking as she led the way:

"It did occur to me that you might need to borrow a costume, and

I had a few old things of my own in mind—but I hadn't imagined you would be so tall. None of my things would do at all."

"It is a nuisance sometimes, being tall. I really don't mind going without a costume."

"Oh, but it would be such a shame. Vera's room is just here. Isn't it funny? I suppose you must be expecting me to show you Christopher's old room, and his things from when he was a boy—but you know, he never actually lived with us."

"Yes, I did know that."

"Oh, did you? I suppose he will have told you, then, that he is Laurence's natural son."

She supposed no such thing; she hoped, clearly, that this would be news to Elsa.

"I think he may have used the word 'bastard.' But that's like him, isn't it?" She couldn't resist that; plainly Mrs. Whitmore had only a very sketchy idea of what Kit was like.

"Yes, oh, yes. Are you and Christopher … "

Elsa looked at her innocently for longer than necessary, and finally said, "Friends? We're friends."

"I see." She knocked on her daughter's door. "Vera dear, can we come in?"

The door opened to reveal a teenaged girl dressed in a costume similar to her mother's, but with a pair of cardboard wings covered in feathers cut from silvery candy wrappers. It was not entirely clear what she was supposed to be. It would have been a silly costume on one of the St. John's sylphs; on Vera Whitmore, it was somehow depressing. She was a tall, thin, dark-haired girl, who resembled neither her small, pretty mother nor her blue-eyed half-brother. In fact, the person she looked most like, to Elsa's mind, was her cousin Peachy. She stared at Elsa with open-mouthed dismay.

"Now, Vera, show some manners! Didn't you say you had something for Miss Nord-ke-vist to wear?"

"Oh, um. You'd better come in." She stood aside to allow Elsa to come in past the cardboard wings. "It's fine, Mom. Go downstairs and talk to Christopher or something." She shut the door in her mother's face.

"You know," said Elsa, "I really don't mind going to the party dressed the way I am."

Vera looked her up and down, and her dismay deepened. Elsa had a feeling that, for the daughter as well as for the mother, she wasn't turning out as expected. She remembered Kit's story of the earnest undergraduate girls waiting for him to propose. Was it so obvious that she was not another of those?

"But it's a costume party," Vera said finally. "Won't you feel stupid if you're not in costume?"

"Not really. But if you have something for me to wear, I'd be happy to try it."

"Well, I just thought … I don't know if it will fit you, but I *am* almost your height." This was true.

She dove into her closet and emerged brandishing a hanger that held a green kilt and blazer and a striped tie.

"Is that your school uniform?"

Vera nodded, blushing fiercely. "I thought it would be funny. The skirt would be *very* short on you, though."

The skirt was very short—it must have been short on Vera—but the rest of the uniform fit Elsa fairly well. She rolled up the sleeves of the blouse, rolled down the tops of her black stockings, and clipped a couple of Vera's barrettes in her hair. Vera studied the black dress where it lay draped across her bed.

"I didn't expect you to be so glamorous," she remarked.

"Neither did I," said Elsa. "It's only happened quite recently. Shall we go downstairs and see what the others think of this?"

Polly was waiting for them in the hall, and gaped at Elsa as she came down the stairs.

"Vera! Was this your idea?"

Vera peered uncertainly around Elsa where they stood, halfway down the stairs. "It's my school uniform."

"I can see what it is! What were you thinking? You know how long it is since your poor brother had a woman in his life! Are you trying to sabotage him now?"

"Sabotage?" Vera wailed. "He said she was his friend! I thought it would be funny!"

"It isn't funny, it's cruel! Making her look like his own sister!"

"She doesn't look anything like me! Why would I try to *sabotage* Christopher?"

"Shh-shh," said Elsa, who was now desperate to get back upstairs before Kit came out and saw her. "You know, I'm not sure that I should wear this after all. The skirt is awfully short."

"There, you see," said Mrs. Whitmore triumphantly. "Poor Miss Nord-ke-vist!"

"It's really all right," Elsa tried to assure the nearly tearful Vera as she followed her back to her bedroom. "I *did* think it was funny."

"Are you Christopher's girl friend?"

"No."

"But do you want to be?"

"Yes. Does that make you think less of me? I always used to be very critical of the girls who wanted to walk out with my brother." *And none of them tried to go to costume parties with him in little school-girl kilts that practically showed off their underwear.*

"I don't know. He's only my half-brother. And I haven't got a complete one to compare. Does Christopher know that you like him?"

"Probably. I'm not very subtle, and he's a good guesser."

At this, Vera revealed the side of herself that thrived on books like *Molly Marchant: A Servant-Girl's Saga*. "Then it's unrequited love on *your* side!" The idea appeared to delight her. "Mom thinks it's the other way around. I won't tell her she's wrong—don't worry. Oh, by the way, *what* is your name really? I *can't* go around calling you Miss Nord-ka-fist."

"It's Elsa, which is a lot easier, isn't it?"

"It is! I've just had a good idea, Elsa. I think my costume would look decent without the wings, don't you?"

So Elsa went to Mrs. Graves's costume party wearing her black dress and the shawl that she had so carefully chosen to complement it, and Vera Whitmore's homemade wings. Kit said she looked like a piece of modern art. Polly was annoyed, but tried to laugh about it. The costumes were supposed to have gone together, with Vera representing her mother's presiding genius, or psyche, or something, and without the wings she looked basically like Polly's gawky teen-aged daughter.

Vera, having discovered that Elsa was both stylish *and* crossed in love, had attached herself to her like a limpet, and made it her business to defend her against both her overly solicitous mother and her heartless brother. Mrs. Whitmore seemed to see more or less what this was about, and didn't like it. Kit was just mystified.

The party was well underway when they arrived, and Elsa did not immediately see Mrs. Graves. In fact, she did not see many people she recognized, but the costumes were partly to blame for that. Mrs. Graves's suite was packed, every room thrown open and full of guests, all the furniture removed from the dining room to accommodate a band and a dance floor. Waiters circulated with trays of hors d'oeuvres and drinks, some legal and some not. Some of the guests had taken their costumes to extremes, with masks and makeup and every type of elaborate transformation. Elsa wondered if it was occurring to Kit, as it did to her, that Peachy could easily be in this crowd and elude detection, if for some reason he wanted to go undetected.

There were also plenty of guests who had contented themselves with a mask on a stick or a symbolic article of clothing by way of a costume, and Elsa thought none of her party really looked out of place. Polly found her friend, who proved to be Mrs. Seely, the woman with the turquoise jewellery. She was one of the ones with a half-hearted costume, obviously assembled out of articles from her own closet and possibly meant to represent a gypsy.

"What a delightful gathering!" Polly gushed.

"Shall we find the refreshments?" Vera suggested to Elsa, limpet-like.

"Yes, let's. Mrs. Whitmore, we're just going to look for refreshments. Kit, come with us."

Vera gave her a sad look.

They wriggled through the crowd into the living room. Elsa secured an innocent drink for Vera by taking something that looked like lemonade, tasting it, and saying, "Oh, it's lemonade—I don't care for that. Would you finish it for me, Vera?"

Vera was enjoying herself, offering Elsa a commentary on all the women's dresses and hairstyles, and casting withering glances at her brother whenever he tried to contribute to the conversation.

They were in the thick of the crowd, pursuing a waiter with a plate of what looked like scallops, when Mrs. Graves met them. Her costume was a mask on a stick and a dress with a lot of feathers. For a moment she looked stymied, as if they were people she recognized but couldn't place. Then she gave Elsa her usual gushing greeting, but all the while her eyes were straying over Elsa's shoulder toward Kit.

"I don't believe we have met," she said, going straight for him. "I am Anastasiya."

He gave her a devastating, little-boy grin, and introduced himself as Kit rather than Christopher. Elsa was astonished; she honestly hadn't thought he had it in him. Vera clutched her arm in a sympathetic agony.

A waiter sidled up with a tray of drinks that were not lemonade, and Elsa was distracted by the need to prevent Vera from trying one. When she was paying attention again, Kit had one of the drinks, but she missed seeing whether he had made Mrs. Graves press it upon him or not. She thought probably not.

Mrs. Graves had a drink too, and was making a series of silly jokes about Kit's costume that seemed designed to get him to admit that it was really his street clothes. *Now how does she know that?*

She began looking warily around the room for the young man in grey tweed. But of course he wouldn't be in grey tweed; who knows what he might be wearing tonight? He might be inside that bear costume that was shambling around the edge of the dance floor.

Kit was cheerily pretending not to get Mrs. Graves's jokes, and had already half-finished his drink. Vera had decided that Elsa was pining, and that it was her duty to stop her.

"I think I see some more of those stuffed mushrooms," she said. "Let's go catch the waiter before he gets away."

"Oh?" said Elsa, looking in the wrong direction until the mushrooms were safely lost in the crowd. "I'm sure he'll come around again if we just stay where we are."

Mrs. Graves was talking about religion. She punctuated some irreverent declaration by crossing herself, and flicked Kit playfully with the feathers on her mask. He batted them out of the way with a nicely judged combination of amusement and discomfiture. At least Elsa assumed it was nicely judged.

"Oh, let's get out of this crowd, Elsa!" Vera cried desperately. "I'm afraid your wings are going to get bent with all these people pushing past us. And I'm *so* thirsty. Let's try to find some more lemonade."

"Okay, let's get you some lemonade," Elsa gave in. Kit clearly—well, probably—knew what he was doing, and she certainly wasn't contributing anything by hanging around.

But moving out of Mrs. Graves's hearing just gave Vera the opportunity to talk about her.

"She's quite old—older than my *mother*—and not at all stylish. Not like you. That dress with the feathers—it's *completely* out of date. I don't think anyone has worn anything like that since 1922. Anyway, how silly to come to your own costume party in something like that. It's barely a costume—what's she supposed to be, a bird? Oh, *poor* Elsa!"

"There are the mushrooms again—did you want one?"

"Only if you do. I was just saying that before to try to get you away from Christopher. How cruel of him to flirt with another woman like that in front of you! I'm ashamed of him. What can he see in her?"

"She is a very interesting woman, and he is just being friendly."

"That doesn't matter—if he knows that you love him, he should have some pity on you. Maybe he can't return your love, but that doesn't mean he has to be a brute. I never thought my own brother would be a brute. Actually it makes me see him in a whole new light. I've always thought him a bit boring—and Mom is so *sorry* for him all the time, which I've *never* understood. But to find out that he's actually a cad—well, I can understand why you're in love with him, if that's the case. I've always thought I would be the type to fall in love with a cad, myself. I mean from what I've read."

"He's not a cad," said Elsa firmly.

Vera gave her a pitying look. "You should just admit that you love him in spite of his faults."

"Of course I love him in spite of his faults, but he is *not* a cad."

They were rescued from this deadlock by the reappearance of Mrs. Whitmore. Vera, to do her justice, would have died rather than breathe a word of Elsa's doomed love to her mother.

"Miss Nord-ke-vist, you didn't tell us that you were a devotee of Orpheus yourself! Indeed, I find you're a celebrity in these circles! Everyone knows you and your wonderful translations, it seems. You should have told me! It was very remiss of you! I assumed, of course, that you were someone from Christopher's church—but you are a free-thinker, like us! I think that really is so refreshing. I've always felt badly about this religious business of poor Christopher's, because you know he wasn't at all religious when he first came to us, and it was really all Charlotte and Gerald's doing—though Charlotte herself was converted by Gerald, in a sort of way, because of course we were brought up quite Low Church."

Vera was frowning at her mother as if she were behaving oddly. And she was, Elsa realized. She had been drinking. Elsa's plan of leaving Vera with her mother and going back to find Kit and Mrs. Graves was foiled. She couldn't very well leave Vera with Polly in this state.

"Let's all go sit down in the dining room and watch the dancing," she suggested, gathering Vera on one arm and Polly on the other. "Only we'll have to find somewhere where I can sit without crushing my wings."

The found a curvaceous Victorian sofa with a view of the dance floor, where Elsa could perch at the end without endangering the wings. Polly tossed herself into the corner of it, and Vera plopped down on the floor at Elsa's feet.

"I don't normally drink," Polly confided.

"No, well—who does, any more?"

"I'm afraid it's gone to my head a little. Or perhaps it is just the atmosphere." No, thought Elsa, it definitely was the drink. "Such an exhilarating atmosphere. It is so wonderful to feel oneself surrounded by so many people who think deeply about the world and our place in it. I am so glad to find that you are one too, dear Miss Nord-ke-vist, even if it does mean that of course your marrying Christopher would be impossible." She gasped stagily, and put her hand over her mouth. "Really, I *don't* normally drink—though I did vote to repeal Prohibition and everything. And of course I've said no more than the *truth*." She gasped again.

"Mom ... " Vera had gone rigid with embarrassment.

"It is a very lively party," said Elsa composedly. "There are some quite impressive costumes, don't you think, Vera? Kit tells me you are interested in designing clothes. What sorts of things do you like?"

"Oh, that's just a silly fad," said Polly, peevishly rearranging herself on the couch. She seemed really annoyed that Elsa had not risen to her bait.

But Vera was gazing up at Elsa adoringly. "Sporting clothes for ladies, mostly. Very practical things—especially for tall women."

"What a brilliant idea! Do tell me about your designs."

"What on earth has become of Christopher?" Polly asked presently, interrupting Vera's description of a golf outfit.

"I'm not sure," said Elsa.

"He's talking with some lady, over there." Vera pointed helpfully across the living room. "He has been talking to her since he came in."

"Oh dear! You must be jealous, Miss Nord-ke-vist!"

"Not at all."

"Huh. No—well, it's probably for the best. Being a free-thinker and an intellectual, I mean. And really—"

"Mom, do you want me to get you some lemonade? They have some nice lemonade—Elsa and I could go get some for you, and a stuffed mushroom. Did you try the stuffed mushrooms?"

"What are you babbling about, Vera?"

"I'm not babbling—I'm trying to be helpful! You always say I'm not helpful, and when I'm helpful you say I'm babbling!"

"Let's go get that lemonade." Elsa got up from the sofa. At this rate they were going to need the bathroom next. "And the mushrooms, too, by all means."

They left Mrs. Whitmore on the couch and wandered out into the foyer, making no very determined effort to find either lemonade or mushrooms. They were both a little dampened in their spirits.

"Is it true that you can't marry Christopher because you're a free-thinker?" said Vera finally.

"It's none of your mother's business whether it's true or not."

"Oh."

"Hallo!" Kit appeared, wriggling out of the crowd in the living room with another half-finished drink. "I've been looking for you."

"Have you really?" said Vera haughtily. "We thought you were too busy talking to that stupid lady with the feathers."

"That's not very diplomatic, dear sister. But I wasn't really talking to her so much as letting her talk to me." He finished his drink and appeared to be eyeing a waiter with more glasses on his tray.

"How much have you had to drink?" Elsa whispered.

"Oh, Elsa. You are sweet."

"I ... But ... That's not an answer."

"I say, Vera—they're playing a waltz. D'you know how to waltz?"

Vera was startled into civility. "Oh! Yes. We learned at school. But I've only ever danced with girls."

"I see. And is dancing with your brother worse or better than that?"

"Oh, I ... "

"Better," said Elsa. "Especially since nobody here knows he's your brother. I'd say you should take him up on it."

Vera beamed. Kit handed Elsa his empty glass, and brother and sister went in to the dance floor together. Elsa watched through the dining-room doors. Vera was predictably awkward, but she managed to maintain a certain poise, and she was clearly pleased. Cad or not, her brother was an excellent dancer. Well, Elsa had known he would be. She was glad she had taken the cardboard wings, which would have been a nuisance to Vera on the dance floor.

Polly was still sitting by herself where they had left her, and Elsa decided to take pity on her and went back to join her. This party was beginning to seem remarkably pointless.

"Kit is dancing with Vera," she explained as she sat down. "It's very sweet."

Polly sighed. "No doubt. He can be very thoughtful that way. It's a shame they see so little of each other, but ... " She dismissed that particular grievance with a wave of her hand. "But he *ought* to be dancing with you, oughtn't he? He came with you, after all."

"I don't really dance," said Elsa.

Polly cocked an eyebrow sceptically. "Well, that's a relief. It reassures me. I mean that you can't really have your eye on him, if you take such a *blasé* attitude about it. I do worry about poor Christopher, you know. I still worry about him. Of course I suppose it isn't my place, but I can't help wondering what will become of him. I think what he really needs is to marry one of these tiresome, domestic little creatures. It looked for a while to us as though he actually intended not to marry, and I thought that so sad. Laurence was tolerant of course—really Christopher can do no wrong in his eyes, ever since he came back from France—but I thought it such a sad mistake. Can you imagine him living all his life without a woman to take care of him? And of course a clergyman needs a wife for so many things—entertaining and charity work and committees and so on. He really needs a woman who would devote herself quite selflessly to all that. A sweet, domestic girl, a Victorian thing, you know, an 'angel in the house.' Not a modern intellectual—like me."

Like *you*? Elsa hoped her incredulity didn't show on her face. But Polly seemed uninterested in the effect of her words on anyone except herself.

"Laurence, you see, had become quite used to doing without a … a *wifely* woman by the time he and I met, and so we were able to get on quite well, and I never felt guilty for not being the kind of woman who could really make a home for him. Domestic things are absolutely beyond me, as I expect you've noticed. But we had such a rare situation—we were so fortunate. Christopher will have become used to all the comforts of domesticity, growing up in my sister Charlotte's house. She is really the perfect homemaker. I suppose it is just as well I wasn't able to raise him—Charlotte is a much more normal woman.

"Oh yes, what was I saying? Well, it seems Christopher made some remark to Laurence recently, not exactly that he intends to marry, but at least that he doesn't intend *not* to, which is really a great relief. Of course he ought to have been more straightforward with us, but he is sadly secretive—he always has been—so one learns to take what one can get. I don't know if I made it clear, but you are the first girl he has *ever* brought home—I mean brought home to us—although I know there were several when he was in university. But there hadn't been any in quite a long time—since the War, really—and then there is all this religion complicating matters. And you know if a man is even the least bit *afraid* of women—and that's what it amounts to, isn't it?—he needs a very meek, nurturing kind of girl. And I hope you won't be insulted if I speak frankly, but you're not really meek *or* nurturing, are you? Of course I like you all the more for it, but I am glad after all to see you're not setting your sights on poor Christopher."

She lapsed into silence, clearly not expecting Elsa to reply, just finished with what she had to say for the time being. Elsa sat trying to decide how much of this was tipsily disingenuous, and how much merely catty. It was hard to say.

She knew most of it was wildly inaccurate. Kit, scared of women? If he wanted a wife—and he did want a wife—it was for both much more and much less than entertaining and church committees. She could imagine him marrying a woman who had her own career. She could also imagine him burdened with a pseudo-intellectual like Polly, useless as a homemaker and helpmeet, wrapped up in some fantasy of companionate equality, but in reality living only for herself.

"Which one is the real you?" he had asked her on the beach, when she had described the two lives she could imagine living. She thought now that she hadn't answered correctly. The real Elsa was a third person who stood outside both of those lives and admired aspects of them, but, if she was not careful, would end up missing the fruit of both of them, the way Polly Whitmore was missing it. And Elsa would realize what she was missing.

Mrs. Graves appeared from the adjoining room, and perched herself girlishly on the arm of the sofa near Polly.

"Good evening!" She beamed down on them. Like everyone, apparently, she seemed a little lit up with drink. "Elsa my *dear*, I am so glad you joined us after all, and brought your very charming friend. He is your friend, is he, and not a secret you have been keeping from me?"

"He is my friend," said Elsa. *And* he's a secret I've been keeping from you—naturally.

"He is my stepson," said Polly, and waited for the reaction.

"Good Heavens!" Mrs. Graves looked her up and down ostentatiously. "He can't be!"

"Well, I did marry very young. I don't believe we've met. I'm Polly Whitmore." She extended a hand.

"Anastasiya Graves. So delighted. Let us get ourselves something to drink, and you must tell me all about him. It is so hot in here, don't you find? Elsa, you will excuse us, won't you? I long to hear more about your friend."

Since the look she gave Elsa, as Polly was getting up from the sofa, had become frankly hostile, Elsa did not bother trying to smile.

Her back was sore from sitting at the end of the sofa with nothing to lean on. She moved down until she could hook her wings behind the low back of the sofa and lean on the cushions. The man in the bear costume came shuffling off the dance floor in her direction, and stopped a short distance away. It was hard to tell whether he was looking at her or not. She did her best to look as though she didn't want to be asked to dance, which wasn't hard, as she didn't. The bear shuffled away.

By and by a shadow fell across her lap, and she looked up to see that Kit was standing over her.

"Mind if I join you?"

"Of course not. Where is Vera?"

"Trying to convince Polly to let her have a gin and tonic." He settled himself next to her, closer than she had expected, so close that his sleeve brushed against her bare arm.

"Mrs. Graves isn't with them?"

"Mrs. Graves? No."

That was good; Polly couldn't have had much time to tell her things about Kit, if that was the case.

He tipped his head back and reached up to flick at the candy-wrapper feathers on the wing behind him.

"They suit you."

She laughed.

"How much *have* you had to drink, Kit?"

He sighed. "Embarrassingly little. The thing is, I was tired to start with. I was up until all hours last night. As you know—you came for Maundy Thursday. That was nice."

"Maybe you should go home."

"Not yet. I'll sober up. I've tried to explain this to you before, but this is an area where I have some experience."

He was slouched so that he could rest his head on the back of the sofa, just under her wing. From a distance, she thought, it must have looked as though he were resting his head on her shoulder— but he wasn't.

"Mrs. Graves seemed awfully intent on getting me away from you earlier," he said. "We'll see whether it happens again."

"You want to make her jealous?"

He looked up at her thoughtfully. "I'm not sure … It might be that she wants to make you jealous. Or she has some other plans for you that don't include me. She has some interest in me, anyway, that I can't quite account for."

She smiled. "Can't you?"

He frowned impatiently. "Don't let's play that game. I'm not fishing for a compliment."

"I'm sorry."

"No, I'm sorry. Good Lord. I really have only had a couple of drinks. I thought it would be a good idea to drink … I thought it would look better. I don't dissemble well, and I want her to think she's getting to me."

And is she? No, of course not. Being jealous of Mrs. Graves—even seeming to be jealous of Mrs. Graves—would be absurd.

"She does have other plans for me—she wants me for Arthur Gallagher. Or she did. When I told her about my … my chequered past, she may have decided I'm not good enough for him."

He looked at her sharply. "Do you think it's that, or do you think … just not useful for her purposes?"

"Purposes? Oh, you mean the pure thingummy, the sacrifice? I hadn't thought about that. It's so obviously made up … "

"But the whole thing is made up. That doesn't mean it's harmless."

"No."

She wondered what Polly had told Mrs. Graves about Kit. That he was afraid of women? That he hadn't had a girl friend since the War, and everyone despaired of his marrying? That might make him sound dangerously apt for their purposes. He *was*, in fact. Professor Hallam had said so.

She wished he would just rest his head on her shoulder, but she had to admire the delicacy that would forbear to exploit her in even so tiny a way for the sake of making Mrs. Graves jealous.

"I enjoyed meeting your father," she said, to change the subject. "I like him."

He smiled. "So do I. I always did, as a matter of fact. Of course, he doesn't believe that. He's attached to the idea that I *hated* him, and then *forgave* him, and am a magnanimous soul and all that. But that's just part of his grandiose narrative of his own life. He's an old man—I don't begrudge him his grandiose narrative."

"But you're wedded to your own diffident narrative of your life. And you're a hero—no one should begrudge you that."

He opened his mouth to object, and then just sighed. "Thanks."

"Now your stepmother, on the other hand—I think I may have made her hate me."

"Oh, I doubt it. Polly doesn't hate people. She feels *so sorry* for them. It can be worse."

"She is very sorry for you, I'd noticed that. I couldn't help wondering if there were something I'd missed. You're not secretly dying of something, are you? I mean, I've seen you in a bathing costume—I know you have got all your limbs."

He laughed. "Well, to do her justice, she has seen me when I've been at pretty low ebb, and I suppose she can't get that out of her mind."

"Yes, I see. Poor Christopher."

"No, now when you say it … it's almost nice." He looked up at her, smiling. "Come dance with me."

For a moment she looked him in the eye. She had not been lying when she told Polly she didn't dance. She had learned how to square dance as a child, but the Revival had been opposed to dancing, Francis hadn't been much of a dancer, and by the time she got to university she was embarrassed by her inexperience and avoided places where she might be asked to dance. She could of course cast aside her embarrassment now and say yes to him. She would be worse than Vera. She could follow him, graceless and uncertain but too proud to giggle prettily about it like one of the sylphs from his parish, and he would become subtly embarrassed and try to put her at her ease—losing all his grace and coordination in the process and ending up dancing badly. They would be relegated to the edge of the dance floor and would look like nothing in the world except a couple involved in a very absorbing and awkward courtship. They would make nobody jealous. Polly would feel pityingly vindicated; Vera would be disgusted. Mrs. Graves would probably give up on both of them.

"No," she said firmly, looking away from him and down at her hands in her lap. "I don't really dance."

"Ah."

"I think," she added after a moment, "that you should probably dance with someone, though. The idea is sound."

"Mm."

After another short silence, and only for a moment, he turned and did rest his forehead on her shoulder. Then he sat up.

A woman in a slim tuxedo, wearing a glittering devil mask and little horns in her blonde hair, had stepped out of the crowd of dancers and was looking speculatively at Kit. Elsa wasn't sure whether she recognized the woman or not. Kit slid off the couch and stood up, stretching in that slightly feline way that occasionally made him seem to deserve his nickname. Elsa felt suddenly weak with a fierce, physical longing for him. As he moved away from her it was as if he was taking all the warmth in the room with him.

He approached the devil-woman, and Elsa could just hear what he said to her.

"I want to make someone jealous—I'll bet you would like to help. Besides … it would look funny, wouldn't it?"

The woman threw back her head in laughter and held out her hand, and they wove their way out onto the dance floor together. Elsa sat wondering whether she hadn't just made one of the stupidest mistakes of her life.

Polly and Vera came back, not speaking to one another.

"I don't know about you, Miss Nord-ke-vist, but I am getting tired! What has become of Christopher now?"

"Christopher is dancing with some other girl," Vera remarked, speaking to Elsa rather than her mother. "In *trousers*. Rather smart, though." She looked up at Elsa soulfully. She seemed to want to say something about "poor Elsa." Elsa was glad that her mother was present, so that she couldn't.

"Oh yes, I see," said Polly.

"I wasn't *talking* to you."

The band was playing a tango. The devil-woman was vamping studiously, leaning into Kit, draping herself around him, and writhing away, prancing with her little shoes. And Kit was meeting it all with the oblivious enthusiasm of an eight-year-old. He ruined her writhing and prancing manoeuvres by getting tangled up in the skirt of his cassock and giggling. At one point he let go of her hand to grab a fistful of the black wool, to her total discomposure. He led her in absurd, improvised steps, grinning at her as if it was all completely hilarious. It was adorable. It couldn't fail to attract Mrs. Graves's attention.

"Well, Miss Nord-ke-vist," Polly drawled on, "I can quite understand your not being jealous of Mrs. Graves—I mean, she would hardly be competition for someone of your age, would she? Though she seemed very interested in Christopher, so clearly she must think otherwise. But that girl he's dancing with now is much younger, and awfully pretty. Quite like you, actually—your colouring, but a bit more … well, a different figure."

I want to make someone jealous, he had told the devil-woman (Elsa wished she knew the woman's name or could think of her in any other way, as this epithet seemed incredibly silly, under the circumstances). Certainly he had intended the woman to think that "someone" was the girl he had just left on the couch, the one who had refused to dance with him. But had he even intended Elsa to hear that? He was not really that subtle, she thought, or that malicious, or—whatever that would have been.

And Elsa knew he hadn't asked *her* to dance in order to make Mrs. Graves jealous. He had asked her to dance because he had wanted to dance with her. And she had turned him down.

"She has nothing to be jealous of!" Vera had decided to start talking to her mother again. "Elsa is much more beautiful than that—that awful trouser woman! Anyway, she doesn't care about Christopher, and she has plenty of other suitors—don't you, Elsa? She doesn't need stupid Christopher!" This betrayal of the brother who had only recently been so gallant as to waltz with her seemed to cause her considerable pain, and Elsa wished she could be more grateful for the show of allegiance.

"It's all right," she started feebly.

"Vera! What a thing to say! Poor Christopher!"

"Oh, 'poor Christopher' *phooey*! That's all you ever say—what about 'poor Vera'? What about 'poor Elsa'? What about—"

"You are making a scene, Vera. We shall have to leave."

Vera subsided onto the couch again, and Polly looked at Elsa for sympathy. She was not inclined to give it.

"Do *you* think I'm to blame, Miss Nord-ke-vist?"

"I think your daughter may have a point," Elsa heard herself saying. She wanted this conversation to stop. "I'm not sure that 'poor Christopher' is really quite the right epithet."

"I can't help it! I was never able to do anything for him, you know, not as I would have liked. I feel it very keenly, even now."

"But I don't think *he* feels it," Elsa said. "I mean—things have turned out well for him. He's happy."

Polly was taken aback. "Well, but—yes, but … don't you think that all this religion is a substitute for something?"

"No, I don't. It's what people substitute things *for*. You astonish me, Mrs. Whitmore. That anyone can have known Kit for any length of time and yet doubt the truth of his calling—it seems incredible to me."

Polly pursed her lips. "You don't sound much like a free-thinker, Miss Nord-ke-vist."

"Don't I? But free is exactly what I am. It is the truth that will make you free, Mrs. Whitmore."

The silence after she said this seemed to stretch out from seconds to minutes, to encompass the whole party. She felt as though a window was open somewhere inside her, and a wind was blowing through, strong and cold.

She went on finally: "You guessed that I didn't meet your stepson at church, but you don't seem to have considered the obvious alternative. It's the other way around. I came back to the Church because I met him."

Polly, having no idea that this was the first time she had formulated these words even to herself, was unimpressed. "I see. Then you're not a devotee of Orpheus. You're a Christian?"

"I am a sinner, but this much, falling for this, I have been spared. This is not the truth or a path to the truth—this is sin and vanity and false doctrine. Actually, I don't know if I should dignify it that much. It's a fake religion out of a fake manuscript."

"Fake?" Now Polly was looking at her with interest. "You mean a forgery? Is that just something you *believe*, or do you have proof?"

Elsa laughed. "Polly, until about a week ago, I wasn't a 'free-thinker,' I was an *atheist*. Absolutely I have proof."

Polly actually clasped her hands in delight. This, it turned out, was the kind of thing she lived for. "Really? Oh, but I want to hear about it!"

They left the party and sat on a bench on the landing by the elevator, and she told them all about it. Vera fell asleep, leaning against the wall, before she had finished, but Polly listened with rapt attention.

"And why haven't you done anything about this?" she asked.

"I don't know exactly what to do. I left the university in—not exactly in disgrace, but pretty nearly. Professor Gallagher—the forger—wanted me to marry him, and when I said no, he took it badly."

Polly, to her surprise, turned pink at this. Elsa recalled how she had met her husband.

"I didn't want to marry him because I don't love him, not because he was my professor," she assured her.

"No no, I quite understand. But what you are saying is that you have no standing at the university, so you can't accuse a professor of fraud. Is that right? But surely you could raise your suspicions here, at the salons. Surely they all have open minds, and would want to know the truth?"

"I don't know whether they have open minds, but Mrs. Graves claims to be the owner of the manuscript. She claims to have been present when it was discovered. If it's a forgery—and it is a forgery—she must know it."

"Then it's a conspiracy!" Polly's eyes shone. "But how thrilling! And how brilliant of you to have uncovered it." She yawned hugely. "Excuse me! Oh, look at poor Vera—I believe she is fast asleep."

"It's time to go home, isn't it?"

"I think so. Will you fetch our wraps?"

"Yes, and I'll get Kit."

"Why not let him stay, if he's enjoying himself?"

Why not indeed? The party had been a waste of time so far, but he might yet be able to find out something useful. She did not think that he really was enjoying himself … but then perhaps she was wrong.

"Well, I'll tell him we're going, at least."

She went back into the party, and the first person she met was Mrs. Seely.

"Have you seen a pr—um, a young man dressed as a priest?"

"Oh, that lovely boy! He's over there, talking with a very pretty girl in men's clothes."

She looked, and there they were on a couch together, Kit slouched languidly, the devil-woman (she really *must* stop calling her that) leaning in, intent and bosomy, talking to him. He was listening with every appearance of politeness, but Elsa could tell he was bored. The woman really did look a little bit like her, she thought. And suddenly she was struck by the certainty that that was what it looked like, to anyone who had eyes to see, when she was talking to Kit: him bored and tired and wishing she would shut up, but listening dutifully because he was a saint; her babbling vampily.

She went to fetch her shawl and Polly and Vera's coats, thinking that perhaps after all she would not tell him they were going. He would offer to leave with them, and there was no need for that.

She found their things and stood holding them, wondering if the person who had just formed those thoughts was really her. Leave Kit at a party without telling him she was going? *What?*

She marched back into the living room and stood awkwardly over the pair on the couch until he saw her and jumped to his feet, looking exactly like someone who had been rescued from something. The devil-woman, very clearly interpreting the situation correctly—it was the least subtle thing in the world—pouted and slid away.

"Thanks," he said. He looked tired and overheated, and as though he might now be genuinely drunk. He carried it very well; it was hard to be sure.

"We're on our way out—Vera's tired, and Polly was getting bored. I just—I came back to tell you. They're in the car downstairs."

Come with us. My love, please come with us! Let us all get out of here.

"Okay, thanks." He intercepted a waiter with a tray of drinks. "You'll be all right getting home?"

"I'll be fine."

"Of course you will. I'll stick around for a bit, but I don't think … " He paused to take a gulp of his drink. "I'm not sure there's much point, but I would like another crack at Mrs. Graves. Seemed like she wanted to talk to me again—I thought she was going to ask me to dance actually, but then she didn't … It's good you're going. I mean, I don't think—Peachy's not here. There's no need for us both to stay."

"Are you sure? I'd stay—if you thought there were any reason … I would stay."

He smiled. "I know. Thank you. I'll be fine."

"Well, I'd better go. I will see you … soon."

"Good night."

She had turned away and taken a few steps before she remembered. She turned back. "Kit! I almost forgot. What time is the—the thing, the Mass, tomorrow night?"

"The Vigil? Your father says he's not going to go. I think he was scandalized when I described the liturgy. Besides, he met an old friend at the prayer meeting who invited him to his house to sing hymns."

"That's all right. He knows we parted ways a long time ago. But what time is it?"

It was a moment before he replied. "Eight."

"Good."

"It's at eight."

"Yes."

"We could—if you wanted—have dinner together beforehand. An early dinner? I could ring you tomorrow morning—I mean, could I?"

"Of course."

"So that we can talk. Over dinner, I mean. About … about that. If you want to talk about it."

"Yes. Very much."

"Good. That's … that is actually my job."

"Oh! Yes, I suppose it is."

"Well, you'd better go."

"Yes. Goodbye."

She left him looking happier than she had ever seen him before.

PART III

Holy Saturday

Chapter Fourteen

THE PRODIGAL SAMARITAN

It was a little after dawn; the morning was clear and cool and quiet. Elsa stood in the open door to her balcony with her cup of tea, looking out at the pale sky.

She had barely slept, but didn't feel the drugged tiredness that usually accompanied a sleepless night. She felt instead the way she used to feel as a little girl on her birthday: a buoyant sense of new beginnings, a little tinged with a consciousness of responsibility, as if she were once again advancing toward adulthood.

Polly had been unflaggingly friendly on the ride home, insisted on dropping Elsa at her door, and then made the taxi wait so that she could finish the story she had been telling about a forged painting. Elsa smiled at the recollection. She wondered if Polly wasn't after all happier that Elsa might be a good match for her stepson than she had professed to be when she thought that she wasn't. At heart, Polly seemed as much a romantic as Vera.

Elsa had sat in her desk chair for a long time when she got home, in front of the flour jar full of tulips, wondering how to pray—which was, she realized eventually, itself a kind of prayer, though a rather thin and weak one. She found the tract that the acolyte from St. John's had given her, and read it. It was written in simple, plain language for the uneducated, and it said things that she had known well at one time. At one time she had prayed often and fluently. She wept a little, and finally she rested her head on her folded arms on the desk and prayed silently, for Kit and for Harriet, whom she loved, for Peachy, whom they loved, for her father and mother and brother and sisters, for Polly and Vera and Laurence Whitmore, for Mrs. Graves and for Arthur Gallagher …

She had managed to get up and crawl into her nightdress before she fell asleep, but then she had woken early, and with a surprising sense of purpose. She had found the pages of hymn translations from the *Bibliotheka*, torn them out of her notebook, set them carefully on fire at her stove, and dropped them into the sink to let them burn to ashes. Then she had sat down at her desk again and written some lines of a wholly different kind of hymn. She had crossed almost all of them out, thinking with chagrin of how she had inwardly mocked that line about "mystic glow" in the hymn on Maundy Thursday. The thing to do would be to get hold of a Septuagint and try to translate some psalms. She got up and made herself a cup of tea.

In the alley below her balcony, a man began singing:
"I heard the voice of Jesus say,
 'I am this dark world's light;
Look unto me, thy morn shall rise,
 And all thy day be bright.'
I looked to Jesus, and I found
 In Him my Star, my Sun;
And in that light of life I'll walk
 Till traveling days are done."

She knew the voice, and at the same time she didn't. She had heard Kit sing in the library stacks, when he had no audience but herself, and she had heard him sing in front of his congregation, and the voice in the alley was certainly his—but he couldn't sing like that.

He also *wouldn't* sing like that in a quiet neighbourhood at the crack of dawn.

She stepped out onto the balcony and looked down. There was an open car parked in the alley by the door directly below her apartment. It was the man in the driver's seat who had been singing. He looked up at her.

He looked very like Kit, in a way. He looked like a statue for which Kit had posed, but which had been intended to represent something else: a god, or a personification of something unspeakably noble. He looked as if he should have had wings. He was wearing a tan raincoat, open over a loud argyle sweater and a tie that didn't match. His battered fedora was pushed back at an angle on his (inaccurately blond) head.

"Elsa," he said, and it was Kit's voice, but that was not how it sounded when Kit said her name.

"Peachy."

"Oh, thank God! Thank God. How could you tell?"

"I don't know. Who else would you be? How did you … How did this happen?"

"I'll tell you all about it. Can I come up?"

"At this hour, looking like that? Absolutely not. I'll come down. Give me a minute to get dressed."

It really took her little more than a minute. She was fishing her keys out of her purse to lock her door when she realized she had forgotten to put on both stockings and a coat. She went back for them, and then ran down the stairs. The car was still there, and the impossible amalgam of Peachy and Kit was standing by the passenger door. She closed the door of the building and stood with her back to it.

The sky was brightening in a cool and matter-of-fact fashion, bathing the alley in a clear grey light. The white wool of her coat, the stitching on her purse, the dashboard of the car, everything was clear and real. The man in front of her was unmistakably real too, every not-quite-right detail of him.

"I must say, you're taking this better than I expected," he said, in Kit's voice but without Kit's accent.

"I'm not sure what you expected me to do. But I may yet do it. I can't promise anything."

He nodded, but—somehow—not the way Kit would have nodded. "That's fair."

"This does explain a lot."

"Does it?"

"It explains why you disappeared, why you couldn't even telephone people and had to write ridiculous letters—why Professor Hallam kept calling Kit 'Peacham.' And at your rooming house, some poet thanked Kit for running an errand for him—but that must have been you."

It explained too why Mrs. Graves had been so interested in Kit herself. It had been obvious to her that he was someone of importance, and she must have been trying to find out why. And when she had heard about Francis, and described someone like an overdone version of Kit, it wasn't the real Kit she had been thinking of: it was Peachy.

"You've been looking for me?" He looked pained. "Is that why—he—came to that party?"

"Of course. We were worried about you. It was all very strange."

He sagged against the side of the car. "I tried to make sure nobody would come after me. I didn't want anyone mixed up in this—this nightmare."

"I know. You were trying to protect Harriet and Kit and everyone. That's what we thought you were probably doing."

"You're not any of you going to forgive me, are you?"

"Don't be silly. You'd better tell me the whole story from the beginning."

He stood leaning against the door of the car, arms folded—a pose that was much more Peachy than Kit—looking down at her. Much too far down. That was another thing he had got wrong.

"You know the beginning—the beginning is when I started coming to the salons with you. I talked with Anastasiya—you knew that. She tried hard to get me interested in what they were doing. I was a challenge, I guess. I didn't make any secret of the fact that I didn't like it. But there was something about her ... something I fell for. I'm not proud of it, but that's what happened. She's scared of something, and I thought I could help. You don't know what it was like. I love Harriet, and I know we would have been all right—I don't know that I would have made her happy, but she didn't *need* me to make her happy, that's one of the things I love about her. But her people! They thought I was an utter waste of space. I couldn't do anything right as far as they were concerned. It was making me crazy. So when I thought I'd found … when there was this woman, and she was in a thorough mess, and I thought I could help, it made me feel better about myself. It was seductive, and I got in over my head. I told her I wanted to save her—she didn't ask to be saved, I just volunteered this, like a fool. But it seemed to be the right thing to say. She said there was something I could do that might help.

"And I knew as soon as I'd promised to help her that I'd betrayed Harriet, that I was in too deep—that's when I quarrelled with Kit, and then with Harriet. I just had to do whatever I could think of to keep them away. You were the one who opened my eyes to it, in a way. You said if I wasn't careful I would drag Kit into something awful. You were right.

"So then I went to the Pure Plain. I think you know how it goes. Quite a few of them have done it, actually, although they told me it never worked for you. You light the candle and read some passage from the book over and over, and you feel yourself … " He swallowed. "It's awful. You feel yourself falling, but not … outwardly. Falling *into* yourself. It doesn't feel like going to a place—I don't know why they call it that. It feels like being dissected. At least that was how it felt to me. I saw all of my faults, itemized, held up in front of me one by one—it went on for ages. And I became convinced that *this* was what—this was who I needed to become. I saw it so clearly—like he was standing on the other side of a bridge, and if I crossed over and took … took him over, became him, I would leave all my flaws behind. It sounds stupid when I put it like that, but it really felt like a revelation at the time, and like something true. You see, I've always thought I wasn't envious of him. I made a point of it. I loved him.

I pitied him—he'd had a hard life, and I hadn't. I didn't care that my parents loved him—that was all right, I didn't mind sharing. I didn't care that girls liked him, either—*he* never cared very much about that. Anyway, that's what I thought. And here I discover that I'd envied him, after all. It felt like the truth.

"And so I … I crossed the bridge, and I turned into him. I was back in the room with the others, and I was like this. Since then I've been hiding as best I could—sleeping in hotels and trying to stay away from people who know him. I haven't been back to the salons, I was too afraid of meeting you. And Ana—Mrs. Graves—has been, well, she's been avoiding me, but I know it's only because she's scared. In the end, as usual, I haven't been much use to anybody."

He stopped speaking and they stood for a long time in silence. She felt a little light-headed. She put a hand on the side of the car; it was indeed cold and real under her fingers.

"Now this, I think," she said slowly, "is where I begin to behave the way you expected me to. You can't have gone to the Pure Plain, Peachy. There is *no such thing*. There can't be. The *Bibliotheka Orphika* is a forgery."

"Damn," he said softly. "Damn, damn, damn." He pushed himself away from the car and strode about for a bit, pushing back his hat and pulling it down again, mussing his hair, but not in quite the right way. "I was afraid you were going to say that. It's not that I don't believe you. Harriet … she didn't betray your confidence, but she did give me a kind of idea that you might have thought something along those lines. And the thing is, I was already starting to think, myself, that it's not the manuscript that did this. I think it was that secretary character. I think … I'm pretty sure he isn't human."

She remembered her first impression of the young man in grey tweed, the mad idea that he was somehow the wrong shape. How she had rarely questioned the fact that she didn't know his name; how she thought of him as something other than a real person. Hallam gabbling about a librarian who had sold his soul to the

Devil … She pulled her coat tighter around herself. Her world had reoriented itself finally last night, and it was easier than she would have expected to look through the opened door onto this new vista: Anastasiya's New Orphics with their idolatrous book-kissing and nonsensical diagrams and muttering about purity and the baseness of matter, all, all enslaved to the Prince of Lies.

"I think you're right," she said.

"And if he's not human … "

"Then it's pretty obvious what he is."

He nodded. "And it is also pretty obvious what I've done. He's offered to turn me back, in exchange for doing obeisance to his master. At the time I thought he meant Orpheus—but I don't think so any more."

She shook her head. "You've fallen for lies. It happens all the time. It *doesn't mean* that it can't be undone."

"No. Maybe not." He stopped striding and leaned against the car again, looking calmer. "I *am* glad I came to you, Elsa. Though I don't know what I thought you could do—perhaps I thought the whole situation would vanish in a puff of smoke on contact with your scepticism."

"My scepticism isn't what it used to be. Were you the bear, last night?"

"Yes. I had some idea of sidling up and talking to you, but then I didn't know what I would say, and you were always with Cousin Vera and Aunt Polly—or Kit—and the whole thing was a shambles. I was leaving when I saw you getting into a car, and I followed you. I slept out here—I was going to knock on your door as soon as it was a decent hour. At least I think I was. I was still trying to work myself up to it. I didn't know how I was going to convince you that I wasn't just Kit acting oddly."

"I don't think you needed to worry about that. You don't look *that* much like him."

"I don't?" He was surprised.

"You're far too tall, and his hair isn't *gold*—it's toffee-coloured."

He looked at her as if that was the silliest thing he had ever heard—a wholly un-Kitlike expression. "Look, I don't … Well. If you tried to turn yourself into Harriet, I daresay I'd be able to pick a few holes in that, too."

"Point taken." She caught her breath abruptly. "I mean … "

"Too late altogether, Miss N. But you astonish me—when I saw the two of you sitting together last night, and him with his head on your shoulder, I thought you must be engaged at least."

"He was drunk. Ah, God! Peachy, he *was* drunk, and we left him in the middle of a horrible cult with people who've sold their souls to the Devil and can change themselves into things—what were we thinking?"

"Possibly we were thinking that he can take care of himself."

"But is that any kind of thing for either of us to think? You're his best friend and I'm in love with him—don't smile like that, you idiot, it's not a happy thing right now. Anyway, your smile's all wrong."

"Okay, well, you're the expert on that. But look—calm down. You didn't know about the Devil and turning into people, and I didn't know that Kit was still there after you left. I honestly didn't. I thought he was in the car with you—I thought the two of you didn't want to be out of each other's sight. When you say 'drunk,' what do you mean? How drunk?"

"Peachy, honestly—how should I know? He wouldn't tell me how many glasses of I-don't-even-know-what-it-was he'd had, just that it had gone to his head because he'd been up all night for whatever it is you do all night in the church on Maundy Thursday! I mean, it's *all* pretty well outside my purview."

"Yes, I see. I expect he'll have been fine, you know. I'm sure he's at home peacefully sleeping it off."

She nodded, trying to feel confident of this. "He would be embarrassed to know we're having this conversation, wouldn't he?"

"Definitely. But he doesn't have to know."

"You would think that, but this is the sort of thing I always seem to end up telling him. I suppose we should wait until a more reasonable hour before knocking on his door?"

"We're not knocking on his door at all! Not unless you know of a way of getting rid of this." He flapped his hands expressively, and very Peachily.

"I don't. That's the point. You've said yourself this isn't about Orphic, Pure-Plain, believe-and-you-can-change-the-world magic, this is about the Devil. Kit is officially more qualified than either of us to deal with that."

He let this pass without pointing out that it wasn't very Protestant. Possibly he didn't notice.

"I can't let him see this, Elsa. I can't. Please don't make me."

She sighed. "I don't suppose I can make you do anything. Let's get ourselves some breakfast. There must be diners open at this hour."

He seemed heartened by this practical suggestion. He opened the passenger door for her. "I know of a good place."

He pulled the car out of the alley and turned onto College Street. He was driving slowly and oddly, holding the steering wheel with tense fists and making the car lurch every time he touched the pedals. She remembered being in a car with Peachy before; he had been a cool and confident driver.

"Have you forgotten how to drive?"

"No! Sort of. I remember the procedure, I'm just not *used* to it."

"I see. How far do we have to go?"

"Not far—the place is just up here on College. And there's nobody on the road."

"After breakfast you'll let me drive, all right?"

"Happily," he said, changing lanes excruciatingly. "It's awful, you know. Being him. I can't even tell if I'm singing in tune." He shuddered. "Playing the piano is out of the question—you must admit I got his hands right." He held one out briefly before clamping it back on the steering wheel. "He has these useless stubby fingers."

"They are lovely hands," she corrected him sternly.

"Ugh. But I didn't get any of the good bits. I don't feel any more inclination toward honesty, or courage, or even any … any greater faith. Don't worry, though—I have worked out what that means."

"Which is what?"

"That this is what he's got to work with, too. He doesn't have a head-start at virtue. He just does the work. Somehow I'd always thought—or not precisely thought, but had it in the back of my mind—that if I were more like Kit, *of course* I could have fought for my country. And, well, he had some personal revelation of God when he was twelve, so obviously it's very easy for him to go on believing—easier than it is for me, who've just always believed but never really got any help with it."

"But you're not *him*, Peachy. You don't have his memories."

"I've got his expletive-expletive claustrophobia—I can barely stand to be in this car, even with the top down. And the insomnia—which he claims he doesn't get any more. If I look like I haven't slept in a week, that's because it's more or less true. Mind you, you're right—I don't have his memories, so I still don't know what did that to him." This seemed to strike him as a grievance rather than a blessing. "Oh. He's told you about the War, I suppose."

"Fortunately for you, yes."

"Yes, that's Peverell Peacham at his finest, right there. His friend's an adjectival war hero, and he lies about it. Who'd want to be him?"

"You would. Obviously."

"Oh, God. With all my heart."

He pulled the car clumsily into a vacant parking spot in front of a diner with an OPEN sign in the window.

It was still early enough that the diner was full of tired shift workers eating breakfast before going home to sleep. They sat in a booth and ordered coffee, and Peachy brooded over the breakfast menu.

"I don't want any of this stuff. I never eat in the mornings—but *he's* apparently ravenous. Maybe I'll have some dry toast. I'm absolutely desperate for a cigarette, too."

"I don't mind if you smoke."

"*I* mind. I don't smoke. I've *never* smoked."

"Do you know how to bake biscuits?"

"Shut up."

They looked at each other and both began to laugh.

Elsa ordered pancakes, and Peachy decided on the spur of the moment that that was what he wanted too, though when they arrived he spent a lot of time cutting them up and pushing them around on his plate. He had taken off his raincoat, and she could see that his sweater was too tight across the chest. That made sense—but the sleeves were also too short, which didn't.

"I'm still worried about her, too," he said, looking mournfully into his coffee cup. "Anastasiya. She's at the mercy of that fiend. I think I was trying not to believe what he really was so that I didn't have to acknowledge how much danger she is in."

"Do you know that for certain?"

He looked up at her. His eyes were certainly the right colour, but the worry in them was all wrong: too blatant and beseeching. "She is terrified, Elsa. I know that. She tried … She got me alone, one evening, that time that you left before I did, do you remember?"

"I had to work the next day, so I went home early. I remember."

"She was still trying to talk me into setting your translation of one of the hymns, and she asked me to stay in order to meet someone, some other musician. I was just trying to be polite. But the other man left before she had a chance to tell him about it—anyway, that was the excuse she gave, when she found me hanging about after everyone else had gone. I did think at the time it might have been an excuse, and that what she was really trying to do was to get me alone. Well, it worked. She seemed nervous, and it flashed into my mind that she wanted to get me on her side for some reason—that she wanted me to rescue her from something, and the only way she could think of to get me to do that was by trying to seduce me. I know that sounds strange, but it's really the impression I had. And I was right. I told her she didn't need to go to the trouble—the poor woman, she was obviously going against her conscience—and that I'd do whatever I could to help her."

"But she never told you that the manuscript was a forgery?"

"I don't think she felt safe to. She never seemed to feel she could tell me very much, just hints about the danger she's in from someone—I figured out pretty early on that it must be that so-called secretary."

Elsa pushed her remaining pancake around on her plate for a minute too. Had she in fact been quite wrong about Mrs. Graves? She had been wrong about so much else. The woman might be in greater danger than any of them, while she, Elsa—and Kit, for that matter—had been treating her quite callously.

"Do you know the fellow's name, by the way?" Peachy asked.

"The secretary? No. I don't know that he has one. Professor Hallam said that he was … that his body used to belong to a librarian who killed himself, and it's just being *used*."

Peachy looked out the window at the bright sun on College Street and shivered.

"Why did I order coffee?" he asked peevishly, looking down at the cold liquid in his cup. "Apparently I want tea. Did I dream the part where you didn't believe in any of this stuff?"

"No, that was real. But becoming less and less real. I sort of destroyed my credibility as a materialist the other day by trying to perform an exorcism."

"You did what?"

"You heard me."

"Did it work?"

"Of course it didn't *work*, it—Well. He wasn't possessed, so … It did something, though. God—the Holy Spirit—did something."

"The Holy Spirit, yet!"

"Absolutely."

"Who did you try to exorcise?"

"Kit."

"*What?*"

"I told you, he wasn't possessed. He was having an attack of … of … "

"Oh. Nerves. He didn't know where he was, and thought the War was still on, and that kind of thing?"

She nodded. "You must have seen him like that yourself."

"A couple of times. Three times. It scared me out of my wits. I never really … never knew how to help—whether one ought to play along, or try to snap him out of it, or what. I didn't really do either. As I recall, I flapped about uselessly like a Victorian maiden aunt. And it was like a reproach to me, you know? Because I wasn't there—how the hell was I supposed to know what it was like?"

"Well, I don't think it's going to happen again."

"You cured him?"

"The Holy Spirit, you buffoon! I said the Holy Spirit."

"I know, I know—but the point is you did something about it, which is apparently more than I ever did. I would do anything for him, Elsa—I wanted to do *something*. I used to almost wish … I used to *daydream* about him breaking down and sobbing in my arms. Which would have been really awkward, actually, but it was the sort of thing that would have made me feel a little useful. I even wanted him to get angry with me for being a coward and not enlisting, so that I could beg his forgiveness—that would have been something, too. But he didn't get angry, he didn't cry—most of the time it was hard to tell what was wrong with him. He didn't need anything, and so there was nothing I could do for him. I just wanted to look after him."

"According to him, you did."

"What? No, that's not true! I did *nothing*, I tell you. Really nothing. I'd get him out of bed in the mornings sometimes and make sure he went to his lectures, but that was no more than he used to do for me when we were both in university. I'd cook occasionally—very occasionally. Mostly I brought home food from my parents. The only thing he ever really asked of me … he had a lot of trouble sleeping, and some nights he'd knock on my door and wake me up for no particular reason, and I'd blunder about trying to make tea or something, and he would have fallen asleep on the couch in the living room before I had finished. *Every single time*. He didn't need me!"

"Is that really what you've been telling yourself? Of course he needed you, Peachy. Why do you think he kept knocking on your door? He needed you to be awake so that he'd feel safe enough to sleep. If he'd actually wanted tea, he could have made it himself."

"Of course you're right," Peachy conceded gustily. "But it was all such trivial stuff. Oh, I know it would have been harder for him if he hadn't had somebody to make sure he got out of bed, and ate, and didn't fall behind in his classes, but he could have got all that and better from my parents—he didn't need to be living with me. And who are we kidding, really? He's Kit Underhill. It would have slowed him down a bit, that's all. Really, that's all I did for him— maybe helped him finish his degree a little faster."

"But … wasn't that worth doing?"

"Dammit! Of course it was."

She pushed away her empty plate. "Let's be clear—I'm not defending all your actions. I think you did more to help Kit than you give yourself credit for, but you also went about telling people he didn't fight."

"I know! That's the kind of terrible friend I am."

"Well? Why did you do that?"

"Oh, I don't know … I had some idea—I used to make up stories when we were boys, and the fun of it was he'd *never* go along with them. It was a joke, you see—the point was to make it believable, but you could *always* ask Kit and find out the truth, that was … oh, it doesn't make any sense, but that was part of the joke. It think I was trying something like that when I first started telling people that we both waited until '17 to enlist. I wanted to hear him say, *No, actually, I enlisted in 1914 and fought at …* wherever it was, and—I wanted him to talk about it. Not for any good reason, just because *I* wanted to know. But he didn't—he went along with the lie, which I never expected, and then I thought maybe that was what he needed after all, maybe he wanted to pretend it never happened, and so I kept it up, even though … I knew it was a bad idea, that it was driving a wedge between us."

Peachy ordered a cup of tea, and Elsa got a second coffee. Something occurred to her, something she had started to wonder about the night before, but—in the troubling way that seemed all too typical where the young man in grey tweed was concerned—had not pursued.

"The secretary … whatever he is … was he there last night?"

He nodded. "You wouldn't have recognized him, though. He has another form that he uses sometimes. It looks … actually, a lot like you."

"What?" A current of terror ran through her.

"He can change himself into a woman—"

"Who looks like me. Peachy, when did you leave the party last night? Where was Kit when you left?"

"I said, didn't I? Sitting on the couch with you. I went down and got out of my costume at that point, and dithered about trying to decide what to do, and I suppose it was half an hour before I saw you getting into the car and thought he was in it too."

"Okay. So you didn't see who he got up and *spent that half hour dancing with*?" She tried to keep her voice from sounding hysterical, but with limited success.

"No! Dancing? Not with you?"

"No, but with a woman who looked a lot like me. Wearing little horns—little *devil horns*! Oh, Lord, what have we done?"

"Shit. Sorry. Language. But shit. You're positive he didn't leave when you did?"

"He was staying because he was still hoping to get some information about what happened to you. I left because Polly and Vera wanted to go home."

"Shit, shit, shit."

"Stop swearing. It doesn't suit you."

"Oh, what? He doesn't swear?"

"He doesn't swear that much."

"That's true," he admitted ruefully. "I didn't see him dancing with—with her—I swear I didn't."

"No, I believe you. And he wasn't—he'd stopped dancing with her when I left, when I went to say goodbye to him. What do you think … what do you think they want with him?"

"The usual thing, I should think. To get him to go to the Pure Plain—or whatever it is—and lose himself."

"What they got you to do." But who were "they"? He was convinced that Mrs. Graves wasn't one of them; but was he right about that?

"I can't see that working with Kit," he said.

"Maybe not. Peachy, I know you don't want to, but we have to go to St. John's. It's half past six—it'll be seven by the time we get there. I don't mind waking him. I just want to know that he's all right."

He sighed, and rested his head in his hands. "We've already agreed you're going to drive, so I don't suppose I can really protest. But you've got to let me stay in the car. If I were him … which I am … I wouldn't want to be faced with me at this hour of the morning."

They paid their bill and went back out to the car. It was an ageing Ford, sufficiently similar to her brother-in-law's car—the car she'd learned to drive on—that she was able to handle it easily. She pulled out of the parking space much more smoothly than Peachy had pulled into it.

They had some trouble getting to St. John's, since Elsa was unused to driving in Toronto, and Peachy had a poor sense of direction, which he claimed was actually Kit's. Finally she drew up in front of a grocer's on St. Clair West, within sight of the spire of St. John's.

The shop was closed, and three teenaged boys were loitering against the empty display shelves outside, smoking and trying to look tough. One of them saw Elsa and Peachy and nudged his companions. They straightened up and disposed of their cigarettes, and a couple of them assumed strange expressions, which Elsa guessed were meant to appear spiritual.

"Good morning, Father!" they chorused.

Elsa kicked Peachy in the ankle from her side of the car. He goggled stupidly at her.

"Oh! Uh—good morning." He nodded vaguely toward the boys. "Who are they?" he whispered in desperation.

"I don't know."

Two out of three of the boys were too busy trying to look as if they had been discussing the doctrine of the Real Presence, rather than girls or cars, to notice anything amiss. They said they were looking forward to the Vigil, and took their leave awkwardly. The third, who wore an apron and was obviously an employee of the shop, remained standing by the empty shelves. When his friends were a safe distance away, he walked over to the car and stood looking down on Peachy with folded arms.

"Who are you, exactly? You're not Father Underhill."

Peachy looked sick and did not reply.

"No, he's not," said Elsa. She recognized the boy now; he was the acolyte who had given her the tract. He had looked at her then and thought she was someone who needed a tract about prayer; somehow she was not surprised that he was not fooled by Peachy's transformation.

"You're not his brother … " the boy pursued.

"No, not quite," Peachy admitted.

"No, you—you look exactly like him and *totally different*. It's real creepy."

"It's hard to explain," said Elsa. She realized she was glad that someone besides herself could tell that Peachy wasn't Kit. "You're Charlie, aren't you? We're in a bit of a fix, Charlie, and we need to speak to—um, to the real Father Underhill."

"You can't," said Charlie. "I've just been over to the rectory with a delivery, and you know that giant weird man who's staying there? He said Father Underhill never came home last night."

He was met with a grim silence. She wanted to ask if he was sure, to insist that they go check anyway. And at the same time it was what she had expected to hear. She had left him at Mrs. Graves's, and he had not come home.

"What giant weird man?" Peachy asked warily.

"My father."

"I'm very sorry," said Charlie. "I didn't mean … "

"My father! Peachy—Kit couldn't very well have come home last night, with my father staying in his house."

"What?" said Peachy.

"He'd been *drinking*."

"What?" said Charlie, eyes wide.

"We were at a party—it wasn't anything terrible." It was very definitely something terrible. "But my father would certainly have been scandalized. I'm sure Kit thought of that. There might be a totally innocent explanation—an almost totally innocent explanation for what's happened to him. Where might he have gone? Your parents' house?"

"We're not going there, either," said Peachy emphatically.

"If I was him," said Charlie, "and I was … uh … in that kind of fix, I'd've gone to the church. There's a couch in the vestry. It's not bad, actually—I've had a nap there before."

"Good thinking," said Elsa. "We'll go there right away. How will we get in?"

"I can get a key," said Charlie. "My boss is a churchwarden. I'll just need to come up with a good story for him."

"I think you're forgetting that you said you wouldn't make me face him."

"I'm not forgetting, Peachy. You can stay in the car, if you have to."

"Excuse me," said Charlie, "but why do you keep calling him 'Peachy'? Peachy is Father Underhill's friend, the musician. I know what he looks like, and you're not him." He frowned at Peachy. "I don't know *what* you are. There's something real fishy about you."

Peachy sank lower in the car seat, and looked up at the boy with an expression of loathing that suited Kit's face very badly. Charlie glared harder and stood his ground.

"You're very astute, Charlie," said Elsa. "There is something fishy. Will you meet us at the church with the key, if you can? It would be a great help."

The boy nodded. "I'll make up a story for Mr. Oates. You'd better go now—there might already be people there to do the flowers. And I don't think Father would want them to find him sleeping in the vestry if they are."

Charlie went back into the dark shop, and Elsa drove around the corner and pulled the car up onto the gravel in front of the rectory, which looked dark and unwelcoming.

"I won't be long," she said. "I'll just go see if the door is already open. If it isn't, we'll wait for Charlie and the key."

"I think it's the side door that they usually unlock," said Peachy, leaning his head in his hand.

She got out of the car and went to try the door. It was securely locked. For good measure she walked around to the larger west door, but found that one locked as well. She turned back to the car, and saw that, in the time she had been gone, a white-haired woman had come up on the sidewalk and entrapped Peachy in conversation.

"And then, you know, Terence *stopped eating altogether*, and I was really worried about him," she was saying when Elsa, quickening her pace almost to a run, reached the car. "But eventually Daphne came home of her own accord, and so it was all right. I knew you would want to know."

"Yes. Thanks." Peachy opened his door and all but sprang out of the car to meet Elsa.

"Sorry to keep you waiting, F-Father," said Elsa. "Oh, hello, Miss … "

"Hello, dear." The woman beamed up at them approvingly. "I was just going, don't worry. I won't butt my nose in. See you tonight, Father."

"Uh—see you tonight."

Since she remained standing there, smiling at them, there seemed no help for it but to turn up the path toward the rectory.

"I think she was talking about cats," said Peachy when they were a safe distance up the path. "I hope to God she was talking about cats. She's still there—what do we do?"

"Go up to the door and fumble with your keys. She'll leave eventually."

"I knew it was a mistake to involve you," he muttered.

They climbed the steps of the rectory porch, and Peachy rattled the doorknob ineffectually.

"Is she gone yet?"

"Not yet. We could go around the back."

But before they could do this, the front door was opened by an elderly woman in an apron, a stranger to Elsa.

"Lose your keys, did you, Father?" She stared hard and critically at Elsa.

"What?" said Peachy. "Oh! Oh, yes. I—er, did. Yes."

The housekeeper stood aside to let them in, looking pained. "Your guest has been asking for you, Father. He seems to think you didn't come home last night—of course I told him I could not say anything about that, but that he must have been mistaken."

"Of course. Yes. I—er, had to leave early." Peachy was doing his best to imitate Kit's accent. It was pretty horrible.

"That's what I told him. He's gone for a walk. I came in early to help with the brass, like we talked about. I expect you forgot."

"Oh! Did I? Yes."

She stood looking at him expectantly for a moment. "You'll need to give me the key, Father." When he stared at her dumbly, she added: "I suppose you have a spare set somewhere."

"Quite. Quite. Upstairs, I think. I'll … go look for them."

The housekeeper *tsk*ed and retreated to the kitchen, leaving Elsa free to follow Peachy upstairs.

"Key to *what*?" he demanded frantically when they reached the landing. "Brass *what*?"

"How should I know? Maybe something in the church? Just look for keys. I'm going to go downstairs and look out for Charlie."

"Why don't we just make a break for it?"

"Because anything you do now is something that Kit is going to have to deal with the consequences of having done later. Just try not to make him look crazy."

He seemed to see the sense in this, and he retreated upstairs, while she went back out onto the porch.

Charlie was not long in arriving, coming around the corner at a run. But when he got to the rectory porch and had caught his breath, he shook his head.

"I couldn't—exactly get the key. Mr. Oates is coming over himself. Said—he was going to anyway—preparations for Easter or something. He's always in and out of the church. He said I could wait until he got here. But we've got to get in there. I don't want him to find Father sleeping in the vestry. It'd—set things back, you know? He's worked hard—Father Underhill has—to get people to respect him."

"I shouldn't have told you he was out drinking."

"Nah, you don't have to worry about me. Where's the other one— the fake one?"

"Upstairs, looking for another key. Something to do with brass?"

"Brass? The sacristy key, maybe. I doubt it'd be upstairs. It's probably in Father's study."

"Let's go find him and tell him that."

Upstairs, they heard noises coming from an open door at the end of the hall. It led to a large, bright room that had obviously been the nursery when the household had included children. There was a frieze of alphabet wallpaper, a window-seat, and a fireplace surrounded by tiles with nursery-rhyme characters. There was also a single bed (halfheartedly made) and a wardrobe and a tidy dressing table, and it was obvious that Kit was using the room as his bedroom. Peachy was opening drawers and tossing things around. Elsa and Charlie both stopped in the doorway as if they had bumped against an invisible rope. They looked at one another.

"You know what he looks like?" Charlie said. "He looks like a picture of Father Underhill done by somebody who didn't really look at him. Like I mean *look* at him."

"Yes, I know what you mean."

"I figured you would. Is it … it's not natural, right?"

"No. It's not natural. Peachy, Charlie thinks that it's the sacristy key we want, and that Kit's keys would probably be in his study, not up here."

"So go down and look!" Peachy commanded.

"No way," said Charlie. "I'm not rooting around in his things. And you're not planning on leaving his clothes flung around like that, are you?"

Peachy turned an exasperated look on Elsa. "Who is this kid, anyway?"

"He's one of Kit's sidekicks. Acolytes. He's obviously very loyal. And he does have a point," she added, advancing into the room to gather up a couple of sweaters that Peachy had pulled out of Kit's wardrobe. "Let's go look in the study," she said when she had tidied the sweaters to her satisfaction. "We'll find the key to the church at the same time, and then we can look for Kit in the vestry. Though he'll likely be woken by all of our traipsing back and forth anyway."

Please, please let him be sleeping on that couch. She could picture it so clearly: the way he would be curled up, the peaceful expression on his sleeping face, the specific untidiness of his hair.

"Why are you pretending to be him?" Charlie was blocking Peachy's exit from the nursery.

"Because that's who I'm pretending to be. Don't ask stupid questions. And get out of my way. I'm bigger than you, you know."

Charlie stood aside with a confident grace. "Yeah, but I already know I can take you."

"One hates to think how."

They were on the landing at the top of the stairs when they heard the front door opening.

"Hell-ooo? Father Underhill?" a female voice piped from below.

"Miss Finch," Charlie whispered. "Stay back."

"Who just walks in people's front doors like that?" Elsa whispered.

"I know! If I did that, my parole officer would have something to say about it."

"Maybe Miss Finch isn't on parole," Peachy suggested acidly.

Downstairs, Mrs. Whittacker had come out to the hall and explained that Father Underhill was upstairs and would be down presently, and they heard Miss Finch saying, "Good, good. I've come to talk to Father about the baptisms."

Peachy shrank back against the wall with a look of horror.

"No, no—dear God!"

Elsa hauled him through the nearest door into an empty spare bedroom. Charlie followed and shut the door quietly behind him.

"How did I let you get me into this?" Peachy moaned. "This was bad enough without adding questionable sacraments and *babies!*"

"Calm yourself and don't be silly. There's nothing questionable about—"

"Don't *start*. I am not baptizing anybody."

"The baptism isn't until tomorrow," said Charlie. "What you have to worry about is the rehearsal for the Easter Vigil. That's in a couple of hours, and if Father Underhill isn't back, and you're still here, you're going to look very stupid."

Peachy scrubbed frantically at his face with his hands. "This is the sort of thing that if it happened in the pictures, they'd play it for laughs. But when it's real, it's not funny."

"Go downstairs," Elsa said, plucking off his hat and tugging at his raincoat. "Talk to Miss Finch about the babies. We'll go down the back stairs and come through the dining room, so it doesn't look like we were up here. You should really change your collar—though you've probably given yourself the wrong size neck somehow, and Kit's collars won't fit you."

"Let's get this over with."

He strode past them out of the spare room and down the stairs. Even the way he walked was subtly wrong. Halfway down the stairs they could hear him saying, "Good morning, Miss Finch. Did I hear you saying something about babies?" He was at least doing a better job of Kit's accent now.

Elsa and Charlie crept down the back stairs to the kitchen and through to the living room, where they sat down and tried to look as if they had been there all the time. After a few minutes they heard a new voice in the hall, this one a man's. Charlie started guiltily.

"That's my boss." He popped out through the doors into the hall. "Hi, Mr. Oates. I was just on my way back to the shop. I was—"

"Very good, Charlie. Since you are here, would you help Father Underhill to find his keys? Where did you say they were?"

"Uh, top drawer of my desk, I think," said Peachy.

Charlie cast him a black look and went into Kit's study. Elsa had come to stand in the doorway. Charlie's boss was a round, sleek man in a striped waistcoat.

"So you're *sure* that will be all right?" Miss Finch piped.

"Oh, absolutely," said Peachy. "No trouble at all. I'll pass on the—I mean, I'll see to it."

"Well, that is a great relief."

Miss Finch took her leave, and Mr. Oates had opened his mouth to ask some difficult question when Charlie returned with a large bunch of keys.

"They were *on* your desk, Father. In a dish."

"Were they really? What a silly place to—for—me—to have put them."

Mr. Oates frowned. Peachy had gone to town with the accent now, and was sounding a bit like a Duke of the Blood Royal, and a bit like a Dickensian chimney sweep. Mr. Oates was clearly more attuned to how Kit sounded than how he looked.

Charlie went to give the sacristy key to Mrs. Whittacker, and Mr. Oates said, "I realize it is a busy day, Father, but I was wondering about the roster for the, er—"

"Oh, quite, quite," said Peachy recklessly. "I'll just go see about that, shall I?" And he dove into the cover of Kit's study.

Yet another person rang the doorbell, and Mr. Oates opened the door.

"Oh, hello!" said a surprised voice. "Is Kit—Christopher—Mr. Reverend Underhill at home?"

"Harriet!" Elsa cried.

She seemed to Elsa like a visitor from another world: neat and fresh in a lavender suit and a white hat with a lavender feather, and carrying a gigantic handbag. She looked cheerful and full of purpose, quite unlike the Harriet whom Elsa had left drooping in her doorway in Annesley a week before.

"Elsa! Hello! You're here early. Visiting, I guess. Gosh, I haven't seen you in ages, it seems like. Are you all right? How silly—of course you're all right. Hello, by the way," she added, smiling on Mr. Oates. "I'm Harriet Spencer. I'm a friend of Elsa's, and of Kit—Reverend Underhill. I didn't realize he would have so many visitors at this hour."

The door to the study opened.

"Kit! What on earth … Why are you wearing Peachy's clothes?"

Peachy staggered slowly out into the hall, his face a mask of anguish, and fell on his knees at Harriet's feet.

"Forgive me, Harriet—forgive me!"

She looked at him sharply. "For what? What have you done with him?"

"I *am* him. I'm not Kit. I'm Peachy."

"He's gone mad," said Harriet, looking around at the others for support. "Has he gone mad?"

Mr. Oates gave an embarrassed cough. "Father … "

"Please don't call me that," said Peachy, still gazing desperately up at Harriet. She edged away from him.

The front door opened once more, and everyone looked toward the newcomer. It was Elsa's father. He stared around the crowd in the front hall, and finally his eyes fastened upon Peachy. A kind of convulsion went through him at the sight. He covered the distance between them in two steps, dropped to his knees on the floor in front of Peachy, and put his huge hands on either side of Peachy's—which was not Peachy's—face. He rested his forehead against the younger man's.

"Lord Jesus, I beg you, release this man from the snare of the Devil that binds him. Sweet Lord, restore him to himself."

There was a moment of complete stillness. Then with a soft noise as of rustling leaves, something seemed to fall away from Peachy. Mr. Nordqvist opened his eyes and found himself face-to-face with an entirely different man. He started backward with a shout.

"Who are you?"

Peachy held out his own hands and turned them over and laughed out loud. "I am Peverell Peacham. And I've never in my life been so pleased to say that."

Chapter Fifteen

FULL OF SHEEP AND ANGELS

In Mrs. Graves's apartment, Kit was waking up. His head hurt—actually, his whole body hurt, but the headache was distinctive—and his stomach felt hollow and queasy. He rolled onto his back and lay for a moment recollecting where he was and how he had got there.

*

It had taken him a tango and a waltz and another tango to realize that the girl in the devil costume was the one who had glared at him in Hart House: the girl who looked like a poor copy of Elsa. He had tried to be nicer to her after that, remembering the uncharitable way he had thought about her then. She had seemed interested in continuing to dance for a while, and then, when she got tired of that and wanted to sit down and talk, he had gone along with that too. He'd felt exhausted by that point; he wondered whether they hadn't somehow been dancing for longer than he realized.

It was like something out of a fairytale, he thought vaguely. *Why did the princesses sleep all day, and why were their new shoes worn out already? Because they had been dancing all night in the fairy realm.*

Was it true, after all, that she was not as beautiful as the real Elsa? She was leaning very close to him now, so that one of her full breasts brushed against his sleeve. The man's clothes she wore didn't really suit her; the real Elsa, with her height and her lack of curves, would have worn them better. Not entirely an appealing thought. Behind her mask, her eyelashes were as pale as the real Elsa's, even

430

though her eyes were the wrong colour. Surely they were a better colour, though; they were blue like his own.

She was talking about something, a lot of strange nonsense. *The Bibliotheka promises that the will is more real than the flesh, that the material is base and false. Base and false. This means—of course—that the individual should be freed from all moral codes and should use the material world in every way for his own gratification.*

"It's a sort of watered-down Gnosticism." He hadn't meant to say that out loud. She had been in the middle of a sentence.

She didn't seem bothered by the interruption. "And don't you think that it is very wise?"

"No, not at all. I think it's very silly." He shook his head. "Not silly—pernicious."

"Pernicious. Because heretical? But surely you agree that flesh is base?"

"If you meant 'sinful'—but you don't, you mean something else. And you went one further, you said *matter* is base, and I definitely don't agree with that. You shouldn't expect me to—I'm a sacramentalist."

They went on talking like this. He could not get out of this conversation by producing the simplest excuse: getting something to drink, seeing someone he knew and wanted to talk to, fancying a breath of fresh air—somehow he couldn't say any of these things. It began to seem less and less strange that he couldn't. Why would he want to? His companion was so lovely. Arguing with her demanded all of his concentration, because …

Well, why? Her point of view was ridiculous. The manuscript was a forgery.

"It's a what?"

For the first time he felt a cold stab of unease. He had not—he *knew* he had not—said that out loud.

"You know," she said delicately, "what it is to lose your hold on reality."

He remembered the smell of acrid smoke, the taste of the dirt. Brass buttons.

"Yes."

"You can see it coming, but you can do nothing to stop it."

"Can I not?" He folded his arms and looked at her challengingly.

And an angel appeared. No, it was Elsa Nordqvist, in Vera's homemade wings, but she had come to his rescue all the same. He jumped up from the couch with relief.

"Thanks," he said.

She was telling him that she was leaving with Polly and Vera, and he was replying at random. He said he was going to stay, because it was what she seemed to expect him to say; it seemed to be what she wanted from him, and he would have done anything … He had somehow got another drink in his hand, and it was half empty. Earlier in the evening she had asked him how much he'd had to drink, and he had teased her for it. If only she would ask again. At the same time he had a hazy idea that it would be good for her to leave.

She was leaving—he hadn't tried to stop her—but then suddenly she turned back.

"Kit! I almost forgot. What time is the—the thing, the Mass, tomorrow night?"

"The Vigil?" The thought of her being there filled him with a bittersweet delight. Honesty compelled him to admit: "Your father says he's not going to go. I think he was scandalized when I described the liturgy. Besides, he met an old friend at the prayer meeting who invited him to his house to sing hymns."

"That's all right. He knows we parted ways a long time ago. But what time is it?"

The party sprang into focus around him. The clichéed dance music was suddenly beautiful. There wasn't enough gin in the world to keep him from understanding this.

"Eight," he said.

"Good."

"It's at eight."

"Yes."

As she disappeared through the door, the other one—the wrong one, the false idea of Elsa—was at his elbow. She wanted to dance again. He turned on her the smile with which he had been watching the real Elsa depart, and she swayed back a little, daunted.

"I'm ready for another round if you are," he said.

*

Mrs. Graves cut in eventually, but that didn't last long. She was a terrible dancer. She kept trying to lead, and he couldn't tell if she was doing it on purpose as a joke, or just because she didn't really know what she was doing. Fortunately by this time he was tired enough that he could plead to be allowed to sit out the next dance with complete sincerity. She called him a poor boy and tucked his hand into the crook of her arm and escorted him off the floor. Before he knew what had happened he had another drink in his hand.

*

Much later, he lay back on one of the couches—not the one where he had sat with Elsa—his feet on the coffee table with its litter of empty glasses and napkins, the skirt of his cassock crumpled around his knees. He was playing with the fringe of his fascia, pouring it through his fingers and spreading the strands out on the couch cushion. He knew he'd had too much to drink, and once he had sat down he had realized he was alarmingly tired, as if he had been through a long illness or a physical ordeal. He had no idea what time it was. Mrs. Graves was perched on the arm of the couch, talking to him.

"Do you remember the story of the Dancing Princesses?" she asked.

"Mm," he said. He wasn't sure whether he meant that to mean "Yes" or "No."

"Every night they were enticed out of their beds and danced to exhaustion in the fairy realm—under the hill. That's what gave me the idea, you know. Your name."

"How apt," he said, and yawned. He hadn't really any idea what she was talking about.

He looked up at her. It occurred to him from this vantage that it was surpassingly odd, if she really wanted to seduce him—and everything else she had done clearly proclaimed that she did—that she was not running her fingers through his hair right now. It seemed an almost incredibly obvious thing to do. Here he was, sprawled out within easy reach of her bony, ringed fingers, drunk and passive with exhaustion, and his hair was undoubtedly doing that thing that it did, that made him look like a little boy who had just crawled out of bed. And she was babbling about dancing princesses. He thought, *Isn't that interesting? You're about as attracted to me as I am to you.*

He smiled up at her. "You're not really Russian, are you?"

"What?"

"I noticed. Earlier. When you crossed yourself. You did it the wrong way. I mean the right way. Depending. Wrong if you were Orthodox."

"What?"

He chuckled. "Elsa didn't think you were. A countess, I mean. Or actually called 'Anastasiya Graves'—I mean, please. I expect you're a lapsed Irish Catholic or something silly."

"*What?*" She slid off the arm of the couch and stood over him. "I've never heard anything so absurd." She torqued up her Russian accent, clutching at it like a slipping garment.

"Well, *really*," he drawled, ratcheting up his own accent, but much more convincingly. "You know something else funny? You and I never met before tonight—did we? And this was a costume party.

How d'you know I'm not a bricklayer or a bookmaker or … a de-
partment-store clerk, or … "

"I suppose I don't," she said, unconvincingly. For a moment she
reverted to her earlier, unctuous manner: "In this place, we all have
the power to be whatever we want to be."

He snorted. "What rot!" he said, rolling the 'r' luxuriantly and
then laughing at himself.

Anastasiya Graves remained standing by the couch, looking down
on him. He wondered whether she were trying to look threatening
or seductive, or whether she thought that to him those were basically the same thing. He sighed and stretched slightly, languidly
readjusting his position on the couch. He was fascinated by the way
that this little display of sensuality obviously put her off, kept her
at bay. He was also—perhaps because the alcohol was beginning to
wear off—somewhat disgusted by what he was doing.

"She could probably have saved you, you know," Mrs. Graves
was saying, with a strained attempt at ironic detachment, "just by
dancing with you."

"It's not her job to save me."

"Ah yes, I suppose you think it your job to save her. Bricklayer,
indeed! And yet she wouldn't even dance with you. Small return
for your devotion, I should have thought."

He thought of how Elsa had refused him, blushing and looking
down at her hands, and how close he had come to seizing them and
saying, "Some other time. At Peachy and Harriet's wedding—or
before that, just the two of us, in my living room, to something
ridiculous on the gramophone. Not here—you're right to not want
it to be here." He hadn't often been turned down as a dance partner,
but her "No" had made him happier than any "Yes" that he could
remember.

"I was devastated," he agreed blandly.

The girl/devil who had danced with him had come back into
the room. He remembered now that she had passed him off to Mrs.

Graves some time earlier, frustrated in her attempt to find out what he knew about the *Bibliotheka*. She had changed out of her costume. In fact, she was dressed as—*was*—a young man in spectacles and a grey tweed suit. Kit wasn't sure how he knew that it was still her. But he realized that she—he—they had made a tactical mistake, a very silly tactical mistake, in presenting him with a male instead of a female opponent.

He kicked over the coffee table and bolted from the couch. He had gained the hallway by the time the glasses had finished crashing and rolling on the parquet floor, but he really was drunk and exhausted, and he had to steady himself by catching hold of a wall sconce, which threatened to come away in his hand. He leaned back against the wall instead. He had run, disoriented, into a blind alley, full of doors leading to bedrooms. There were still party guests in some of them; he heard voices and laughter. The door to his left was half open.

The young man in grey tweed caught up to him.

"Whatever made you do that, Father?"

Kit recognized his voice. He was the man who had come into the library after Hallam. The thing that used to be a librarian, but had been hollowed out and filled with evil. Suddenly he began to laugh. The creature cocked a sandy eyebrow at him.

"You were dressed as yourself too," said Kit.

"It strikes you as funny."

"It really does."

"But we are not opposite numbers, you know," the young man said casually. "Perhaps the Spirit deigned to light on you for a moment, when some bishop laid his hands on you—perhaps. It's a matter of belief for you, unfortunately. I have no need to believe anything. I am inhabited by my master at all times. Indeed it is the master who speaks to you now."

Kit drew himself up and made the sign of the Cross. The creature wrinkled its nose and pushed up its spectacles with a display of nonchalance.

"A rude gesture, certainly. But not ultimately all that effective."

"I don't know," said Kit cheerfully. "It makes me feel better."

"It's a survival tactic, isn't it—this insouciance? In reality, you feel things deeply—for good and ill—but you try to protect yourself with flippancy."

"Oh, well done. But I don't think amateur psychoanalysis is your best strategy with me."

"I'm right, aren't I?"

"You're right, but I can tell you you're right because I already knew that about myself. I'm probably too self-involved to be got at that way."

"You misunderstand my intent. I was merely making conversation. My strategy for 'getting at' you is simpler." He went on, in a reasonable voice, like a detective in a novel explaining how he had solved the mystery. "At first I thought the female disguise might help, but you don't have that horror of the feminine that I thought you might. That would have made you vulnerable, of course, as would a desire too naïvely suppressed—but you happen to be quite clear about what you want, and matter-of-fact about denying yourself. It would all be admirable if it weren't so stupid."

"Is there a point to this?"

"Oh yes. You see, you *are* self-involved. Wrapped … up … in yourself. Oh, you don't really consider it a vice, in spite of what you say. You just keep yourself to yourself. Private. Inviolate. If I wanted to get at you, I'd just … "

He felt its incursion as vividly as a hand sliding under his clothes—but it wasn't on his skin, it was inside of him, gently and lasciviously reaching under some outer layer of his mind. The horror of it was unspeakable. For a moment he stood paralyzed by it. But only for a moment.

He grabbed the thing by its grey tweed lapels, hauled it toward him and, with one hand on the back of its head, slammed its face against the wall. He could hear the nose breaking, and for a moment he was caught in the grip of a sickening satisfaction. It was mercifully replaced by revulsion that what he had just smashed into the wall was a human face. He dropped the limp form and pushed through the half-open door. As he swung it shut, the creature was gathering itself up and crawling away from him. Kit slammed the bolt to and managed to cross the floor to the toilet before he fell to his knees and was sick.

Some time later, when no one had rattled the doorknob or knocked, and the sounds of the party had died to subdued voices and departing footsteps, he rose shakily from the tiles, ran water into his cupped hands and rinsed his mouth, and wiped his face on his sleeve. He sat for a moment on the edge of the bathtub, trying to think of a better plan and failing. He couldn't even summon the initiative at this point to untie his shoes. He slipped down into the tub, curled up, and fell asleep almost immediately.

*

So that was where he was: on his back in Mrs. Graves's bathtub, hung over and sore from having slept in a bathtub, but otherwise sound and in possession of his faculties. On the whole, it could have been a lot worse.

The sun was bright on the tiled wall above him. He sat up in the tub, and his eyes fell on the towels folded over the rail beside the sink. He remembered now that in Elsa's account of her first visit to Mrs. Graves's salon, she had mentioned putting the towels in the tub before she had slept there. How sensible of her. He yawned and stretched gingerly, favouring his sore shoulder.

He heard footsteps and men's voices from the hall. One voice he recognized as belonging to the devil in grey tweed. The other was unfamiliar.

"I wish you had seen fit to tell me last night," the unfamiliar voice said. "One might almost think you don't have my best interests at heart." The doorknob rattled. "Yes, well, you weren't lying about its being locked. I wonder which of these keys it is. I don't think I have ever had to unlock the bathroom before."

The keys jangled as he tried them in the lock. *He's doing this for my benefit*, Kit thought. He cast his eyes around the bathroom. The window was high in the wall, and he recalled that they were at the top of the building anyway. He leaned back in the tub and clasped his hands behind his head. He had an idea why the devil had not tried to get through the door on his own before the morning. And there was just the possibility that the other man was merely some friend of Mrs. Graves, helping to clear her apartment of stragglers from the night before.

The door opened. The man with the keys was the one who had been presiding over the meeting at Hart House. He was wearing silk pyjamas and a dressing gown, his greying curls unkempt, his chin unshaven. He looked as though he had slept more comfortably than Kit, but not as long. Kit had no recollection of having seen him at the party.

The devil, behind him, showed no sign of ever having had a broken nose, but, as Kit had suspected, he also seemed reluctant to enter the bathroom. He looked warily at the man in the tub.

Kit yawned ostentatiously.

"Sorry to be monopolizing the facilities. I'm just on my way out."

He grabbed the sides of the tub in order to suit the action to the words, but the man in the dressing gown stood over him, effectively preventing him getting out. Kit sat back down and looked up at him questioningly.

"Something I can do for you? Besides getting out of the bathroom, I mean—since you don't seem to want me to do that."

The man was about Kit's height, but slighter, and there was a daunting intensity in his expression. He was a man very used to having his own way, Kit thought. Obsessed with it, even. The kind of man who would invent a system for subduing the world to the mastery of his own mind, for fun—and then sell his soul for the chance to make other people believe in it.

"You're Arthur Gallagher, aren't you?" *And as far as you're concerned, I'm not getting out of this bathroom alive, am I?*

"I am. And you, I am sorry to say, are in my way."

"Actually, you're in my way—and I offered to get out of the bathroom."

"How much has she told you?"

"I have no idea what you mean. But I will say that if you speak her name—well, if you speak a certain name, which might be the one you mean—I'll knock you down."

Gallagher gave a derisive snort. "Your chivalry is quaint, but extraordinarily misguided." His lips twitched; he was toying with the idea of calling Kit's bluff by saying something repulsive about Elsa. Instead, he turned toward the devil in grey tweed. "Get him out of the bathtub, will you?"

The young man stood for a moment looking at Kit with distaste. Then he rolled his shoulders back and stretched his neck a little, like an athlete beginning to warm up. Both the grey tweed and the young man fell gently away, and the false Elsa stood there in a tiny white cotton nightdress, her pale hair down around her shoulders, her nipples making hard points under the thin fabric.

She stepped gracefully into the bathtub, sliding the nightdress higher than necessary on her pale thighs.

"I'm getting out!" He scrambled awkwardly to his feet, grabbing at a shelf beside the bath and knocking over several bottles. One of them broke in the tub, spilling a strong, choking perfume.

He got out of the bathtub, but she was out before him, and stood between him and the door.

"Oh, come on," said Kit. "Really? You're going to play this game?"

"I think we might," said Gallagher, behind him.

"I thought we'd already established that I'm not afraid of women."

"Oh, that's right. Well, you can easily get away, then. You could hit her, for instance—knock her down."

Kit glared at him over his shoulder, and Gallagher laughed. "It must be excruciating, being such a gentleman." Looking past Kit, he added, "I don't know why you were so sure this wouldn't work." He gave Kit a shove in the direction of the false Elsa. "Now! Tell us what you know about the manuscript."

"What manuscript?"

"We know she told you something. What was it? How much does she know?"

"How much does who know?"

The professor made an impatient noise. The false Elsa took a step toward Kit, her head tipped a little to one side. The face was not Elsa's, but it was like hers: the same high cheekbones, the same slender, mobile lips and arched, pale brows. The vacant expression of the too-blue eyes was giving way to something worse, a kind of sulky reluctance. This was obviously for his benefit too.

But it's not how she would look.

"Isn't it? He thinks it is."

Her long fingers were pleating the fabric of the nightdress up around her hips. The voice was wrong—too high—the hands the right shape, but too delicate. She was Gallagher's idea of an improved Elsa: softer, shyer, more voluptuous. He was repelled, but he was also sickeningly aroused.

"Really—why did you think this wouldn't work?" Gallagher drawled.

"It isn't working." He spun around and struck Gallagher hard in the face.

The man's head snapped back. He slipped on the tiles, but grabbed the towel rail and stayed upright. Kit ducked around the false Elsa and dove toward the door. Something caught him in mid-step, like a blow on the inside of his skull, and the next thing he knew he was prone on the bathroom floor. He gasped for breath, his vision dissolving in bright spots. He tried to heave himself up from the floor, and failed. Someone's knee caught him in the centre of his back and forced him down again.

"She's … not—that heavy."

The false Elsa hit the back of his head so that his cheek bounced painfully against the tiles. Gallagher, dabbing at his bloody nose with a facecloth, knelt down in his field of vision.

"What dib she tell you … aboud de maduscribt?"

"Say that again?"

"The *Bibliotheka*," he said more clearly, taking away the facecloth. "Tell us what you know."

"Never heard of it. Sounds like—the German for 'library.'"

"Greek, you ignoramus. It's Greek." Gallagher got to his feet. "Get him to talk first. How much she knows—*how* she knows, damn her—who else knows."

The false Elsa gave a low whimper.

"*Do* it! You can have your way with him after—eat him or possess him or whatever the hell you want. She will regret that she ever took this bastard into her confidence—just as she will regret everything that she has done to oppose my will."

Kit tried again to get up, and again there was that pressure, at once brutal and slitheringly intimate, of something trying to unfurl itself inside his mind, and he dropped gasping onto the tiles. She was trying to turn him over. She had no more strength, physically, than the real Elsa—probably less—but she had him in her power with that trick. He tried to get a purchase on something, and caught hold of the pedestal of the sink. He clung to it as she tried to flip him onto his back. She succeeded only in twisting him at the waist.

"This is … ridiculous. What are you even trying to do?"

"You know what I'm doing," she breathed, her voice low and sorrowful. That was the worst part of it—the way she was pretending she didn't like this any more than he did. "In a moment, you'll even want me to do it. Apparently part of you already does. Try to tell me *now* that flesh isn't base."

She had discovered that the pockets of his cassock had slits in them that gave access to the pockets of his trousers—and the buttons of his trousers. She had started expertly undoing them. He tried to curl up to get away from her moving fingers, but in the process lost his grip on the sink, and instantly, as he had anticipated, she had hold of his wrist, and was dragging his hand toward her. He clenched it into a fist, but he could still feel her thigh as she pressed his hand to it, drawing his knuckles across her soft skin, up under her nightdress, her mind pressing into his.

The professor was leaning on the edge of the bathtub, nursing his bloody nose and watching.

"That's right," the false Elsa murmured. "Show me. Let me in. Let me see. Let me see everything, and then I will show you … I will comfort you. You will see what you need to do. That is how it works. But first let me inside."

He felt something give inside him like a rotten floorboard. She turned him easily under her, drew his open hand up under the white fabric to her breast. Her other hand reached down between her legs, gathered up the skirt of his cassock, and slid inside his trousers.

"Don't—please don't."

She smiled sadly. He could close his eyes, but that would make it worse. If he closed his eyes, his imagination, as treacherous as his body, would turn her into the real Elsa.

But the real Elsa …

He caught hold of her wrist, and pulled his other hand away from her breast. He could lift the real Elsa easily—he'd done it when she tried to defend him from Hallam—and she was taller and stronger than this simulacrum. So much stronger.

"I'm—not—afraid of you … "

What I am afraid of …

She took the bait; she followed him eagerly in. His hands dropped limply away onto the tiles, and he lay open to her—him—*it* as it slid into his mind, probing along the scar left by the falling church and the agonizing slog through no-man's land afterward. He felt his back arch, his heels sliding on the tiles as he writhed weakly against the shock of the unnatural invasion. His vision was filled for a moment with her pale face, evilly smirking, then that was mercifully replaced with blackness. His body was subdued, unresponsive—but that was just a relief, he'd been a bit sick of it. He could feel only the devil walking along that seam in his mind, poking at it with satisfaction. *Hmm, yes,* it was saying. *This will do nicely.*

He was unable even to flinch away, but the places that it touched were no longer painful; the whole wound had been cleanly healed. He could recall clearly—more clearly than in the worst of his night-mares—every ragged outline of the ruined church, the sound of every mortar, the smell of the smoke, of the earth as it rained down on him. But the terror that had held him at intervals after that he could remember only as a series of bare facts: at such-and-such a time I was frightened to be in a car, or a basement; at such-and-such a time I couldn't sleep. Surely the thing would be able to tell that. But somehow it couldn't. It mistook his revulsion at its violation of his thoughts for pain; it touched the healed place and imagined that it had discovered a fresh wound.

Oh! Lord! This is why you made me like this, after all.

And it could not hear that. It was busy preparing something for him, very pleased with itself.

See how you like this, Father! it chuckled.

It rolled him into the thing it had prepared, and drew back to watch.

The bathroom and the false Elsa and Professor Gallagher were gone. He was in St. John's, lying on his back in the empty chancel. It was morning, or afternoon, or both at once; light streamed in the clerestory windows on both sides, tremendous shafts of it, and light blazed in the stained glass above the altar. He felt very peaceful there. The church shook as if it had been grasped from above by a giant hand. The beams began to splinter, and plain glass from the highest windows rained glittering down.

Chunks of yellow brick fell out of the walls, and more sunlight poured through. The posts of the rood screen were coming down behind him like felled trees. The statue of St. John rolled past. One of the angel-shaped pavement candlesticks crashed down beside him with a huge noise like a bell. The curve of her neck rested lightly on his outflung arm; her wing warded off the roof-beam that had been about to fall on him. He lay there unafraid.

The great eastern window was coming down, but in pieces: a glass palm tree fell across the altar without shattering; a cloud floated down to settle in the choir stalls.

A stained-glass sheep was snuffling affectionately in Kit's hair. The Shepherd stood over him, no longer grave but smiling, gently amused. A longing that was like nothing he had ever known, and that had been echoing through all his adult life, rose up in him.

The stained-glass figure was gone. The floor beneath Kit was beginning to crumble, to subside gently on top of cushioning mounds of candles and baskets and choir music and acolytes' surplices. They cradled him as he sank down into incense-scented darkness.

For a long time he lay at rest, neither breathing nor feeling, all the workings of his body stilled. To think that it should be so good! He had always been very satisfied with his body: It had been strong and obedient, and people—himself included—had liked the way it looked. But this rest was good too.

Then he heard a sound: a voice, or an instrument, or a rush of wind and water and beating wings, wordless, or thundering out in verse upon verse of poetry, or one great word, its syllables not yet finished. But what it meant was that it was time. Time! Now! Come!

He rose up out of the earth, which fell away from his naked limbs. He was on a wide, empty plain, and in the impossibly far distance, the sun was rising—but not the sun, something else. He was whole, and himself. He brushed the dirt out of his hair, and felt the warm breeze on his skin. Between him and the sunrise stood towering a flame, or a man, and in his hands he held a great balance.

I know how this goes!

He shouted it delightedly at the sunrise and the angel.

Let it be now! Say it is now!

Let me be judged, that I may hasten the time when I may see Him.

But he knew—and somehow it could not diminish his joy—that it was not really now. When it happened, though it might be like this, it would not look like this. What it would look like he was not ready to see. But that was all right.

He sat back down in the loose earth, hugging his knees, and watched the sun that was not the sun but more than the sun rise, and the angel go about his work with the balance, until the vision faded and he was sitting on the floor in a bathroom, between the sink and the toilet, with his back against the tiled wall. He remembered having once been here before, a long time ago. He leaned his head back against the wall and laughed.

There was a young man absurdly clad in a woman's white night-gown, clutching a towel around himself and leaning on the edge of the bathtub, looking ill. And there was a grey-haired man in a dressing gown, with a bloody nose, shouting at him.

"I said: Find out how much he knows about the manuscript! What's so goddamned difficult about that, you useless halfwit? What the hell have you done with him instead? You've driven him mad, like Hallam—did I ask you to do that? Well, did I? Why have you done that?"

The young man shook his head slowly, looking at Kit. "I haven't. I haven't touched him. He's—protected."

"Protected?"

"Full of … " He swallowed hard as if trying not to throw up. "Sheep, and—and angels."

"Well, *do* something about it! Aren't you supposed to be so powerful? Aren't you supposed to be at my beck and call?"

The young man glared at him petulantly. "You know what your problem is, Gallagher? I don't think, at bottom, you really believe in God."

Gallagher stared as if this were the baldest non sequitur.

"That's what this is about, you fucking moron!" the devil shouted at him.

Kit grabbed the edge of the sink and got to his feet. He held the memory of the vision carefully in his mind, like a handful of water. But he was back in the present, and he didn't feel particularly good, in a variety of ways that he didn't want to think too much about.

"What do you think you're doing?" Gallagher tried to sound menacing.

"Leaving. Look. I am not going to tell you anything about your rubbish fake manuscript. And I don't think your cut-rate Mephistopheles is up for having another go at me. So I think I'm just going to walk out of here."

And he did. Once out of the apartment he stopped in a corner of the stairs, leaned against the wall, and laboriously, because his hands were shaking badly, did up the buttons of his trousers.

Chapter Sixteen

THE POWERS OF DARKNESS

"I don't know whether I forgive him or not," Harriet said, slipping a gramophone record back into its sleeve and flipping efficiently through the stack before sliding it into its proper place. She had started out pacing Kit's living room, and then gravitated toward the gramophone with its untidy pile of records.

"I think if you don't know, you haven't forgiven him," said Elsa. "Yet."

Harriet nodded. "That makes sense. But you think I might still. And that makes sense too. It's remarkable how much sense you manage to make right now, Elsa. We're in quite a nonsensical situation. And *what* am I doing?"

"I think you're putting Kit's records in alphabetical order."

"I'm not—I'm organizing them by colour. Where is he in all of this, anyway? Is he over at the church? Does he know that we're all in his house?"

"No, and no—we left him at Mrs. Graves's last night, and he didn't come home. And before you suggest that we go charging in there to rescue him—"

"I wasn't going to suggest that! My gosh. That would be a little bit embarrassing for him, don't you think? It's just his bad luck that we all happened to show up at his house—otherwise he would have been able to sneak in, and nobody would have known. Poor Kit."

It was a natural thing to think, but all the same Elsa found she couldn't bear it. "Harriet, what are you suggesting?"

"Well … " She hesitated delicately, then forged ahead: "He's been seduced by Mrs. Graves, hasn't he? Just as Peachy was. We know she's a seductress." She had finished with the records and begun pottering along Kit's bookshelf.

"And you're ready to forgive *him?*"

"I've nothing to forgive him—he's not my fiancé. Nor yours, the last I heard."

"No, but Harriet—he hasn't been seduced by Mrs. Graves."

"I'm sorry," said Harriet indignantly, "but I think he has. He is a man, you know, Elsa. He is flawed like everyone. I'm sure he didn't set out to be seduced, but you can't pretend it couldn't happen."

"I'm not pretending that it couldn't happen. I'm just maintaining that it didn't. And I'm not doing it just to be loyal. Peachy fell for Mrs. Graves because he wanted to protect her—he wanted to guard her and shield her and look after her and—Kit's not like that."

"He's not a gentleman?"

"He's not a mother hen!"

To Elsa's surprise—she had thought that was probably unforgivable—Harriet exploded into laughter.

"He *is*, you know—Peachy is. He tries to be so many other things, and so flighty and unreliable, but what really makes him happy is if he can do something for you. I don't think I ever gave him enough to do."

"You're kind of a mother hen yourself, Harriet."

"I know."

"You're just more efficient about it."

"Thanks. I did think about this, you know. I thought we had something in common, wanting to help people, wanting to solve people's problems for them. But I should have … I should have tried to give him more encouragement."

"Harriet. Forgiving him is one thing. Blaming yourself is another thing entirely. I *don't* think you should do both."

The back door opened, and they heard the voices of Mr. Nordqvist and Peachy raised in argument in the kitchen.

"Perhaps we had better go see what that's about," said Elsa.

Harriet followed her through the dining room. Elsa's father had taken Peachy out to walk around the rectory garden half an hour ago. Peachy had gone meekly at the time.

"That is mere superstition!" Mr. Nordqvist was protesting. "Can you find any mention of such a thing in Holy Scripture? I tell you, you cannot."

"No, look—I know that I'm not in a position to convince you, I know I'm horribly compromised and all that. Believe me, I understand that. But it's not as if I'm talking about doing divinations or—or sprinkling it on the garden to improve the roses or something. We *know* we're dealing with demonic powers—it's *absolutely* orthodox and traditional. And anyway, sir, with the greatest respect—have you got a better idea?"

"Prayer! Prayer, and faith in the Lord Jesus, Brother Peach!"

"Well, obviously, yes—yes, obviously, that too. You know, sir, 'Peachy' is actually short for … "

He was interrupted by Charlie, who burst through from the dining room in a threadbare cassock, carrying a cut-glass decanter of something.

"I've got it," he said, putting the decanter on the kitchen table.

"What is it?" Harriet asked.

"Holy water."

Mr. Nordqvist shook his head.

"I have to get back to the rehearsal," said Charlie. "It's not looking good. Mr. Oates is trying to make excuses for Father Underhill, but I don't think Mr. Cox is buying it."

"It's very good of Mr. Oates," said Elsa. "Peachy, just what exactly are you planning to do with that?"

"I'm not sure yet. Right now I'm going to look for something to pour it into. That thing's a bit unwieldy. If we have to take it somewhere."

"Perhaps you should have some saints' relics as well," Mr. Nordqvist suggested. "Some magic candles? Or a golden calf."

"Pappa."

"I think I remember unpacking something that might do," said Harriet, opening a cupboard.

Charlie was still standing in the doorway.

"Can I … " he started. "Can I tell them Father Underhill's being held captive by devils? Because it's his first Easter at St. John's, and it was his idea to change the liturgy, and … it's really not good for him to miss this rehearsal."

"No," said Elsa firmly. "You cannot tell them that. We don't know that that's the case."

Charlie nodded sadly and went out.

"Here we are," said Harriet, turning from the cupboard with a silver flask in her hand. "I knew I'd seen one somewhere."

"I cannot be a party to this," said Mr. Nordqvist regretfully. "You must do what you feel to be right, Brother Peach. I believe that your heart is good. But it is not my path. I shall be in the garden if there is any news of Brother Christopher."

"Can somebody tell me again what Elsa's dad is doing here?" Harriet asked when the back door had closed behind him.

"Not really," said Elsa. "I'm not sure anybody but God actually knows."

"I'm terrifically grateful to him," said Peachy. "I hope he doesn't think I'm not. He's just a little intense."

Elsa thought she needed to find an excuse to leave Harriet and Peachy alone in the kitchen. It needn't even be a particularly good excuse. The trouble was, neither of them seemed to want to be alone with the other. Harriet was still reeling from the sight of the man she'd thought was Kit turning into Peachy, and still unsure whether she could forgive him for his betrayal, no matter how strange the circumstances had been. That was fair, but she was still, Elsa thought, trying to fit the irrational truth of what had happened into the conventional framework of a man leaving his fiancée for another woman.

As for Peachy, he was just afraid of not being forgiven, and Elsa couldn't blame him for that. She tried lamely to help them find a funnel.

"What I was thinking is that we ought to prepare ourselves in advance, and pick our moment," Peachy explained. "There's a meeting this afternoon—not a salon at Anastasiya's, but one of the Purists' shindigs. Gallagher runs those. He seems to steer clear of the other crowd, and I didn't know he was involved at all until I went to one of the Purists' meetings. I only went to find out about them for Ana—for Mrs. Graves. She can't attend, because they're men only. But her secretary always changes form after he gets inside Hart House. Changes into his female form, I mean. Just because Gallagher likes it, I think. That's why I thought the meetings might be our best opportunity. He'd be easier to deal with as a woman."

Harriet was looking at him as if she wondered how much of this he was making up. "What do they do at the meetings?" she asked. "Is that where they taught you to turn into Kit?"

He shook his head. "No, that was different. Private. These are just meetings. They sit around and talk about what they're going to do with the power they're acquiring, how they're changing the world with their minds. Encouraging each other. It sounds silly, but when you hear them … " He shivered. "They're deadly serious. I think it's also where they make their plans to … to sacrifice people."

"*Sacrifice*? You mean kill people?"

"From the sound of it. It's like an inner circle—you don't hear any talk of that kind of thing at the salons, but when you get in the heart of it, you find out what they do to get the real power. At least that's what they're peddling. Not penny-ante stuff like turning yourself into your best friend. They claim the manuscript requires sacrifices. Obviously it's not really the *manuscript* that wants them, but I think the sacrifices may be real. Pure … uh, virgins and that kind of thing."

"That's horrible! And you think that, if we go to this meeting, we'll find Kit? You think he won't have come home before then?"

"He may—I hope he will. But I think we have to have a plan."

"Because you think he's a prisoner somewhere. You don't think he's just been … that Mrs. Graves has just … you know, that he's spent the night at her apartment."

"Kit? Hah! Not a chance. Besides—Anastasiya isn't really like that."

"Isn't she?" Harriet frowned. "It seems to me that's exactly what she's like. I'm not trying to blacken his name, you know. I do think it would be unlike Kit to let himself get seduced. But I also think I'm being realistic, even if you two won't consider it. You idealize Kit, that's obvious, and Elsa's … "

"Unrequitedly in love with him," Elsa supplied.

"Unre*what*edly?" Peachy gave her an incredulous look. "That's not what—"

"Don't tell me again that's not what it looked like at the party! He was flirting with me at the party to make Mrs. Graves jealous. That's all. So stop it."

"He was *what*?"

"He was trying to find out what had happened to you. Mrs. Graves seemed to be the person most likely to know."

"Yes, but toying with your affections to do it?"

"Of course not! You're starting to sound as bad as his teenage sister. He was playing a part. We were simply there to try to find out what happened to you."

"And now we're trying to work out what happened to him," said Harriet, "and what I can't understand is why we're jumping to the conclusion that he's in the toils of this strange cult, rather than, say, in Mrs. Graves's apartment, with Mrs. Graves. Because to me what seems most likely is that, you know, he was at this party, and by everyone's admission he'd had too much to drink, and this Graves woman got her hands on him and just exploited the situation a little."

"No!" said Peachy and Elsa at the same time.

Harriet sighed. "It's just that I'm having a hard time understanding why this Graves woman would seduce *you*, and turn you into Kit, and then not want the real thing when she had him in her hands."

"But that's not what happened. She didn't … she didn't seduce me. Not really. And she didn't turn me into Kit."

"I see. So I'm not to blame her, I suppose. Well, that's too bad, because it doesn't leave me with many options for who else to blame."

"I know," said Peachy miserably.

"I'll take this back to the church," said Elsa, picking up the decanter of holy water.

"Let's go with her," said Harriet. "If we're going ahead with your plan, we ought to have other things. A Bible, and maybe a cross or something like that. Certainly a Bible."

They crossed the rectory lawn and went around to the front door of the church, finding the closer side door locked. Inside the church, at the back, a cluster of acolytes in faded and ill-fitting cassocks were standing around a table, going over some portion of the evening's service. Elsa recognized the two youths from the grocer's, holding matching unlit torches and looking even more ostentatiously spiritual.

A sad-eyed man who was in charge of the rehearsal was saying, "Now the Celebrant—if he were here—would take the thurible and cense the fire. And if he is here tonight, hopefully that is what he will do. And if he isn't, God help us."

Charlie dutifully pretended to hand the silver chains of the censer to the empty spot at the end of the table where Kit should have been.

"I think he will be here," said Elsa thoughtfully, as they walked up the aisle away from the acolytes. She was thinking of her father's vision. He had seemed sure that it represented a real scene, and that it had not happened yet.

Elsa didn't know where the holy water had come from, so she

walked through doors at random, hoping that Peachy and Harriet would wander off. Instead they stuck with her.

In the vestry she looked again at the empty couch where she had so hoped to see Kit curled up asleep. She had slipped out as soon as she had been able to get the key from the stunned Mr. Oates, but by the time she arrived in the dark and silent church, she had known without looking that Kit was not there.

Mr. Oates put his head in the vestry door now. "Any news?"

"No news," said Peachy.

"Ah. Well, if I can be of any assistance … The miracle worker, where is he?"

"My dad? He's in the rectory garden, digging a bed for vegetables."

"Is that what he's doing?" said Harriet.

"He talked Kit into letting him dig up most of the back garden to plant squash and onions. He was scandalized that Kit was planning to fill it with rosebushes."

"How sad!" said Harriet. "It would have made a lovely rose garden."

"I should not venture to question the word of a man of such spiritual stature," said Mr. Oates reprovingly. "I shall go offer my humble assistance. I stock many varieties of vegetable seeds, which I would be most happy to contribute."

Peachy stood in the vestry door after Mr. Oates had left, looking out into the chancel.

"What's the matter?" asked Harriet.

"It's just that the organ is out there, open and unattended. And I've got my own hands back."

"Play us something," Harriet suggested.

He bounded across the chancel and slid onto the seat at the organ, clasped his hands gleefully for a moment, and then brought them down on the keyboards in a tremendous chord.

Harriet put her own hands to her face, and tears started in her eyes. Elsa hugged her. They went out to sit in one of the choir stalls by the organ. Peachy began playing something quite simple: the tune of the hymn that he had been singing that morning under Elsa's balcony. The acolytes processed down the aisle and into the middle of the choir, Charlie Boult swinging the smokeless censer at the head of the procession. The two with the torches were beginning to slouch and fidget and look less spiritual.

From the far end of the church, Elsa heard the rattle of a door being opened and the bump of it swinging shut again. Peachy had begun to spin an elaborate fantasia out of the hymn melody. Someone was running down the aisle. Elsa looked up. It was Kit. He vaulted over the rail in front of the organ console and flung himself on his friend. Peachy smacked both keyboards in his surprise, and the organ gave out a horrendous, squawking roar.

"Sorry! Sorry!" Kit released him and backed away, laughing. "But it's you! You're back. You're all right."

"Sure, *I*'m all right." Peachy stared up at him. "You look like hell. What happened to you?"

"What? Nothing. Uh—things. Not important."

Elsa thought Peachy's assessment was pretty accurate. Kit's face was bruised, he was unshaven and pale, and his cassock was a crumpled mess. His eyes were a little too bright, and there was a sort of brittle giddiness about him, totally different from the languid intoxication of the previous night.

"We were just developing a brilliant rescue plan," said Harriet, sliding out of the choir stall. "But as it probably wouldn't have worked, it's just as well you turned up now."

"Oh," said Kit. "I had no idea. I'm sorry you were put to the trouble … "

"Actually, I thought you *would* turn up," Harriet went on. "Some rather extraordinary things have happened in the meantime. We'd tell you all about it, but I think these people need you to be in their rehearsal. Actually they seem quite anxious about it."

"Yes, it's crossed my mind that they might be," he said. He went down into the chancel. He looked as though he could only focus on one thing at a time, and that only with some difficulty.

"Well, isn't that a relief?" said Harriet, looking around at Peachy and Elsa, still sitting on the organ bench and in the choir, respectively.

"He didn't need to be rescued," Peachy said stiffly. "I know where he's been." He got up from the organ. "I don't feel like playing any more. I'll be over at the rectory."

"Maybe we'd better stop treating his house like a train station café, now that he's back," said Harriet.

"Maybe, but he and I need to have words."

Harriet sat back down with an unconvincing shrug, and affected to become interested in a hymnal. Peachy left the church.

Elsa sat watching the rehearsal. Kit was taking the brazen-it-out approach rather than the candidly-explain-everything one. He had apologized to Mr. Cox for missing the beginning of the rehearsal, but offered no excuse for his lateness or explanation for his appearance. He insisted on carrying on from where they were, and said that he would catch up on the earlier part of the service. And then he didn't last long. They reached a part in the rehearsal where he should have gone up the steps to the altar. He turned away suddenly.

"Let's finish this later. I mean you carry on without me, and I'll get caught up after. I've got to … " He started down the chancel without even trying to finish his sentence.

Mr. Oates, returned from communing with Elsa's father, had been watching the rehearsal from the front pew. He got to his feet now. "Ah, Father, that reminds me," he began.

"Not now," Kit snapped.

Mr. Oates looked starkly shocked and sat back down. Kit left the church, and Elsa got up to follow. Harriet moved out of her way to let her get out of the stall, and then seemed to think better of this and got up too.

Kit had reached the rectory steps by the time Elsa came out of the church, but there he stopped suddenly, holding onto the railing, and bent over the flowerbed, retching.

She ran the rest of the way across the lawn. He had straightened up by the time she reached him, and was wiping his mouth with his handkerchief. She felt needlessly maternal noting that he hadn't actually vomited; he must not have had anything in his stomach to bring up.

"I shouldn't have been rude to Mr. Oates," he said, looking past her. "He probably wants the roster for the … " He sighed.

"I think he was just trying to give you an excuse to duck out of the rehearsal."

"What? Why? I can't even remember what I did with that roster." He turned away from her toward the door. She stood uncertainly at the base of the steps. "You can come in, of course," he said, but as though his heart weren't in it.

He had gone inside by the time she came through the door. She found him standing by the lone side table in the hall, holding the silver flask that she had last seen in the kitchen, with the stopper out, looking at it with alarm.

"What in God's name did I just drink?"

"Holy water." She couldn't resist adding, "What does it taste like?"

He made a face. "Not good. Salty."

Peachy appeared through the living-room door, hands in his pockets.

Kit's voice wobbled on the edge of hysteria: "Why is there—a flask of holy water?"

"Oh, that. We were making preparations to burst in and rescue you from the peril we imagined you were in," said Peachy stiffly. "Foolish of us, wasn't it? When you were—well … "

"When I was, well, what?"

"Well! I'm just a fraction too much of a gentleman to say. But did you expect me not to notice Anastasiya's perfume wafting off your clothes? Or did you expect me to imagine that there's some innocent explanation for that?"

Kit stared at him for a moment. "Yes, actually."

"Oh, is that so? And what is it?"

"I think you've rather forfeited your right to hear it."

"Really? And how about Elsa? She's right there, you know."

"Peachy … " she tried feebly to interrupt.

He went on undaunted: "And has *she* forfeited *her* right to the 'innocent explanation' of why you ditched her at—"

"He *didn't*!"

"Why you ditched her"—he was shouting now—"to spend the night in Anastasiya's—*augh*!"

Kit had flung the rest of the flask of holy water in his face.

Peachy sputtered and blinked and flailed blindly with one fist; Kit dodged around him and grabbed him by the front of his loud sweater. He pushed Peachy back against the wall on the opposite side of the hall, and pinned him there.

Harriet, coming through the front door at that moment, gave a shout of alarm. She ran past Elsa and fell upon Kit, tugging determinedly at his arm.

"Don't you dare hurt him!"

"Harriet!" Elsa cried. "Don't be silly!"

Peachy, obviously mortified by this, was roused to fight back in an undignified and effeminate style. Elsa tried to pull Harriet out of the way. The empty flask clanged on the floor. Kit, caught between the flailing Peachy and the clinging Harriet, proved that he had been restraining himself before. He shook free of Harriet, trod hard on Peachy's foot, and slammed his shoulder into Peachy's chest. Peachy fell back, gasping, and Elsa succeeded in hauling Harriet away from Kit. Harriet turned on her, tears of rage in her eyes.

"Don't try to keep me out of this! You're all trying to keep me out of things, and I'm sick of it! I won't have it!"

"Oh, shush!" said Elsa unkindly.

Harriet drew back a hand in fury, and Elsa winced in anticipation of the slap which she thought she deserved. Kit caught Harriet's wrist, looked horrified with himself, and released it. Peachy, still winded, flung himself sideways at Kit with a sort of desperate groan, and Kit shoved back hard to avoid falling forward and knocking Harriet against Elsa. Peachy staggered back through the open study door. Kit turned and ran after him.

Harriet and Elsa looked at one another, and suddenly they were both shaking with laughter.

"Goodness! I almost hit you! I'm so sorry."

"Not at all—I tried to *shush* you! I'm sorry Kit stopped you hitting me."

"I'm not the one who disappeared for three weeks!" came Kit's voice from the study.

"Maybe we should leave them alone to sort this out," Elsa said, making a small move toward the back of the house.

"Maybe we should," said Harriet, not moving at all.

Elsa stepped back beside her, so that she could see through the door into the study.

Peachy had dodged behind Kit's desk chair. "*I'm* not the one who slept with Mrs. Graves!"

The chair, to Peachy's misfortune, had wheels. Kit seized it and spun it out of the way. Peachy made an ungainly attempt to clamber over Kit's desk. Kit grabbed him by the collar and hauled him back.

"Nobody slept with Mrs. Graves, you ass!" Peachy's collar popped half off and slipped out of his grasp, and Peachy dove for the other side of the desk. Kit didn't attempt to pursue him. "Not that that's much credit to either of us. She's an awfully half-hearted seductress—I don't think she even fancies men."

Peachy rubbed his throat and goggled at him. "You *goddamn* egomaniac. Just because she didn't fall for you and your holier-than-thou, swanking around in your cassock pretending to be celibate act, that means she doesn't like men?"

Kit gasped as if he were about to laugh. "I wouldn't have put it like that."

"We should definitely go," Harriet hissed. "They've obviously forgotten we're here."

"Definitely," said Elsa. "Obviously."

"But wouldn't your famous honesty compel you to put it *exactly* like that?" They were shouting at each other across the desk now. It was becoming a caricature of a fight, and they both seemed to know it. "I mean, she must have tried to seduce you, because my God, why wouldn't she? But you're so heroically goddamn chaste, it didn't occur to you that she might have scruples herself, that she might be tormented by her own conscience, poor woman, even as she tried to win you to her side, to defend her, to—"

"What absolute rubbish!" Kit shouted across Peachy's expatiations. "What I am is *constant*. It's not really that hard. And I haven't had *anywhere near* as much encouragement as you have."

"Hah!" Peachy crowed. "That's only because you're too wrapped up in your own bullshit to damn well *do* anything about it!"

Harriet clapped a hand over her mouth, eyes wide, as if she hadn't realized her fiancé even knew words like "bullshit."

Now Kit really did laugh, rather hysterically. "That's incredible, coming from you! Is it even remotely possible that what you were doing for the last three weeks *wasn't* being 'wrapped up in your own bullshit'?"

Harriet looked like she might faint. Elsa had to try hard not to laugh herself.

"Oh, I know," Kit went on, "why don't you tell me, because I *long* to hear about it. I mean, it's been three weeks since I got to hear about the insupportable misery of being Peverell Peacham—*I don't know how I've lived!*"

"Maybe my misery isn't particularly impressive, but goddammit, *somebody has to talk about something!*"

"Like WHAT? How we're both bloody cowards who sat on our arses until 1917—"

"So you do think I'm a coward!" Peachy yelled triumphantly. "Well, of course you do. When were you going to tell me so?"

"I was saving it up until you accused me of fornicating with a middle-aged, lesbian—Don't try to hit me again, you idiot."

Peachy swung at him from the other side of the desk anyway. Kit dodged nonchalantly, and Peachy fell forward onto the desk with the force of his inept blow. He gave a groan of mingled pain and self-pity. Kit leaned against the edge of the desk and looked down at him in silence.

"We should leave them alone now," Harriet whispered.

"Yes," Elsa whispered back. "We should."

They remained standing in the hall.

"I don't think they're going to kill each other after all," said Harriet.

"No."

"But that never really did seem likely, did it?"

"No."

Kit put his hand lightly on Peachy's head for a moment. "I don't think you're a coward," he said.

"How could that possibly be true?" Peachy's voice was comically muffled against his arms on the desk.

"Come on, get up. It is true. I think when you didn't enlist, you were … you were listening to what God was telling you to do. Even if you didn't realize it."

Peachy pushed himself up onto his elbows. "I didn't, that's for sure. But you're the expert."

"Where have you been for the past three weeks?"

"I've been in Toronto, trying to avoid you and everyone who knows you, because I'd turned myself into a kind of copy of you. Indistinguishable to most people. Elsa was the only one who could tell I wasn't actually you. Elsa and some annoying squirt of an acolyte, for some reason. I can't expect you to believe it, but … "

Kit nodded. "I think I've seen the sort of thing. So you were going to people the world with copies of yourself … and instead you turned yourself into me? Even I don't think that's a good idea."

"No, *only* you don't think it's a good idea."

"That's not true. Harriet doesn't. Your parents don't. I promise you, they don't. None of your friends—none of *our* friends do. If you can't see that I'm the one who's lived in your shadow and not the other way around … "

"I'm stupider than you thought? No, I can see that. It's not the point. The point is, you're a better man: You don't resent me for it."

"Sometimes I do. I keep quiet about it because I owe you a lot. Sometimes I resent that, too. Most of the time I don't, because I love you. My dear … can we finish this conversation later? I feel quite sick—I slept badly and I … had a difficult morning. I'd like to lie down for a while in my own bed."

Peachy opened his mouth, presumably to launch into a flood of apology, but then shut it again and nodded.

"I think I can let you do that, yes."

They looked out into the hall at the two women.

"We were going to leave," said Harriet.

"But then we didn't," said Elsa.

And all four of them laughed.

Kit got halfway up the stairs before he stopped and turned back. He looked down at the others with a curious expression.

"Mrs. Graves … I don't think she's lesbian, actually."

"Nobody but you did think that," said Peachy.

"No—I thought he was right," said Elsa.

"But I was wrong. She's a man. She's Arthur Gallagher."

After a space of strained silence, which no one seemed to want to break by asking whether he were quite mad, he sat down on the stairs and went on.

"Last night, Mrs. Graves and another woman were passing me

back and forth between them. The other woman, the one who … the one I was dancing with, was—"

"The secretary, in female form," said Peachy. "Elsa mentioned."

Kit nodded. "Mephistopheles *manqué*, or whatever. She was trying to sell me on the virtues of the *Bibliotheka* and its nonsense, and I thought—just *thought*—about the fact that it's a forgery, and she latched onto that somehow. Then in the morning, she—he, at that point, but he turned back into a she—showed up with Gallagher, who was very keen to know how much I knew about the manuscript."

"Showed up where? Where were you?"

"In the bathroom," Elsa supplied. "He slept in the bathtub."

Kit looked straight at her for the first time since he had returned. He smiled slightly and nodded.

"Okay," said Peachy, "bypassing the question of how you knew that—how does any of that prove that Mrs. Graves … I mean, it's preposterous!"

"That's not a meaningful word in this context," said Elsa.

"It doesn't prove anything," said Kit. "But when I went to sleep, it was Mrs. Graves and Mephistopheles, and it was Mephistopheles and Gallagher when I woke up. I expect you'll find that nobody's ever seen Gallagher and Graves together. Graves is obviously an impostor of some sort—at the very least, she's not a Russian countess. She kept trying to lead when we were dancing last night. And then there's the weird fact that she and Gallagher have basically the same handwriting—or one of them writes the other's letters. We could never figure out which of them was pulling the other's strings. But if they're not separate people … "

"He's right," said Elsa. "I know he's right. I don't know why I didn't guess it myself."

"Because that's not the sort of thing you guess," Harriet said.

"She's a man," said Peachy, on a rising note of hysteria. "She's a man? Anastasiya is a *man*?"

"She's a fictional character," said Elsa. "She's *played* by a man."

"Yes, but—a man. A male, masculine—"

"Shush, Peachy," said Harriet. "She didn't want you, and she didn't want Kit. She wanted Elsa. That's all there is to it. Kit, when you say they were keen to find out what you knew, you don't by any chance mean that they—in order to find out—that they tortured you?"

"No, no." He said it with conviction, but as he looked from one face to another it was clear he was himself realizing that it wasn't true. "Sort of. Not tortured, exactly." There was another long pause. "They did … They … She—she pretended to hate it, but … "

They stood waiting for more, but finally he shook his head and got to his feet. "I'm sorry. I'm going upstairs." He stopped again. "Oh. I didn't tell them anything, if that's what you were asking."

"It *isn't*," said Peachy. "And nobody thought you did. We have met you."

When he was gone, Harriet said, "What do you think happened to him?"

"I don't know," said Elsa, but that wasn't true. "Yes, I do. The woman—the devil—who looked like me—did something to him."

"Did what?" Harriet persisted.

"I think he was … I think he might have been raped."

They looked at her in horror. Harriet said, "And we've been here thinking that … "

"We didn't just think it," said Peachy. "I absolutely yelled it at him."

He dug his hands into his pockets and started resolutely up the stairs.

"Do you think maybe you'd better let him be by himself?" Harriet called after him.

"Kit? No." He stopped on the stairs and looked down at her. "If I were going to make another scene begging forgiveness, then yes. But I'm not." He gave her a wry smile and then went on up the stairs.

Harriet stood looking up at the stairs until after he was gone, and for the first time since Peachy had reappeared that morning, Elsa felt sure of his future happiness. After what Gallagher had done to Kit, her own hope of happiness might be ruined—but Peachy's clearly was secure.

"Tea," said Harriet. "Don't you think?"

"What?"

"We should make tea."

She shook her head. "I think I should go."

"Where?"

"Anywhere—away. Somewhere he doesn't have to look at me. Besides, I need to find Arthur Gallagher and kill him with my bare hands."

"Impractical," said Harriet.

"Not necessarily," said Elsa through clenched teeth.

No, what would keep her—barely—from avenging herself on Gallagher was the thought that Kit wouldn't like it.

She didn't get farther than the porch. She sank down on the steps, feeling scalded inside with rage.

It was what she had feared in the library, exactly what she had feared: the powers of darkness had been at him and torn him up somehow. They had left him enough intact that she must still love him, but they had made him unable to look at her.

Unable to approach the altar, which is much worse.

Charlie Boult came over from the church, in his street clothes again, looking pleased with himself.

"I got Mr. Cox to write down all the stuff Father needs to know for tonight, so I can tell him later when he's feeling better. It's not hard—Father Underhill came up with the service, and Mr. Cox even admitted he did a good job with it, which, if you knew Mr. Cox, is really something." He grinned. "*Was* he captured by devils? He looked kind of like he might've been."

She nodded.

Charlie whistled. "Well, I'm glad he's all right."

He's not! she wanted to shout at him. *How could you be so perceptive before and not see this now?*

"Not surprised," Charlie added. "But glad."

"I'll tell him," said Elsa.

She remained sitting there as Charlie ambled back across to the church.

Was it a revenge that Gallagher had prepared especially for her? Had he known not only that to hurt Kit would hurt her, but that to do it in this precise way would destroy her best hope of happiness?

But this was not something that happened to you.

And that was true. Sorrowing or raging, even for his sake, not for her own, was no real use to him.

It was unlikely, in fact, that Gallagher would have taken such a finely honed revenge. Neither he nor Mrs. Graves had ever really learned very much about her.

Neither he nor Mrs. Graves … She experimented with superimposing the two images in her mind. It worked surprisingly well. She remembered a number of odd things Mrs. Graves had said about the essence of womanhood, and about Elsa being more real than she. Gallagher had done exactly the opposite of what she had imagined she would do if the power of the *Bibliotheka* were real. With all the prestige and privilege he had as Professor Arthur Gallagher, he'd wanted something that he thought he could only get by becoming Mrs. Anastasiya Graves. And what was it that he'd wanted? A different type of adulation, perhaps, or simply some insight into what he imagined to be the mysteries of womankind. Whatever it was, the fear and discontent that Peachy had detected in Mrs. Graves—that Elsa had been aware of too, even if she had callously tried to ignore them—testified eloquently that he hadn't got it.

She found Harriet sitting at the kitchen table, waiting for the kettle to boil.

"You came back," said Harriet happily, popping up from her chair.

"Yes." She looked at the stove. "He should eat. He obviously hasn't eaten." She remembered what the transformed Peachy had craved for breakfast. "I'll make pancakes."

Some part of her still wanted to bang cupboards and slam things around, but she found herself instead handling Kit's belongings very gently. She got out a pan and found where he kept flour and sugar and eggs. By the time Peachy came down to the kitchen, she had a stack of pancakes keeping warm in the oven.

"Fantastic! I was just coming to see if there were something for him to eat. He claims not to be hungry, but that's obviously untrue." He began putting things on a tray. "You were right about what happened. I told him what you said, and he said that was about the size of it, but that it was mostly metaphysical, and that he was saved by a beautiful vision of St. John's falling on top of him—he was becoming a bit incoherent at this point—and he's ashamed to have been so affected by the other business and not to be able to shrug it off and carry on."

"Did you tell him that was ridiculous?" asked Harriet.

"Nope. Didn't even think it."

"Oh, of course. I didn't mean … "

"Ah, you made tea. Perfect."

"Naturally we made tea," said Harriet in a small voice. "I hope it's still hot."

"Here," said Elsa, "take a mug for him instead of a cup and saucer. Easier to manage if your hands are shaky."

"Good thought."

"Tell him we're—tell him we're glad he's safe. For that matter, tell him he *is* safe, and that I said so. It will make him laugh, but it's not really funny, and he knows it."

Peachy went away with the tray.

"I hope he's actually hungry," Harriet remarked. "That was a huge pile of food."

"Clearly I am expressing my love through pancakes. Shall I make some for you, my dear?"

"That would be nice."

As she poured more batter into the pan, it occurred to her that perhaps what Harriet wanted most just then might not be pancakes. She turned to look at her.

"I think I've become a Christian again. At least I mean that I *want* to be a Christian again."

Harriet smiled and bounced a little in her chair. "And is that a cause or an effect of being in love with a vicar?"

"Neither, I think. I'm pretty sure they're parts of the same thing."

"Yes, that sounds about right. You see, it never really made sense to me, you being a materialist. You're too poetic."

Elsa sat across the table from Harriet and watched her eat pancakes. She tried to explain some of what had happened in the last few days. Harriet was right; they had been keeping her out of things a bit, and that was no true office of friendship.

"And I realized it isn't just God, either," she said. "It isn't some kind of chilly, intellectual deism. That would be too easy. It's all this fiddle about incarnation: blood, and bread, and candles, the Word made flesh, and people being raised from the dead, not just their souls but their bodies too. It is—it has to be—absolutely all of it."

Harriet nodded, crossing her fork and knife on her empty plate. "That's what I think too. Well, not the candles—I don't think the candles are important."

"Maybe not."

"They're okay if you like them, though. I think. This is what I pictured, you know."

"What is?"

Harriet got up and took her plate to the sink, where she deposited it, looking pleased with herself, but did not wash it. It was a fact that she had probably never washed a dish in her life.

"Eating your cooking and talking about religion in your kitchen."

"Harriet, it's not my kitchen."

"No, of course not." She stood looking out the window above the sink. "There's a nice view of the back garden from here. It really is a shame about the roses." She turned to look at Elsa. "I don't want to meddle, you know, but—you *did* hear Kit say that he was just being constant, and that he hadn't had much encouragement?"

"Yes."

"And you *do* know what he meant by it?"

"Mm. I don't think he really meant me to hear that."

"But you did hear it! You can't go on—the two of you can't go on pretending that—" She gestured hopelessly. "Oh, I said I wasn't going to meddle."

"No, I don't blame you. But I think I *can* go on pretending I didn't hear it. I think it's the least I can do."

"Yes, I see." Harriet folded her arms and leaned back against the sink. "You want to beat him at his own game."

"What?"

"You know, generous self-denial—I love you but I'm not going to tell you because I don't want to be a burden to you, et cetera et cetera."

"No … "

"No—I see. You want to give him the opportunity to declare himself in a more appropriate style. Because … you care about that sort of thing."

"No!"

"Oh, but you think he does."

"No!"

"Well, there you are then." She looked smug. "You're welcome."

After that, Harriet said she was going upstairs "to check on the boys," and left the kitchen. Elsa washed her plate and the frying pan and the bowl from the pancake batter, and put everything back in the cupboards. She felt a little trapped by Harriet's logic. It was obviously true that what Kit said meant that he was in love with her, had been in love with her for some time, and that Peachy had known about it. Harriet seemed to have known about it too. Polly Whitmore had known about it, for crying out loud. Then she remembered something else. On the golf course, Peachy had been moping about how Kit would be a better match for Harriet than himself, and Elsa had said, "But he's not available, is he?" and Peachy had said that no, he wasn't. It was the second time she and Kit had met. She had imagined that he wouldn't even remember her name.

Harriet came back down and leaned in at the kitchen door.

"Elsa, come see."

"See what?"

"They're both asleep. It's precious."

She followed Harriet upstairs and looked into the nursery. Peachy was sitting on the floor by Kit's bed, his head lolling back against the mattress, his mouth hanging open slightly, his hands slack in his lap. Kit was curled up under the knitted counterpane. He was in his undershirt, and one bare arm lay outside the cover, his hand not far from Peachy's shoulder. In the white-painted nursery, on Kit's narrow bed, they looked as much like overgrown little boys as they had the first day Elsa and Harriet met them on the beach.

Please let them be all right, Lord. Please heal them both—let them wake up whole and happy.

"Elsa!" Harriet whispered with sudden urgency. "I'd completely forgotten!"

"Forgotten what?"

Harriet shut the door carefully behind her and scurried to the stairs.

"The whole reason I came here in the first place!" she said excitedly. "The Bibliotheque thingy."

"Yes?"

"I have it in my handbag."

"Harriet! No you don't."

"Shh! Come on, I'll show you."

Harriet found her handbag in a corner of the living room, and tugged out of it a brown, leather-bound volume. Elsa could see immediately that it was not the *Bibliotheka Orphika*, although it was an old-looking book and rather like it.

"I took it from Professor Gallagher's office," Harriet explained proudly. "Did you know I have a natural aptitude as a pickpocket? I lifted the college keys from a janitor on Wednesday, and tried them out to find the one to Gallagher's office. Then, once I had the correct one, I got a copy made and returned the set to the Annesley porter with an entirely believable story about finding it somewhere. Then I went back into the office on Friday, when the university was closed and I thought it should be safe. It actually took me a long time to find this. It was in the bottom of a drawer, under a bunch of things, and the drawer was locked too, but he'd left *that* key in another drawer. I thought it would help for you to get a good look at it—you know, to prove that it's a forgery."

"That was very resourceful of you," said Elsa, taking the book and wondering how she could tell Harriet that all that ingenuity had been wasted. She wondered what this book actually was. She opened it.

And there Eurydice, the soul's truth, will stand before you, awaiting her rescuer …

It was an amateur effort, though a thorough one. The pages of the book were not even parchment; they were thick paper, artfully stained to look old. Tears and imperfections had been drawn in with ink. The Greek script was meticulous, uniform, easily recognizable.

Elsa sat down in Kit's chair, which was fortunately right behind her. She looked up from the pages.

"Harriet, it's not the *Bibliotheka Orphika*."

"It's not?"

"No, it's better than that. It's Gallagher's draft of the *Bibliotheka*, in his own hand."

Chapter Seventeen

TO THEM THAT LOVE GOD

Kit woke some time in the early afternoon to the gentle whisper of rain on the rectory roof. He stretched and lay on his back looking at the faded alphabet frieze around the ceiling of the nursery. Out of habit, he picked out the letters of his name: C, a boy playing cricket; H, a horse and rider; R, a blonde girl reading a book … He used to think that the blonde girl looked like Elsa, but he didn't see it any longer. Nobody looked like Elsa to him now except Elsa.

He felt better than he usually did when he slept during the day. He felt cared for, and he found he was past being embarrassed about it. He'd actually cried on Peachy's shoulder, and Peachy, surprisingly, hadn't seemed embarrassed about that.

He had nodded sagely when Kit had tried to explain how ashamed he was to be going to pieces like this.

"It's damned easy to start thinking that way, as if your soul's the only real part of you and your body's not important—I should know, I fell into that trap myself. It's dead wrong, of course. *You* know that."

"Yes … you're right, I do. So wait—what does that mean? I should be ashamed, or I shouldn't?"

"It means it's not wrong to be upset about what happened—you were pretty attached to your blessed virginity, and—"

"Wait, no, she didn't—she just pawed me about a bit. That was all that physically … "

Peachy rolled his eyes dramatically. "Okay, I take it all back. You *are* overreacting."

And Kit had punched him, but not hard at all.

Peachy had gone now, and with him—or, more likely, with someone else who had come in quietly to clean up—the empty dishes and some of Kit's discarded clothes. He could hear voices downstairs. He had always found it comforting to have people awake in the house when he was trying to sleep; less so, he realized now, when he wanted to take a bath.

He wrapped himself in his dressing gown and crept circumspectly to the bathroom, mercifully unobserved, and filled the tub. He sat in the warm water and rested his head on his knees and listened with a detached interest to what was going on downstairs. It sounded as if people were moving furniture.

He tried to discern Elsa's low, beautiful voice among the others, but he couldn't hear it. That was all right. She had made him pancakes—objectively delicious pancakes—and told Peachy to tell him that he was safe. She probably—certainly—had better things to do with her Saturday afternoon than hang about his house waiting for him to pull himself together. He would see her again soon; she was coming to the Vigil. He lay back in the bath and thought about that.

By and by the voices downstairs ceased, and there were no more noises of moving furniture. The bath water was cooling, and Kit stood up and got out of it. He took his time shaving, pulled on his dressing gown again, and went back to his room. He needed to go over the notes for the Vigil, but he had time. The rain was still falling softly outside, which put paid to his idea of spending an hour in the garden. He put on work clothes anyway; if his interpretation of the furniture-moving noises was correct, he thought there might be work to be done in the house. Then he considered the possibility of baking bread. Or better yet, hot cross buns. He hadn't had time to make any yesterday. If Elsa came back before the Vigil, he would have hot cross buns to offer her—a pleasing thought. And he would make sure by that time he wasn't still dressed in an old flannel shirt and patched trousers.

At the base of the stairs he narrowly avoided a collision with a thing that looked like a small Roman mausoleum, but which he recognized after a moment as the discarded sideboard from Polly's front hall. The leopard-skin rug was rolled up and propped next to it, and the mismatched gilt chairs stood near the open door. It was what he had thought. Polly must have found some way to deliver them herself; the Peachams wouldn't have helped her to fill his hall with ugly furniture on Holy Saturday. He leaned out the door into the porch to see if there was any more.

There wasn't, but Elsa was sitting on the porch, under the window of his study, with a book open in her lap. It looked almost as though she had been guarding the door. She looked up.

"You're still here," he observed.

"Yes—I hope … "

"I'm so glad."

She was dressed in her school clothes, the sleeves of her plain blouse and her black cardigan rolled up, her pale hair untidy, her face untouched by makeup. He felt as if he were seeing her for the first time, as if he had never really noticed how beautiful she was.

"I didn't hear you come down the stairs," she said.

"I didn't," he admitted guiltily.

"You slid down the banister!"

"Clearly I need to grow up."

She shook her head, smiling. "Don't you dare." She looked down at her book, a little pink creeping into her cheeks.

He looked out at the rain falling gently beyond the roof of the porch on the rectory garden.

"Is everyone else … "

She launched into an explanation gratefully: "Peachy and Harriet went to his parents' house; my father is gone to Mr. Oates's shop to talk about seeds; Mrs. Whatsit, your housekeeper, went home; the Altar Guild and the acolytes are in the church, fussing with lilies; and Polly and Vera left their—their kind gift of furniture, and promised to be back for the service. I thought I would sit in the porch so as … so that you could have your house to yourself."

"You didn't have to do that."

"It's no hardship. It's nice out here."

"It is." It was warm, in spite of the rain. "Do you mind if I join you?"

"I've been sitting on your porch waiting for you to wake up. What do you think?"

He came out onto the porch and sat down beside her, with his knees drawn up, not entirely at ease.

"What are you reading?"

She held out the open book. It was written in Greek.

"No, really, what are you reading?"

"John's Gospel." She turned the book so that he could see the spine. It was his Greek New Testament from university.

"I'm sure I have that in English somewhere."

"I've read it in English. I'd never read it in Greek."

"Ah. I suppose not." He felt a little ashamed of his happiness. He hoped it didn't look too much like triumph.

She closed the Bible and set it aside. "Actually, I haven't been able to concentrate very well on it. There are so many things … " She sighed, and smiled at him. "You're feeling better?"

"Altogether better. The pancakes were tremendously helpful. I'm sorry that I made you worry."

"Kit! Don't say that. I'm the one who should … I am so sorry I left you last night. I'm sorry that I involved you—exposed you to any of that vileness. I would do anything to put it right, to keep you from having been hurt."

"But you did! I thought I explained that to Peachy with stunning clarity. It was because you healed me that I was able to let her—to let Mephistopheles walk in my mind without learning anything that could really hurt me. She tried to show me a vision of horror, and instead it was transformed into beauty … into love."

"I see."

"I'll tell you what happened," he said, and he did. It was much harder to describe what had happened in the bathroom than what he had seen afterward; he launched into the description of the vision eagerly once he got to that point. But it seemed important for her to know the whole thing.

"So you see how you did protect me, after all."

"I see how you were protected," she said slowly. "I don't see that you need think I had anything to do with that. Not unless you want to."

"I do, rather. But," he added, with a sudden insight, "it doesn't change the way I feel about you, if that's what you're worried about. That was a settled thing a long time ago."

She did not reply. He wondered if he had been idiotically misinterpreting everything since that moment at the party when she refused to dance with him.

She sat looking out over the wet lawn. He followed her gaze past the parish hall toward the yellow-brick mass of the church standing solidly against the grey sky. He looked back at her, watching her fingers smooth the fabric of her skirt over her knees, and he was struck by a powerful sense of her uniqueness. If he had tried to recreate her from his own imagination, he—even he—would have got her wrong.

"It's a lovely view," she said, still looking at the church. "It's almost elegant on the outside. But the inside is homey."

"I like it."

"I think I can tell you what it was like," she said thoughtfully. "My conversion. I felt like Elizabeth Bennet: It's been coming on very gradually, but I think I can date the beginning to when I first saw his beautiful house … "

"Wait—in that analogy, Mr. Darcy is … "

"God. Yes."

"I don't know what I think about that," he said, but he thought she could probably tell from his grin that it wasn't true.

"Yes, you do," she said. "You think it's all very apt, but you wonder where it leaves you."

"No … I'm pretty clear about how I fit in around here. I'm part of the furnishings. I try to be worthy of the honour."

"I can't tell whether that is exquisitely humble or a little vain."

"You're not meant to be able to tell. I think it's a bit of both."

She reached out a hand and touched the side of his face, her fingers cool and gentle. He pulled her hand down and kissed her palm. Now she was kneeling over him, cupping his face in her hands, pushing her fingers into his hair. He put his hands on her waist and felt the warmth of her skin through the thin fabric of her blouse, the muscles of her stomach tense under his palms. She was looking down at him with an intense and protective affection. There was no sound but the delicate percussion of the rain, hemming them in and isolating them from the world. When her lips finally touched his, it seemed like the conclusion of a long and tender debate.

It was a soft, slow kiss. It was like waking in the morning in the sun and nestling back into the bedclothes. She drew back a little, steadying herself with a one hand on the window sill. He tightened his arms around her so that she lost her balance and fell against him, laughing. He felt the collar of her blouse pressed against his cheek, and the smooth curve of her collarbone. He kissed her throat, just brushing his lips across her skin. She shivered.

He released her, and she sat back down, a little distanced from him. She straightened her clothes self-consciously. He stretched out to lie on his back on the boards of the porch, his hands clasped behind his head. He felt surprisingly good: keyed-up, but not un-bearably so, and at the same time oddly calm. He realized it was because he had been worried about how that would go—if it ever came to that. But he needn't have been; she had taken it all in hand.

"Remarkably," she said, looking out into the rain, "we seem to have been unobserved."

"All things work together for good … "

"Oh! Shocking!" She looked down at him, glowing.

She had come out to sit in the porch so that they wouldn't be alone in the house together. He had felt her desire and her care for him pulling her in opposite directions, and he had felt the compromise that, in her strength, she had made between them.

"I love you so much," he said. "But I think you should finish your MA."

"*What?*"

"I think you should finish your MA and make a start on your PhD. Before we marry. I'm being ruthlessly practical. It's the way that you affect me. I don't want the world to lack the work that you would do, just because I distracted you from your calling. I think … I honestly think that would be a sin."

She stared down at him in silence for a moment, then she shook her head wonderingly. "How much of my PhD do I have to do?"

"Not much. I don't really know how it works. Just find a topic, I suppose, that you're excited enough about to carry on with."

"Kit, if it's a precondition to marrying you, I could get excited about the genitive absolute in Plato."

"It's not a precondition, my dearest love. If you decided the life of study wasn't what you wanted after all … "

"I don't know any more quite what I want, other than you. Which is just what you want to avoid, isn't it?"

"Well, it's … it's flattering and lovely. But yes."

"I shall have to think about it. Not think, I mean—p-pray?"

"It's only that I don't think being a vicar's wife should be the whole story of your life."

"You don't think I'd be happy? Or … "

"I don't think you'd be as happy as you could be. But mostly I don't think you'd be useful."

"I'm a good cook! I know how to keep house. I—"

"I didn't mean useful like that."

"No, I know you didn't. You meant … useful to the Lord, I suppose." She smiled, and then hid her face in her hands for a moment. "It's the nicest thing you could possibly offer me, and I don't know how to accept it graciously. I have a lot to learn."

"Oh, my love. So do I."

She raised an eyebrow at him. "*You* can learn after I finish my MA."

"Not just that!"

"You're blushing," she remarked clinically. "Quite beautifully. Kit, talking of my MA—no, quite seriously, now. Did you know that Harriet broke into Gallagher's office to try to steal the *Bibliotheka*?"

"She didn't!" He half sat up, but subsided onto his elbows. "'Tried' to steal it, you said."

"Yes—but what she actually found was a draft copy in Gallagher's own hand."

"Proof!"

"Unmistakably. I'd show it to you, but I already convinced her to take it back."

"Wouldn't it be safer to hold onto it, though? What if he's realized it's gone and destroys it when he gets it back?"

She shook her head. "It doesn't matter. You told me yourself that I shouldn't try to take revenge on him."

"I suppose I did. To be fair, that was before we knew he'd sold his soul to the Devil."

"I've been thinking about this all morning—well, in between the other things I've been thinking about: what I've put you through, and how you said what you were was *constant*." She smiled wryly. "I've been thinking about how close I came to losing my own soul. You were right about that, too. I was in deeper with the cult than I had any inkling of. But I think I was saved by my own scepticism.

"I don't know why that should be true. But somehow, God's grace has worked in my own life through my reason. And if that means anything, it's that I shouldn't abandon reason. There are two things I could do, Kit. I could tell Gallagher that I have the draft, and that

I could destroy him with it if I wanted. With any luck he wouldn't think it was a bluff. After what he did to you, I don't know that it would be a bluff. I could be very happy ruining him. And it would accomplish what I need—he would have to let me go back to my degree. Or I could return the draft without letting him know that I've seen it, and publish my own findings about the hymn with the emended line, and the anachronistic language, and the unified style of the manuscript, all of which cast doubt on its authenticity. It's good research. It wouldn't be impossible to find a reputable journal that would publish it. It wouldn't necessarily destroy Gallagher's career, and it wouldn't necessarily advance mine. But it might, and if it did, it would be through my own honest work, not through blackmail.

"If you tell me that you'd rather I go and ram the draft manuscript down Gallagher's throat, I'll do it."

"I don't want *you* to do that. I wouldn't mind doing it myself." After a moment he added: "I did get to hit him, you know."

"Did you?"

"Mm-hm. I gave him a bloody nose. Mind you, after that he stood and watched while his fake version of you pinned me on the floor and … Sorry. I was just thinking how little she was like you, actually."

"That stands to reason. I think you knew me better five minutes after we first met than he *ever* will."

"You may be right." He sighed. "About the other, you are *certainly* right."

"I thought you would agree. I just wanted you to understand why it might take a little while."

He hadn't thought, when he suggested she should finish her MA, about the obstacles to her resuming her studies. He was beginning to wish he hadn't said it. But it had been the right thing to say.

"But don't worry," she said, gathering her feet under her and getting up, suddenly businesslike. "We can be quite happy in the meantime. I am going inside to put on some more water for tea. You stay where you are."

He stayed. They were alone with the rain for another half an hour. They drank their tea and talked about St. John's and Anglo-Catholicism, slightly shy now that they were finally, fully revealed to one another, slightly embarrassed by their shared happiness. The rain abated, but the sky remained heavy with clouds. Elsa's father was the first one to return to the rectory, his pockets full of packets of seeds given to him by Mr. Oates.

*

Eight o'clock was the latest that Mr. Cox had been willing to push the Holy Saturday liturgy, and it wasn't quite dark enough to feel like midnight, but Kit didn't mind.

"There's a good congregation," the crucifer, Henley, reported, popping back into the vestry from an unauthorized excursion to peek at them.

Kit had to suppress an urge to peek out in his turn. He felt a little bit younger than Henley himself. Everyone who had seen him at the rehearsal had been anxious about his health, but his joy now seemed to be infectious. The mood in the vestry was fizzing excitement. As they made their way through the basement to emerge at the back of the church, Mr. Cox had to shush everyone several times.

There was a moment on the stairs coming up from the basement when Kit looked back at the shuffling crew of assembled acolytes and shot them a conspiratorial grin, because several of them were smiling at him encouragingly, and he was reminded of something he couldn't quite place. Coming out into the fire-lit church he identified it: It was looking back to count the men whom he had led home from that disastrous raid on the German trenches almost a decade ago. There was nothing particularly similar about the situations; he wasn't even in charge of the liturgy, he was just one of the participants, following Mr. Cox's directions like everyone else. But that was—that had always been—a happy memory. When he had counted them, they had all been there. Every single member of his party had survived.

Chapter Eighteen

THE NIGHT IS COME

The Vigil began in a kind of homey magnificence, the faces of the acolytes and the sacred ministers lit by the jumping flames of the New Fire at the back of the church. Elsa was glad that she had watched the rehearsal; she had an idea of the shape of the service now, and remembered the terms for the participants and the parts of the church. She sat in a pew full of Kit's family: Peachy and Harriet to her left with Dr. and Mrs. Peacham; Laurence Whitmore on her right with his wife and daughter. She could see Charlie Boult in the firelight, solemnly handing the chains of the thurible to Kit, as the fragrant smoke curled and billowed around them.

She felt her attention to Kit, to his voice and his face in the firelight, and to the words of the service and their meaning, fused like strands of molten glass, *parts of the same thing*, as she had told Harriet. It was beautiful, but it was not—it would never be—simple.

In the afternoon they had baked hot cross buns, with people coming and going from the rectory, her father wanting to discuss with Kit what had happened to Brother Peach, Polly and Vera returning with a second load of awful furniture in their borrowed car. Kit had gone over the details of the service with Charlie, with a seriousness and minute attention that didn't surprise her, but that she had never seen at work before. But of course he cared whether the deacon and subdeacon were on his right and left or vice versa, just as she would have cared whether a verb form were found in all extant manuscripts or only the oldest.

Peachy and Harriet had returned from the Peachams' house with a loaded picnic basket, and they had all eaten dinner lounging on the dining-room floor and listening to Peachy and Harriet discuss the renewed plans for their wedding. They wanted to have it at St. John's, by licence, so that neither of their families could be said to win. Kit pointed out that, as he was *part* of Peachy's family, that might not hold strictly true. Harriet said that was all right with her, and then began to sketch out plans for serving the wedding breakfast on the rectory lawn. Kit did not object. She had easily talked Peachy into accepting the job of playing for Sung Mattins.

They pretended to be totally absorbed in their own happiness, but Elsa could tell that they were dying to ask what had happened at the rectory while they were gone. She couldn't believe that it wasn't written plainly on her face, as she could see it was on Kit's, but they had not yet reached the point where they could casually kiss or even touch in front of other people. They certainly couldn't talk about what had happened on the porch; what would they say? Peachy and Harriet had to be content with conjecture.

Now the procession with the tall Paschal candle was moving slowly down the aisle, and the sidesmen distributed flame from the candle to the hand candles held by the congregation, little flames springing up across the nave. The procession reached the chancel, and Kit and the deacon and subdeacon took seats between the choir stalls, and they began the long series of readings and psalms. Elsa thought that her father would have liked this part of the service. She imagined him trying to introduce plainchant into the Tree of Life meetings, and how they would react the first time he said something about, "Brother Christopher, my future son-in-law … " She recalled her attention sternly to the liturgy.

Then the Gloria began. The church was filled with ringing bells, organ and choir in full voice, a triumphant tumult of sound. The Peachams had brought bells, and had a couple of extras, which they offered to Elsa and to Vera Whitmore. The party in the chancel was sweeping up into the sanctuary, the acolytes were lighting the candles amid the riot of lilies, the sacred ministers changing out of their purple vestments into white and gold. And from the back of the church came a hollow, thudding crash.

In the joyous chaos of the great Gloria, only a few heads turned toward the source of the new noise. Vera, at the end of the pew, was the only one in their party who immediately looked back, and then for a moment she tugged on her mother's sleeve in vain to get her attention.

"Mom! Look! Mom! Look!"

By this time there had been a few shouts of alarm from the back of the church. Elsa glanced over her shoulder, and her voice gave out at the words "Lamb of … "

The doors at the back of the church had burst inward. Outside stood a pale shape that Elsa had seen briefly once before. Inside the doors stood Arthur Gallagher.

The singing and bell-ringing died gradually away as more and more people looked back and saw the thing outside the doors. It wasn't, on the face of it, very obviously frightening. In the oddly thick darkness that cloaked the church steps, it was hard to get a clear view of it, but it looked like nothing so much as a bundle of grey tweed. Yet there was a horrible purposefulness to the way it swayed in the doorway, as if pushing against an invisible barrier, seeking a weak spot, looking for a way in.

Gallagher had ducked around the stone font and dropped to his knees on the floor beneath it. He looked as if he had been running.

Most of the choir kept going until the end of the Gloria, and the organist, with his back to the door, played on undaunted. No one in the sanctuary seemed to have noticed anything amiss. They were carrying on with the liturgy. The sacred ministers went unperturbedly up to the altar steps, deacon and subdeacon parted and stepped back, and Kit turned to face the congregation, and the thing outside the doors. It drew itself up, filling out and billowing grotesquely in the doorway. There was no mistaking that it recognized him as its opponent.

There was a moment's stillness. Everyone in the choir and the sanctuary had now seen it, and there was a frightened shuffling and whispering. Several children in the nave had started to cry, but most of the adults seemed too shocked to make a noise. Eyes were turning from the apparition outside the door to the man at the altar.

He held up his open hands and, in a clear, deliberate voice that carried across the crying and the shuffling and whispering, sang: "The Lord be with you."

A ragged chorus answered, fervently and tentatively and with varying degrees of speed: "And with thy spirit." From Elsa's pew it rang out immediately and with force.

Kit went to the missal stand at the end of the altar and turned his back on the door. The deacon and subdeacon forgot what they were supposed to be doing and swayed helplessly in place for a moment before scurrying to follow him.

"Lord of all life and power," he sang from the Missal, in the same carrying voice, "who through the mighty resurrection of thy Son hast overcome the old order of sin and death … "

The thing outside the door thumped against the stonework and gave a furious moan that shook the beams of the church ceiling. Kit finished the prayer and was answered with a confident "Amen."

Several people had left their pews and edged tentatively toward Gallagher where he was sitting on the floor under the font. Elsa strode down past them.

Mrs. Barrington was kneeling beside him by the time Elsa reached the font.

"Was that … that object chasing you?" Mrs. Barrington asked, her tone stern rather than solicitous.

Gallagher looked up at Elsa standing over him and did not reply.

"Did you come in here for sanctuary?" asked another Altar Guild lady, who had reached him by this time.

"No," said Gallagher, still looking steadily up at Elsa. "I came to find her."

"To find Miss Northquest? But what does she have to do with you?"

"Do you know this man, Miss Nordwest?"

"She is the only one who can save me," said Gallagher, before Elsa could reply. He still crouched on the floor beneath the font, but his posture had become subtly more confident, his voice stronger.

"Save you? What do you mean? How can she save you?"

"Do you know what he means, Miss Northquist?"

"She knows," said Gallagher. "If she truly loved me, she could have saved me long ago."

"Loved you!" Mrs. Barrington exclaimed.

Elsa felt a sudden ache in her throat. In spite of everything that had changed, the man still had power over her. Even now he could ruin her tenuous happiness. In front of the ladies of the Altar Guild, he had revealed her as a woman with a past, linked somehow with a man on the run from the powers of darkness, but cold-hearted, deficient in love. Totally unsuitable to be a vicar's wife. And it was all true.

"How could I save you now?" she asked, standing over him.

His eyes were burning, and he was breathing hard. "By doing what you wanted to do all along—by becoming me."

She shook her head slowly. After all, he was lying; he had not come here to find her, or not primarily. He was not trying to ruin her happiness. The man was terrified. He was trying the only thing he could think of on the spur of the moment to save himself from the horror to which he had pledged his soul.

"It's true," she said, "that at one time I did want that. I don't any more. And, Professor, there has to be—there *is*—a better remedy than that."

"There is no remedy! You have seen to that. If you had not begun spreading the story of a forgery, I would not have tried him beyond the limits of his patience, and he would not have called in my debt tonight—I might have lived another year or more, I might have found a way to outwit him at last, I might … " His voice trailed away.

The Gospel reading was finished. The three acolytes with the cross and torches were shuffling down the nave with faces like men going before a firing squad, the sacred ministers following. Elsa remembered from the rehearsal that they were headed for the baptismal font. She held out her hands to the man on the floor.

"Come," she said. "Get up. We're in the way."

He reached for her hands and then stopped. "At midnight my soul—whatever that may be—is forfeit to that thing and its Master. Do you think I would hesitate to throw you to him, to save myself?"

"Yes," she said. "You are hesitating right now."

He let out a sharp, choked laugh, and grabbed her hands. She yanked him ungently to his feet and then pulled her hands away. After all, she did not trust him very much.

The group around the font parted to let the acolytes pass through and process around to stand behind the font. As they turned their backs on the open doors, the creature outside began its groaning again. The sacred ministers walked in front of the acolytes and turned toward the font. Mr. Cox stood in position on one side, holding the book for Kit to read from.

Kit looked at him and, in a discreet undertone which was nevertheless audible to everyone at the back of the church, said, "Mr. Cox, could somebody please close those doors?"

Mr. Cox nodded gravely, and there was a moment's hesitation while he sought out someone to whom to relay the order. Several of the sidesmen, however, had heard it too, and they hastened forward without further urging and clapped the doors shut, shooting home the heavy bolt that held them.

Kit smiled, and looked out at the congregation and said, "Let us pray."

This time, a faint ripple of nervous laughter answered him.

Beyond his strong voice, as he went on with the thanksgiving over the baptismal water, they could hear something bumping and scrabbling furiously against the wood of the doors. But the doors remained shut.

"Do you here, in the presence of God and of this Congregation, renounce the Devil and all his works, the pomps and vanity of this wicked world, and all the sinful lusts of the flesh?"

"I do," came the chorus of voices.

Kit paused, looking at Gallagher, who had not spoken.

The professor's face was chalky. Very slightly, regretfully, he shook his head.

After a moment, Kit went on: "Do you believe the Christian Faith as it is set forth in the Apostles' Creed?"

"I do," said Elsa with the rest of the congregation.

"Will you endeavour to keep God's holy will and commandments, and to walk in the same all the days of your life?"

"I will," they answered, "God being my helper."

Gallagher remained silent.

"Almighty God, our Creator and the rock of our salvation, who hast given us new birth by water and the Holy Spirit, and bestowed upon us the forgiveness of sins, keep us faithful to our baptism, and so make us ready for that day when the whole creation shall be made perfect in thy Son … "

The procession returned decorously to the sanctuary. The organist began to play, and everyone fumbled for their hymnals. With the doors shut, the people were regaining their confidence; those toward the front were probably beginning to think they might have imagined what they had seen outside. It would have been easy to do; after all, it had been so hard to tell what it was.

"*The Lamb's high banquet called to share,*" sang the choir and the congregation, "*Arrayed in garments white and fair … *"

"I could have spoken the words," said Gallagher, under the cover of the singing, "but they would have been a lie, and that could not possibly help. That could not possibly save me. Could it?"

"I don't know," said Elsa wretchedly. She hated this man; she wanted to go on hating him, and from a safe distance. She did not want to hear the desperation in his voice; she did not want to care what became of him. But she had spoken the words: *I do, I will.*

This is the first and great commandment. And the second is like unto it …

"Why would it be a lie?"

He shook his head hopelessly. "I don't regret—not really. Not as I should. I don't regret the things that *worked*."

"What things? What did you do, exactly?"

He spoke in an eager whisper: "I set out to make a fool of Martin Hallam. That was how it started. He had some stupid book by a man named Persimmons that he was terrifically excited about. He thought he had found a formula that Persimmons had searched for in vain. He wanted my help in testing it—a tedious business with pentagrams and blood and a long chant in barbarous Latin. I agreed to help only because I wanted to laugh at him. I didn't expect it to work—but that thing came when we called, materialized in that shape in Hallam's office in University College, and then turned itself into something that looked like an undergraduate and made quite civil conversation."

The people in the last pews were turning to look at them again, and Elsa wanted to draw Gallagher away into a corner, or simply shush him. But he remained in the aisle, and went on with his story.

"And as it turned out, I was better prepared to deal with it than Hallam. He just went to pieces. He didn't know what he wanted, but I did, although I hadn't known it until that moment. It was a simple request. I wanted the *Bibliotheka Orphika* to be real. It was something that I had made up: a *jeu d'esprit*, to use your own frighteningly accurate term. I had never shown it to anyone—I was ashamed of it, of the fancifulness of it. But I was also so proud of it.

And if it were real—ah! There would be nothing to be ashamed of. I wanted to have found it somewhere in Egypt, and I also wanted to be asked to produce a critical edition. Of course that meant ideally I should be two separate people—but that proved hardly a difficulty." He smiled painedly. "With the Devil, *all* things are possible."

"No doubt." And how easy, no doubt, to promise your immortal soul as payment when you didn't believe you had such a thing. Once again Elsa was staggered by the grace that had allowed her to escape a similar fate.

"*Protected in the paschal night,*" the people sang around them, "*From the destroying angel's might … *"

"That was ten years ago," said Gallagher. "The terms of our agreement were clear … and at the same time fiendishly unclear. The cult—the salons—all of that was meant to provide him with devotees, worshippers for his Master. The corruption of pure souls. I thought it was a means for me to evade my own final payment. I really believed that it could work that way. Perhaps if I had done a better job of it … "

"You made a deal with the Devil. It never works that way."

"Do you want to know what I do regret? I regret that I did not ask him to make me a gift of you. I regret that I was so determined to win you on my own. Of course I see the psychology of it. I became obsessed with you after I had achieved all my desires with the *Bibliotheka*. That had become too easy. My pride would accept no help in the pursuit of you. And I did not do it so badly at first. No, you don't know—you had no thought that I was pursuing you, at first, because I did it *well*. I invited you to my office, I showed you the manuscript, we spent happy hours together while you pored over my handiwork … and came up with the theory that it was written by one man. I had underestimated you. What could I do after that? I tried—in my pride—to reduce you to something I could control. I thought I had enough sway over you as a man that I might offer you marriage with one hand and take away your intellectual curiosity with the other. I regret that—I regret thinking that such a high-handed approach might ever work with you. I regret descending to threats and pleading. But more than that, even now, I regret that they didn't work. I've seen what you really are, and it's … it's not what I thought. It's not as good as I thought. But I still want it."

"That's very flattering."

It obviously wasn't meant to be; but it was the truth, and that was something.

"*O all sufficient Sacrifice,*" the hymn rolled on, "*Beneath thee hell defeated lies …* "

The sidesmen taking up the collection had arrived at the back of the church, and frowned at Elsa and Gallagher. She realized she had left her purse in the pew with the Peachams and Whitmores. But Gallagher had already taken out his wallet and tossed a handful of bills into the plate. The sidesmen stared at him in surprise.

"How did you determine that the manuscript was forged?" Gallagher asked, turning back to Elsa.

"I—I had the idea when I heard you use a turn of phrase that sounded like the author. At first it was just an idea. Then I found the line of the hymn to Apollo in Gruber's edition of the Cambridge Florilegium in last April's *Antiquarian Record.*"

"I never checked Gruber's edition! How did you happen upon it?"

The hymn ended just as she began to answer: "I didn't—" She dropped her voice to a whisper. "I didn't 'happen upon it.' I sought out all of your sources looking for just such a slip."

She heard Kit's voice from the sanctuary: "Almighty God, giver of life and health … "

Gallagher shook his head. "Again I have underestimated you. Yet it does not make you more desirable in my eyes. If you continue to outwit me, I could overcome my infatuation. I could learn to think of you as a colleague. A rival, even. Save me, and I will do it. I will see you reinstated at the university, I will foster your career, argue with you in print like an equal—that's what you want, isn't it?"

She stared at him, appalled. "What do you think I am that you can make that kind of bargain with me? *I* can't save you."

"But you can! Why do you think I let you attempt the Descent so many times? I knew you were immune to it—he had told me so from the beginning, that he would try, but he knew he hadn't the power to take over your mind the way he did with others. And you are the one who worked whatever miracle was worked on *him*," he pointed down the aisle toward the altar. "You filled him with … something—you made him proof against the Devil. You did that!"

"I *did not*. God did that."

"But you were—you were the instrument, if you like. He—it—saw your hand in it. As you saw my hand in the *Bibliotheka*. It was your work."

"It was God's work! And Kit's faith, not mine. All I did was pray, without even knowing what I was praying for."

But that was not strictly true. In that moment in the elevator, she had believed with her whole heart that she could speak those words and be heard. And if what had brought her to that moment of certainty was love, it was not love of a particularly shining purity; it was carnal, selfish love for an attractive man who had always treated her well. Why should that kind of love be the vehicle for any kind of grace?

Maybe if you were handsomer and younger, Arthur Gallagher; maybe if you flattered my pride by treating me like a man; maybe if you had blue eyes and an English accent and an eager, passionate, boyish innocence; maybe you're right: if I loved you, if you were loveable, I could save you.

Something like heavy fists thudded against the closed church doors, and the wood groaned under the force of the blow.

"Therefore with Angels and Archangels, and with all the company of heaven, we laud and magnify thy glorious Name, evermore praising thee and saying … "

"Kneel," said Elsa to Gallagher.

They knelt on the cold tiles by the font. The choir began the *Sanctus*, an elaborate setting of the Latin words.

"Monteverdi," said Gallagher absently. "I remember this from my childhood."

Elsa thought of her own childhood, of the joy that she used to feel at Revival meetings, standing and singing beside her father. She held out a hand toward Gallagher.

"Here," she said.

He took it.

Lord, please let him live. Let him repent and live. Let the devil go away from our doors unsatisfied. Let him live.

On their knees on the floor of the church they listened to the words of the Consecration, while the devil outside hammered at the doors.

"The Peace of the Lord be always with you," said Kit.

"*Et cum spiritu tuo,*" said Gallagher.

Elsa looked at him, and he gave a slight shrug.

"We do not presume," Kit began, and the congregation joined in around them, "to come to this thy Table, O merciful Lord, trusting in our own righteousness … "

Elsa and Gallagher were still looking at one another.

"I don't know this one," she whispered.

"Neither do I."

They listened to the prayer, hands clasped between them. Gallagher turned to look at her again, a different and urgent expression in his face.

"Do you forgive me?" he said.

She thought about it for a moment, and said what she wanted to be true, because that, she thought, was the way to make it so: "Yes. I do."

The choir began the *Agnus Dei*. The acolytes were kneeling in the sanctuary to receive Communion. The music finished, the congregation began filing out of the pews.

The doors at the back of the church burst open once more.

Gallagher let go of her hand and pushed her roughly away from him. "Go! Don't be near me!"

From the open doors a fissure had begun to open in the floor of the church, a crack snaking toward Gallagher where he knelt in the aisle. It broke around the font and snaked onward. The heavy weight of stone shifted, and the font tilted sideways. Outside the door, Elsa could not see the devil's grey tweed form any longer. There was nothing but yawning darkness, cold and hungry. She felt a crashing wave of vertigo as she looked out, as though she were looking down—and down and *down*. Shuddering, terrified, she looked away.

Gallagher got clumsily to his feet, but he remained standing in the aisle. Elsa stood for a few moments longer frozen between him and the orderly procession of people going up for Communion. She wanted more than anything to join them, but she could not turn her back on Gallagher while the cold depth outside the door gaped for him. Yet she couldn't help him this way. Not knowing what she intended, she took a small step toward him.

Mr. Oates was in the aisle beside her.

"Come on, man," he called to Gallagher. "Come with us—there isn't any other way."

But before Gallagher could move, the crack in the floor opened directly under his feet, and he lost his balance and fell back, grasping at the lip of the tilting font. Mr. Oates rushed forward and caught the huge weight of stone as it toppled. Baptismal water splashed over the front of his suit. Several men ran to his aid to support the font and roll it sideways onto the floor.

"Clear out!" one of the men shouted. "Stand back!" They had to drag Mr. Oates clear, panting and staring at his wet hands.

The floor was crumbling away, breaking up and rolling and sliding out through the open door into the hungry darkness. Gallagher scrabbled desperately for a foothold on the shifting surface.

"What did he want to come in here for?" a miserable female voice moaned from one of the pews. "Oh, God, make it go away!"

The aisle was clogged with people, some of them still trying to move up to the altar, others turned to stare back at the dark doorway and the disintegrating floor. A few had headed for the side door, but when they got it open, there was blackness outside it as well. Elsa looked for the other members of her own party. The Peachams were already on their way back down from the altar rail; Peachy and Harriet were out of sight, and the Whitmores had remained helplessly in their pew. No one moved toward Gallagher. They looked at the darkness outside the door, and it was the most they could do not to turn away.

There was a confused shuffling in the chancel, as people moved out of the way to either side. Kit strode through the chancel and down the aisle. He had taken off the white chasuble and left it behind, and he came down to the crumbling back of the church in his alb with the gold-embroidered stole crossed in front. Several of the acolytes followed him, an impromptu procession, trying to look as though this were something they had rehearsed. Peachy and Harriet were in the crowd that tagged behind the acolytes. All stopped short of the crumbling floor, and only Kit went forward.

He reached Gallagher a few feet from the door, and grasped him by both arms. Gallagher clung to him, and Kit hauled him up onto the solid floor until there was a moment when they were almost embracing.

Peachy and Harriet had arrived behind Elsa. "Get out of it!" Peachy shouted urgently. "Kit! You'll be caught in it yourself!"

Kit pushed Gallagher to safety, and looked past him for a moment at Elsa and Peachy and Harriet. He was smiling, but when the smile died away, it was replaced by a look of apology. He turned toward the door.

The ground was slipping away so steadily under his shoes that the few steps he took to reach the door were at a run, and when he went through the doorway it was in a leap, arms outstretched, launching himself forward into the consuming darkness as if to embrace it.

Invisible hands caught him, and casually, in one brutal motion, snapped his head back. For a moment his body hung limply in the huge grasp, then it fell like a doll to land on the church steps. The darkness began to fold in on itself and recede, and the prosaic light of a streetlamp glowed through the rain.

She felt nothing, thought nothing; even grief seemed a distant, if a certain, prospect. She didn't move, as if she were waiting for some motion from the crumpled shape on the steps that would not move again.

Around her, people were making noises of relief, of amazement and anguish. Someone—his father—was stumbling out onto the steps and gathering up his body, awkwardly cradling the broken neck, trying to close the open eyes.

And there was another light, piercing impossibly down the length of the church from the stained-glass window over the altar, out through the open door into the heart of the retreating darkness, falling on a flight of stairs beyond and below the earthly stairs outside the church.

Elsa felt someone trying to hold her back, and there were voices calling her name—versions of her name, anyway—but above them was one voice in particular, one that had never sounded so commanding: "Don't do that! Let her go!"

Chapter Nineteen

ALL THE KINGDOMS OF THE WORLD IN A MOMENT OF TIME

The airless, placeless darkness lasted only for a moment. It was replaced by a dim, cold *somewhere*, with dark rocks. He felt the impact as he hit them, dropping limply on his side, but it was like a noise heard underwater, indistinct and distorted. A sentence presented itself to him dispassionately: *He was dead before he hit the ground.*

He gathered himself up and looked around. He was in a tremendous valley, its walls so high and so close together that no sky was visible, just mounting heights of dark rock on either side. It was so cold that for a moment he felt stupidly surprised he could not see his breath in the air.

For a long time, or what might have been a long time—he was no longer able to gauge the passage of time with any accuracy—he was alone in this desolate landscape. At first he simply sat on the stone floor of the valley. The air felt stale, and there was a smell. At first it was the merest hint, but it grew, or rather he grew more conscious of it: a smell that was like something he had always known, and like nothing in the world, unplaceable, banal, and awful. There was a sound, too, that grew in the same way, throbbing in some unjudgeable distance. It was the sound of weeping.

And that was odd, because he did not, himself, seem to have any tears to shed. It was so cold, and he was so alone; he would have liked to weep, but he seemed to have forgotten how.

He got to his feet and tried to brush the dust of the stones from his alb. It wouldn't come off, though he went on trying for some time. He wrapped his arms around himself to try to get warm, but this didn't work either. In the opposite wall of the valley he could dimly make out the shape of a wide, dark arch. He took a step toward it.

His foot landed in nothingness, and it was only by throwing himself violently backward that he was able to keep from toppling off the precipice that he hadn't known he was on. This time he hit the ground hard, skinning the palm of one hand. He scooted back from the edge across the rocks, his heart banging in his chest, all his muscles shaking. His panting breath made a cloud in the cold, stale air.

"I know … " He paused to draw breath.

" … that my Redeemer liveth … "

He got to his feet again.

" … and that he shall stand at the latter day upon the earth. And though after my skin, worms destroy this body, yet in my flesh shall I see God."

He looked over the edge of the precipice. It went on down, below as above; he was on a narrow ledge on one side of a fissure, not at the bottom of a valley. The floor of the fissure was as distant as the sky, and he could not see it. But it was from down there that the sound of weeping came.

He sat down on the very edge, letting his feet dangle. Awkwardly reaching across with his left hand to dig in his right pocket, he found his handkerchief and drew it out. He moistened it on his tongue and used it to clean his scraped palm. It stung appropriately. He took his time with it.

Metaphysically, he though, *what is this? Where is this?*

He had felt the fatal injury, not as pain—it had been too quick for that—but as a definite sensation with a clear conclusion. Well, it was what he had expected when he had flung himself out the door, though he had imagined it might be a bit more dignified, might involve more of a struggle. But where Gallagher had been headed … was that where he was?

He tried to think in terms of categories, theologians, schools of thought … The only thing this accomplished was to wake in him a nostalgia for his days in college—not so long ago, in fact, but not adequately appreciated at the time. He remembered specific scenes, professors' voices, conversations with his fellow students, sitting on the floor in the apartment with Peachy, trying to decipher his notes and identify the places where he had fallen asleep in class.

From there his memory moved to other things, and he remembered an early conversation with Peachy—more of a monologue, really—about saints and the propriety of being named after them. (Peachy had always a little regretted not having a proper saint's name himself, although his middle name, satisfactorily, was George.) And, "How did you get a name like Christopher if your parents weren't even Christian?"

But his "parents" hadn't named him; his mother had done that on her own. He remembered her telling him the truth about that once, when he was nine years old, and they were eating at a café in Paris. By this time she used to talk to him as if he were her contemporary, which was both flattering and difficult. They were sitting at a sidewalk table, and he was eating the ham and cheese on toast that went by a fancy name in France, cutting it up into little pieces, because that was what you did, savouring each bite and the fresh spring air. She was smoking a cigarette, but casually, the way she did in France, not with the belligerence with which she smoked in public in England.

"I always liked the name Christopher," she said. "It was the name of the first boy I was in love with. I was quite a little girl—not much older than you are now. I don't know what ever happened to him. Something quite conventional and sad, no doubt. But he made an impression on me. I thought of him when I had to come up with a name for you."

That was what it was always like with his mother: she *had* to come up with a name for him, like a chore; but then she had thought of someone she had loved, which must mean … But you never really knew where you stood with her.

They had been waiting for his father, of course, whom in those days Christopher had to call "Uncle," because the poor man didn't know that he knew any better. He hadn't known Christopher was going to be there, either; usually Adele Underhill came to France with either her lover or her son, not both. When he joined them at the café table, he had tried to be polite about it.

"So you brought Christopher with you. Was there some problem with his school?"

She gave him an irritated look; she always knew what you were thinking really. "They're on Easter holidays, Laurie. And there's an exhibit that I want him to see. I think he'd like it."

It was an exhibit of swords and armour. He'd loved it. And it was the first time he was aware of his mother going out of her way to do something just to make him happy. It was almost the last time, too. A year later, he thought of that exhibit in the hospital after the crash, while he sat by her bed. He couldn't get it out of his head; it was like somebody was talking to him about it, gently and insistently, reminding him of that day of walking around the museum with her, of how happy he had been. It seemed almost grotesque at first—a stupid, trivial thing to be thinking about when she was dying, which he knew she was. Then he realized he wasn't thinking about it just to remember it, but so that he would know what to do now. He'd asked the nurses to send for Laurence Whitmore. He had gone out of his way to make a scene about it, which wasn't entirely necessary, and he had made sure that his mother heard, so that, should his father arrive too late after all, she would at least know that someone—it didn't particularly matter that it was him—had loved her enough to try to fetch him.

That was how it had turned out, too. His father had been hours too late, but she had died thinking that she would see him again, which was better than nothing.

And she'd died thinking that her son could look after himself. The scene he made with the nurses had amused her.

"You might be a bit too much like me," she said, after he had returned to her bedside and was holding her hand, because it seemed like the thing to do. "But if I'd wanted to prevent that … I ought to have started sooner."

And where was she? Now, when he was here—where was she?

Not here. Nowhere near here. That he had prayed for and believed for eighteen years, give or take. He smoothed out his handkerchief and used a clean corner of it to dry his eyes.

"What *are* you playing at?"

He looked up. The false Elsa was perched on a crag of the rock wall opposite, by the dark arch, a little above him. He could see her clearly in spite of the dimness; she was no farther away than the far side of a large room, in spite of the chasm between them. She was naked, except for a pair of cardboard wings like the ones the real Elsa had worn to the costume party. She crouched indecently on the rock, white thighs splayed, looking down at him with a sullen expression. He looked away.

"You are acting," she went on, "as if you still have a body. As if it isn't a thing you have left behind."

"Yes."

"Do you think that your physical strength can somehow, possibly save you?" She sounded pityingly curious.

"No … 'He delights not in the strength of the horse: he takes not pleasure in the legs of a man.'" He swung his own legs carelessly over the pit. "Only it *did* just save me. So there's that."

She made an unimpressed little "huh" noise. He took his time refolding his handkerchief, but did not replace it in his pocket.

"This is not the way that we generally like to do this," she said by and by, conversationally. "I will be frank with you. You're not an awful lot of use to me with your virtue intact."

"I don't know what that could possibly mean," he said. Virtue wasn't a thing that you carried around carefully, trying to keep it in one piece; it was a process, it was little things that you had to do every waking moment, and that he very frequently did not do, had not done; it was work.

"I could tempt you, of course, with other selves, other possibilities. The way I did all the others. But I know you too well. There's no other person you would prefer to be. Still, I could offer you a self who possesses things you're never likely to have: power, influence, great wealth … But I don't even need to do that."

She gathered her pale feet under her and jumped off the rock. Her cardboard wings carried her down to the foot of the empty arch, where there was a flat place like a balcony. She squatted near the edge of it.

"All I need to do is offer you this." She pointed down.

He looked, and where there had been only darkness there was now something like the glimmer of still water, and he could see his reflection looking up at him.

Only it wasn't his reflection. The vestments were the same, but the face was older, the hair completely grey. It was still a face that you could be vain about, and the man looking up at him was vain about it … oh, certainly he was.

"He's no one in particular," the false Elsa was saying. "Rector of a small parish in a working-class neighbourhood, a place known only for its famous choirmaster. Beloved by his parishioners, but you couldn't call him powerful or influential—certainly not rich. Underpaid, in fact. One wonders he is even able to support his family, which I believe is numerous. But of course his wife works—teaches, as I understand, at the university, and has published books—and so that must help."

"And none of them notices?"

"Notices what?"

"What has become of him."

"Of course they don't notice. He is universally loved."

"That could be. But he doesn't love universally. Or at all, I think—except himself. Maybe that's what happens if you make that kind of a sacrifice for your own sake."

The false Elsa made an angry noise and a snatching motion with her thin hand, and the reflection disappeared.

"I don't think you understand," she hissed, holding her closed fist out over the pit. "This version of you is entirely within my gift. The real Kit Underhill died at thirty, on his way out of the church after his quaint attempt at recreating the ancient Easter Vigil. Tragic, of course, and quite unexpected. Some sort of undiagnosed illness, it seems. A weak heart, perhaps."

"I do understand that I'm dead, thanks. But everyone in the church saw how I died." The air seemed to grow colder around him, and he realized what he had said. "No, it—it doesn't matter if they did or not."

"Doesn't it?"

"Of course not! Of course not!" He scrambled to his feet and backed away from her toward the rock wall.

Oh, but it did matter.

She crouched like an animal, smiling predatorily through the foul air at him. There was more than a little of her real form in that smile.

"It's not enough that I had to give up my life, *which I loved*, but I've got to not care that no one knows I did it? It's too much! How can you ask that much?"

And worse than all of it was his scorching sorrow at his own pride.

"You're right," she cooed triumphantly. "It *is* too much. But *I* don't ask that much. I never would."

"I'm not talking to you!"

"You should be. I am the only one who hears you."

Deny it! Deny it! he told himself furiously, and he didn't.

"No, you're not," said the same voice—but so different.

She was standing in the dark archway behind the false Elsa. There were droplets of rain on her hat and on the black wool of her sweater. She was out of breath from running down the stone steps that he could see dimly behind her.

The false Elsa frowned up at her. "What are you doing here?"

"I don't know," she admitted. "Perhaps I am refusing to face facts. Or perhaps I am facing them truly for the first time."

She had spared barely a glance for the false Elsa, but went on looking across the chasm at Kit.

"He abandoned you, to die for the sake of a man you hate, who would never have crossed his path if it had not been for you. Can you honestly say that you brought him anything but unhappiness?"

"Of course not," she said, before Kit could stop her.

"What were you to him?" the false Elsa pursued. "Not his wife or his fiancée—certainly not his mistress. You never even held his hand or kissed him in public. Did he, in fact, die without ever hearing you say that you loved him?"

"He did."

"Then it's obvious what you are doing here after all, isn't it?"

"Yes." She took another step closer to the edge, still looking across the darkness at him. "We never got a chance to present a united front, you and I."

He could feel her presence as if they were touching, as if their bodies were clasped in the closest embrace. Looking across the pit at her, he felt her intention as clearly as if she had spoken it in his ear. She could do it, too; he had had no faith a moment ago, but this he believed completely. All that he had to do was pretend that he didn't.

"Elsa, I am no good at this."

She stepped right to the edge now. He felt a lurch of vertigo on her behalf; he wasn't even afraid of heights, but he remembered that she was.

"That's all right," she said. "I love you."

She turned on the false Elsa, seized the long curls of its hair in one hand, wrapped them around her fist, and hauled the creature by its head toward the edge of the pit.

It gave an undignified squawk. It scrabbled feebly at her strong hands. "What is this? 'Love saves the day'? How trite, how ridiculous!"

"No doubt. Some things—are worth—being ridiculous for."

"He abandoned you!" it wailed. "What sort of love is that?"

"What *sort* of love? It's a sort that you should recognize. The thing is, I didn't come here to sacrifice myself. That's what he did. I came here—I believe I really came here to take him back. And I didn't come alone."

From the stairs behind her came a familiar voice, raised exultantly, in the top of its form:

"Alleluia! Alleluia! Alleluia!

O sons and daughters, let us sing!

The King of heaven … "

And joining him, growing nearer and stronger, an uncertain chorus: " *… the glorious King,*

O'er death to-day rose triumphing.

> *Alleluia!"*

Behind the two Elsas, the doorway was filling with people. There were faces that he recognized, confused and fearful, and some that he didn't. They were the Easter Vigil congregation. Some still held lit hand-candles, and others were clutching hymnals. Charlie Boult and the two torchbearers and the subdeacon processed down the stairs with as much dignity as was compatible with not tripping on their albs in the dark. A knot of choristers came down, singing heartily. But out in front, leading and marshalling the whole crowd, was Peachy.

"That Easter morn, at break of day,

The faithful women went their way

To seek the tomb where Jesus lay."

All the Kingdoms of the World in a Moment of Time
They shuffled out onto the stone ledge and pressed in at the
doorway. There was Polly Whitmore, with her hat knocked sideways,
holding onto her sister's arm, and Charlotte and Gerald Peacham,
following their son with complete faith, matter-of-fact and without
surprise. There was Harriet, glowing, singing with all her heart.
There were Miss Finch and Mrs. Barrington, and Mr. Oates nearly
tumbling down the stairs in his eagerness, and a family whose name
Kit could not remember, with half a dozen children, wide-eyed and
excited. There was Mr. Cox, frowning out at the dark chasm, plainly
assessing it as a practical problem, considering how best to get across.
The false Elsa, squirming in the real Elsa's grasp, glared around at
them all with annoyance, as if they were a swarm of insects.

"*An angel clad in white they see,*
Who sat, and spake unto the three …"

It lied, Kit thought. *They did see.* Suddenly the whole thing
seemed so insignificant: his little life, the little bit of bravado with
which he had ended it. It was all so small, like a thing you could hold
in your hand, and so dear. As he had felt united to Elsa a moment
ago—and in a completely different way—he felt the presence of
Someone, who had come in with the Easter Vigil congregation with
their candles and incense and hymn books. And again he knew how
this was going to go, and knew it with a joy that was also sorrow—
because this was still what he wanted, but he was ashamed to want
it, still more ashamed to know that it was going to be granted him.

"*That night the apostles met in fear;*
Amidst them came their Lord most dear,
And said, 'My peace be on all here.'
Alleluia!"

"He is here!" the false Elsa gasped, annoyance melting into horror.
"How—how did He … "

In desperation it grabbed the hands that held it, and the false
and the true Elsas swayed for a moment on the edge of the pit.
Several people rushed out of the doorway. Kit saw Charlie realize

that he was holding something that could serve as a weapon, draw back his arm to swing the thurible, and freeze in anguished indecision. Harriet was right beside him, and Polly Whitmore and her sister. But it was Peachy who strode forward, still singing—"*When Thomas first the tidings heard*"—grabbed the real Elsa around the waist, and hung on.

With his weight behind her, she flung the false Elsa out over the edge of the pit. It fell, twisting and kicking, then caught itself with a flapping of cardboard wings and sailed sulkily down, the white human shape dissolving in the distance into flapping fabric: a tangle of grey tweed, tattered and grubby.

Kit felt the rain on his face before anything else. The blackness of the rocks tipped upward and filled with faint stars, and somewhere nearby a streetlight came on.

Chapter Twenty

THE PROSAIC FUTURE OF DINNER PARTIES

To Elsa it seemed that the dark landscape broke apart and dissolved, and she and Peachy and Harriet and Charlie and all the others fell through starlit darkness until the slick flagstones of the walk in front of St. John's were under the soles of her shoes, and felt as though they had been there all along. Something sparkled in her vision, and she didn't know whether it was tears or the rain.

Kit lay where he had fallen on the church steps, the upper half of his body across his father's lap. Whether Laurence Whitmore had noticed or cared where the rest of the congregation had gone, leaving him alone with his grief—whether it even seemed to him that they had gone anywhere—Elsa couldn't guess. When Kit started to breathe again, with a startled convulsion like a man waking suddenly from a dream, his father nearly dropped him.

Elsa was conscious of everyone moving and talking at once, while she remained again silent and still.

"Yes, I know it was a miracle, thank you—" This was Dr. Peacham, shouldering through the crowd gathering around Kit. "But he could still have a broken neck. And manhandling him like that—"

"Torches! Crucifer!" This was Mr. Cox. "Back into the vestry now, before the hardware gets any wetter!"

Dr. Peacham was kneeling on the steps beside Kit, pulling back the damp fabric from his neck to feel that his spine was intact.

"Do you notice any numbness?"

"Um … " Kit blinked up at him. "Yes, but … not the kind you mean."

"Does anything hurt?"

"Just my hand. I … " He held it out like a child. "I scraped it on the rocks. Before you got there."

Professor Whitmore was looking at his son almost with horror. The brown bats, Elsa thought, had been put in a more peculiar perspective still.

Peachy, Elsa noticed finally, still had his arms around her. He squeezed her gently.

"You did it," he said, in a voice brimming with emotion. "You actually did it."

She turned to look up at him. "*We* did it, Peachy!"

"What? Oh, I guess so. You, and me—a little bit, anyway—and Our Lord."

She hugged him back. Harriet collided with them in her eagerness to embrace them both, and Elsa wriggled out of their arms to leave Harriet and Peachy clinging to each other.

"Peverell," Harriet was saying, "you were magnificent! Shouting at everyone like that to let Elsa go, and the way you led us out there, and made sure we all came along, and the way you stepped up and did just the right thing—helped Elsa when none of us could manage. It makes me wish—it's crazy, but it almost makes me wish I *hadn't* forgiven you yet, so that I could do it now, only ten times more. I love you so much."

A police officer came across the wide expanse of St. Clair to investigate the crowd on the church steps.

"Has anything happened?" he asked.

"Of course something has happened, Officer," said Mr. Cox with dignity. "It is Easter."

"Yes?"

"Christ is risen."

"He is risen indeed!" chorused the departing torchbearers and

Charlie Boult, and the rest of the congregation joined in, raggedly. "Alleluia!"

"Oh, quite, yes." The policeman touched his hat and backed away.

As he left, a tall figure in a dark coat strode into range of the streetlight and waved cheerfully: Elsa's father, returning from his hymn-singing evening. He did not ask if anything had happened.

Kit got to his feet on the steps, and pushed his wet hair back from his forehead. He looked around at the congregation, momentarily at a loss. He folded his hands.

"*Ite, missa est,*" he said.

There was general laughter. Several people said that they should all get out of the rain, and someone recalled that there were refreshments in the parish hall, and this, under the circumstances, was greeted with more laughter. The crowd began to split between the people who just wanted to get into the dry hall and have something to eat, and those who wanted to follow the resurrected vicar around and stare at him. Mrs. Peacham said something practical about towels and fireplaces, which gave these people a good excuse to troop over to the rectory. Elsa had the impression that some of them would have picked Kit up and carried him if he would have let them. She saw Charlie still standing on the steps, last of the acolytes left, finally taking off at a run for the sacristy with the dripping thurible slung over his shoulder.

Kit was turning and looking for her through the crowd. She made her way to his side, and he reached for her hand. He pulled her to him and kissed her, chastely but emphatically. She laughed, and he blushed.

"You're soaking wet," she said. "Let's go inside."

On the rectory porch, Mr. Nordqvist caught up with them, and clapped Kit on the shoulder in a congratulatory gesture that nearly knocked him down.

"I knew it would all turn out well!" he declared. "Praise the Lord!"

Everyone on the porch who had not noticed that he had only

then joined the party gazed with awe at this man who was able to take such a great miracle in his stride.

In the crowded hall with its clutter of tatty Neoclassical furniture, Kit scanned the faces around them.

"What happened to … "

"I'll find out," said Elsa.

He let her hand go reluctantly, and surrendered himself to the fussing of his step-mother and foster-mother and most of the Altar Guild. She found Professor Whitmore by the door.

"Sir, did you see what happened to Professor Gallagher? After we had all … while we were gone?"

"Oh." He roused himself from his daze with an effort. "That man? He dared to show his face for a moment, but he fled back inside the church at a glance from me. The monstrous coward. Though I suppose … " He hesitated. "I suppose he was ashamed."

She pulled back on the damp hat she had just taken off, and took the shortest route back to the church, through the hall where the parishioners who were not milling in the rectory were refreshing themselves with steaming cups of tea and talking very loudly and giddily.

Half-vested, dripping acolytes were also talking loudly and giddily in the chancel as she passed through from the hall. The scar of crumbled bricks was visible at the back of the church, running under the tilted font. There was only one person left in the nave, sitting stiffly at the end of a pew.

It was not Arthur Gallagher. It was a tall, angular woman in a man's dark tweed suit, her yellow hair unwaved, her face pale and faded-looking without makeup. It took Elsa a moment to recognize Mrs. Graves. Gallagher's suit fit her fairly well.

"I don't seem to be able to change back," she said when she saw Elsa standing in the aisle beside her. "I—I took this form when I … "

"When you ran away from Kit's father. You didn't think he would attack a woman."

She nodded. "That must have been what I intended. I was conscious only of wanting to flee from myself. But I don't seem to be able … The power that effected the transformation seems to have been withdrawn." Her hands shook as she smoothed her hair back from her face.

Elsa stood looking at the woman in the pew, thinking about that. Arthur Gallagher was, in one sense, no more. She wondered whether it was a punishment, or grace. Maybe it was both.

She said what she had come to say: "Won't you come over to the rectory and tell Kit that you're sorry?"

Mrs. Graves started, eyes wide. "He didn't die?"

"He did die. He is alive again."

Mrs. Graves looked up at her with a horror more real than Professor Whitmore's.

"You went after him. Like … "

"Yes. Like Orpheus, I suppose. What else could I possibly do? We all went after him. And it worked. Unlike Orpheus. God made it work."

She left Mrs. Graves sitting in the empty church, and followed the acolytes back to the rectory.

"I can't believe I *shoulda* hit somebody with the thurible," Charlie was saying as they walked ahead of her, "and I *couldn't*."

The others murmured in sympathy.

One of the torches said, "But nobody could blame you. She *looked* like a woman."

"She looked like Father Underhill's girl friend, is what she looked like," said Charlie.

"His *what?*"

"You didn't see them kissing outside just now?" asked the other torch.

"Come on," said Charlie pityingly, "did you actually need to see that to know she's his girl friend?"

"Fiancée, probably."

"Nah, girl friend—she doesn't have a ring."

"Anyway, Charlie, did you really think that devil-woman looked like her?"

"I dunno—didn't it?"

"Well, kind of. Wouldn't've fit into one of her dresses, though, if you ask me."

"Nobody," Charlie growled, "did ask you. There's not gonna be any of that. We clear?"

Elsa hung back so that they wouldn't realize she had heard.

"What I want to know," said the crucifer, who had not yet spoken, as they were mounting the rectory steps, "is did he ought to have taken off his chasuble or not."

"What?"

"When he went down to the back door. Liturgically, you know. Did he ought to have taken it off? Because when you think about it, offering himself instead of the professor was like an *extension* of the Mass, right—so ... "

"Yeah, that's ridiculous."

"No, but—you know! It's a consideration."

"Not having the Altar Guild pitch a fit because he wore the best white chasuble out in the rain—*that's* a consideration."

"I don't think it was," Charlie said slowly. "An extension of the Mass. I think that was just him, and that's how he meant it. I think that might actually be why he took it off."

After a moment one of the torches said, "We could ask him."

They went inside the rectory laughing about that. Elsa followed them after a moment, wondering if they *would* ask Kit, and how many other questions and congratulations would come between her and an opportunity to talk to him again. There could be hundreds. She could wait. He was alive; there would be time. He would never belong exclusively to her, but it was not because she thought he could that she had gone down the dark stairs after him.

The rectory was a chaos of people making tea and lighting fires and running up and down stairs with towels and bottles from Kit's pre-war liquor cabinet, and talking and laughing and giving one another dazed hugs. In the living room Elsa saw her father listening raptly while Mr. Oates and Mr. Cox told the story of the events that he had missed.

Vera Whitmore was helping Mrs. Barrington find dry clothes in the rummage-sale boxes in the dining room, and emerged waving a white lace thing and calling, "Elsa, Elsa! This would be *perfect* for you!"

The parish was divided in how to take Elsa. Some people wanted to shake her hand with matter-of-fact enthusiasm, as if she had just won an election; others stared at her from a distance with wary awe. The couple of sylphs who had followed their mother into the rectory gave her looks of tragic resignation. Others seemed simply curious.

"I have been attending this church for forty-two years," one little old man informed her, "but I don't believe we have met."

"Well, I'm new," she admitted. "I'm—I'm Father Underhill's girl friend."

Kit came through the door from the kitchen, nursing a teacup full of something which was certainly not tea. He was naked to the waist, except for a towel slung over his shoulders, and his hair, still damp, was the untidiest she had ever seen it. One of the sylphs saw him and retreated into the living room with a little squeak.

"Kit, really!" said Harriet, following him out of the kitchen. "I know it's your house, but you can't wander around like that. Peverell, go upstairs and get him a dressing gown."

But Peachy was trapped in a corner by the organist, who was waving his setting of the *Te Deum* in his face, shouting superlatives and demanding to know why he hadn't written a Mass.

*

Elsa woke in Kit's living room for the second time in as many weeks.

It was barely dawn. She crawled off of the chaise where she had slept, and stretched.

The Whitmores had gone home, eventually, along with most of the Altar Guild and the churchwardens and choristers. Kit had fallen asleep on the floor by the fireplace, and been carried upstairs—or halfway upstairs, before he woke and protested—by Mr. Nordqvist and Charlie Boult. Shortly after that, Elsa's father had accepted an invitation from Mr. Oates, with whom he had left, deep in a debate about infant baptism.

Dr. Peacham was asleep on one of the couches in the living room, and his wife lay with her head in his lap. Harriet and Peachy were similarly arranged on the other couch. Through the open door to the dining room, Elsa could see acolytes curled and sprawled amid the rummage-sale boxes.

She yawned, and padded on stockinged feet out into the hall, closing the living-room door quietly behind her. Kit was standing in the open front door, in his pyjamas and dressing gown, looking out into the rectory garden, where the first rays of sun were slanting palely across the grass beyond the long shadow cast by the house.

He turned toward her, and she saw that his face was wet with tears. He crossed the space between them in a couple of steps, caught her in his arms, and held her tightly. She could feel him trembling.

He rested his forehead against hers for a moment, and smoothed her hair back from her face.

"Thank you," he whispered.

She kissed him. "Any time."

He leaned back and took a swipe at his eyes with his sleeve. "I'm afraid this isn't quite what you signed up for."

"What isn't? You, alive, on Easter morning, crying to see the sunrise?"

"The state I'm in … I don't know if it will go away—I don't know if I want it to go away." He pressed his knuckles to his lips. "I have to go on as if … not as if it didn't happen, but as if it *did*. I don't know how to live, day by day, in the light of that fact. What am I to say to people? How am I to act? The only thing … the only thing John's Gospel reports about Lazarus after he came out of the tomb is that some time later he was at a dinner party." He smiled tearily. "And then I think … maybe that's helpful after all."

"Oh, Kit … But you have always lived in that light, haven't you?"

"I … have, but—I haven't always had to look at it." He let go of her. "When it comes down to it, I'm scared of it. I'm scared to go on living."

"That makes sense," she said.

"It does?"

"Yes."

"Oh. Dr. Peacham says that at most I was dead for a couple of minutes. He says it's not impossible for people to be revived quite naturally within that time—drowning victims and so on."

"That's true. Is that comforting?"

"A little bit."

She shook her head. "The thing that I think we all imagined about you, Kit, is that, if anyone could take this in his stride, it would be you."

He laughed weakly. "Not what you signed up for at all, then."

"Not at all," she whispered. She laid a hand on his chest. "I love you more in this moment than I ever have, but not as much as I will. I don't need a spirit of prophecy to tell you that."

He took her hand and kissed it. "Thank you. I could be a bit scared of that, too—but you know what? I'm not."

"Good."

They went to stand in the doorway together. He leaned against the door frame, and she leaned against him. His arms were warm around her.

"Do you have a Mass to get ready for?" she asked.

"Soon," he admitted.

She thought about the first Mass of Easter morning, in the

church with the crumbled floor at the back where he had run to his death the night before.

"Shall I talk to you about the future?" she said. "The prosaic future of dinner parties?"

"Well, it was a dinner party with Our Lord—I'm sure it wasn't all that prosaic."

"Exactly."

"Talk to me about the future."

"Well, I've thought about it a little bit. Instead of sleeping last night. I've lost my scholarship by dropping out, so it will take some doing to finish my MA. But it's not an insurmountable problem. I think Professor Kluge will take me back, and I will do my best with Saint Eustacia. I'll need to decide what subject to pursue for my doctorate—I don't think the saints' lives will yield enough for a doctoral dissertation, and … in spite of everything, I'm still not that keen on them—the Lives, I mean, not the saints. In the meantime, I can work through the summer and save money for expenses. Mrs. Barrington says her son's firm needs a secretary, and that I might be suitable. It would pay more than Fortini's and make better use of my skills—I'm not honestly all that good at selling jewellery. Mrs. Peacham has offered to let me stay with them to save the cost of rent. I've already more or less said I'll take her up on it. I hope you don't mind—I didn't think you would mind. She says they have a spare room, so I wouldn't have to stay in your old bedroom, 'because that might be a little odd.' I'm sure they'll understand my not going to church with them. Because I'll come here, I mean. I'll be busy during the week, and I wouldn't want to miss any opportunity to see you." She turned a little in his arms to look up at him. "Actually, I'd come even if … " Suddenly she felt tears springing in her own eyes. "Even if you were … if you were dead. I would still come to church. I think."

He tightened his arms around her and kissed her.

Presently he said, "Talking of bedrooms … You know the reason

I sleep in the nursery is just because it's the biggest room on that floor—and I don't have to go on doing that. Eventually, I mean."

"Yes? Well. Yes. It is an *awfully* big room."

"Too big—do you think?"

"Oh, my dear. *Of course* not."

Someone was coming up the path through the rectory garden, walking awkwardly as though in ill-fitting shoes. The figure paused for a moment, daunted by the sight of them in the doorway. It was Mrs. Graves.

"I didn't think that we would see her again," said Kit. She felt him tense warily against her. For a moment she was distracted by how thrilling that was.

"No, it's Arthur Gallagher we won't see again. She's what's left of him."

They moved a little apart, and were standing in the doorway hand in hand when Mrs. Graves reached the porch. She did not come up the steps, but stood on the path looking up at them.

"There are no words to express adequately what I must say, but all the same, I am compelled to try. I am profoundly sorry. You have shown me finally how much I was in error, not only in my allegiance, but in all of my actions—in everything that I have imagined." She paused for a moment, looking dissatisfied. She looked up again. "You are lovers?"

"We are," said Kit.

"I am so glad. I did what I could to keep you apart, and it gives me the greatest possible joy to know that I did not succeed. It makes me believe that I might be forgiven. No … it makes me believe that I have *been* forgiven."

"What are you going to do?" Elsa asked.

She shrugged. "I will write a suicide note to be found at Arthur Gallagher's house. I see no need to distract the police with an insoluble mystery. But I also see no need to waste your good research on the real provenance of the *Bibliotheka*. I will—he, I mean, will have taken that secret to the grave, leaving you free to publish your findings, if you like. Clearly that is what you had intended to do … "

"It is."

"I am sure you should have no difficulty finding a receptive audience. It is to be hoped that the cult will disintegrate on its own after that."

"But you, Mrs. Graves," Elsa pursued. "Dr. Graves, I suppose—you did earn a PhD after all, even if it wasn't under your present name. What will *you* do?"

She hesitated, then looked up at them uncertainly. "I think … I shall go back to Egypt, and see if I can find a real manuscript."

"You'll write to us?" said Kit.

She stared. "You would wish that?"

"Yes, I think so. I feel a certain sense of responsibility—I'd like to know how you do."

"Oh!" said Elsa, letting go of Kit's hand to clasp hers in sudden excitement. "You should look for St. Eustacia's house. It should be in the desert there somewhere—the *Apophthegmata* gives a detailed description of the location—but nobody has ever made a thorough search for it. I can let you have my notes on the *Life,* for what they're worth."

"Miss Nordqvist—are you offering me a research topic?"

"Yes," said Elsa, "I suppose I am."

Kit leaned against the door frame and laughed. Then he straightened up, slipped his arm around Elsa's waist, and said, "Come inside the house. We'll make tea."

ACKNOWLEDGEMENTS

And those whom we have forgotten, do thou, O Lord, remember …

I could not have written this book, or really any book about friends, without Alexandra Bolintineanu, from whom I learned so much of what I know of friendship. She also provided a lot of practical help with the plot—so much that I can no longer remember which bits were her contributions. Victoria Goddard's assistance was similarly monumental, and similarly impossible to catalogue at this point, though I can say that probably her best piece of advice was, "It's midnight on Holy Saturday. I think he should actually die."

For a long time, these two were the only ones who had read the manuscript. Pat Kennedy, the third person to see it, was a great pleasure to work with as an editor. Her advice was invaluable, and her moral support has also been tremendously helpful.

Fr. Mark Andrews didn't ever hear much about this book while I was writing it, but he helped all the same. Come to think of it, he is probably the main reason I thought to write a book with a priest as a hero.

Susan Dunning helped me come up with the details about the *Bibliotheka Orphika*, and provided me with the phrase "the genitive absolute in Plato." Her husband, Andrew, assisted with the layout, but any stylistic infelicities that remain are entirely my fault.

The Toronto Reference Library provides a wonderful free service to anyone who wants research assistance, and I'm grateful to Katherine Vice for her enthusiastic help in finding sources on life in 1920s Toronto. Again, all remaining historical inaccuracies are my responsibility.

I owe heartfelt gratitude to all the friends who have encouraged me and read my writing over the years, and to my family, who have always supported me in anything I've wanted to do. Finally, my husband, Mike, who wasn't my husband when I started writing this book. It's dedicated to him because I set out to write something that he would be proud of.

HISTORICAL NOTE

As I suspect often happens with historical novels, there are some quite inconsequential details in this book that are real, while all the major things are fictional.

All of the characters are my own invention, with the single exception of Canon Plumptre, who really was rector of St. James in 1925. It is highly unlikely that he would have had an Anglo-Catholic curate, but I assume it would have tried his patience if he did. The Lloyd George Apartments, where Elsa lives, are now called the Epitome Apartments, and the unit I assigned to Elsa is the one where I was living when I began writing this book. Annesley Hall is the oldest purpose-built women's university residence in Canada, and my best friend and I lived there as undergraduates, though never in adjacent rooms.

Most of the details of the University of Toronto are as real as I could make them, right down to the small elevator in the stacks at the old library, which has been modernized but is still there. And, most inconsequentially yet most importantly, the Peachams attend the real-life Anglo-Catholic church of St. Thomas's on Huron St., where I am a parishioner and acolyte. The sanctuary has been extended since Kit's childhood, and the inscription "God With Us" was replaced in the 1930s by a magnificent reredos with polychrome statues of saints, and a new inscription which reads, "Sic Deus Dilexit Mundum": God so loved the world …

St. John's, its rectory, parishioners, and nearby businesses on St. Clair West are completely fictional—the site of St. John's was and still is part of a park. The banner embroidered with the wrong patron saint is a detail borrowed from St. Thomas's. The ceremonial of the Easter Vigil at St. John's (along with the other Holy Week services) is also largely borrowed from St. Thomas's. It is, as I hope I have made clear in the story, completely anachronistic for 1926. However, it would have been perfectly possible for someone to construct such a service based on the information available in the contemporary edition of *Ritual Notes*, which is what I posit the fictional characters at my fictional church did.

ABOUT THE AUTHOR

Alice Degan is an academic, novelist, and Anglo-Catholic living in Toronto with her divinity-student husband. She studies and teaches medieval literature, and writes fantasy and something she likes to call metaphysical romance. *From All False Doctrine* is her first published novel.

You can follow her and sign up to her newsletter to hear about new releases at: **www.alicedegan.com**.